A KINGDOM TO CLAIM

OTHER BOOKS AND AUDIOBOOKS
BY SIAN ANN BESSEY

GEORGIAN GENTLEMEN SERIES
The Noble Smuggler
An Uncommon Earl
An Alleged Rogue
An Unfamiliar Duke
The Unassuming Curator
A Provincial Peer

HISTORICAL
For Castle and Crown
The Heart of the Rebellion
The Call of the Sea

FALCON POINT SERIES
Heirs of Falcon Point
The Danger with Diamonds
From an Unknown Sender

HE IS A WARRIOR. SHE IS A HEALER.
TOGETHER THEY WILL FIGHT TO SAVE THEIR KING.

A KINGDOM TO CLAIM

SIAN ANN BESSEY

SHADOW
MOUNTAIN
PUBLISHING

Visit us at shadowmountain.com

Library of Congress Cataloging-in-Publication Data

Names: Bessey, Sian Ann, 1963– author.

Title: A kingdom to claim / Sian Ann Bessey.

Description: Salt Lake City : Shadow Mountain, [2024] | Summary: "Aisley lost everything in a Viking attack. Almost seven years later, the Vikings are again rallying on Wessex's borders, and Aisley fears for her life. Brecc finds himself inexplicably drawn to Aisley. However, a Viking attack tears them apart, and King Alfred is forced into hiding. Brecc must reconcile his loyalty to King Alfred with his growing love for Aisley."—Provided by publisher.

Identifiers: LCCN 2023056569 (print) | LCCN 2023056570 (ebook) | ISBN 9781639932474 (trade paperback) | ISBN 9781649332721 (ebook)

Subjects: LCSH: Alfred, King of England, 849–899—Fiction. | Soldiers—Great Britain—History—To 1500—Fiction. | Vikings—Great Britain—History—Fiction. | Great Britain—History—Alfred, 871–899—Fiction. | BISAC: FICTION / Historical / Medieval | FICTION / Romance / Historical / Medieval | LCGFT: Historical fiction. | Romance fiction.

Classification: LCC PS3552.E79495 K56 2024 (print) | LCC PS3552.E79495 (ebook) | DDC 813/.6—dc23/eng/20240116

LC record available at https://lccn.loc.gov/2023056569

LC ebook record available at https://lccn.loc.gov/2023056570

Printed in the United States of America

Publishers Printing

10 9 8 7 6 5 4 3 2 1

For Hannah, Sophie, and Ellie
You make me want to keep writing.

ACKNOWLEDGMENTS

A HUGE THANK-YOU TO ALL those at Shadow Mountain and Covenant Corporation who have worked so hard to bring this book to the world. I am especially grateful for my incredible editor, Samantha Millburn; my cover designer, Emily Remington; my marketing manager, Amy Parker; and my product director, Heidi Gordon.

Thanks also to Brooke Loeffler, for creating the marvelous map at the front of the book, and to Benjamin Merkle, whose book *The White Horse King* taught me so much about the life of King Alfred the Great.

Writing a historical novel set so long ago is extremely challenging. I could not have done it without the support of my family and many dear friends in the writing community. Thank you, Kent, for going so many nights without a proper dinner. And thank you, Traci Abramson and Sarah Eden, for keeping me going when the going got tough.

Finally, but most importantly, thank you, readers, for reading my books and for begging me to write another Viking novel. I hope *A Kingdom to Claim* brings you much enjoyment.

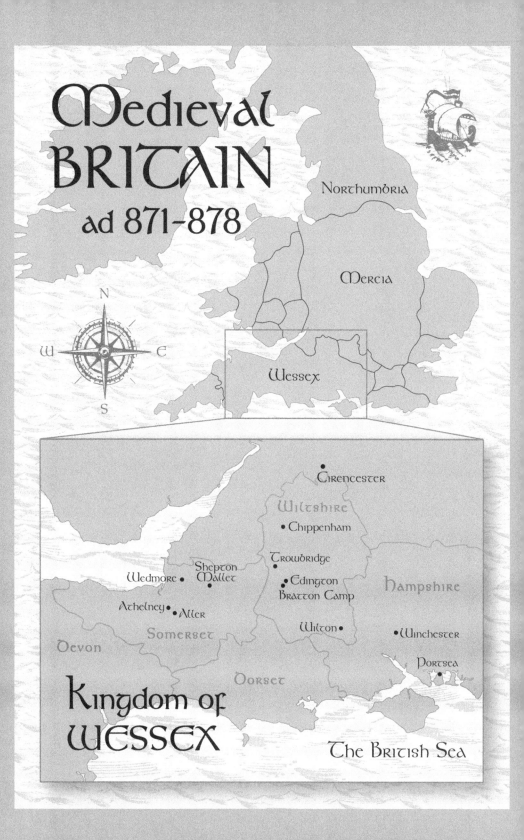

Medieval BRITAIN
ad 871-878

Northumbria

Mercia

Wessex

N
W · E
S

Cirencester

Wiltshire

· Chippenham

Trowbridge ·

Shepton Mallet ·

Wedmore ·

· Edington
Bratton Camp

Hampshire

Athelney · · Aller

Wilton ·

· Winchester

Somerset

Devon

Dorset

· Portsea

Kingdom of WESSEX

The British Sea

PRONUNCIATION GUIDE

IN ORDER TO MAINTAIN THE historical integrity of this novel, I have remained true to the names of the people who actually lived through the events depicted in *A Kingdom to Claim*, along with the places where the various incidents occurred. I have also used fictional names and titles as well as some Saxon and Norse vocabulary that would have been common during the 800s. These words may be unfamiliar to modern readers. For this reason, Shadow Mountain is making available an audio pronunciation guide on *A Kingdom to Claim*'s web page on the Shadow Mountain website.

The QR code below will take you to that audio pronunciation guide, a recording in which I pronounce each of the unfamiliar words. This web page will also include a listing of the words and where they are found in the book as well as a time stamp for where they are found in the recording so you can jump to any word you want to see or hear. I hope this will enhance your reading experience as you enter the world of medieval Wessex with Aisley, Brecc, and King Alfred the Great.

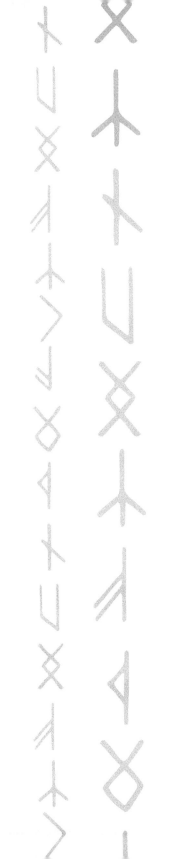

GLOSSARY

Ceorl: Also known as Freemen, they owned their own land and were allowed to bear weapons.

Danegeld: A land tax levied by the crown, used to pay off Viking invaders in exchange for peace.

Danelaw: A code of laws established by Viking invaders in Britain.

Ealdorman: Title given to a man of high status in Anglo-Saxon England. Forerunner of the title "earl."

Folkmoot: A general meeting of the people in a town, district, or shire in Medieval Britain.

Fyrd: A local militia in an Anglo-Saxon shire, headed by the shire's ealdorman and comprised of all freemen.

Mail Byrnie: A short chain mail shirt that covered from the upper arms to the upper thighs.

Mummers: Medieval actors, often associated with masked mime.

Pottage: Thick soup or stew.

Scop: Medieval bard or poet.

Shield Boss: The round conical or convex center of a shield. Usually made of metal.

Thegn: Anglo-Saxon nobility.

CHAPTER 1

Trowbridge, Wessex
May AD 871

THE PUNGENT AROMAS OF ROASTING venison and sweet mead filled the banquet hall. Servants flitted between the long tables, replenishing goblets, bread baskets, and platters of fruit and meat. At Aisley's right, a scop plucked at his lyre, his melodic chants recounting the Saxons' victory against the Vikings at Ashdown almost six months earlier, and from their positions at the head table, two of the king's thegns raised their cups and cheered. Others in the room took up the shout, expressing their loyalty to the new king and a resolve to purge their land of the plundering horde from the north.

Aisley wrapped her narrow fingers around the wooden goblet before her. At only twelve years of age, she had never before attended a banquet of this grandeur—certainly none that boasted the King of Wessex as its guest of honor. And the men's passionate outburst was a discomforting reminder that she did not truly know what was expected of her. Was she to respond in kind? Or were the females in the room—especially the young ones—exempt from such displays of eagerness?

Hazarding a glance at her mother, who was seated beside her, Aisley waited for some softly worded direction. But her mother's lips were pursed closed, and rather than reflecting the tangible eagerness in the room, she appeared troubled. Indeed, if the barely noticeable lines running across her forehead were any indication, the scop's efforts at engendering enthusiasm for King Alfred's cause seemed to have fully missed their mark with her.

"Mother?" Aisley could barely hear her own voice above the surrounding cacophony. "Is something amiss?"

"I must procure more milk thistle and parsley," her mother said. "There is barely enough dried milk thistle seed in the crock for one cup of tea."

Understanding, like a weighted ball, settled in Aisley's stomach. She turned her attention to the head table once more. As Ealdorman of Wiltshire and King Alfred's host, Aisley's father was seated there, to the left of the king.

Though not more than twenty and one years of age, the king's presence exuded authority. His hair and beard were brown, his dark eyes bright and alert. Only two years the king's junior, Aisley's older brother, Wulfhere, sat at their father's left. His broad shoulders and ruddy cheeks were a picture of good health and a stark contrast to her father's sallow skin and pinched expression.

"Father is in pain," Aisley said.

Her mother gave a tight nod. "He would not countenance missing the royal banquet, even if his health suffers because of it."

The weight in Aisley's stomach moved to her chest. "But you can help him. Your medicinal tea has repeatedly brought him relief from the discomfort that plagues him."

"We have been fortunate that he has responded so well to it," her mother said. "I pray such providence continues."

It would continue. It had to. Over the last few years, her father's more vigorous activities had been curtailed by bouts of gnawing pain and swollen feet. Her mother claimed it was his liver. The tea she occasionally steeped for him appeared to help above all other treatments, but nothing had successfully cured him of the malady, and recent attacks had seemed to last longer and be more painful than the previous ones.

Aisley watched her father lower his knife to the trencher of meat before him. The blade shook slightly in his trembling fingers. She slid her hands beneath the table and clasped them tightly on her knee. She was not sure if God listened to the silent prayers of young girls who were as unlearned as she, but if He did, she hoped He would facilitate an end to the merrymaking so her father might retire to his bed with his pride intact.

"I will seek out some milk thistle and parsley at first light," she said.

"There is likely some parsley in the kitchen garden," her mother said, "but you will have to search the hedgerows for the milk thistle."

"I will find them," Aisley promised, attempting to smother her fears for her father's well-being with determination.

Her mother's expression softened slightly. "Mayhap you can harvest the milk thistle's seeds this time."

Aisley's grip on her clasped fingers tightened. Her childhood had been filled with long rambles through the nearby woods and fields with her mother, where she'd been taught how to recognize all manner of flowers, leaves, and berries. Along with being charged with memorizing the names of each plant, she had also been tutored in their curative properties. She'd long since been the only person her mother trusted to procure plants for her remedies, but although Aisley had watched her mother prepare herbs for a soothing salve or restorative tea more times than she could count, she had yet to make one herself.

"But if I were to make an error . . ." She swallowed. She would not—could not—be the person responsible for causing her father to suffer.

"Your aptitude for healing is undeniable," her mother said. "You are ready to do more than gather the plants."

"How can you know that? I have never assisted anyone in their healing."

Her mother offered a ghost of a smile. "How many times have you come to the aid of your brother with a dock leaf when he has encountered nettles? Or offered a sprig of heal-all to your sister when she has complained of pain in her throat? To assuage the discomfort of others comes so naturally to you, you do not recognize your gift."

Aisley stared at her mother. Was it true? She had never been as confident among strangers or so good with horses as her brother. Her younger sister, Diera, was prettier and better with a needle than Aisley. Indeed, there were times when the comparisons had stung. More often than not, her mother publicly praised Aisley's siblings' obvious talents, leaving Aisley wondering if she was good for anything more than gathering flowers to decorate the banquet hall. "I . . . I do like plants," she said as the first tendrils of awareness caught hold.

"And you give them the respect they deserve," her mother said. "That fact alone sets you apart from most."

Aisley's gaze returned to her father. He turned from speaking with Wulfhere to reach for his goblet. Even from a distance, his wince at the slight movement was unmistakable.

Desire to alleviate his pain surged through her. "Can Father not excuse himself to rest?" Even as she voiced the words, Aisley knew it was a futile thought.

Before her mother could respond, however, the gray-haired thegn sitting on the other side of the king rose to his feet. "Silence in the hall!" he called. "The king wishes to address his subjects."

Instantly, the scop's thrumming ceased, and all eyes turned to look upon King Alfred. Flickering candles augmented the light coming from the fire in the center of the room, illuminating the row of powerful men seated on either side of him at the head table.

With a polite bow, the thegn reclaimed his place, and the recently crowned monarch silently surveyed the room. "Kendryek, Ealdorman of Wiltshire, has provided us a fine feast," he said, acknowledging Aisley's father with a nod. "You have my thanks."

Aisley's father bowed his head. "The good people of Wiltshire are honored by your presence at Trowbridge, Sire."

"Just so." The gray-haired thegn thumped his goblet on the table, and others at the head table immediately echoed the action.

A muscle in King Alfred's jaw twitched. It was the only outward indication that he'd heard the boisterous shout.

"Over the last few years, the Saxon people have claimed hard-fought victories against the Vikings, but we have also borne grievous losses." He clenched his fists. "My brother, King Aethelred, died of a wound inflicted by a Viking spear. Many have had crops, possessions, and loved ones torn from them in a treacherous and brutal fashion." Conviction filled his voice. "Those sacrifices cannot be for naught. We must fight the pagan invaders to defend our families, our homes, our land, and our Christian way of life."

This time, the men's cheer filled the hall, and the thegn at King Alfred's side handed him a glittering horn. A layer of gold covered the horn's tip, and multicolored gems glistened from the highly polished surface. Mead overflowed its rim as the king handed the horn to Aisley's father. With a respectful bow, Aisley's father accepted the glistening offering and raised it to his lips.

"What is the meaning of the golden horn?" Aisley whispered. She'd never seen anything so ornate. "And why is father kissing it?"

"He is pledging his devotion to the king," her mother replied. "King Alfred is the ring-giver at this banquet. Each of his thegns and warriors will be given the opportunity to kiss the horn and swear to remain true. In exchange, the king will gift them something of great worth."

Aisley watched with wide eyes as the king handed her father a bulging leather purse. The coins within clinked, and her father passed the horn to her brother.

"Wulfhere is to receive a prize also?"

"Of course." Her mother straightened her shoulders. "Wulfhere is most certainly of an age and sufficiently noble to participate."

Wulfhere took the horn and kissed it. Mead dripped from his fingers onto the table below.

"A horse for your loyalty, Wulfhere," the king said. "It shall be delivered to your father's stable within the week."

The shock in Wulfhere's eyes quickly turned to satisfaction. "I am most grateful, Sire."

"Devotion is worth a great deal more," King Alfred said. His gaze shifted to the young man seated on the other side of Wulfhere. "Is that not so, Brecc?"

Wulfhere passed the horn to his neighbor. The thegn, who appeared of a similar age to the king, raised his dark eyes to meet his liege's. "You speak the truth, Sire. And all that I have, I give to my king and the good people of Wessex." He raised the horn to his lips, and the king set another leather purse on the table. It was smaller than the one he'd given to Aisley's father, and rather than passing it to the thegn named Brecc, King Alfred pulled open the leather tie and withdrew a treasure.

"A ring from the ring-giver," King Alfred said. "An appropriate gift, I believe."

The green stone embedded in the gold ring sparkled in the candlelight. A gasp followed by a low murmur echoed through the room, but Aisley did not turn to discover the source. Her attention was fully focused on the stunning ring now lying on Brecc's open palm.

"I am honored, Sire," he said.

"Already, you have served me well. I ask only that you continue to do so with steadfastness."

Wrapping his fingers around the ring, Brecc bowed his head low. "It shall be done." He then offered the horn to the dark-haired thegn at his left. It had barely left his hands when the door to the hall burst open. The flames on the candles at each table danced as a gust of cold air entered the room. Two men dressed in riding cloaks walked in.

Aisley did not recognize either one, and if the frown upon her father's face was any indication, they were strangers to him also. Her father shifted on the bench as if he were planning to rise. He winced, the pain he was surely experiencing slowing his movements. Brecc was first to his feet, quickly followed by Wulfhere, whose hand went directly to the dagger at his waist. Other thegns rose, but none else reached for a weapon.

"The strangers are known to the king's men," Aisley observed softly.

"So it would seem," her mother said, not taking her eyes off the new-comers, who were now in deep discussion with Brecc and the gray-haired thegn. "And they come bearing news so urgent that it could not wait for the end of the banquet."

"What news, Warton?" It had taken little more than a glance at the war-rior's grim expression for Brecc to know the report was not good.

"The Vikings are amassing at the border." Warton, the taller of the two warriors who'd been charged with guarding the stretch of river near Winchester, kept his voice low enough that no one else in the banquet room could overhear their conversation. "Teon and I remained hidden long enough to see them readying their boats. They are heavily armed, and there can be no doubt that they intend to take to the water soon."

Warton's companion, Teon, nodded. "There's thousands of 'em, sire. And there's no mistakin' their intentions."

Brecc's stomach tightened. Although he'd guessed Warton and Teon's sudden appearance in the banquet hall did not omen well, to be days—weeks, at best—from another battle against the Viking horde was the worst possible news.

"We must inform His Majesty immediately," Ormod muttered.

The older nobleman had been King Aethelred's adviser before the for-mer king's untimely death, and King Alfred had continued to rely heavily on Ormod's counsel when the responsibility of the crown had been abruptly thrust upon him.

"I do not believe His Majesty would wish the banquet to end in panic." Brecc had no need to turn around to know that all eyes were upon the uninvited visitors. "Mayhap it would be prudent to have those at the head table reclaim their seats and Kendryek's guests resume their meal. A quiet word in the king's ear would cause less alarm than a public announcement."

"Agreed," Ormod said, his frown disappearing as he swung to face the room once more. "Let the feast and ring-giving continue! And if Ealdorman Kendryek does not object, these latecomers would be happy to share in the generous spread."

Kendryek nodded his approval, and at Ormod's signal, the other thegns took their seats once more.

"The ring-giver's ceremony must continue." Ormod lowered his voice so that only Brecc could hear. "Now, more than ever, the king must have his men firmly behind him. When the opportunity allows, I shall inform him of the warriors' message. You find a place for Warton and Teon to eat without fear of being questioned. After traveling such a distance in so short a time, they will need their strength if we are to quit Trowbridge straightway."

Brecc glanced at the place he had vacated at the table. Meat filled the trencher he'd shared with his fellow thegn, Arthw. But the food no longer held appeal.

Arthw had taken up the embellished horn, and King Alfred was watching him expectantly. Arthw's hesitation was so faint it was barely discernible. But Brecc had caught it. His companion knew what was to come. With the arrival of two of the king's warriors, no one seated at the head table could be in any doubt. What they did not know was how soon they would be called upon to act.

"Come," Brecc said to Warton and Teon. "You must eat." He led them to the back of the room, where a small table was pressed up against the wall. "You there," he called to a nearby servant girl. "These travelers require food and mead. Fetch an extra trencher and goblets, if you please."

The girl bobbed a curtsy. "Right away, sire."

She scurried out of the room, and Brecc scoured the area around the table. "It appears that there is no bench to spare, but I daresay food, drink, and a place to set them is a start."

"To be right honest, sire, after spendin' so long in a saddle, I'm more th'n 'appy to stand fer a bit," Teon said.

Brecc acknowledged the warrior's comment with a wry smile. "I imagine you'll be back in that saddle before you are ready. I thank you both for bringing us this intelligence in so timely a fashion. The king will know how to act after Ealdorman Ormod has spoken to him."

Warton and Teon remained silent. If the Vikings were coming, they would be called upon to fight. They both knew it.

The servant girl reappeared with a flagon of mead and two goblets in hand. Brecc stepped away. With Warton's and Teon's needs being met, he should return to the head table. He scanned the large room. Most of its occupants had accepted Ormod's request and had resumed their eating. Brecc's gaze stopped at the table where Kendryek's wife and daughters sat. The ealdorman's wife was watching her husband, a concerned look on her face. One daughter—whose flaxen hair was the image of her mother's—was fiddling idly with a ribbon on her gown, her attention on the glittering horn at the head table. The second daughter, whose long tresses glinted red in the firelight, seemingly had no interest in the ring-giver's gifts. Instead, she was looking directly at Brecc.

Startled by the intensity in the girl's eyes, Brecc held her gaze for two long breaths before giving her an acknowledging nod and looking away. The king's horn had traveled the length of the head table and had returned to the monarch. Ormod was speaking with him now. The thegn's head was turned away from those gathered in the room, but if King Alfred's lowered eyebrows were any indication, he was not pleased with Ormod's report.

Squaring his shoulders, Brecc crossed the room in long, brisk strides. Regardless of the young girl's knowing mien, it was not possible that Kendryek's copper-haired daughter comprehended the imminent threat looming over their people. He released a tense breath. He could only pray that she—and thousands more innocents—would be spared from ever knowing the worst of what was to come.

CHAPTER 2

DAWN WAS BREAKING. THE FIRST tendrils of light infused the sky beyond the woods, illuminating the mist hovering over the meadow. Aisley raised the hem of her gown and stepped over a large rock. It was a somewhat pointless endeavor. Already, the lower portion of her gown was wet and speckled with mud.

Beneath the hawthorn bush ahead, a cluster of purple flowers drooped under the weight of the morning dew. Aisley stepped closer and smiled. She'd been right. They were milk thistle. And there were enough that she would not need to seek out more.

Crouching beside the plant, she withdrew the small knife from the basket in her other hand and gently pushed aside the largest leaves. A shout reached her from the direction of the longhouse. She paused her work to look over her shoulder. A thin trickle of smoke floated above the kitchen roof. Cook was no doubt about her morning work. But it was early for other members of the household to be in the courtyard.

Aisley eased her fingers around the prickly thistle stem, pressed the blade against it, and sliced it in two. Dropping the purple head into the basket, she repeated the procedure with each flower until the colorful blossoms all but covered the parsley she'd picked in the kitchen garden.

A horse neighed, and another shout was followed by the clip-clop of many hooves hitting cobbles. Rising to her feet, she tightened her grip on the handle of the basket. Why were the horses out of the stables at this hour? Surely the king's men would not rise so early after a late night of feasting.

With mounting curiosity, Aisley lifted her damp hem and ran across the meadow toward the house. Pausing at the courtyard entrance to catch her breath, she studied the scene before her. The king's men milled between the waiting horses. Some held spears and shields; others had helmets tucked beneath their arms. Every face was grave; every exchanged word was brief.

One of the strangers who'd interrupted the feast last night crossed Aisley's view. She swallowed hard. He and his companion were the reason for this new sense of urgency. She was sure of it. Soon after the ring-giving ceremony had concluded, the king had requested that the women and children leave the room so that he might speak privately with the thegns and ceorls in attendance. Her mother had been too consumed with her father's health to speculate upon the reason for the meeting, but Aisley knew full well that along with the thegns, those freemen, farmers, and independent landholders made up the backbone of Wiltshire's fyrd. They were the men who were expected to respond when the king issued a call to battle.

With rising concern, Aisley stepped around a restless horse and scoured the area for any sign of her father. Upon their dismissal from the hall the night before, Aisley's mother had insisted that Aisley and her sister, Diera, retire to their beds. Aisley had known better than to contradict her mother's firm directive, even though curiosity over what the men were discussing had burned within her. She'd watched the thegn named Ealdorman Brecc speak with the latecomers, noted his grim expression when he'd turned back to the head table, but she had not expected an immediate call to arms. For that was what this was. There could be no doubt about it.

A middle-aged thegn at Aisley's left shouted at Taber, her father's youngest stableboy. The lad cinched a leather strap beneath a nearby black mare and came running. Aisley turned the other direction and made for the house. Giving three saddled horses wide berth, she rounded a small group of ceorls and barreled directly into someone else's firm chest.

Her unwitting target gave a surprised grunt.

"Oh!" Untangling herself from the folds of a thick woolen traveling cloak, Aisley stumbled back a few steps. "Forgive me, sire." She looked up and found herself gazing into the dark eyes of Ealdorman Brecc. Warmth flooded her cheeks. Of all the gentlemen to whom she might have exhibited herself so poorly, it had to be this one. Raising her chin slightly, she attempted to reclaim a small measure of poise. "I beg your pardon." She managed an inelegant curtsy. "I should have been minding where I was going."

"No harm done. I daresay your small stature does you a disservice. It must be difficult to see past so many men and beasts."

It was. But Aisley did not especially like being reminded of her lack of height. Especially by a relative stranger. "I believe it was my speed rather than my stature that must be blamed, sire."

"Of course." Ealdorman Brecc's eyes flickered with something that looked suspiciously like humor. "I stand corrected."

Aisley stiffened. She did not wish to be laughed at any more than she wished to be pitied for her small bone structure.

"I confess," he continued. "I had not thought that one of Ealdorman Kendryek's daughters would be in the courtyard at this hour. Let alone be in so great a hurry."

The importance of her early-morning assignment flooded back. The unexpected chaos had waylaid her, but with the noisy preparation occurring in the courtyard, there could be no doubt that her father was awake. And she must reach him before he departed his bedchamber.

"I am fulfilling an errand for my mother," she said. "If you will excuse me, I must go to my father immediately."

At her words, a shutter fell across Ealdorman Brecc's face, snuffing out any hint of humor or congeniality. "If you wish to speak with your father, I suggest that you find him forthwith. We shall be leaving within the half hour."

We? Was the thegn referring to the visiting dignitaries only? Or had Wiltshire's fyrd truly been called to arms? New voices reached her from the courtyard entrance, and with increased panic fluttering in her stomach, Aisley spotted two local landowners leading their mounts through the gate. Their presence was the only answer she needed. The local militia who rode with the ealdorman of the county to fight for the king were gathering. And they would all expect her father to ride at their head.

Scarcely remembering to offer Ealdorman Brecc an acknowledging nod, Aisley ran into the house. She crossed the great hall with hurried steps until she reached her father's chamber. The door was open. Her mother stood within, her long, pale hair hanging loose against the blanket covering her shift.

"You cannot do this, Kendryek." There was no mistaking Aisley's mother's desperation.

"Edla," her father pled. "You must understand. I have no choice in the matter."

"There is always a choice," her mother said.

Aisley's father stood beside his bed, his traveling cloak around his shoulders, the fingers of one hand tightly wrapped around the bedpost as though to keep him upright. Her mother stood before him. At her right, Wulfhere was dressed in his traveling clothes, and he held a large round shield and a spear.

"I accepted the ring-giver's coins," Aisley's father said. "I am honor bound to do King Alfred's bidding and to ride against the Vikings at the head of Wiltshire's fyrd."

The Vikings. In Aisley's hand, the basket trembled. The bloodthirsty heathens had swept across Northumbria and Mercia, leaving death and pillage in their wake. Now they had their cold-blooded hearts set on adding Wessex to their conquests.

"You are ill," her mother said. "The king will understand."

"I can lead our men, Father," Wulfhere said.

Her father shook his head. "I shall be glad to have you beside me on this journey, Wulfhere, but this is something I must do."

"In your current condition, the journey alone may kill you." Aisley's mother's voice broke.

"If it is God's will that I die, who am I to question it?"

"But what if it is not His will." Her mother stepped forward, her hands clenched. "What if He wishes you to stay here and rest that you might lead the people of Wiltshire uprightly for years to come?"

Aisley's father lifted his free hand and ran it down her mother's hair. "It is my understanding that our God is a majestic being of truth and honor, of virtue and light. Holy writ tell us that He wishes every person—no matter his or her circumstances—to emulate those qualities. If I am to be a man of truth and honor, I must do what I believe is right, regardless of the sacrifice it requires."

Her mother's lip trembled. "No. This is too much."

"Wulfhere will be with me."

"You would have me lose my husband and my son?" she cried.

"I am not ill, Mother," Wulfhere said. "I do not intend to die."

"So you say," she countered. "But when the Vikings attack in a manic frenzy, you will have little control over who falls."

Wulfhere's jaw tightened. "I am as likely to kill ten Vikings as they are to injure me."

Aisley did not wish to hear this talk of dying. Neither she did wish to listen to her parents contend with one another. She raised the basket in her hand and stepped into the room. "I have parsley and milk thistle for your tea, Father."

Her mother and Wulfhere swung around, obviously startled by the interruption.

Aisley's father released his hold on the bedpost, and with an ill-concealed flinch, he moved across the room toward her. "You picked these for me?" he asked, gesturing to the plants in the basket.

"Yes. They will need to dry for a few days, but there is more in the crock ready to be used for your tea. The herbs will ease your pain. They always do."

He offered her a sad smile. "The healing properties in your mother's teas are quite remarkable, but I fear there is not time to prepare any before I must leave."

Aisley felt the sting of tears. "Must you truly go, Father?"

"Yes, child." He cupped her cheek in his hand. "All will be well, you shall see."

She hung her head, but he gently raised it until her eyes met his. The whites of his eyes were yellowed, and she recognized the pain in their depths.

"Have courage, Aisley," he said. "And I shall do the same. We shall be brave together."

Her heart felt that it might be breaking, but she nodded. "Yes, Father."

His expression softened. "Good girl."

Outside, a horn sounded.

"It is time, Wulfhere," he said. "Bring me my sword, if you please."

Wulfhere crossed the room and retrieved the sword leaning against the wall in the corner. Aisley's father reached for her mother's hand. Raising it to his lips, he pressed a kiss to her fingers. "God willing, I shall see you again ere long."

Her mother took an unsteady breath, though whether her battle was with frustration or sorrow, Aisley could not tell. "I pray it is so," she said.

Word of the latest Viking incursion into their county had reached the men of Wiltshire mere hours ago, and yet Brecc could not fault them for the speed in which the fyrd had gathered. Ever since first light, willing warriors—some on foot, some on horseback—had entered the ealdorman's courtyard in a steady stream. And now that the sun had swept away the last vestiges of early-morning mist, the previously open space was full of men, horses, and wagons. Already, the makeshift army had closed ranks behind Ealdorman Kendryek and his son and were anxiously awaiting the order to move out.

Seated upon their mounts, the king's thegns formed two solid lines behind the standard bearer, and from his position near the entrance to the ealdorman's house, Brecc watched Ormod for a signal that the king was ready.

Somewhere nearby, a wooden shield clattered to the ground, the metal-domed boss at its center hitting the cobblestones with a clang. Brecc's horse snorted, skittering away from the unexpected noise and causing a similar reaction in the horse beside them.

"Steady, Noori." Brecc leaned forward in his saddle to set a calming hand upon the stallion's strong neck before turning to speak with the thegn at his right. "My apologies, Arthw."

"Can't blame the horses for being jittery," the habitually taciturn gentleman responded. "It's long past time that we were away."

Brecc silently agreed. He had no great desire to go to battle, but this waiting—especially when the Vikings were marching across the countryside in a lethal swathe—did little to help their men's morale. "I daresay the king has good reason for the delay," he said.

"Caught up in his prayers like his brother before him, I wager," Arthw muttered.

Scops regularly sang of the miracle at the Battle of Ashdown, when the delay caused by King Aethelred's prayers facilitated an unexpected two-fronted attack and won the Saxons a glorious victory.

"If that is the case," Brecc said, "we can hardly grumble. Our monarch's devotion to God is undoubtedly one of our greatest strengths."

Arthw's expression suggested that he felt otherwise, but he pressed his lips into a firm line and turned his attention back to Ormod.

"I beg your pardon, sire."

At the sound of a young lady's voice, Brecc swiveled his head. Kendryek's daughter—the same one he'd spoken with earlier—stood beside his horse. Surprised that Noori had not reacted to her sudden appearance, Brecc raised his eyebrows. "You wish to speak to me?"

"Not especially," she said. "But in this great press, I cannot reach my father."

Brecc's eyebrows notched a fraction higher. It appeared that the girl was wont to speak her true feelings, even if they were not particularly complimentary.

She lifted the small linen sack in her hand. "It is exceedingly important that my father receive this before he leaves, and I wondered . . ." Her voice trailed off as though she'd only just now considered the inconvenience inherent in her request.

"You wondered if I would be so good as to give it to him," he guessed.

She nodded. "Yes, sire."

"You understand that I will not be riding with your father and that it is highly unlikely that we will cross paths unless I make a particular effort to seek him out?"

She nodded again, and this time, he caught the glisten of tears in her arresting green eyes. "I know it is much to ask, but you are the only gentleman within reach with whom I'm acquainted."

"Forgive me. I did not realize that we were acquainted."

"You are Ealdorman Brecc." There was no mistaking the pink rising in her cheeks, but he had to give her credit for maintaining her composure at his subtle rebuke.

"That is true, but I have yet to learn your name."

"Aisley," she said. "My name is Aisley. And I would forever be in your debt if you would do me this great service."

At Aisley's guileless pleading, Brecc felt his resistance waiver. True, seeking out Kendryek when they made camp for the night would be inconvenient, but it would give him an opportunity to stretch his legs after having been on horseback all day. And the ealdorman should not be so hard to find among an army of ceorls.

He eyed the small sack curiously. "May I ask what is so vital that it must reach your father without delay?"

"Medicinal herbs." She paused, and this time, there was no denying the tears in her eyes. "My father has been ill for many months. Partaking of a tea made from these herbs will assuredly ease his present suffering and might offer him greater strength when fighting the Vikings."

"Both outstanding outcomes," Brecc said.

"Then, you will take them?" Hope rang in her voice, and he could not help but smile.

"Very well."

"You have my deepest thanks, Ealdorman Brecc."

"And a lifetime of debt, if memory serves."

"Yes." She raised her arm. "That as well."

Brecc leaned down to take the bag from her. It weighed very little and smelled of parsley. He slipped the string around his belt and tied it firmly. "I will look for your father this evening," he promised.

"It is requisite that he steep the herbs in boiling water, and when the liquid has cooled, he must drink it all."

Brecc's lips twitched. Had the ealdorman ever dared counter any of his rather remarkable daughter's demands? "I shall tell him."

A horn sounded, snapping Brecc's attention back to Ormod. The king's mount waited beside him, a groom ready to assist the monarch into the saddle.

"He is here at last." Arthw's voice carried to the nearby ceorls, and several of them turned their heads to watch King Alfred exit the house.

Brecc took a deep breath. The time had come. They were heading to battle. "If you will excuse me, Aisley," he said. "It appears that the king is ready to depart."

His words were met by silence. Surprised, Brecc glanced at the spot where the girl had stood only moments before. She was gone.

CHAPTER 3

AISLEY STOOD AT THE LONGHOUSE window, flexing the fingers on her right hand. They were sore, and her palm where she'd pressed against the pestle was purple. When her father and Wulfhere had left the bedchamber for the courtyard, Aisley had not paused long enough to ask her mother for directions on how to make the herbal blend her father used. Instead, she'd raced to the cold storage room as fast as her short legs could carry her. Trusting her memory of the many times she'd watched her mother prepare the herbs, she'd exchanged her basket of fresh plants for the crocks containing the remaining portion of dried milk thistle and parsley. After pouring the precious plants into a mortar, she'd ground them with a pestle until her hand had pulsated with pain. Luckily, there had been several small linen bags lying on the shelf beside the crock, and as soon as she'd emptied the contents of the mortar into one of them, she'd chased after her father.

She hadn't been fast enough. She'd never seen the courtyard so crowded and knew that if her father and Wulfhere were to ride at the head of their men, they would both be far closer to the road than she could ever hope to reach in the press. She flexed her fingers once more before resting her hand on the windowsill as she watched the last of the warriors filter out of the courtyard. Finding Ealdorman Brecc so close to the house had offered her a moment of hope after her initial despair. It had been forward of her to ask the thegn for his help—particularly when he'd had so many other matters to attend to. No doubt, her mother would be mortified to learn what she'd done. But she would never find out. And if Aisley's boldness helped her father, it was worth any amount of indignity.

"What is all the noise about?" Diera walked in, rubbing sleep from her eyes, and Aisley was reminded of how early it was. So much had happened already this morning, it was hard to believe that she was normally still abed at this hour.

"The king's men have left," Aisley said.

"Could they not have spared the household by doing it a little more quietly?"

"It is possible," Aisley said. "But last night, the king called for the fyrd to gather. Hundreds of Wiltshire's men were here by dawn."

"Did father go with them?"

Aisley nodded. "As did Wulfhere."

Diera's eyes widened. "Is it another battle with the Vikings?"

"Yes."

The single word carried a heaviness that even a nine-year-old could feel. Diera's chin quivered. "Where is Mother?"

"In her chamber, I imagine." Aisley had not seen her mother since fleeing her father's room.

Diera took off toward their mother's chamber at a run. Aisley moved away from the window, her shoulders slumped. She was not sure which was harder: leaving to fight the bloodthirsty Vikings or being left at home to await news.

The fire crackled. Someone tossed another branch on the flames and sparks swirled heavenward. Brecc rose from his position on the ground beside the log where King Alfred sat. His thigh muscles ached, and he grimaced. At only twenty years of age, his body should not be complaining over so simple a movement, but after a hard day's ride, Brecc doubted there was a man in the camp who was not feeling the effects of too long in the saddle or too many furlongs on his feet.

"If you would excuse me momentarily, Sire." Brecc bowed to the king. "I believe I will take a walk before retiring for the night."

"Most wise," King Alfred said. "By Ormod's calculations, we are over halfway to Wilton, but we have another long ride on the morrow if we are to head off the Vikings before they take the town."

The prospect of another full day in the saddle was unpleasant, but Brecc had no cause to complain. All day long, farm laborers and yeomen had been leaving their fields to join the army of men marching toward Wilton on foot. Carrying nothing more than rudimentary weapons and a small sack of vittles, they had joined the ever-lengthening convoy. Even now, men were slipping into the field where the men were encamped, finding a place to rest among those who had already claimed a spot.

"I shall return shortly," Brecc said.

King Alfred offered an approving nod and turned to his adviser, who was seated at his other side. "What think you, Ormod?"

"I beg your pardon, Sire?" Startled, Ormod turned his attention from the scrap of manuscript in his hand to the king. "You wished my opinion on a matter?"

"Yes." The king rose. "On whether you would accompany me on a circuit around the camp."

Brecc smothered a grin. Based on Ormod's expression, the older gentleman would prefer to remain exactly where he was. But before Ormod could suggest that King Alfred take his walk with Brecc instead, Brecc slipped away.

There were hundreds of men gathered in the camp. Half a dozen fires burned, but none so large or so bright as the one at which the king sat, and there were surely men of lower standing who were positioned too far from the flames to experience any warmth. Brecc frowned. He hoped those brave souls had access to a blanket of some sort. Or at the very least, a warm cloak. His fingers went to the small bag tied at his waist, and he scanned the growing throng in the semidarkness. Kendryek was a thegn. He would not be too far distant from the king's escorts, but if Brecc gauged the man's character aright, neither would he wish to be too far removed from the men he had pulled from working the land to do the king's bidding.

Moving past the inner circle of thegns, Brecc started toward the wagons carrying the Wiltshire men's shields and spears. The temperature dropped as he stepped farther from the fires, and he looked upward. Like heavenly candles, a profusion of stars twinkled in the night sky. They would become brighter as the darkness deepened, and the cold would become more bone-chilling. As grateful as Brecc was that they were not having to contend with rain, cloud cover would have kept them all warmer.

He pulled his cloak more securely around himself and surveyed the clusters of men nearby. Most were conversing in small huddles, their voices low. A sense of determination hung in the air. Along with an underlying whisper of fear.

"I am seeking Kendryek, Ealdorman of Wiltshire," Brecc said, approaching a large man with hands the size of frying pans.

The man pointed a stubby finger toward a small grove of trees. "He wus 'ere not long ago, but I reckon you'll find 'im near th' ash trees now. Needed t' set 'imself down fer a bit, I'm thinkin'."

If Kendryek was suffering from as much discomfort as his daughter had suggested, the laborer's assessment was undoubtedly correct.

"I thank you," Brecc said.

"You'll likely find 'im with 'is son," the local man added.

"Of course." Brecc nodded politely and walked the short distance to the small copse.

At least a dozen men were seated beneath the trees, some of them leaning against the thick trunks. One sat slumped, his hood over his lowered head.

"Ealdorman Kendryek?" Brecc asked.

Immediately, the lowered head lifted, but it was the man beside that gentleman who rose.

"Who comes inquiring for Ealdorman Kendryek?" the man who stood asked.

"Ealdorman Brecc."

The man bowed, and in the semidarkness, Brecc caught the glint of his pale-colored hair. The same color as his mother's and youngest sister's long tresses. This was Wulfhere.

"Forgive me, Ealdorman Brecc. I did not recognize you in the dark."

"No apology is necessary," Brecc said. "I could say exactly the same."

"Ealdorman Brecc, you are welcome." Kendryek spoke, and if the catch in his voice and the fact that he had yet to stand were any indication, the gentleman was in considerable pain. "Pardon me for not rising to greet you. My body is not as young as it once was and is protesting our long march."

"I, too, am feeling the effects of too much time in the saddle," Brecc said. Not as much as Kendryek, to be sure, but his comment seemed to put the older man at ease.

Kendryek drew his hood back and gazed up at Brecc. "How may I assist you, sire?"

"I have something that belongs to you." Brecc tugged at the string looped around his belt, and the small linen bag loosened. Pulling it free, he stepped closer and offered it to the older man. "I was told that the bag contains medicinal herbs."

Kendryek's gaze dropped from Brecc's face to the small sack. "My wife gave you this?" There was wonder in his voice.

"No, sire. It was given to me by your daughter, Aisley."

His head shot up again. "Aisley?"

"Aye. She was most insistent that it reach you straightway." Brecc inclined his head. "I have undoubtedly waited far longer than she had hoped but not so long that you cannot brew some tea before bedding down for the night, I hope."

"I shall have someone see to it immediately," Wulfhere said, reaching for a drinking vessel on the ground beside his father.

Kendryek tightened his fingers around the small bag. "Bring me the hot water, and I shall steep the tea myself."

Offering a brief bow to his father and to Brecc, Wulfhere disappeared into the darkness.

"May I offer you a portion of grass upon which to sit until my son returns, Ealdorman Brecc?" There was a hint of humor in Kendryek's tone, and Brecc found himself unaccountably glad to hear it. "I should be most interested to hear exactly how my young daughter managed this seemingly miraculous task."

Attempting to ignore his aching muscles, Brecc lowered himself to the ground. He had intended to make his delivery and complete a circuit around the field before returning to his earlier position beside the fire, but talking to Kendryek about his green-eyed daughter's unique petition for aid was far more appealing than overhearing muttered conversations among anxious warriors or listening to Ormod discuss battle strategy with the king.

"She came upon me as we were preparing to leave the courtyard," he said. "I believe she had hoped to hand the bag to you herself but was unable to reach you in the press of men and horses."

Kendryek shook his head slightly. "She must have fetched this as soon as I left my bedchamber. It is hard to believe there was enough time for her to prepare the herbs, but somehow, she managed it."

"I received the impression that you are very important to her."

Kendryek sighed. "She is a rather remarkable young lady," he said. "Her mother is learned in the art of healing and has taught Aisley well. But Aisley possesses something greater than a knowledge of which plants contain curative powers; she has the gift of caring deeply for the well-being of others."

"A powerful combination, to be sure," Brecc said.

"Aye. And an uncommonly rare one." He sighed again, and this time, the emotion felt deeper. "I pray she will be given the encouragement to nurture her gift. If so, she will be a blessing to far more than her ailing father."

"How much longer will this take?" Diera asked. "We've been tying up weeds for two-and-a-half ages."

Aisley giggled at Diera's creative measure of time. Her sister disliked hanging plants up to dry almost as much as Aisley disliked working with a needle.

"Patience, Diera," their mother said. "There are times when we are all required to do things we would rather not do." She stepped onto the wooden stool and hung the string she'd just tied around a bunch of lavender on a hook in the ceiling beam. "It is a life lesson that is best learned at a young age."

Aisley heard the resentment in her mother's voice and looked up from the thyme she'd been sorting. It had been over a fortnight since her father, Wulfhere, and the other men had ridden out of the courtyard to confront the Vikings. Since then, conversations had been stilted, expressions anxious, and an unsettled aura had filled the house. Aisley, Diera, and their mother felt it, certainly. But so, too, did the servants.

Aisley wished there were some way of receiving word on how the men were faring. The continued silence was torture. It hung over the fields empty of laborers, the stables without stablehands, and the business establishments in town devoid of merchants. Unfortunately, it was a scenario that had been repeated all too often over the past year, and Aisley knew that if the laborers stayed away overly long, the repercussions would be far more serious than a pall of silence. The harvest would be impacted, and food would become scarce.

"How much longer do you think we shall have to wait before we receive news of the battle?" Aisley asked.

Diera darted a nervous glance her way, obviously surprised that Aisley had dared voice the question everyone was wondering.

"Why do you think I should know such a thing?" her mother snapped. Unfortunately, no amount of time outdoors gathering herbs and medicinal plants had fully erased the pinched expression on her face. "There is no reasoning with a Saxon man when he has his mind set on something. I daresay it is the same with a Viking. They will fight until they no longer remember what it is they are fighting for."

"The last time Father gathered the fyrd, he said that they must fight to protect the people of Wiltshire and their land," Diera said. "I do not think he will forget that."

"Honor above all else," their mother responded bitterly.

Aisley furrowed her brow. "Is that not a good thing?"

Her mother reached for the bunch of thyme in Aisley's hand, the lines cutting through her pursed lips deepening. "It depends upon whom you ask."

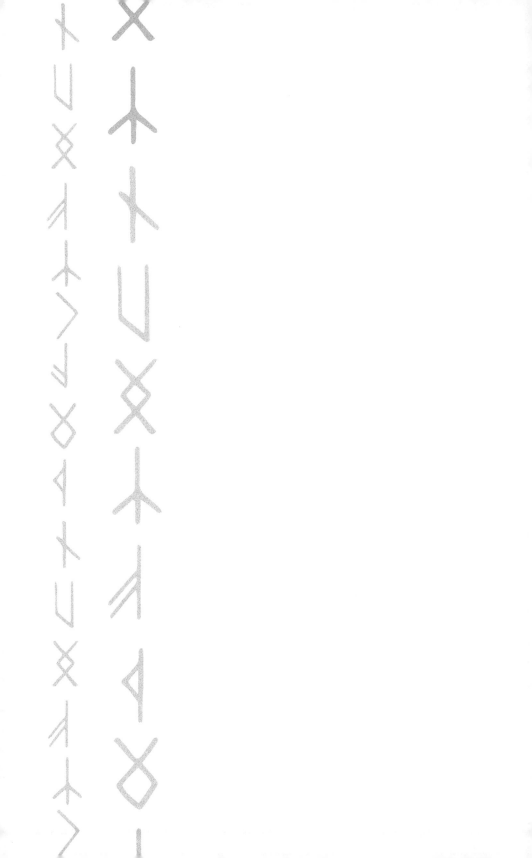

CHAPTER 4

THEY WERE OUTNUMBERED. BRECC EYED the men lining the ridge above them grimly. Too many to count, and there was no telling how many bloodthirsty Vikings lay waiting in the ranks beyond his vision. Tightening his grip on the handle mounted beneath his shield boss, he pressed his shoulder against Arthw's at his right. The gentleman grunted his approval. The closer the warriors stood to each other, the better. Their overlapping shields formed a formidable barrier, but all it would take was one weak link—one man to fall or to abandon his comrades—and the blockade's effectiveness would be compromised.

"Looks to be a large gathering of chieftains," Arthw muttered. "I'd wager this battle is one they aim to win."

Brecc nodded. The chieftains' metal helmets glistened in the early-morning light, and though they were not yet close enough for him to identify the extravagantly molded face guards, he knew the intimidating headgear's purpose. The chieftains' warlike appearance was meant to engender fear in their foes—as were their howling battle cries. The Vikings' similarity to a pack of ravenous wolves was all too real.

From somewhere on the hilltop, a blood-curdling cry rent the air, and suddenly, the Vikings were racing toward them, swords and spears raised as they poured down the hill in a torrent of fearsome shouts.

"Hold your positions!" At King Alfred's shout, the men at the front of the shield wall tensed. "With trust in God's strength and mercy, victory shall be ours!"

"We fight for Wessex!" The shout came from somewhere in the midst of the nearly four thousand men who were standing in tightly packed rows behind Brecc.

The call was immediately picked up by others. "For Wessex!"

Keeping his eyes on the hillside, Arthw shifted slightly. "And so it begins."

The Vikings were close enough now that Brecc could identify which were armed with swords and which were wielding axes. A horn sounded, and an instant later, the sky filled with spears arching over the grassland toward them. The response was instant. A single shout, and more spears took to the sky, this time directed toward the Vikings.

Brecc raised his sword. The Saxon counteroffensive had begun.

Cries of agony mingled with shouts of fury. All around, the clash of metal hitting metal and the thud of spears penetrating wooden shields reverberated down the Saxons' line of defense.

Brecc lunged at the nearest Viking, the tip of his blade catching the man's thick leather garment on his arm. The heathen swung his raised ax toward Brecc, but Brecc countered the attack with a blow that knocked the man to the ground. Out of the corner of his eye, Brecc spotted another volley of incoming spears. "Forward," he yelled.

As one, the front line surged up the hill. Two, three, four steps. It was all that was necessary. The spear that should have hit his shoulder sailed past Brecc's ear, missing him by a fraction. Arthw cursed as a spear penetrated the soil at his feet. They both knew that if one of them fell and a fresh warrior did not step forward to fill the gap immediately, the floodgates would open, and there would be no holding back the Vikings then.

"The shield wall is holding." Arthw grunted, lowering his head as yet another spear sliced through the air between them.

Behind Brecc, a man shrieked. The sound sent chills down Brecc's spine. Such a gut-wrenching sound did not accompany a superficial flesh wound. The man at Brecc's right stumbled, his shield shifting against Brecc's. With a roar, three Vikings attacked, wielding their spears with deadly precision. Brecc's neighbor cried out, his knees buckling. The moment the man's shield dropped, another Saxon warrior pushed forward, stepping over his comrade to press his shield against Brecc's.

"Stay the course! We have them." It was Ormod's voice.

Already, the field was littered with fallen men. The clatter of metal attested to the ongoing battles along the Saxon shield wall, but many of the Vikings had dropped back. For the first time since their initial war cry had rent the air, the Saxons' adversaries were unsure. Brecc turned his head. Determination shone in every Saxon's eyes. Despite the unlikely odds, victory was within reach.

Another shout. This one closer. Brecc ducked as an airborne spear whistled past him. Beside him, Arthw gasped. A hiss of pain followed. Brecc swiveled. The spear had partially entered his comrade's arm. The wooden shaft wavered before toppling to the ground, drawing the spear's tip out of Arthw's forearm as it fell.

Brecc kicked the spear aside. Someone else could use it against their enemy. "How bad is it?"

"'Tis nothing." Arthw was speaking through clenched teeth. "It caught the edge of my byrnie."

"Call another man up," Brecc urged.

Arthw kept his eyes forward, his jaw tight. "There's no need. The heathens are retreating."

It was true. The spear that had pierced Arthw's arm must have been one of the last to fly. The Vikings were running toward the ridge, leaving their dead and wounded behind. A cheer erupted. From the Saxon army's rear, farmers and laborers began running onto the battlefield, carrying their pitchforks and scythes aloft.

"It is too early for jubilation," Arthw said grimly. "The Vikings may have withdrawn, but they are not gone."

Bodies, bleeding and broken, lay scattered across the slope. Brecc swallowed the bile in his throat. Did the Viking chieftains ever consider the price their greed exacted? Many of the casualties were Saxons, most certainly, but there were numerous Vikings among the dead, and those who were injured might yet die of their wounds. Brecc glanced at Arthw. His companion's face was pale, but he remained upright, holding his shield in place.

"Your wound. How bad is it?" Brecc repeated.

"Not so bad that you'll be claiming my purse," he said.

Brecc scowled. The practice of searching those who'd died in battle for valuables had never sat well with him. To walk away with an associate's possessions after he'd died in the service of his king and country was abhorrent. "I have no interest in your coins," he said. "Unless you intend to spend them on my next meal."

Arthw eyed his blood-soaked sleeve. "I fear my need for a healer may surpass my desire for food at present."

Brecc's thoughts instantly turned to Ealdorman Kendryek's young daughter. Would that she and her mother were close enough to be of assistance.

His eyes scanned those lowering their weapons along the shield line. Had the ealdorman survived the battle despite his weakened state?

"Remain here," Brecc said. "If there is help available for your wound, I shall find it."

Arthw's grudging acceptance of Brecc's offer was a far greater indication of his level of discomfort than any words could have been. Lowering himself to the ground with a wince, Arthw nodded. "If all you can find is sufficient water to rinse off the blood, it would be welcome."

The king was standing not far away in deep conversation with Ormod. Three or four other thegns hovered nearby, their attention flitting between the mounting disorder on the battlefield and the king and his adviser's serious discussion. Brecc started toward them. If anyone knew where help could be had for the wounded, it would surely be these men.

"What is being done for the injured?" Brecc called, caring little that Ormod would consider his question a blatant and ill-mannered interruption.

"My question exactly." The king offered Brecc an approving look, even as his adviser frowned. "We must seek them out from amongst the dead."

"I agree wholeheartedly, Sire," Ormod said. "But we must not act too hastily."

"If we do not act hastily, more men will die," Brecc said. "I left Arthw back there. He will not admit to it, but the cut in his arm, caused by a Viking spear, is significant."

"Arthw, you say?" King Alfred said. "Ormod, enough is enough. Look at the destruction around us. We must assist our injured immediately."

Ormod glanced at the ridge. It was clear of all invaders. "Very well, Sire." He inclined his head. "I shall have men locate and gather the injured."

"Water," Brecc said. "Where might we find some?"

"We have men filling barrels at the river," Ormod said. "They will be here shortly." For the second time, he eyed the ridge anxiously. "I would remind you, Sire, that the Vikings are wont to return to a battlefield if they have not yet tasted victory. It might be wise to assign watchmen whilst our attention is so diverted by those in need of aid."

"A point well taken," King Alfred said. "See it done, Brecc."

Brecc bowed. "Right away, Sire."

The nearby thegns watched his approach. Dunlap, a broad-shouldered warrior from Dorset, spoke for them all. "What word, Brecc?"

The chaos was magnifying around them. Men's shouts cut through stunned silence. Running feet raced to assist crippled, dragging limbs. And blood. So much blood.

Brecc attempted to focus on the thegns. "The king wishes watchmen set up around the battlefield until we are sure the Vikings have fully retreated."

Dunlap nodded his approval. "I shall take the north side and will gather some men to join me." He jerked his head at the other two landowners. "You two take east and south. Brecc here can watch our backs to the west."

Grateful that Dunlap had made his assignment easier, Brecc turned to the west and toward the river. Already, men were returning, staggering under the weight of barrels full of sloshing water.

Brecc picked up his pace. "Take it to the last position of the shield wall," he ordered. "That is where you will find the men who battled the Vikings face-to-face."

"Very good, sire." The dark-haired man grasping the barrel with both hands puffed out his response but did not stop.

Satisfied that the water carrier was on course to find Arthw, Brecc scoured the area for more thegns. Few laborers would wish the responsibility of rounding up those of higher status to stand watch. Particularly if those ceorls were intent upon lining their pockets with the wealth of others.

Not more than thirty paces distant, a man rose from a crouched position on the ground. Another remained sitting at his feet. The many warriors milling between them made identifying the gentlemen difficult, but the byrnies they wore spoke of wealth, and Brecc started toward them. He was almost close enough to hear their voices when the standing gentleman turned, and Brecc recognized him.

"Wulfhere," Brecc called. "How do you and your father fare?"

"Uninjured, praise the heavens." Wulfhere ran the portion of his sleeve protruding from beneath his byrnie across his forehead. The chain mail rattled. "Although, I am not sure my father could have lasted on his feet much longer."

"I lasted long enough. That is what matters." The ealdorman spoke from his position on the ground. "A rousing win for the king, do you not agree, Ealdorman Brecc?"

"Indeed." Brecc could not think on the injured and dead littering the ground beyond them. Or of Ormod's worry that the fighting was not over yet. "I pray the violence is truly behind us."

Wulfhere cocked his head to one side, his eyes narrowed. "You witnessed us routing the Vikings yourself."

"I did."

"And yet you harbor doubts?"

"If the Vikings have proven one thing over a year filled with deadly battles, it is that they cannot be trusted."

Wulfhere snorted. "What is to distrust here? They will not wish to return only to be beaten again."

Perhaps. Brecc turned to face the ridge. Half a dozen men wearing Saxon tunics and byrnies were making their way up the rise. The watchmen led by Dunlap, no doubt.

"It is good to be wary." Kendryek attempted to stand, but he lacked the strength.

"If I may be of assistance." Brecc offered the older gentleman his hand, and Kendryek accepted it with a reluctant sigh.

"You have my thanks, sire."

Wulfhere frowned. "There is no reason for you to be upon your feet now, Father."

Kendryek's gaze followed Brecc's, his wan complexion and pained expression hiding his thoughts. "It is good to be wary. Especially when it comes to the Vikings."

"The battle is over," Wulfhere said, offering his father his arm and allowing Brecc to step away. "Our men are leaving, and it is time we do the same."

Wulfhere was undoubtedly correct. Those who had scavenged the battlefield were making their way toward the road. Those who had opted to forego the easy pickings were already gone.

"Then I shall wish you Godspeed," Brecc said with a slight bow.

A horn sounded from the hillside. Brecc pivoted, his breath catching. Dunlap's men were racing toward them, their shouts reverberating through the dreadful silence that had suddenly descended upon the battlefield below.

"Rebuild the shield wall! The Vikings have regrouped. They will be upon us in minutes!"

Half a furlong away, the king and Ormod stood as though frozen. Arthw, the bucket of water beside him forgotten, was attempting to rise from his place on the ground. He stumbled, and Brecc took off, racing across the grass toward him. Wulfhere's curse was the last thing he heard before the Vikings' chilling shrieks reached them.

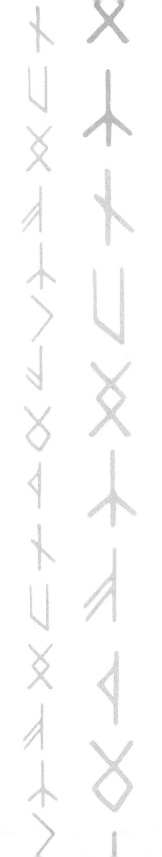

CHAPTER 5

THE STABLES WERE UNNATURALLY QUIET. Aisley stood just within the doorway, blinking as her eyes adjusted to the dim light. The rustle of straw, thud of hooves against the hard-packed ground, and gentle nickers she associated with the building were absent. She missed them. The emptiness did not feel right. Or good.

Drawing her shawl more closely around her shoulders, she moved inside.

"Taber?" she called softly. "Are you here?"

"Aye." The clatter of a pail being set down on the other side of the stables was followed by hurried footsteps. Moments later, a boy of about nine years of age appeared, brushing his hands down his straw-covered tunic. "'Ow can I 'elp you, mistress?"

"I saw you out in the fields yesterday," she said. "With Daisy."

Taber shifted his feet anxiously. "Tryin' t' 'elp, I were. Mildritha in th' kitchen were tellin' me that Cook's right worried 'bout the peas and beans in the fields." He shrugged. "With all th' men gone, the weeds are takin' 'old, and there's been no one scarin' off th' birds."

"Are the peas close enough to harvest that the birds have started their pilfering?" Aisley asked.

"Aye. An' Cook's that worried 'bout it, she's plannin' t' send th' maids t' start harvestin' soon."

Aisley frowned. When she'd spotted their old plow horse in the field with Taber, it had been a welcome reminder that not every single horse had left with her father and the fyrd, and the realization had drawn her to the stables. She'd known this morning's visit would not be like the ones she usually made when she stopped to greet each of the horses in their stalls, but she'd determined that any time spent in the stables with Daisy translated to less time for needlework. Her visit had been intended as an escape rather than a reminder of their current difficulties.

"What must be done?" she asked.

Taber shrugged helplessly. "I don' rightly know, mistress. I've been walkin' Daisy twice a day, jus' t' keep 'er old legs movin', so I thought I might as well take 'er up an' down th' rows t' see if she couldn't scare off some of them vexin' birds while she were takin' th' air. Problem is, th' weeds are comin' on strong without anyone t' tend to 'em. The paths between th' rows are gettin' choked up. But I don' know 'nough 'bout such things t' start pullin' at plants."

Aisley stared at him, her thoughts whirling. Their stableboy might not know much about plants, but she did. Would her mother allow her to labor in the fields if it meant saving their crops?

"I'm glad you told me, Taber," she said. "I will speak to my mother about the crops and the weeds and the birds."

"I don' know what it is 'bout them birds. It's not like anyone 'ere told 'em that th' peas are ripe or th' men are gone. Wiley they are." He scratched his head. "With all the easy pickin's and freedom they 'ave flyin' all over, I'm thinkin' it wouldn't be so bad t' be a bird."

"If you were a duck, you might end up on someone's table," Aisley warned.

Taber grinned, erasing the worry that had shown on his face only moments before. "Nah. A hawk's what I'd be."

Aisley suppressed a giggle. It probably wouldn't do to tell Taber that he seemed far more like a sparrow than a hawk.

"I'd best go speak to my mother about the crops," she said. "Tell Daisy that I shall visit her soon."

"Aye, mistress."

Aisley hurried out of the stables and into the courtyard. Clouds filled the sky, and she paused to look up. Would they have rain by evening? A large black bird flew over the longhouse and landed on the rooftop. It cawed. Three more crows appeared, settling beside the first. The cawing intensified, and Aisley shuddered at the ugly sound. Birds—ducks, hawks, and sparrows included—certainly had their place. But surely the world could survive without crows. No one wished those harbingers of death close by.

♛

The hillside was littered with bodies. Moans of the injured punctuated the gusts of wind that prefaced the storm that was assuredly coming. Brecc turned his face to the sky and closed his eyes, shutting out the devastating destruction before him. It was finished. The conflict at Wilton would be forever remembered as the battle the Saxons won and then allowed to slip through their fingers.

They'd had no time to regroup. No time for the shield wall to function as it should. The Vikings had surged back over the ridge to tear through the unprepared men of Wessex, hacking them down indiscriminately until thousands lay dead and dying.

Brecc took a deep breath and released it slowly. He'd walked through hell today. By some miraculous means, he had emerged on the other side still whole. But far too many others could not say the same. Arthw was gone. As were a goodly portion of the other thegns. Brecc lowered his head. He was not sure how the young king would fare without his experienced warriors. By God's grace, Ormod had survived. He would be King Alfred's anchor through the maelstrom ahead. Even now, he was assisting the king with the distasteful task of brokering an agreement with the Viking chieftain, Guthrum. Danegeld would be required. The churches would be stripped of their wealth, and the Saxon people would suffer.

Swallowing against the bitterness in his mouth, Brecc crossed the short distance to the river and dropped to his knees at its bank. He lowered one hand, allowing the water to trickle through his fingers before scooping it up to his lips. He drank and then repeated the process. A persistent stinging on his right cheek reminded him that a Viking blade had very nearly reached his throat. He rinsed his cheek with another scoopful of water, grateful that the water ran clear when he lowered his hand. His byrnie had saved him more than once this afternoon. Had he been dressed as so many of the laborers and farmers had been, he would not have been so fortunate.

A wagon rolled toward him, a man on horseback riding alongside it. Brecc rose to his feet. Drying his hand on his tunic, he studied the approaching rider. Hair so blond it was almost white. A blue tunic stained with blood and dirt but recognizable nonetheless.

He stepped forward. "Greetings, Wulfhere."

The ealdorman's son raised his hand, and the wagon driver reined the horse to a stop.

"Ealdorman Brecc," Wulfhere said, guiding his horse a little closer. "I had not thought to see you again."

"Nor I you," Brecc replied. "I am grateful to know that your life has been spared."

"Aye." Wulfhere's eyes flashed. "Although the same cannot be said for my father."

Brecc's heart sank. It should not have come as a surprise, given the older man's weakened state, but the news was a blow. A vision of the ealdorman's daughter, Aisley, flashed before him. Her desperate desire to spare her father from unduly suffering was a meaningful indication of how difficult his death would be for her.

"I am truly sorry. Although I did not know him well, it was readily apparent that your father was a good man."

"He was." Wulfhere's jaw moved as though he were working to contain his emotions. "I shall return his body to Trowbridge, where he shall be given a burial befitting a gentleman of his station."

Brecc's gaze darted to the wagon, its presence on the battlefield now clear. The serviceable vehicle had come from Trowbridge bearing weapons; it would return carrying its master. And all Wiltshire would mourn the loss.

"Your mother and sisters—"

"They shall be well cared for," Wulfhere interrupted before he could finish. "Upon learning of my father's death in battle, the king granted me the position of Ealdorman of Wiltshire in my father's stead."

The depth of Brecc's relief that Aisley would not be forced to relocate from her home and that she would continue to have her needs met was both unexpected and startling. He had only spoken to the girl twice, and yet her welfare mattered to him.

"I am glad to hear it." This news would alleviate the loss for every member of the ealdorman's family. Mustering a strained smile, Brecc took a step back. "Godspeed to you. I shall slow your journey no longer."

Aisley pressed her thumb against the edge of the peapod. It popped open, exposing a row of perfectly round green peas within. She ran her finger along the inside, watching with satisfaction as the peas dropped one by one into the large bowl on her knee. There was something wonderfully satisfying about the simple activity, and Aisley was glad to be productive.

Her mother had been aghast at Aisley's request that she work in the fields, pulling weeds. But upon learning that the crops were suffering due to the men's absence, she had reassigned a few of the household servants to the fields. Unfortunately, that had left Cook shorthanded. It hadn't taken Aisley long to convince her mother that she was perfectly capable of shelling peas and that she could complete the assignment in a manner worthy of an ealdorman's daughter.

"How are the peas coming along, Aisley?"

Aisley started. She hadn't heard her mother enter the kitchen. Straightening her spine, she held out the bowl for her mother's inspection. "I have only a handful left."

"She's been doin' marvelously, mistress." Cook wiped her wet hands on a rag and moved away from a large pot of water to bob a curtsy.

"I'm glad to hear it. But you've been here long enough for one day."

Aisley glanced at the small pile of unshelled peapods. She was so close to finishing; it seemed a terrible shame to walk away now. "It would not take me—" She stopped as the clatter of hooves reached them. Far more hooves than Daisy could claim.

Her mother's gaze darted to the window, and the next moment, Diera flew through the door.

"They're back," she gasped. "Father, Wulfhere, all the men, and their horses."

"You've seen Father?" Aisley had already set down the bowl of peas and was making for the door.

"Well, no. Not yet. But his men would not return without him, would they?"

With her mother and Diera close at her heels, Aisley ran into the courtyard. Already the large square was filling with men and horses. The wagon rolled slowly up to the main door of the longhouse, and the man riding beside it turned to speak to the driver.

"It's Wulfhere," Diera cried, waving.

Aisley glanced at her mother. She was exhibiting none of Diera's enthusiasm. Her face had paled, and her gaze had yet to leave the wagon. Aisley turned her attention to the back of the vehicle. Swords and shields lined one side. A gray blanket covered whatever lay on the other.

Wulfhere dismounted. He must have seen them standing outside the kitchen, because he started toward them, his gait stiff and his face grave.

"Dear God." Her mother's murmured words were barely audible. "Let it not be so."

"Mother." Wulfhere reached them and bowed politely to their mother.

"Tell me," she demanded.

"He is gone," Wulfhere said. "Killed by a Viking spear on the battlefield."

Aisley stared at Wulfhere, attempting to comprehend his words. No. It could not be. Not her father. She swung back to face the blanketed object in the wagon, understanding and tears releasing simultaneously. "Father is dead?" she whispered.

Wulfhere offered her a curt nod. Diera looked from him to their mother and started to sniffle.

Their mother stood stiffly, her hands clasped tightly at her sides. "I warned him." Her voice wavered. "I told him not to go."

"You did," Wulfhere said. "It would have served him well to listen."

"What good is that knowledge now?"

He looked away. "I should have supported you when you spoke to him of your concerns."

Their mother released a short breath. "This is no more your fault than mine."

"Agreed." Something flashed in Wulfhere's eyes. "If the blame is to fall anywhere, it should be placed firmly upon King Alfred's head."

"But you said it was a Viking who took Father's life." Aisley swiped at her tears.

"Aye. In a massacre that never should have happened." Bitterness filled his voice. "Thousands of men killed—and for what? Nothing. Worse than nothing. Wessex has lost its men and its gold."

"The king agreed to pay the Danegeld," her mother said.

"Aye." Wulfhere snorted. "If he was willing to barter our gold for peace, he should have done it before the slaughter."

"I do not understand." Aisley looked from her mother to Wulfhere, desperate for clarity. Nothing made sense. Her father was gone, and yet they appeared more anxious to place blame than to grieve his loss.

"You are too young to apprehend what has happened," Wulfhere said.

"I am old enough." Aisley raised her chin. "Father would have explained if he were here."

Wulfhere released a frustrated grunt. "The king has agreed to pay the Viking chieftain a great deal of gold on condition that the chieftain and his men leave Wessex. Churches will be stripped of their treasures, and taxes on the citizens of Wessex will increase to pay the debt."

"We are ruined," their mother said, the first hint of fear entering her voice. "Without your father, we can pay nothing. We have nothing."

"The danegeld will make life more difficult, but we shall manage," Wulfhere said. "I am the Ealdorman of Wiltshire now."

Their mother gasped. "The king has given the position to you?"

"He has."

She smiled. It was her first real smile since Aisley's father had ridden out of the courtyard. Aisley looked away, emotion churning within her. Wulfhere's appointment may have allayed her mother's anxiety, but it had done nothing to alleviate the aching emptiness in Aisley's chest. She stifled a sob. Her father was gone. Even if the Vikings were no longer an imminent threat, from this moment on, nothing in her life would ever be the same.

CHAPTER 6

Chippenham, Wiltshire
January AD 878

IT WAS BITTERLY COLD. AISLEY'S breath hung in the air in frozen puffs, and she had long since lost all feeling in her toes. Diera stood at her side, her nose the color of a beetroot—a sure sign that her sister had been out in the elements too long. But whatever discomfort Diera was experiencing was obviously insufficient to dampen her enthusiasm for Chippenham's market. Despite the January chill, eagerness shone in her blue eyes. There were simply too many stalls laden with beautiful things for her to contemplate cutting their visit short.

Aisley had never visited this particular market before, but she thought it likely that this week it was larger and grander than usual. King Alfred was in residence at the royal court, and he had invited thegns and their families from around Wessex to join the festivities leading up to and including the celebration of Twelfth Night. Never one to turn down the opportunity to sit at the king's table and partake of a royal feast, Wulfhere had declared that they must all travel from Trowbridge to Chippenham for the holiday.

Local vendors, their carts filled with eggs, butter, and cheese, vied for the attention of the king's visitors with those who had come to sell from farther afield. The town square was a vast tapestry of colors, with jostling customers milling through the stalls and haggling voices and potent aromas filling the air.

They wove through the crowd toward the far corner of the square, where an inn appeared to be doing an even better business than the merchants bartering outside its door. A table covered with fine fabrics drew Diera's attention.

"Oh, Aisley." She pointed at a bolt of dark-blue linen. "Have you ever seen the like?"

At present, the sight of a warm fire would have interested Aisley more, but she forced a smile. "It is exquisite, though far too costly to purchase, I am sure."

"How can you possibly know that?" Diera huffed. "Wulfhere would never say such a thing."

Aisley suppressed a sigh. It was true. Wulfhere rarely refused Diera anything, and his penchant for acquiring extravagant clothing was almost as great as Diera's. Not more than a fortnight ago, he had purchased a new fur-lined traveling cloak when the one he'd used last year remained in excellent condition. Aisley winced at the thought. It had been over six years since the Battle of Wilton, and yet there were far too many commoners in Wiltshire who had yet to recover from the loss of their husbands and fathers. Women working themselves to exhaustion to provide for hungry children in tattered clothing. Aisley's heart ached for them. Wulfhere did not watch over his people the way their father had, and it filled her with a torturous mixture of guilt and sadness.

Like a moth to a candle, Diera moved closer to the finely woven fabric. Aisley hung back, her gaze shifting from the linen-laden table to the two gentlemen standing just beyond the merchant's display. One had his back to her, his dark wavy hair uncovered despite the bitter cold. The other had his head covered by the hood of his traveling cloak and appeared to be leaning against the wall of the inn, as though needing the support of the stone structure. As she watched, the hooded gentleman ran an unsteady hand across his pale face. Concern filled her, and she took an involuntary step toward them before catching herself. Surely the gentleman's companion could offer assistance if it was truly needed.

"You are skilled in a great many things, my friend." The gentleman groaned before continuing. "Unfortunately, healing is not one of them. The fresh air you suggested as a cure-all is doing nothing to improve my symptoms."

Aisley's breath caught. She had been correct. The gentleman was unwell. And she could not simply stand idly by if her knowledge of healing remedies might be the means of easing his suffering. Allowing instinct to overcome whatever common sense she owned, she circled the merchant's table and came up behind the ailing gentleman's companion.

"I beg your pardon, sire." The dark-haired man swung around, but Aisley kept her focus on the one leaning against the wall. "I do not mean to intrude, but am I correct in believing you are unwell?"

The gentleman shifted so that his forehead now rested against the wall. "I daresay I do give that impression." He took a couple of deep breaths. "Forgive me—" With another groan, he staggered around the corner of the inn. Moments later, the sound of retching reached her.

"Rheged's timing has always been impeccable." There was humor in the dark-haired man's voice. "I would hazard a guess that if whatever is plaguing the poor fellow's stomach does not kill him, the mortification of reliving that undignified exit may do the job."

"Set all jesting aside, sire," Aisley said, indignation infiltrating her mounting concern. "Your friend is obviously in dire straits." She turned from anxiously watching the corner of the building to face him.

Deep brown eyes gazed down at her from beneath raised eyebrows. Instantly, a flood of memories assailed her. The courtyard outside her home in Trowbridge. The shouts of men preparing to leave for battle. A handsome thegn on horseback taking the bag of herbs she had so desperately wanted to give to her father. Aisley's mouth went dry. The gentleman's hair was shorter than it had been six years ago and a scar the length of her little finger now ran across his left cheekbone, but there could be no denying that she'd seen those expressive eyes before.

"Ealdorman Brecc." The words came out in a rush, and she lowered her head to curtsy. When she raised it again, all hint of amusement was gone from his eyes. He stared at her as though trying to put together fractured pieces of those same memories, and despite the cold, a new and decidedly uncomfortable warmth flooded Aisley's face. She had been only twelve years of age when they'd met. And even then, their interaction had been minimal. It had been forward of her to greet him as though they were acquainted. "Forgive me," she said, attempting to quell her burgeoning discomfort. "You likely have no recollection of the time that was both our first and our last meeting."

He issued a sharp intake of breath, his look of puzzlement disappearing. "It was at Trowbridge," he said. "You are Ealdorman Kendryek's daughter."

"I am." Why his mention of her father should cause a lump to form in her throat, she could not say. She attempted to swallow past it. "My name is—"

"Aisley."

Shock drew her eyes back to his. "Yes."

He held her gaze. "I should have known you instantly. Your copper-colored hair is almost as distinctive as the green eyes you inherited from your father."

"I would contend that at this precise moment, my face is likely as green as this young lady's eyes." At the sound of the other man's voice, Aisley swung around. The ailing gentleman had reappeared and was standing unsteadily with one hand pressed to his stomach. "Given that fact," he continued, addressing Ealdorman Brecc as though she were not there, "I should like to submit that you will either have to throw me over your shoulder to return me to my chambers or abandon me in this corner of the market so I may die without an audience."

"How long have you been feeling so poorly, sire?" Aisley asked.

"An eternity." He moaned.

Ealdorman Brecc cleared his throat. "I believe the symptoms started soon after his meal last evening."

A sickness likely triggered by something he had eaten, then.

"And have you taken anything that might offer you some relief from your discomfort?"

The gentleman Ealdorman Brecc called Rheged raised his head long enough to glare at his companion. "Nothing more than a walk in the bracing fresh air."

"Which seemed a far better choice than remaining hunched over a bowl in your putrid-smelling bedchamber," Ealdorman Brecc countered. "Besides, I've heard tell that a short excursion outdoors can be an excellent curative."

"Indeed," Aisley said. "But perhaps not the best option when one barely has the strength to stand upright."

Ealdorman Brecc crossed the short distance to his friend, drew Rheged's arm across his shoulder, and placed his own around the gentleman's waist. "He was not so weak as all this when we set off."

"True." Rheged grimaced. "Nor so discourteous. Rheged, second son of Ealdorman Bernard, at your service."

Aisley smiled at the common—and yet currently ludicrous—greeting. It seemed that Ealdorman Brecc had also caught his friend's unreasoned words, for he chuckled softly. "Rheged, may I introduce Aisley, daughter of the late Ealdorman Kendryek, sister of Ealdorman Wulfhere of Wiltshire. Aisley, this poor sop may be of little service to you for the next day or two, but he is a noble enough fellow to make good on that promise in the future."

"Of course," Rheged muttered. "Unless Brecc opts to leave me here after all."

"Since that is not even a possibility," Ealdorman Brecc said, tightening his grip and guiding Rheged forward, "you'd best brace yourself for the short walk needed to reach our mounts."

"An infusion of wormwood and mint is an excellent remedy for an unsettled stomach," Aisley said.

Ealdorman Brecc paused, and at his side, Rheged stumbled to a halt. "Where might we find those herbs? Are they for sale at the market?"

Aisley looked out at the stalls and carts filling the square. They continued down the adjoining streets for as far as she could see. Even if there were a merchant selling curative plants, there was no telling how far away he was, and Rheged was in no position to comb the area for a stall that may or may not exist. She took a brief mental inventory of the supplies she had brought with her. "I have some dried wormwood in my bedchamber," she said. "And thyme, which is almost as efficacious as mint."

If Ealdorman Brecc was surprised, he did not show it. "And you are willing to offer them to Rheged?" he asked.

"Of course."

Ealdorman Brecc smiled, and Aisley's stomach fluttered.

"I thank you for your kindness," he said.

"It is nothing." She pressed a hand against her middle, offering a silent prayer that the unexpected flurries were not early symptoms of Rheged's illness. "Fetching the medicine is a worthy reason to return to the royal residence. My sister and I have been at the market long enough. It is past time that we escape the cold."

"Your sister is here?" Ealdorman Brecc's gaze traveled across the milling crowd.

"She is." Battling her inexplicable reluctance to point out Diera and their attending servant to the thegn, Aisley gestured toward the stall where her blonde-haired sister was handing a piece of blue linen to the vendor. "She is speaking with the fabric merchant."

He nodded. "I see her now. Mayhap if she has completed her purchases, she will be willing to leave."

Rheged's shoulders were slumped, and his head was lolling lower and lower.

Aisley offered him a worried look. "I shall ensure that she does," she said. "She is well used to me quitting an activity so that I might assist with an injury or illness."

"I am most grateful for your help." Rheged's voice was low.

She took a step back. "You'd best be on your way, Ealdorman Brecc. I shall meet you within the half hour at the doors to the great hall."

CHAPTER 7

BRECC PACED THE SHORT DISTANCE between the entrance to the great hall and a nearby tree before scouring the open area between the royal estate's buildings once more. A black cat skulking in the nearby shadows, a groom walking two horses toward the stable, a maid scurrying from the kitchen to the well with a bucket in hand, and three thegns talking loudly as they crossed to their quarters on the other side of the large square. There were people aplenty, but the one person he wished to see had yet to appear.

Turning on his heel, Brecc walked back to the large wooden doors. Releasing a tense breath, he rolled his shoulders and attempted to suppress his rising concern for Rheged. He had never seen his friend so weak. Not even the leg wound Rheged had received at the Battle of Wilton had laid him so low.

Helping Rheged reach his bed had been far more taxing than it should have been. By the time they'd reached the estate, Rheged had been unable to steer his mount unaided, and Brecc had been silently berating himself over persuading his friend to make the outing to the market ever since. He'd enlisted a stablehand to help him carry Rheged to his chambers and had left him dry-heaving over a bowl so that he could meet Aisley to claim the promised medicine.

Aisley. Her striking green eyes were unmistakable. Brecc shook his head slightly. It should have come as no surprise to learn that the girl who had gone out of her way to deliver medicine to her father had become a stunningly beautiful young lady who not only took note of those struggling around her but also offered her assistance. Brecc had thought on her occasionally over the years. He had known that the loss of her father in battle would affect her acutely, and that awareness had been uncommonly difficult to set aside.

The whisper of lightly running feet reached him, and he turned to see Aisley herself hurrying across the grass. His heart warmed at the sight. She was yet wearing her cloak, but the hood had fallen from her head, and her long, copper hair was flowing freely behind her. She had grasped a fistful of her light-blue gown in one hand and was holding up the hem—no doubt to prevent a fall. In her other hand, she clutched two small bags.

"I pray I have not kept you waiting long." She panted as she came to a stop before him. "My sister—" She bit her lip as though catching the words before they could escape. "I had hoped to be here sooner."

"It is enough that you have come now," Brecc said.

She raised the pouches, a short length of string, and a remnant of linen fabric. "I have brought wormwood and thyme," she said. "Tie the herbs in small linen bundles and place them in boiling water to steep. They will make a potent drink that should calm Rheged's stomach and allow him to rest."

Brecc took her offerings and eyed them uneasily. "I have no notion of quantities. Do I place everything you have given me in the fabric?"

She shook her head. "Cut the fabric before you begin. There should be sufficient for half a dozen doses. If he tolerates the first drink, offer him another before sundown. And another before you retire for the night."

Brecc shifted uncomfortably. He was more than willing to watch over Rheged and encourage him to take the treatment Aisley suggested, but he had no desire to follow up one error in judgment with another. "Encouraging Rheged to visit the market was a mistake on my part," he said. "I must not risk another." He hesitated. "His condition has worsened, and he needs someone well-versed in the healing arts to administer the herbs correctly."

She tilted her head to meet his gaze, and a crease appeared along her brow. "You realize that I am in no position to enter a thegn's bedchamber."

"Not as a noblewoman entering alone," he agreed. "But in the capacity of a healer, with me at your side, it could be done."

The crease along her forehead deepened. "It would be unseemly still. If someone were to come upon me—"

"I shall ensure that that does not happen."

"How?" Her mesmerizing eyes held his, and it suddenly became unaccountably difficult to think clearly.

"I cannot say exactly, but—" He broke off. There was no time for this. Rheged was waiting. "Forgive me. I should not have unduly pressed when you have already shown such kindness." He inclined his head. "I am in your debt." And then, with long, brisk strides, he started back toward the building that housed the thegns.

"Ealdorman Brecc."

At the sound of her voice, Brecc turned his head.

"If you remain in the room with us, I will come," she said.

Relief brought a smile to his face. "I am most grateful."

"We shall need hot water."

He nodded. "I guessed as much. I set a pot over the fire in his bedchamber. It should be at a boil by now."

Shutters covered the window to the bedchamber, shrouding the room in shadows. In the fireplace, flickering flames offset the darkness and the chill, and a large pot bubbled over the fire, sending steam up to the rafters.

Releasing the clasp on her cloak, Aisley slid it off her shoulders and set it across the back of a nearby wooden chair as Ealdorman Brecc approached the gentleman lying on the bed. A bowl sat on the floor. It was empty, but an imperceptible aura of illness hung heavy in the stale air.

She was a fool for being here. Common sense along with years of training told her that. Her mother would be aghast to know that she had entered a young thegn's bedchamber. And yet, Aisley could not shake the conviction that she was where she needed to be.

"Is he awake?" She spoke softly, not wanting to startle Rheged with her presence.

"I think not." Crouched at the bedside, Ealdorman Brecc placed a hand on his friend's shoulder and shook it gently. "Aisley is here, Rheged. She has brought the herbs that will help your stomach."

"Nothing will help," Rheged muttered.

"I think it might be worth putting her treatment to the test," Ealdorman Brecc said.

"Of course you do." Rheged rolled onto his back and tossed an arm across his eyes. "You do not need to imbibe whatever foul concoction she offers me."

"How do you know it will be foul tasting?"

"How do you know it will not?" Rheged countered.

Smothering a smile, Aisley unfolded the piece of linen Ealdorman Brecc had set on the wooden table in the corner.

"Do you have a knife I may use, sire?" she asked.

Rheged stiffened, his arm dropping from his face. "No blood-letting," he said with more vigor than he'd shown since Aisley had met him.

"Truly, Rheged?" Ealdorman Brecc handed her the dagger from the belt at his waist. "You are well on your way to convincing Aisley that you are a fearful mouse of a man."

"Rather that than a bleeding pig of a man."

Ealdorman Brecc raised an eyebrow. "Mayhap there is some fight left in you after all."

"No fight," Rheged said wearily. "Merely a modicum of self-defense."

"You have nothing to fear from me or Ealdorman Brecc's blade, sire." Aisley sliced the last piece of fabric into three small squares. "I am using the knife to create sachets for the herbs so that you may benefit from their curative properties without filling your cup with leaves."

Ealdorman Brecc rose to his feet and moved to stand beside her. "Show me," he said, "so that I may do it when you are no longer here."

With a nod, Aisley poured a portion of each of the herbs onto one of the fabric squares. Raising the corners of the fabric, she drew them together and tied the small bundle closed with a short piece of twine. "You see," she said, setting the sachet on her palm and holding it up. "It is not so difficult as all that."

"I believe you made it look far easier than it is," Ealdorman Brecc said.

"And she has yet to tell us how it will taste," Rheged mumbled.

Ealdorman Brecc tossed her an apologetic look, but Aisley was glad to see a spark of interest—no matter how small or petulant—in Rheged. She dropped the sachet into an empty goblet and crossed to the fireplace.

"I've heard tell that the worse the curative drink tastes, the more efficacious it is," she said, covering her hand with the rag lying on the hearth and reaching for the pot of boiling water.

"That sounds like a poorly framed justification for causing a man to feel more wretched than he did before," Rheged said as she poured the steaming liquid onto the sachet of herbs in the goblet.

Ealdorman Brecc placed his hands on his hips and glared at his friend. "I am of a mind to leave you here to wallow in your misery alone. You do not deserve this young lady's aid."

A flash of something that looked suspiciously like panic flickered through Rheged's sunken eyes. He attempted to raise his head and shoulders from the pillow, only to give up in defeat moments later. "As you see," he said. "I am fully dependent upon you both." He sighed. "It is a humbling position to find oneself in, but that is no excuse for rudeness. You have my apologies."

"Apology accepted," Aisley said, carrying the steaming cup to the bed. "I have seen illness and injury influence a person's natural disposition in a variety of ways. It is never pleasant for anyone." She glanced at Ealdorman Brecc. "When the herbs have steeped a little longer, this exceptionally foul-tasting liquid will be cool enough to drink. If you would be good enough to raise Rheged to a sitting position, I shall take charge of ensuring that he swallows the brew."

Rheged opened his mouth as if to object, but one look at Ealdorman Brecc's stern expression was enough to cause him to close it again. Aisley smiled. The soothing drink would be a pleasant surprise for the dejected gentleman.

♔

Brecc was twice amazed. Not only had Aisley successfully persuaded Rheged to drink an entire goblet of her herbal tonic, but she had also done so with the patience of a saint. A few sips with lengthy pauses between had made the process painfully slow, but it seemed to have worked. Rheged had held the liquid down and was already showing signs of improvement.

"There," Aisley said, setting the empty goblet on the table. "That was not so terribly bad, was it?"

"No." Rheged cleared his throat awkwardly. "I daresay I have not been my best self since you arrived. I am grateful to you for assisting me regardless of my whining."

"I believe I have listened to a full year's worth in one day," Brecc said. "Which means you have expended your entire whining allotment until Twelfth Night a year from now."

Rheged chuckled. It was the first time he'd shown any hint of amusement in hours, and secretly, Brecc was immensely grateful to see it.

"I can make no such promise, but I shall attempt to finish off the day without complaint."

"A worthy—albeit meager—goal," Brecc said.

Aisley reached for her cloak. "It would be best if you kept to your bed and limited yourself to wormwood and thyme infusions until the morrow," she said. "As encouraging as it is to see your improvement, you must not overextend yourself too soon."

Rheged's hopeful expression fell, and he gave Brecc a knowing look. "Well played, Brecc. Well played."

Brecc grinned. He'd known Rheged for years. His friend lived for large, boisterous social events. There was little that would prevent him from attending a dance or feast. Except perhaps the admonition of a quietly spoken young lady who may well have saved his life. "I cannot imagine what you mean," he said.

"Forced to sit out this evening's festivities, and I am not permitted to complain even once."

"Why would you wish to attempt dancing when your legs have the strength of jelly?"

"Or eat roast venison and duck when I could have wormwood and thyme hot drinks?" Rheged asked. "It makes no sense whatsoever."

Aisley's lips twitched as though she were holding back a smile. "Do not be overly downhearted, Rheged. From what I was told when we arrived at the royal residence this morning, there will be plenty more feasting ahead. And I daresay you will enjoy it all the more for having missed it this night."

With a resigned sigh, Rheged leaned back against his pillow. "I hope you are right. And I also hope that Brecc is forced to dance in my stead. Knowing that he is doing something he dislikes so much will make my loss easier to bear."

Brecc shook his head in disbelief. Rheged was definitely returning to his usual self, and it was time to end this conversation before it became any worse. "Come, Aisley," he said, donning his cloak as he walked to the door. "I shall escort you back to your quarters, and we shall let this jester rest."

"You do not need to trouble yourself, sire. It is not far."

"I gave you my word that I would ensure that no one would question the time you have spent here," he said. "I intend to keep it." Without waiting for a response, he opened the door and glanced up and down the passage. It was empty. Turning his head slightly, he listened. No footsteps echoed off the flagstones. "Come," he repeated. "There is no one in sight."

Moving ahead, Brecc led her to the outer door. There were three servants in the courtyard, but they were intent upon their chores—running in and out of the kitchen with laden arms and seemingly no interest in anyone or anything else.

Brecc stepped outside. Dusk had fallen. The biting wind tugged at the edges of his cloak as he waited for Aisley to join him. "The weather has not improved since we were at the market, I fear."

She drew her hood over her head. "A good excuse to cross the courtyard quickly, then."

"Aye." That and removing her from the entrance to the men's quarters in a timely fashion.

They walked along the courtyard's perimeter, staying close to the buildings so as to glean a modicum of protection from the wind.

They passed no one, and when they reached the ladies' residence, Aisley stopped. "You have my thanks, sire. There is no need for you to go any farther. The bedchamber I share with my sister is just beyond this door."

"Will I see you at the banquet this evening?" he asked.

Her hood hid a portion of her face from him, but he caught her soft smile. "My brother has been talking of little else. He has heard wondrous things about the king's festivities during the week preceding Twelfth Night. He would not countenance me missing it."

"In that respect, your brother and Rheged are very much alike. Rheged has looked forward to all the food, dancing, and mummery for months."

"Which explains his despondency now," she said.

"Fleeting despondency is a far better state than the one he was in before you gave him of your herbs. He was gravely ill, and I had begun to worry that he might not recover."

"I am grateful that he responded so well to the treatment."

"Your father hoped you would continue to develop your gift for healing. I believe he would be very proud of what you accomplished this day."

She raised her head. "He . . . he told you that?"

"He did. I spoke to him at length when I delivered the herbs you gave me before we arrived at Wilton."

"I . . . I never knew if he received them. Wulfhere has shared very little of what happened then." She shrugged. "I was young, and he returned from the battle full of rage. I did not wish to anger him further by plying him with questions."

"It was a harrowing time that few would wish to revisit, but you may ask me anything you wish to know about the battle and the days immediately leading up to it. Unfortunately, I was not with your father when he died, but if I can answer your questions, I will do so."

To his dismay, her beautiful eyes filled with tears.

"That is most generous, sire."

"Brecc," he said. "I wish that you would call me Brecc."

"Brecc." She offered him a hesitant smile. "I should very much like to hear your memories of my father. Mayhap we can speak again before we each return to our homes."

"It shall be done." He inclined his head and took two steps back. "But now, you had best remove yourself from this inclement weather."

"Yes." She turned to reach for the door handle, but before she could grasp it, the door swung open.

"Aisley! Wherever have you been?"

Brecc studied the elegant woman standing in the doorway. Ealdorman Kendryek's wife had changed very little in six years. Her resemblance to her youngest daughter—who was currently standing at her elbow—was even more striking now that Diera was no longer a child. They both wore an air of refinement, but neither exhibited the aura of gentle kindness he recognized in Aisley.

"Good evening, Mother."

"Diera told me you raced out of your room hours ago carrying a goodly portion of the herbs we brought with us."

There was no hiding the accusation in the older woman's tone, but whether it was over Aisley's use of their precious herbs or her unexplained absence, Brecc could not tell.

"Someone in the castle was in need, and so I—"

"I am quite sure somebody in the king's household could have sent for a healer. You are a guest here. There was no call for you to become involved."

"That is true, Mistress Edla." Brecc stepped out of the shadows. "But your daughter was good enough to offer her assistance regardless."

"Ealdorman Brecc." Aisley's mother and sister dropped into hasty curtsies. It seemed that Kendryek's widow recalled who he was. So much the better. "Forgive me," she continued. "I did not see you there."

"I consider it a fortuitous meeting," he said. "I had hoped to express my thanks to you for sharing your knowledge of the healing arts with Aisley. You taught her well."

Mistress Edla appeared to stand a little taller. "Even as a child, she learned quickly."

Brecc was quite sure that was true. He was equally sure that Aisley's gift had been nurtured by a compassionate heart rather than merely an ability to memorize by rote. Now was not the time to make that distinction, however. If Aisley was to avoid her mother's censure, this was the time to appeal to the lady's vanity. "You have much to be proud of, Mistress Edla," he said. "Aisley's skills and timely intervention likely saved the life of one of the king's thegns. I daresay the king himself will wish to thank you when he hears of it."

At their next meeting, Aisley might accuse him of exaggeration, but Brecc was not beyond using either that or flattery. Besides, three hours ago, Rheged had certainly acted as though he were inching dangerously close to death. And King Alfred had always looked upon Rheged fondly. The monarch would surely be glad to know that his faithful warrior had recovered from so sudden and violent an illness.

"I am very glad to hear it." If Mistress Edla had been standing before a looking glass, she might have been accused of preening. Straightening her shoulders, she smoothed her hands down her dark-green gown and gave Aisley a pointed look. "If the king intends to single you out, Aisley, you had best be dressed appropriately. And as the banquet begins within the hour, you have no time to waste."

Aisley's mother had offered him the perfect reason to take his leave, and yet Brecc hesitated. Had he done enough to prevent Mistress Edla from putting Aisley through an inquisition after he was gone? He glanced at the young lady standing before her mother and sister. Her head was high, her expression composed.

"I am quite sure the king will be far more interested in the welfare of his warrior than on my choice of attire," Aisley said, "but if he should happen to speak to me, I shall be sure to tell him who guided me through the healing arts."

Mistress Edla tucked her arm through Aisley's. "I daresay he would be most interested to know such details."

Brecc smiled into the rapidly deepening darkness. It appeared that Aisley had picked up on his ploy to deflect interest from Rheged by appealing to her mother's conceit, and she was willing to utilize it herself. Mentally adding *perceptive* to Aisley's growing list of admirable qualities, he retreated another step. "If you will excuse me, ladies, I, too, had best prepare for the banquet."

"Of course." Mistress Edla inclined her head. "Good evening to you, Ealdorman Brecc."

"Ealdorman Brecc," Diera echoed, dropping into a small curtsy.

With her movement restricted by the position of her mother's arm, Aisley simply offered him a small smile. "Good evening, sire."

He bowed and turned away. If he hastened, he might have time to speak with the king or his adviser before the banquet began. A word in King Alfred's ear about Aisley's efforts this day might not be a bad thing after all.

CHAPTER 8

AISLEY HAD NEVER SEEN SO large a great hall nor so many people gathered in one place. Long tables laden with food and drink lined the perimeter of the room. Benches filled to capacity with the king's guests ran along both sides of all the tables except the one at the head of the room. There, King Alfred, his wife, and his closest thegns sat with an unobstructed view of the reveling visitors.

Wulfhere was seated at the far end of the head table. It was a position of honor, and he had claimed it with gratification. If he had been disappointed that he was too far removed from the king to engage in a private conversation, he was currently hiding the emotion well. He and the thegn seated at his left appeared to be in great spirits, their reddened cheeks and loud laughter hinting at rather too many goblets of ale.

For her part, Aisley was glad that she, Diera, and their mother were seated on the other side of the room. It made it far easier to quietly observe those around her without feeling that she, too, was on display. Her gaze drifted past the glowing fire in the center of the room to the musicians who were slowly circling it and then—inevitably—to Brecc. He and Ealdorman Ormod, who was seated at his left, exchanged a few words. Brecc nodded at something the king's adviser said and speared a piece of meat in the trencher before him with his dagger. Raising the piece of venison to his mouth, he looked out across the room, and his eyes met hers.

For three long, pounding heartbeats, he held her gaze, and then a jester ran between them, tossing five balls into the air in quick succession. Aisley blinked. All around her, the crowd cheered. The jester stumbled into an overly dramatic bow. The crowd laughed, and at the head table, the king's laughter joined in. Brecc smiled. He was surely responding to the jester's antics rather than to having noticed her, but Aisley's heart warmed regardless. There had been little reason for him to smile earlier today. She was glad that his worry for Rheged had lessened enough for him to enjoy the evening.

As though Diera had somehow sensed the direction of Aisley's thoughts, she leaned closer and spoke over the chatter and the music. "You must tell me before I die of curiosity. Has the mysterious ailing thegn whose name you refuse to divulge recovered enough to attend the banquet this evening?"

"To the best of my knowledge, no one has ever died purely of curiosity," Aisley said dryly. "I believe your life is safe."

"Truly, Aisley? That is all you will tell me?"

Aisley gave a weary sigh. What would it take to stem her sister's unending questions? She had deflected most of Diera's and their mother's earlier questions by claiming that the gentleman she had assisted was relying upon her discretion and that she was not at liberty to discuss him or his malady. Unfortunately, Diera remained completely undeterred.

"There are a great many people here," Aisley said. "Even if I were to attempt to answer your question, I could easily miss seeing someone."

Her sister raised a disbelieving eyebrow. "He was under your care. If he is here, you would know it."

There was truth to Diera's claim. There was also an empty space on the bench beside Brecc. Aisley reached for a piece of bread. She prayed that Rheged owned sufficient sense to keep to his room, for she harbored a rather strong suspicion that if the thegn were to walk into the great hall, Brecc would rise from his seat and promptly walk him back out again.

Mayhap answering Diera now, while there was nothing of substance to report, was the best way to put an end to her questions. "He is not here," she said.

"Well then." Diera did nothing to disguise her disappointment. "If I cannot see him for myself, I shall be forced to rely upon your observations." She leaned closer still. "Is the gentleman anywhere near as handsome as Ealdorman Brecc?"

Aisley tensed. Diera could rightly claim that this question had nothing whatsoever to do with Rheged's condition or her treatment of it. And yet

Aisley had no desire whatsoever to answer it. What was she to say? She supposed Rheged was of a goodly stature and healthy build. During the short period he'd been outside his bed, he'd been doubled over in pain, and she had not noticed such things. Indeed, she could scarcely recall the color of his hair. A rather discomforting realization given that she knew full well that Brecc's hair had the lustrous sheen of a raven's wing and fell in soft waves to his shoulders.

"I truly cannot say." Making a concerted effort to avoid looking at the head table, Aisley placed a piece of bread into her mouth and took her time chewing it.

"Do not be ridiculous." Diera was losing patience. "Either he was pleasing to the eye or he wasn't."

"He was unwell, Diera. No one looks their best under those conditions."

"Not so handsome, then." Her sister leaned back, a satisfied gleam in her eyes. "I confess, I would have been hard-pressed to believe you had you told me otherwise. Few gentlemen are so fine as Ealdorman Brecc."

It was suddenly hard to swallow her bread. Aisley reached for her goblet and took a small sip of mead. The fruity drink washed down the morsel, and she silently berated herself for acting like a fool. What did it matter if Diera singled out Brecc? Nothing. Aisley set down her goblet and tucked her clasped hands beneath the table. That was right. It meant nothing.

♛

Never before had Brecc envied a court jester. He had no desire to play the buffoon, to maintain a comedic or overly energetic role before the masses, and yet, as he watched Aisley's expression of wonder from across the room, he found himself wishing that he—not the whirling juggler—was the one who had so fully captured her attention.

Since he'd seen her last, she'd changed into a lavender-colored gown with embroidered embellishments at the neckline. Her hair, twisted into a coppery crown around her head, shimmered in the candlelight, and as he watched, she offered the jester a shy smile in exchange for a small ball.

"I do not recognize the two young ladies who have so entranced our jester," Ormod said. "Do you?"

With a start, Brecc realized Ormod was speaking to him. "I beg your pardon?"

"The ladies." Ormod gestured to the distant table where Aisley sat. "Who are they?"

Another glance in that direction told Brecc that the jester had offered Diera one of his other balls and was encouraging both ladies to throw them. Diera was smiling coyly. Aisley appeared distinctly uncomfortable.

"They are the sisters of Ealdorman Wulfhere," Brecc said. "And the older lady sitting beside them is their mother."

"Ah, yes." Ormod strained to see beyond the jester. "A striking woman, if I remember correctly."

"You do."

"And one daughter looks much the same."

"Both daughters have much to recommend them." Why he should feel so irritated that Ormod noticed only Diera's physical resemblance to her mother, Brecc could not tell. Her kind-hearted disposition notwithstanding, in his opinion, Aisley's hair color and diminutive stature set her apart in the best possible way. "I learned only this afternoon that the oldest, Aisley, is also a gifted healer."

"Is that so?"

"Aye. She was good enough to offer her assistance to Rheged when she came upon us at the market, and I am grateful to report that he is already feeling much improved."

Ormod eyed the vacant spot on the other side of Brecc. "I wondered what had become of the fellow. He's not one to miss a banquet if he can help it."

"True. And I daresay he would have come tonight had I not insisted that he rest. Less than three hours ago, he was deathly ill."

Ormod appeared suitably impressed. "An extraordinary healer indeed. Or else a young lady blessed with good fortune."

"In this instance, I would wager it is the former," Brecc said.

"If that is so, I wonder how she came by her skill. It is not common amongst the nobility."

It was the very opening Mistress Edla had wished for, but before Brecc could enlighten Ormod further, the king rose to his feet, and a sudden, expectant hush fell over the room.

"My friends!" King Alfred's voice carried across the large space. "We have enjoyed a fine meal together, but the queen informs me that the evening would be incomplete without some dancing. What say you?" A ripple of excitement traveled the room, and the king offered his wife a satisfied smile. "It appears that our guests are in agreement with you, my dear." At the queen's nod, the king clapped his hands. "Ladies and gentlemen, take your places for the carole."

The scrape of benches being tucked beneath tables filled the room. Servants scattered, clearing the center of the floor as the lutist joined the psalterist in the corner and began to play a familiar tune. Brecc hesitated only until he saw a broad-shouldered gentleman lead Diera into the dance circle, and then he rose. Ormod's surprised expression was understandable. Brecc could not remember the last time he had participated in a dance. But this evening seemed a good time to make a change.

Mindful that the dance would begin at any moment, Brecc crossed the floor in long, rapid strides. Already, the number of participants had grown to fill the space between the tables and the fireplace in the center of the room. They blocked his vision of the table where Aisley had been seated, and it suddenly struck him that he might not reach her before she was escorted onto the floor by another. Squaring his shoulders, he wove through a chattering group of expectant dancers. If she was no longer in her seat, he would simply have to ask another young lady to join him. At this point, he was committed.

A couple sidestepped him, and suddenly, he was standing before a table with Aisley gazing up at him.

"Brecc!" In an instant, her look of stunned disbelief turned to concern. "Has something happened to—" She caught herself. "Your associate. Has he taken a turn for the worse?"

Unsure as to whether he should admire her overarching concern for Rheged or be disheartened that she seemingly saw no other reason for him to be standing before her, Brecc shook his head slightly. "As far as I am aware, your patient is resting still." He cleared his throat. "I came to see if you would like to join me in dancing the carole."

Her eyes widened. "I had thought you did not dance."

"I do not often participate," he said, "but I am fully capable of performing the steps."

Color tinged her cheeks, but she rose immediately. "I should be honored."

The music rose in volume, and behind him, he sensed movement in the dance circle. "We shall have to cut in," he said, reaching for her hand. It was small and warm and fit in his perfectly. Tightening his grip, he drew her toward the circle and tapped the shoulder of Ealdorman Lufian. The gentleman ascertained his need in a glance. With a grudging nod, he released the hand of the lady at his right and slid to the left. Brecc and Aisley slipped into the gap and were quickly absorbed by the dancers.

♛

Aisley stepped to the right, her feet keeping time with the music as the body of dancers circled around the room. They moved slowly and smoothly, yet her heart raced. Brecc rarely danced, but he had left the head table and crossed the entire length of the great hall to dance with her. Why would he do such a thing? Was he simply wishing to please his king? Or had he felt sorry for her when another gentleman had so quickly claimed Diera? Her pulse slowed a fraction. She did not desire his pity.

The carole's refrain began, and as was the custom, the dancers sang to the music. Brecc joined in, his voice deep and melodic. She glanced at him, and he raised an amused eyebrow.

"Does it surprise you so much that I can recall the steps and the words to the song?" he asked when the chorus ended.

Silently praying that he would attribute the warmth flooding her cheeks to the fire they were circling, she chose honesty over denial. "In truth, I am beginning to think that your dancing and singing are not nearly so impressive as your ability to read minds."

He laughed. "I shall choose to take that as a compliment rather than as a reflection of how badly out of practice I am with the carole."

His modesty extracted a smile from her. He had not placed a foot wrong during the entire dance, and he surely knew how well he carried a tune. Her brother, Wulfhere, would have drawn attention to his talents. She found that she much preferred Brecc's understated confidence—a confidence that she guessed could withstand a little teasing.

"You may if you wish. Though that is undoubtedly why I am receiving such pitying looks from the other young ladies in the circle," Aisley said. "They know that it is only a matter of time before you stand upon my feet."

He shook his head. "More fool me. I had hoped you would pay those astute ladies no mind. At least, not until your throbbing toes were too painful to ignore."

The carole's refrain began again, and as they rounded the corner beside the musicians, Brecc took an extra step and slid his foot into hers. Aisley gasped, her eyes instinctively darting to his face. Mirth twinkled in his dark-brown eyes, and she smothered a smile.

"Nicely done, sire," she said. "But I fear you will have to try that again." She tossed him a saucy look. "It seems that you missed my toes." Before he could respond, she turned away and began to sing.

She heard his chuckle above the music, and then he was singing too.

CHAPTER 9

BRECC PASSED THROUGH THE WIDE gate and exited the royal estate. The sun was slowly rising above the horizon, casting a pale-blue light over the mist hanging across the River Avon. Pulling his cloak more closely around his shoulders, he followed the path that ran along the estate walls until he reached the fork that led to the bridge and the entrance to town. A goose honked, and above Brecc's head, a *V* formation of the large birds sailed southward, no doubt seeking warmer climes. If Brecc had wings, he'd be tempted to follow after them.

Moving away from the gravel path, he crossed the ice-crusted grass to the riverbank. The sound of his footsteps followed him, magnified by the imprisoning mist. He would be hard-pressed to see much of the river this morning. At least, not until the mist rose. It would have been wiser to wait, but after a fitful night, he'd been more than ready to quit his pallet and set his mind on something other than a petite young lady who had so fully captured his attention that he had deigned dance three caroles, and who had made him smile more in one evening than he had done in the previous six months.

He'd spent half the night attempting to reverse whatever charm Aisley had placed upon him. Less than one day in her presence should not cause his thoughts to deviate so fully from their normal course. Mayhap she'd actually placed her spell upon him in her youth and it had been lying dormant during the intervening years. Now that he thought on it, his memories of her observant nature, her burning desire to aid her father, and her expressive green eyes were more firmly seated than most recollections from so long ago. But those memories did not stir the same feelings in him that he'd experienced while holding her hand last night.

A dog barked in the distance, and from the other side of the royal estate wall, a cockerel crowed. It would not be long before the sounds of servants starting their work in the king's stables and kitchen broke up the steady rush of running water coming from the river. Releasing a frustrated sigh, Brecc started along the riverbank. If he were fortunate, the morning mist would rise by the time he reached the riverbend, and the waterway would open to his view.

He spotted the small hooded figure as soon as he rounded the bend. The person was bent over at the water's edge and appeared to be gathering something on the ground. Disinclined to enter into a conversation with a stranger, Brecc veered right, moving off the path so as to pass by without interrupting the other person's activity. He'd taken only four steps through the damp grass when his foot landed upon a stick. The wood cracked, and with a cry of alarm, the figure at the riverbank leaped upright, causing the hood of their cloak to drop. A curtain of copper-colored hair tumbled out.

"Aisley!" Brecc froze. "Whatever are you doing here?"

She placed a hand to her chest. "Currently, attempting to calm my racing heart. As of a few moments ago, gathering cowslip."

"Gathering cowslip?" Brecc stepped closer, and for the first time, he noticed a small basket lying at Aisley's feet that appeared to be filled with greenery.

"I could hardly believe it when I saw it." Enthusiasm rang in her voice. "Cowslip usually blooms in April and May, but just look at this." She picked up a stem from the basket and held it out to him. He caught the flowers' faint perfume. Or mayhap it was Aisley's perfume. He could not rightly tell. "Every part of the plant can be used for one ailment or another."

Brecc shook his head slightly, as though the action would somehow clear his mind.

"You are out here in the early hours of the morning to gather plants all alone?"

"I do not make a habit of requesting a servant to assist me at this hour, especially as I rarely see another soul." She cocked her head to one side and looked at him curiously. "Why are you here?"

Over the last few weeks, an inner voice had sounded a warning, and experience had told him that it should not be ignored. Even to his own ears, the reason sounded ludicrous. But it was better than the alternative. He was not prepared to tell Aisley that he was here because thoughts of her had prevented his sleeping.

"I enjoy coming to the river when it is quiet," he said. "It is a good time to watch the watercraft arriving."

She was still studying him. "Is there a particular boat you are waiting for?"

Brecc hesitated. How much more should he share? And how had she gained such remarkable perception? "Might I suggest that of the two of us, you are the one better versed in mind reading?"

Her smile was so slight, he barely caught it. "When one prefers to sit and watch over participating, it becomes easier to catch things that are not spoken."

It was a phenomenon he was all too familiar with. And if he were being fully honest with himself, that same type of instinct told him that he could trust Aisley. He did not wish to alarm her, but she was a native of Wessex. She knew the threat the Vikings posed to their people, of the continued skirmishes occurring along their borders. His concerns should come as no real surprise.

"Reports recently reached King Alfred that the Viking chief, Guthrum, is amassing a large number of men along Wessex's border," he said. "The king has scouts monitoring the Vikings' movements and is confident that they would get word to him should the Vikings' movements develop into anything truly threatening."

"But you are less sure," she guessed.

"I have seen how quickly the Vikings can rally. If Guthrum breaks the oath he made after the Battle of Wilton and chooses to launch an attack from the water, his men could travel the Avon far more quickly than a Saxon could ride to Chippenham, no matter how speedy his mount."

She turned to look downriver.

The water was clear of all boats. Brecc prayed it would stay that way.

"This Guthrum," she said. "He is the one who led the Vikings at Wilton, is he not?"

"He is."

She remained silent. Brecc waited, sensing her warring emotions.

"Do you know how my father died?" she asked softly.

He had promised to answer her questions, but it would not be easy. For either of them. "Allow me to carry your basket," he said, "and we shall walk a short distance together."

She handed him the basket filled with cowslip, and he offered her his other arm. When she'd slid her hand around it, he led her back to the path.

"I spoke to your father twice before he died," he began. "The first time was when I sought him out after our first day's ride so that I might give him the herbs you sent."

"How was he then?"

"The journey had been difficult for him, but your gift lifted his spirits immensely. He spoke very fondly of you."

"I am not sure that I have yet thanked you for making that delivery," she said. "It was very impertinent of me to ask it of you."

"It was my honor. I saw how much the tea eased your father's discomfort."

"Did it truly?"

He nodded. "The next time I saw him, we were on the battlefield. He was weak but insistent that he participate. He held the line with Wulfhere beside him. The Vikings were unprepared for the heart with which we fought that day. Ultimately, they were forced to retreat."

Aisley's wide eyes met his. "But the Saxons were not the victors."

"We let down our guard." Bitterness filled his voice. "It should not have happened. When the Vikings retreated, our men—exhausted yet exhilarated—broke ranks to celebrate." He paused as the memories of that awful scene came flooding back. "I saw your father. He had given his all."

"It was the illness that took him, then?"

Brecc shook his head. "The Vikings returned, and we were unprepared for them. They swept through the battlefield like howling fiends, slaughtering everyone in their path. Your father was too weak to fight or to run."

Silent tears were rolling down Aisley's face. "He did what he set out to do," she whispered.

"Aye." He stopped, set the basket on the ground, and raised his hand to gently wipe the tears from her cheeks. She was cold, and he longed to comfort her but did not know how. "He was a good and honorable man, Aisley. He fought for his home, family, and people, and loth though he was to leave you, I believe he was at peace with knowing that his life would likely end on that quest."

"No matter whether it was his illness that took him or the actions of an invader." Her voice broke.

"They both take equal amounts of courage, I believe."

She managed a watery smile. "The last words he spoke to me were of courage. He said that we must be brave together."

"Losing your father at a young age most certainly required that."

She looked up at him then, the discernment he was beginning to recognize shining in her tear-filled eyes. "How old were you?"

"Eight years of age. My father was an adviser to King Aethelwulf. He and the king died within a few months of each other. As you know, the kingdom then fell to King Aethelwulf's older son. Prince Alfred was only ten years of age at the time, and as we were experiencing similar losses, we spent much time together." He shrugged. "It seemed natural to continue that close association even after he became king."

"You were brave together," she said.

"I suppose that is true."

She took a deep, unsteady breath, then picked up the basket. "It might be best if I return to the longhouse before my mother and sister awaken."

Brecc nodded. "Even if you return bearing a bounteous crop of cowslip, I believe that would be wise."

Her tears had stopped, but he suspected her emotions were too fragile for further conversation, so without a word, he offered her his arm, and they started back the way they had come.

Already, the mist was rising, leaving everything in its wake dripping with moisture. A loud plop sounded from the river.

Aisley started, and Brecc gave her arm a comforting squeeze. "A duck diving for its first meal of the day," he said. "There is a whole family of them living beneath the willows over there." He pointed to the large tree hanging over the river. "At first, they were rather loud in their disapproval of my being on their portion of the riverbank each morning, but we've smoothed things over, and they now tolerate my presence without a single quack."

This time, Aisley's smile reached her eyes, and Brecc felt the tightness in his chest ease. He'd likely shared more than he should have with her, but she had lived with the weight of not knowing about her father's final days for too long. She might need time to ponder what he'd told her and to grieve anew, but he was fully convinced that Aisley was every bit as courageous as her father. She would manage as nobly as Kendryek had.

"I thank you for talking to me so freely." They were approaching the entrance to the royal estate. Her feet slowed to a stop, and she withdrew her arm from his.

"If my account has caused you pain, I am truly sorry."

She shook her head. "Your show of trust and understanding means more than I can say."

"I believe you have exhibited similar amounts of those qualities."

"Then we are even." She smiled again, and his heart warmed. "Good day to you, Brecc."

"Good day, Aisley. Oh, and watch for the cats patrolling near the stables. If caught unawares, they will make almost as much noise as the ducks."

She nodded. "A valuable warning. I shall avoid all creatures, great and small, and wish you a similarly quiet return."

CHAPTER 10

WHEN BRECC ARRIVED BACK AT the thegn's longhouse, Rheged was out of his bed and donning his clothes for the day.

"You appear much improved," Brecc said.

"I am." He reached for his belt. "And though I appreciate how much Aisley's brew helped me, I am ready to eat some real food."

Brecc chuckled. If Rheged's renewed vigor had been an insufficient clue to his improved health, the return of his appetite was testament enough.

"How was the river?" Rheged asked.

"Quiet," Brecc replied.

Rheged grunted. "As it always is at this time of day."

"It's not that I wish it to be any different." Brecc dropped onto a nearby stool.

"It's just that you fear one day it will be," his friend finished for him.

"Think on it, Rheged. It is well known throughout Wessex that the king and all his closest men and warriors are here. For the Vikings, that means only one location must needs be attacked to decimate the Saxons' leadership."

"Guthrum took the danegeld. He made an oath to leave Wessex in peace."

"How much longer do you think that will last?" Brecc asked. "Until the gold is gone? Until their avarice overcomes their honor?" He rose and paced across the small room. "The Vikings have a history of breaking their oaths. It makes no difference which pagan god they pledge to, the oath means nothing to them when their coffers are empty. We have only to look to our neighbors, Mercia and Northumbria, to see that."

"What you say is true, but the king has men positioned at our borders. They will ensure the Vikings do not come upon us unawares."

Brecc ran his fingers through his hair. There was little point in pursuing this conversation. He and Rheged had exchanged a similar one when the royal party had first arrived in Chippenham almost a fortnight ago. Little had changed since then. Brecc's disquiet remained, as did Rheged's belief that all would be well. Thus far, Rheged seemed to have the right of it. But Brecc could not shake his conviction that should it happen, news of an imminent Viking invasion would travel far more quickly by word of mouth along the river than by a single scout navigating the countryside on horseback. The men who plied the waters to make a living were a tight-knit group. Not only would they pass along such a warning quickly, but they would also hasten to remove themselves and their boats from harm's way.

"I pray you are right, my friend," Brecc said.

"I am. You shall see." Rheged gave Brecc's shoulder a good-natured slap. "But whilst we are on the subject of rumors, I should like to know why you unexpectedly chose to take up dancing on the one night I was not there to witness it."

Brecc glared at him. "Who have you been speaking with?"

"Ah!" Rheged grinned. "Surely you are aware that one of the most important rules of rumors is that one never shares the identity of one's informant."

"That is ridiculous."

"So is the notion that you willingly danced the carole."

Brecc raised his eyes to the ceiling. "You were gone. I took your place on the dance floor. You should be thanking me."

"For enjoying the evening whilst I lay languishing upon my pallet? I think not." Rheged leaned forward. "Who was the favored young lady? My informant was rather vague on that subject."

"How very unfortunate for you." Brecc slid his arm beneath his pallet and withdrew his sword. "I am scheduled for some sword practice. Do you wish to join me?"

"That was a remarkably blunt change of subject."

Brecc slid his sword beneath his belt and started for the door. "Are you coming?"

"Aye. On one condition." Rheged folded his arms and waited until Brecc turned back to face him. "If I win, you tell me who you danced with."

"Agreed."

Rheged's eyebrows shot up in surprise. "Agreed? Just like that?"

"You heard me."

"Very well." Rheged claimed his sword from beneath his own pallet. "Prepare to tell me everything."

Brecc smothered a grin. Under normal conditions, he and Rheged were fairly evenly matched competitors. But these were not normal conditions. Brecc's overarching concern about Guthrum's plans and his recent emotionally charged conversation with Aisley had left him in desperate need of a challenging physical outlet. He would fight especially hard today. And Rheged had not eaten for over twenty-four hours. Brecc reached for the door. "Never fear, you may concede at any time."

Aisley completed her second circuit around the inner walls of the royal estate, having barely noticed the lush greenery, the half dozen buildings, or the clear blue sky. Her thoughts were on her father—on what he must have suffered during the long journey to Wilton and the battle there and on how much she missed his steadying presence. Memories of his voice, his smile, and his kindness filled her and melded with words, expressions, and gestures she'd shared with Brecc these last two days.

Not many gentlemen would have been so forthright with a lady. Somehow, he had managed to separate the gruesome reality of what he'd experienced with the information she'd so desperately desired. He had shared more with her during a short walk along the riverbank than Wulfhere had shared with her in six years. Without resorting to descriptions that would invite nightmares, he had offered her enough to bring a blessed level of closure to a chapter of her life—of her father's life—that had been unsettled for so long.

Gratitude welled within her, and she wiped away another tear. She had shed many since escaping her mother, Diera, and the other women in the longhouse. Thankfully, her mother had been too pleased by her unexpected collection of cowslip to question her further on her early-morning outing.

For her part, Diera had been so fully engrossed in an elaborate tapestry she and some of the other women were creating that she'd barely acknowledged Aisley's return to the longhouse. It was just as well. Their distraction had enabled Aisley to slip away again, this time to walk the estate and sort through her thoughts alone.

She reached a large oak. Slowing, she set her hand against the gnarled bark, drawing strength from the old tree's solid presence. Her eyes stung. She closed them, raising her head to face the sky above. The cold air caused her cheeks to tingle.

"What is it this time, Aisley?" At the sound of her brother's voice, Aisley's eyes flew open. "Are you plotting a way to add oak bark to one of your tinctures, or are you merely daydreaming?"

In her present condition, Wulfhere's sarcasm cut deeper than it should. "Neither. I am simply taking a moment to enjoy nature."

"In these frigid temperatures?" Wulfhere eyed her disapprovingly. "Your nose and eyes are so red, you have likely done damage to them."

If she had damaged any part of her body during this day's activities, it was her heart. Deep sorrow would certainly do that. The facial discoloration her tears had caused would fade, but mayhap it was for the best that Wulfhere thought she was suffering from the cold.

"You are right," she said. "I should return to the longhouse."

He grunted, seemingly surprised that she had agreed so quickly. "I am going that way. I shall walk with you."

They started toward the women's longhouse in silence. Aisley's feelings were too raw to discuss their father, but as the silence between them lengthened, she felt compelled to say something. "Have you enjoyed the royal festivities as much as you imagined you would?"

"Arriving late certainly put me at a disadvantage," he grumbled. "The best accommodations were already taken, and I have yet to be introduced to many of the guests. But the food and drink have been adequate."

Adequate? That was hardly the word Aisley would have used to describe the feast they had enjoyed the night before. "I thought last evening was quite splendid."

"I am sure you did." He eyed her curiously. "Was there any particular reason that Ealdorman Brecc asked you to partner him in the carole?"

"Because he wished to, I imagine." Aisley had self-doubts aplenty on that score, but a modicum of pride prevented her from sharing them with her arrogant brother. "I thought you were too far into your cups to notice."

Wulfhere scowled. "Not so far gone as all that. And I daresay I was not the only one to wonder why he would single you out."

When he could have had his pick of any of the other ladies in the room. The words went unspoken, but they hung in the air between them. After all, what gentleman in his right mind would consider a petite young woman with reddish hair and a liberal sprinkle of freckles across her nose when he could choose a tall, elegant lady with hair the color of ripened wheat and skin as white as snow?

"If you saw him approach our table, you surely know that Diera had already been asked by another."

"I noticed," he said, "and it caused me to realize that I have neglected acquiring suitors for you both for far too long." He appeared unusually thoughtful. "Two advantageous marriages would go a long way to replenishing the family's dwindling finances."

Shock rendered her momentarily speechless, but when she found her voice, it shook with indignation. "You would sell your sisters to the highest bidders to cover your mismanagement of funds?"

"You know nothing of my financial dealings."

"I know enough to recognize excessive spending on clothing and the horses in our stables," she said. "I also am fully aware that the people of Wiltshire never suffered from so much poverty when father was ealdorman."

Wulfhere reached for her arm and pulled her to a halt before him. "Leave Father out of this discussion," he growled.

"Why?" She thought she had cried herself dry, but tears were pricking the back of her eyes once more. "If he was so important to you, do what you know he would have wished you do. What he would be doing if he were still here."

"And just what do you think that is?"

"Taking care of the people under your stewardship," she said.

He released her arm with a snort. "Further proof that you speak out of ignorance. I have taken care of you, Diera, and Mother since the day Father died. And I shall continue to do so by finding you and Diera wealthy husbands."

Aisley was beginning to feel nauseated. "And the common people of Wiltshire? What of them?"

"Their misfortune can be placed firmly at the feet of King Alfred," he said. "He was the one who ordered the men to enter a battle when he was incapable of leading them to victory. He was the one who drained Wessex of all its wealth to pay for that mistake. Wiltshire lacks men to work the fields and money in the coffers because of the miscalculations of our king."

No hint of sorrow for their suffering. No concession that he might have done more to ease it. Six years before, King Alfred had been young and inexperienced, certainly, but if Brecc's account of the Battle of Wilton was to be believed, it was the men who had broken ranks and begun a premature celebration, not the monarch.

Revulsion clawed at her throat. "You accept no blame and would malign the king while staying as a guest in his residence?"

"I speak the truth as I see it." He lowered his voice. "And believe me, I am not the only nobleman in Wessex to feel this way."

"And what will you and these others of whom you speak do when the ring-giver offers you each his gifts at the banquet this evening?"

"We shall accept them willingly." Wulfhere began walking again, crossing the short remaining distance to the women's longhouse in long strides and forcing Aisley to run to keep up with him. "Only a fool would turn down such a gift."

"It is given in exchange for loyalty to the king," she reminded him.

"Aye. And he has it." He waited for Aisley to take hold of the door-latch. "For now, at least."

"Wulfhere!"

"Good day, Aisley," he said.

She watched him walk away. Her heart that had ached so acutely such a short time ago now felt numb.

CHAPTER 11

"WHAT DID YOU DO TO Aisley?"

"I beg your pardon." Brecc looked up from his unenthusiastic contemplation of the roast goose on the trencher before him.

"You heard me." Seated beside him at the high table, Rheged studied Brecc with narrowed eyes. "Or mayhap it was not something you did but something you said."

"I cannot imagine what you are referring to."

"Is that so?" Rheged put a piece of meat in his mouth and chewed it slowly, his gaze gliding past Brecc to settle on Aisley. "Just because you had me on my back with the tip of your sword at my chest before I could so much as catch my breath this morning, it does not mean I did not discover who you danced with last evening."

Brecc should have guessed as much. "It was no secret."

"No. But you treated it as such. Which made it particularly satisfying to uncover." Rheged's calculating gaze returned to him. "You fought me this morning like a man possessed. And this evening, Aisley has not once turned to look at you. Not because she is fully diverted by the people at her table, for she has scarcely exchanged a word with anyone there, but rather because she seemingly does not wish to look this direction."

Brecc's stomach clenched. It had been easier to brush off Aisley's seemingly ill-disposed behavior before Rheged had confirmed its reality. "I truly do not know why she would avoid looking at anyone seated at the head table," he said.

"Not everyone," Rheged corrected him. "She has watched her brother's interactions with those at the end of the table on more than one occasion."

"You would make an excellent spy," Brecc said dryly.

"I daresay, but in this instance, I need more information to unravel the clues."

"To the best of my knowledge, Aisley enjoyed dancing the carole last evening," Brecc said. "I have nothing more to share with you." His conversation with Aisley at the river was private. As far as he was concerned, it was well within his rights to be troubled over how badly it might have affected her—especially given how wan she appeared this evening—but that interaction had nothing whatsoever to do with Rheged.

"Then I shall simply ask her," Rheged said. "She assisted me when I was ailing; it is only right that I should offer to do the same."

It was a noble suggestion, and Brecc's instant indignation mixed with irritation was wholly irrational. It was also undeniably existent.

"The king is ready to begin the ring-giving ceremony," Brecc said. "You'd best wait until that has concluded before you leave the table."

Rheged gave an accepting nod, and Brecc breathed a silent sigh of relief. Regardless of what gifts the king bestowed this evening, when the goblet was returned to the monarch, Brecc would be the first to leave the table—and the first to reach Aisley.

Aisley dipped a piece of bread into the meat juice at the bottom of the trencher she shared with Diera, keeping her eyes averted from the activity at the head table. Ealdorman Ormod had voiced his acceptance of King Alfred's gift and had passed the jewel-encrusted goblet to Brecc. She did not need to watch to know that Brecc would kiss the rim. His allegiance to the king was certain. As was his remarkable awareness of the activities of those around him. He had been the first of all the thegns to leap to his feet when the messengers had arrived at her home in Wiltshire to warn of the Viking attack all those years ago. He was likely the only one who had been diligently watching the river since the king's party had arrived in Chippenham. And he had arrived at her table the night before, moments after Diera had left to join the dancers.

Aisley knew what it was to unobtrusively study others and recognized that capacity in Brecc. It was undoubtedly one of the reasons he had ascertained her feelings so well when they had spoken at the river. It was also the reason she could not face him this evening. She had battled a maelstrom of emotions all day. Her mother and Diera had not noticed. Neither had Wulfhere. But Brecc would.

If he saw the abhorrence in her eyes when Wulfhere accepted the ring-giver's gift, he would not rest until he discovered its source. If he sensed how badly she wished there had been no pity or obligation involved when he'd asked her to dance, he might dissemble to spare her feelings further. And that would be worse. She wanted Brecc to always speak the truth to her. Even if it hurt.

"I would contend that the ring-giver's gifts are overly modest this year." There was no mistaking the criticism in her mother's voice. "A small pouch of coins for an oath of full allegiance asks a great deal of each thegn."

Each thegn, or simply her son?

"Given that so much of Wessex's gold was given to the Vikings in exchange for our freedom, it is understandable," Aisley said.

"It is the churches that have lost their treasures, not the king," her mother retorted. "Else how could he have put on twelve days of feasting for so many?"

"Mayhap he considers the banquets and entertainment to be part of his gift giving," Aisley suggested.

"Hush." Diera patted Aisley's arm to draw her attention to the end of the head table. "It is Wulfhere's turn."

Their brother exchanged a meaningful glance with the thegn seated beside him and accepted the king's goblet.

"Who is the thegn sitting next to Wulfhere?" Aisley asked. Someone whose devotion to the crown was as insincere as her brother's?

"Hush, Aisley!" This time it was her mother. "We must see what Wulfhere receives."

Performing every expected gesture, Wulfhere bowed to King Alfred and raised the goblet to his lips. The king acknowledged the action with an inclination of his head before handing Wulfhere a small leather purse. Aisley watched as Wulfhere loosened the leather ties and withdrew a small piece of jewelry. He set it on the palm of his hand. The muscle in his jaw twitched, but then he offered a polite smile.

"I am honored, Your Majesty."

"That is all?" Aisley's mother hissed. "A silver brooch no wider than a chestnut?"

Aisley swallowed against her suddenly dry throat. "Mother!" She kept her voice low. "We can barely see the gift from here. It may be far more valuable than you believe." A generous gift might have bought Wulfhere's allegiance until the next ring-giving ceremony; a gift that he considered insultingly parsimonious may well do the opposite.

"King Aethelred would never have given his thegns so little. During his reign, a pouch such as the one Wulfhere received would have been brimming with jewelry."

Aisley refrained from pointing out that with no means of acquiring more jewelry in the meantime, King Aethelwulf's generosity was likely the primary reason that King Alfred was forced to be more sparing with his gifts. Regardless of its accuracy, in this state of mind, her mother would not have taken the observation well.

"Wulfhere is leaving the table," Diera said.

A quick glance confirmed Diera's remark. Several of the thegns who'd been seated at the head table were now on their feet. With most of the food consumed and the ring-giving ceremony over, it seemed that the evening's celebration was over.

"Signal him, Diera," their mother said. "I wish to see the brooch."

Diera rose to do her mother's bidding, and Aisley knew that it was time for her to leave. Wulfhere's self-seeking disposition would undoubtedly overcome civility, and she had no desire to listen to him and their mother belittle the king for his gift.

Determined to remove herself while she still could, she came to her feet. "If you would excuse me," she said. "I believe I will retire early."

"Surely not before you have seen your brother's gift," her mother said incredulously. "Wulfhere is almost upon us."

Which was precisely why she wished to go. "I am sure there will be many who wish to view it. I shall undoubtedly see Wulfhere on the morrow. He can show it to me then."

Her mother frowned, clearly displeased. Already, the great hall was filling with people who had left their seats to mingle with other guests. Wulfhere's voice rose above the rest, and their mother turned to greet him.

It was exactly the distraction Aisley needed. Without another word, she reached for the cloak she'd set beneath the bench and stepped away.

Slipping around the table, she fumbled with the fabric of her cloak. The milling people made it difficult to draw it over her shoulders. She tugged at it, and suddenly, the fabric lifted.

"Allow me." At the sound of Brecc's voice, Aisley's heart leaped—only to begin thumping wildly as panic settled upon her. Ignoring Brecc had been much easier when he'd been on the other side of the room. Now that she was within arm's distance, his tall, broad-shouldered presence was far harder to disregard. "May I speak with you for a moment?"

"Why?"

Lines appeared on his brow. The question had surprised him.

"I wished to inquire regarding your health. At the banquet this evening you appeared . . ." He paused as though choosing his words carefully. "You did not seem quite yourself, and I was concerned that mayhap I had caused you undue suffering."

She shook her head slightly. "I confess, I shed many tears after our conversation this morning, but I remain grateful to you for your openness. Some tears were of sadness for what my father was forced to endure and a renewed sense of loss that he is gone; some were of anger for the length of time I was forced to wait to learn the details you shared."

"I am sorry."

"There is no need." Donning her cloak in the crowded room had been a mistake. She started toward the door and the cooler outside air. "I do not desire your pity, Brecc."

He caught up to her in two long strides. "My pity? Whyever would you think that I felt pity for you?"

"Why would you not? You know me as a young lady who lost her father too soon, who was left in ignorance of the circumstances too long, and who is far more used to observing her sister dance the carole than participating in the dance herself."

They had reached the door. If he accepted her response, he could leave her now. But there must have been something in Aisley's voice, some hint of the desperation she felt to truly know his answer to this question, that caused him to do the opposite. Clasping her elbow firmly in one hand, he opened the door with the other. "Come," he said, propelling her forward.

The cold air swirled around Brecc's ankles and stung his cheeks. He took a deep breath, hoping the icy lungful would do something to clear his head. Aisley's question had left him reeling. Had he truly given her the impression that his interactions with her were motivated by pity? If so, he had significant repair work to do.

The door to the great hall opened again, emitting half a dozen laughing, talkative people.

He lowered his head to Aisley's ear. "I was not so wise as you and did not reclaim my cloak before leaving. If you are not opposed to conversing in the company of horses, mayhap we could relocate to the stables." He managed the ghost of a smile. "I might be easier to understand if my teeth are not chattering incessantly."

"Very well."

Keeping his hand on her arm, he guided her away from the path that led to the women's and men's longhouses and toward the large building at their right. A faint flicker of candlelight showed between the chinks in the stable door, guiding them to the entrance. As they stepped closer, Brecc released Aisley's elbow and reached out to feel for the latch. A gust of wind swirled around the corner, and Aisley's cloak flapped. He sensed her pulling the fabric closer.

"I have it," he said, grateful that his fingers were not yet so chilled that he could not manage the lever.

The door swung open, and a band of pale-yellow light illuminated their way inside. A candle flickered on a nearby shelf. Brecc closed the door carefully. Somewhere nearby, a horse nickered and a hoof hit against the hard-packed floor.

A shadow materialized in the darkness. "May I 'elp you, sire?"

The stableboy could not have been more than eight or nine years of age. His ruffled hair sported a few pieces of straw, and Brecc guessed that they'd disturbed his sleep.

"Where is the stablemaster?" he asked.

"In the loft, sire. Would ye have me fetch 'im?"

"That won't be necessary."

The lad looked from him to Aisley, confusion clouding his expression. "Will ye be needin' a mount, then?"

"No mount," Aisley said, coming to his rescue. "But Ealdorman Brecc would benefit greatly from a blanket. Once he has something to protect him from the cold, we shall leave you and your horses in peace."

Understanding lit the lad's face. "The wind's bin 'owlin' all evenin'. Not the kind of weather t' be outdoors without a coverin', I'd say."

"And you would be right," Aisley said.

The boy looked pleased. "I'll find a blanket. If I go t' the back, there'll be some that are a bit fresher 'un the ones up 'ere."

"That would be ideal."

The boy needed no second bidding. He disappeared in a flash.

"I thank you for explaining our appearance to the lad," Brecc said, "even if he is now convinced that I am a fool."

Aisley laughed softly. "If it is of any consolation, you accepted his bafflement very well. Most gentlemen I know would have attempted to justify their cloakless condition no matter how senseless the argument."

He studied her in the candlelight. "The truth is important to you."

All hint of humor in her expression disappeared. "It is."

"Then we have that in common." He reached for her hand, grateful when she did not pull away. His fingers were cold, but she did not flinch. "I give you my word that I will always speak the truth to you. And to that end, you must believe that not once did I approach you out of pity.

"We lost our fathers at a similar age. The circumstances were different, but a child's emotions are less complicated than those of adults, so I would surmise that our feelings regarding those difficult events were alike. I never wished for pity. Love, certainly. Reassurance, and even, on occasion, some assistance. But not pity. I would never offer you something I did not desire myself.

"As far as your second insistence is concerned, I provided you with the information you lacked simply because I could tell how much you longed to know the details of your father's last days. Recalling my experiences at the Battle of Wilton is not something I do often. The memories are unpleasant and, to this day, occasionally rob me of sleep. Pity is not a strong enough motivator for me to willingly entertain those thoughts." Her eyes had not left his, and he knew he must finish before the stableboy returned.

"Your third assertion should be the easiest to address, yet somehow, it is the hardest." He took a breath. "I asked you to join me in the carole because not only did I wish to dance with you above all the other ladies in the great hall, but I also wished to dance with you above my normal desire to remain seated."

She caught her lower lip between her teeth, and it seemed to him that her lips might be trembling.

"Is that truly so difficult to believe?" he asked.

"Yes," she whispered.

The rustle of the stableboy's footsteps in the straw was drawing nearer.

Brecc wanted to ask why she would ever have reason to doubt her worth, but there was no time for that discussion now. "We will speak of this again," he said. "Until then, I would have you know that if my legs were not longer than Rheged's, he would have beaten me to your table this evening. And if I had not had the good fortune to see you slipping away, he would have held you captive in the great hall with his entertaining stories, and I would have been left awaiting a turn to speak with you whilst simultaneously wishing that the curative you gave him had not been nearly so effective."

At her tremulous smile, Brecc's heart swelled. Flooded with the overwhelming desire to kiss her, he tightened his grip on her hand and drew her closer. Then reason stumbled into the circle of candlelight in the form of the stableboy.

"'Ere you are, sire." The lad held up a ragged blanket that smelled strongly of horse.

Brecc released Aisley's hand and attempted to gather his wits. "I thank you," he said, taking the blanket.

The boy bobbed his head and waited expectantly until Brecc draped the blanket across his shoulders.

"We had best be on our way," Aisley said.

It was a good reminder.

"I shall return the blanket on the morrow," Brecc told the stableboy.

"Right you are, sire." The lad bobbed his head a second time and then heaved open the door. "Good evenin' to ya both."

CHAPTER 12

AISLEY LAY ON HER PALLET, staring up at the shadowy outline of the rafters above. Beside her, Diera slept peacefully, her even breathing an echo of the gentle snoring coming from their mother's pallet. Aisley had been under her covers with her eyes closed when her mother and sister had returned from the great hall the night before. Their whispers had been loud enough for Aisley to gather that Wulfhere had been as disgruntled about the brooch he'd received from the king as their mother had been. Diera had made no protestations. She rarely did. Especially if the end result involved the acquisition of fine things.

Grateful that they'd assumed she was asleep, Aisley had shut out the murmuring and allowed her thoughts to dwell on Brecc. In the quiet of the stables, he'd held her hand and promised to tell her the truth. She wanted to believe his kind words, but trusting one man's declaration over years of comments that had convinced her she was inferior was difficult. Mayhap that was why she loved working with healing plants. In that sphere, she knew she excelled and could make a genuine difference. Her mother grudgingly admitted that Aisley's skills had likely surpassed her own. But in all other ways, Aisley fell short. She was not so pretty or tall or elegant as Diera, not so outgoing or confident as Wulfhere. Indeed, up until her recent interaction with Brecc, Aisley had been largely overlooked in public settings.

She had learned to expect the lack of attention; she was comfortable with it. The way Brecc made her feel, however, was not comfortable at all. She placed her hand on her stomach, hoping the extra weight would calm the fluttering that began whenever she considered the way he had looked at her in the stables, or the way it had felt to have her hand in his.

No, this sensation was not at all comfortable. Stifling a groan, she rolled onto her side. It would be horribly cold outside her covers, but continuing to lie here awake would be even more torturous.

The decision made, she donned her outerwear with as much speed as her fumbling fingers allowed. Not wanting to awaken anyone else, she picked up her shoes and tiptoed across the room. Opening the door, she stepped outside. The winds had abated, and a frosty silence hung over the buildings on the royal estate. Pausing long enough to put on her shoes, she tucked her hands beneath her cloak and stepped onto the path.

The first sounds of morning reached her as she walked. A bird singing from a treetop, a horse neighing in the stables, the clatter of pans from the kitchen, and a woman's voice—likely the cook—scolding someone for being too slow. The servants were already hard at work. It would not be long before the paths between buildings were filled with people.

Passing the kitchen, Aisley continued toward the stables. Footsteps approached, coming from the direction of the men's longhouse. Raising her hood, Aisley lowered her head slightly. Given the choice, she would rather not engage in conversation with a stranger. Especially while she was alone.

"Aisley?"

Her head shot up. "Ealdorman Rheged!"

"Rheged," he corrected. "Please call me Rheged."

"Very well." She studied his face. He had color in his cheeks—no doubt enhanced by the cold air—and the listless look was gone from his eyes. "I am glad to see you so much improved from the time I saw you at the market."

"Aye. That was a rough go. I am indebted to you for your assistance."

"Not at all." She eyed him curiously. He was without a cloak and carried a long sword in his belt. "May I be so bold as to inquire where you are off to?"

"You may." He patted the sword at his side. "I was forcibly reminded only a day ago that my swordsmanship could use some work. I thought some early-morning practice would be worthwhile."

"Such diligence is impressive."

"Well, there we are, you see. If I cannot be praised for my skill with a sword, I shall try to attain it for diligence in practice."

Aisley giggled. "Such a fine character trait must surely be worth something."

"Most certainly. And that is precisely what I shall tell Brecc when he claims he bested me the last time we sparred."

"Claims?" At the sound of Brecc's voice, Aisley's heart tripped. "Are you still refusing to admit defeat?"

Brecc stepped up beside them, but Rheged ignored him. "Pay him no mind, Aisley. It was an unfair battle. I was weakened by illness and lack of food, and he was a man possessed."

"Would you like a rematch?" Brecc asked, pointing to Rheged's sword. "It will take me only a moment to fetch my weapon."

"I believe I will take my chances with a pell," Rheged said. "It is far less likely to exploit an inequitable advantage."

Brecc smiled, but this time, it did not reach his eyes. "Fair enough. But do not destroy the pell completely."

"I shall make no promises," Rheged said. He bowed to Aisley. "Good day to you, Aisley."

"Good day, Rheged."

He offered Brecc a jaunty nod and set off toward the stables and the barn beyond. Brecc watched him go in silence.

"Were you at the river?" Aisley asked.

"Aye." He turned and offered her an apologetic smile. "Forgive me; I was lost in thought."

"Is it what you have seen or what have *not* seen there that worries you the most?"

His brow furrowed. "I did not speak of worries."

"No, but you clearly have them."

He shook his head slightly. "I am beginning to wonder if I might rue the day that I promised to always speak the truth to you."

"Of all the worries you may have, that one should never enter your mind again. If it would help to talk, I am a good listener. If you need time for quiet contemplation, we can walk in silence." She waited, barely daring to breathe. And then he smiled.

"I should like that very much," he said.

"To which 'that' do you refer?"

"Walking with you. And talking. And thinking. I believe I should like to try a little of them all."

Aisley's heart lifted. "Then we shall."

♕

Offering Aisley his arm, Brecc led her away from the cluster of buildings and toward the path that ran along the inside of the royal estate walls. She said nothing, clearly waiting for him to initiate a conversation. And yet he felt no undue pressure to speak. She truly seemed content to simply walk, and he found her presence at his side remarkably assuasive.

"Rheged thinks me a fool for concerning myself so much over a Viking invasion that has yet to materialize." He sighed. "Mayhap he is right."

"There was no sign of anything at the river this morning?" she asked.

He shook his head. "It is likely a far-flung hope that word of Viking movements would reach Chippenham that way. But it is a hope I have been willing to keep alive, if only to bring a measure of peace to my own mind." He frowned. "It has helped, but I have been unable to fully assuage my unease since our arrival here."

"There may yet be a reason." Her grip on his arm tightened. "May I share a personal experience?"

"Of course."

She nodded, taking a moment to compose her thoughts. "When I was very young, I fell into a creek that ran along the outskirts of my father's property." A smile crossed her lips. "I think it likely that I was attempting to pick flowers beyond my reach.

"Thankfully, my father arrived in time to witness the accident and to pull me from the water. Afterward, he told me that he received a distinct impression that he should remove himself from the stables, where he was seeing to one of his horses, and go to the creek. The feeling did not make any sense to him, but he chose to act upon it and, by so doing, undoubtedly saved my life." She looked up at him. "He believed that God willingly offers us warnings and instruction but that few of us listen."

"I am no priest or holy man, Aisley. It is hard to believe that God would send a message to me when He could choose someone of far greater influence."

"My father was no priest either," she said. "And I most certainly am not. Yet there have been times when I have felt prompted to offer particular herbs to someone who is ailing, without any understanding of why the herbs might help. My father's counsel has caused me to wonder if those feelings might come from a divine source."

Brecc's thoughts reeled. Surely Aisley's suggestion was unreasonable. Some men of the cloth might even consider the notion that God would communicate with a lowly girl, a father, or a warrior to be an offense against heaven. And yet, regardless of the startling nature of the concept, it did not feel blasphemous to Brecc.

His free hand rose, his finger feeling for the scar that ran across his cheek. Why had he turned at the precise moment the Viking warrior had aimed his blade at Brecc's throat? He'd not heard the heathen's approach above the horrific sounds of the battlefield, and he'd barely caught his breath from dispatching one of the Viking's comrades, but the impression to step aside had been strong enough that he had acted upon it. His face was forever scarred, but his life had been spared.

"Even if what you say is true," Brecc said, "why would God choose me? King Alfred is a pious man. He spends hours with the priest, speaking with God each day. He is fully committed to doing God's will. He would be a far better conduit for a heavenly message."

Aisley's faint smile hinted that she had pondered similar questions. "Do you recall hearing the priests tell the story of David and Saul or Esther and the Persian King? It seems to me that God has already established a pattern of communicating with those who might righteously influence a ruler." She paused. "Have you spoken of your concerns to King Alfred?"

"I have. He listened, but he believes that Guthrum will honor his oath." Brecc gave a troubled sigh. "It is what King Alfred would do, and as a man of his word, it is difficult for him to conceive of a leader doing otherwise."

"Guthrum is not guided by the same morals."

"No," Brecc said grimly. "He is not."

They passed the entrance to the estate. The gates were open, and Brecc could see the glisten of the River Avon in the distance, through the trees. In less than twenty-four hours, the thegns would leave this place for their respective homes. The king and his retinue would relocate soon after. Mayhap the Viking threat would come then, when the leadership of Wessex was scattered. Brecc wished he had a better understanding of the Viking chieftain's way of thinking.

"No matter what lies ahead for Wessex," Aisley said, "the king will benefit from having you so keenly alert to the Viking threat."

Her words were kindly meant but did little to lessen Brecc's underlying frustration. For the best part of a fortnight, he'd felt more helpless than helpful. He was ready to have the Twelfth Night celebrations behind them and some normalcy restored.

"Will you return to Trowbridge on the morrow?"

"I believe that is what my brother has planned, although my mother and sister refuse to speak of anything but the Twelfth Night banquet, so I do not know the details of our departure."

Brecc did not especially wish to consider the details of Aisley's departure either. He had come to know her uncommonly well in a few short days, and he would miss her.

The thought startled him with its intensity and truth.

"I will go with the king, but I have yet to learn his plans for our removal from here." He glanced at her. "Mayhap I could persuade him that a visit to Trowbridge would not go amiss."

The warmth of her smile lit a fire in his chest. "You would be most welcome."

They had reached the large oak. He drew her off the path and under the tree's protective limbs. She looked up at him, her beautiful green eyes capturing his. Dear heaven, how had she come to have such influence over him in so short a time?

"I shall do everything in my power to visit you there soon." He raised his hand to brush some hair from her face. The strands ran softly through his fingers.

She nodded, but the enthusiasm he had hoped for was missing. "I pray it will not be too late."

He lowered his hand. "Forgive me. Have I misstepped?"

She looked away. "Not at all."

"Aisley?" Gently, he touched her jaw, guiding her eyes back to his. "Tell me what is troubling you."

She met his gaze without flinching. "Wulfhere informed me yesterday that he intends to find wealthy suitors for me and Diera forthwith. He wishes to use our marriages as a means of filling his coffers."

Her words were like a physical punch to the stomach. Did Wulfhere truly see his sisters as nothing more than property to be bought and sold?

Brecc had the ear of the king and a valuable parcel of land on the southern coast, but he had no hidden stash of gold. Upon his father's death, Brecc had been left sufficient funds for his needs; amassing a fortune had never been his focus. Truth be told, up until three days ago, he had not given more than a fleeting thought to providing for a wife and family sometime in his distant future. At twenty-seven years of age, he was still young, and his life was devoted to defending the crown, which left little room for anything—or anyone—else. Even now, he was not sure that he was ready for marriage. He simply knew that the thought of Aisley married to another made him want to beat Rheged in a sword fight even more handily than he had the last time.

"Wulfhere cannot do that." Even as Brecc spoke the words, he knew they were false. The ealdorman was fully within his rights to arrange marriages for his sisters.

"He can, and he will." She swallowed, and the hurt in her eyes was almost Brecc's undoing. "So, if you do intend to come to Trowbridge, I would ask that you not delay your visit too long."

"I shall come," he promised.

She nodded again, and this time, a single tear rolled down her cheek. He caught it with his thumb, his palm cupping her jaw as his fingers disappeared beneath her hair. Her skin was so soft. He took an unsteady breath, willing himself to take a step back. Now. Before it was too late.

"I will watch for you," she whispered. "Every day."

His heart pounding, he drew her closer. He hadn't truly wanted to retreat. He knew that. But was this what she desired? Lowering his head, he hesitated one excruciatingly long moment, and when she did not pull back, he brushed her lips with his. Her breath caught, but then she leaned into him, and his lips sought hers once more.

She smelled of thyme and some other flower she must have been gathering recently, and she fit in his arms as if she were always meant to be there. He pressed her closer, losing himself in the deepening kiss. And then, somewhere nearby, a cockerel crowed, announcing the beginning of a new day. Slowly, reluctantly, Brecc relaxed his hold on Aisley. She took a stumbling step back before raising her head to meet his gaze. Soft color tinged her cheeks.

He smiled gently. "I believe that irritating bird was determined to wish you good morning."

"Good morning?" She gasped and turned away. "I must go!"

"Is there somewhere you must be straightway?"

"Yes. No." She started toward the path, and Brecc hastened to follow after her. "I do not suppose we are the only people in the vicinity to have heard the cockerel's wake-up call. If I am not in my chamber when my mother and sister arise, they will want to know what I was about, walking the grounds so early."

"I see. And am I to gather that you are not well versed in dissembling?"

"I am not," she admitted, the color in her cheeks deepening. "And there are some things I would rather not share with them."

Admiring her wisdom, Brecc offered her his arm. "Come," he said, picking up his pace. "You shall be there before the troublesome cockerel crows again."

CHAPTER 13

AISLEY PAUSED AT THE DOOR, waiting for her eyes to adjust to the dimmer light inside the longhouse. Humped blankets covered each pallet. A light snore and an occasional sleepy murmur were the only sounds. Hardly daring to breathe, Aisley crossed the floor on stocking feet. Releasing the clasp on her cloak, she draped it over her pallet and slipped beneath the fabric.

The beams of daylight illuminating the chinks between the shutters were brighter now than they had been earlier. It would not be long before someone awoke. Especially if the cockerel continued his alarm. She closed her eyes, wanting to block out the commonplace scene in the longhouse so she might relive the wonder of her experience outside.

Brecc had kissed her. She ran her fingers gently across her lips, recalling the thrill that had coursed through her when he'd drawn her close. Being in his arms had felt so right. She swallowed the lump in her throat. He had promised to come to Trowbridge, but she knew the king dictated Brecc's movements. Brecc might be delayed for months, and if Wulfhere's determination during their last conversation was any indication, he would make good on his threat to have her married before then.

She willed her tears to stay away. Her mother might notice if she'd been crying, and she could not use the cold outside as an excuse. If Wulfhere or her mother were to ever find out what had transpired between her and Brecc . . . She clenched her fists. Neither of them must ever know. Nor Diera, for that matter. Her sister was incapable of keeping a secret. This would have to be a sweet memory she kept to herself.

"Aisley?" Diera's sleepy voice was barely coherent.

"Yes."

"Is it morning already?"

"It is." And had been for some time.

Diera groaned. "Why does it always come so early?"

Aisley smiled into the semidarkness, grateful for the extra hour she'd been gifted. "I fear you will have to ask someone far cleverer than I to receive a good answer to that question."

"If you two do not cease your chatter, you will make enemies of all the other ladies in the longhouse." Their mother was not one who arose with a cheery disposition.

"I apologize, Mother," Aisley whispered.

"As do I." Diera paused. "Do you think we can stay abed until others have risen?"

"Yes." The rustle of their mother's pallet suggested she was settling into a new position. "And I do not wish to hear another word from either of you until then."

Brecc wiped the sweat from his brow with his sleeve and surveyed the fresh gouges in the pell. Slashing at the inanimate object with a wooden sword had not been nearly as satisfying as pinning Rheged to the floor, but Rheged's refusal to enter into another practice bout with him had remained firm. And Brecc had been desperate.

"Are you ready to tell me what this is all about?" Rheged stood leaning against the barn wall, his arms folded.

"No." Brecc sheathed his sword and swiped at his brow again. Like Aisley, he was disinclined to share their private moment together with anyone else.

"The threat of a Viking attack?" Rheged was undaunted. "Word on the river? A rather lovely copper-haired distraction? Ormod's lack of bathing? Or something else entirely?"

All of them. With the addition of Wulfhere's callous threats and the exception of Ormod's neglect of his personal hygiene. Brecc had not noticed that, but thanks to Rheged, he undoubtedly would now. And he would have to sit beside the man all the way through the Twelfth Night feast.

With a groan, Brecc ran his fingers through his hair. The strands were damp. He would do well to bathe before this evening also. "Which of us is going to apologize to the king for damaging the pell so badly?" he asked.

"Responding to a question with another question that is wholly unconnected to the first is against the rules."

"Whose rules?"

"Mine," Rheged said. He took a step away from the wall. "We have been friends long enough for me to recognize that this rage you are battling is not normal. I will listen if you need an ear."

Brecc released a deep breath and allowed his shoulders to drop. Rheged was right. He must let something go. "If I had my choice, it would be Ealdorman Wulfhere who was the target of my blade."

Rheged's eyebrows shot up. "Well, I had not anticipated that response. Any particular reason why?"

"He's an ale-bibbing thegn with more avarice than nobility."

"Agreed," Rheged said without hesitation. "Anything else?"

It was Brecc's turn to raise an eyebrow. "Agreed?"

"Of course. I have spoken to the man. It does not take more than one conversation to ascertain that he is more interested in eating at the king's table than in protecting the crown."

Brecc grunted. Mayhap Rheged was more observant than he'd previously thought. "What else do you know of him?"

"He has two very attractive sisters who, up until now, he has kept hidden in Trowbridge, and his closest associate amongst the thegns is Ealdorman Gimm."

Brecc frowned. He should have guessed as much. Gimm hailed from Dorset and was as unreliable as the weather. He and his fyrd were always the last to arrive to battle and the first to concede. His men were never placed in the front line because they did not have the training or determination to stand firm when the Viking hordes attacked.

"What have you recently learned of Wulfhere?" Rheged turned the question back on him. "Something unpleasant, I'd wager."

"In that, you are correct." He would not betray Aisley's confidence by saying anything more, but it was comforting to know that should he be called upon to act against the thegn, he would likely have Rheged's support.

"In fact, I think it might be worth the king's while to visit the good ealdor-man in Wiltshire to gain a better gauge of his leanings."

"And to check on his sisters," Rheged said.

Brecc started for the door. "Aye. That too."

Aisley had not seen Brecc all day. It was hardly surprising. The cold weather had kept the women indoors all morning, and by afternoon, preparations for the Twelfth Night feast were well underway. After they had dressed for the occasion, Aisley had spent extra time plaiting Diera's hair into elaborate loops. Diera had offered to return the favor, but Aisley had opted for a nar-row plait that circled the top of her head and left her remaining hair hang-ing freely down her back. Now that she was in the great hall, surrounded by all the exquisitely dressed ladies and gentlemen, however, she wondered if she should have chosen something a little more splendid.

Brecc had entered soon after Aisley, Diera, and their mother had taken their seats. Dressed in a maroon tunic with embroidery at the neckline and sleeves, he'd appeared even more handsome than he had before. Her stom-ach had fluttered the moment she'd spotted him, but when he took his seat at the head table and turned to smile at her, the fluttering had spiraled into a frenzied swirling. Eating would be all but impossible unless they made no further eye contact.

It was her third royal banquet in as many days, but this was the grand-est yet. The hall was decorated with boughs of evergreens, the smell of pine and juniper mingling with the aromas wafting off the overflowing platters of food. The king and queen sat in state at the head table, watching with obvious amusement as the costumed mummers circled the room, entertain-ing the guests. Beside them, the thegns looked on with varying levels of enthusiasm, while those seated around the room offered applause, laughter, and cheers at regular intervals.

The main doors opened, and four servants walked in carrying the larg-est platter Aisley had ever seen.

"The Twelfth Night cake," her mother said, sitting a little taller so as to watch the servants parade the enormous fruited loaf around the room. "I wondered when it would be brought in."

"And look!" Diera pointed to the wooden circlet seated atop the loaf. "The crown for the Lord of Misrule."

The mummers bowed affectedly as the servants and their precious cargo passed by, no doubt practicing for the obedience they would be forced to offer the person in the room who discovered a bean in their piece of cake.

"Can you believe it?" Diera clapped her hands excitedly. "Someone will be crowned the Lord or Lady of Misrule in the very room where the king and queen of Wessex sit."

"I hope it will not grow overly unruly." Aisley had attended enough Twelfth Night celebrations to know how raucous they could become. The person who found the bean would be crowned sovereign for the remainder of the day, and all within his or her sphere would be obliged to obey his or her every command. It was a special honor, but as the guests would expect the Lord or Lady of Misrule to be clever, outgoing, and humorous, Aisley offered a fervent, silent prayer that no bean was located anywhere near her portion of the cake.

With their circuit of the room complete, the servants set the Twelfth Night cake on the head table and began portioning it. One by one, the guests received their piece. The room hummed with excitement. Several groans of disappointment followed until a male voice rose above the rest.

"Ladies and Gentlemen, behold, this evening's Lord of Misrule!"

Aisley's gaze shot to the head table, where Rheged was on his feet, holding a small white bean on the palm of his hand.

A cheer arose, and then someone shouted, "All hail, the Lord of Misrule!" Bench legs scraped along the floor as the guests all rose and bowed to Rheged.

One of the servants handed Rheged the wooden circlet, and with a look of pure delight, the gentleman set it upon his head. It wobbled and then slid sideways, obviously a few sizes too small. Rheged caught it in his hand and grinned.

"My first command of the evening is that Ealdorman Ormod shall wear this crown on my behalf. I am not abdicating any of my power to him, mind you, simply the care of my headpiece." With obvious forbearance, the older gentleman accepted the circlet and placed it upon his head. It fit perfectly. Those in the room cheered their approval, and Rheged beamed. "And now, I believe it is time that the mummers paraded around the room like a flock of chickens."

The guests roared their approval, and the mummers gathered themselves together, tucked their hands in their armpits, and began flapping and clucking like a disoriented cluster of hens. Aisley began to laugh. She could not help herself. The mummers' various animal masks only added to the ridiculousness of their antics.

Rheged resumed his seat, watching with amusement until the mummers' arm flapping began to slow.

"Enough, mummers," he called. "You have been worthy chickens, but it is time for you to go to roost." To the sound of much laughter, the actors retired to the corner of the great hall and sat upon the floor to rest. Rheged surveyed the guests, and a hushed anticipation descended over the room. "I believe a role reversal is in order," he said. "One who has never been—nor ever will be—a thegn shall experience it this night." He looked directly at Aisley, and her breath caught in her throat.

"No," she whispered. "Please, no."

"Aisley, sister of Ealdorman Wulfhere," he called. "Come take your place at the head table. There is room enough here between me and Ealdorman Brecc."

The guests seated around her cheered and clapped their approval. Wulfhere appeared stunned. Brecc was glaring at Rheged as though he wished the man would choke on his words.

"Go, Aisley!" Diera poked her ribs. "People are waiting."

Attempting to stay the trembling threatening to consume her, Aisley stumbled to her feet. More cheers sounded. She did not look at her mother. There would be no reassurance found in her countenance. Instead, Aisley set her gaze on Brecc. He had turned from glaring at Rheged to watch her slow approach. His eyes shone with apology. She recognized his helplessness and simultaneously realized that only she had the power to make this situation tenable. Lifting her chin a fraction, she approached the head table.

Bobbing a brief curtsy to the king and queen, she moved to stand before Rheged. "I have obeyed your call to become a thegn, oh Lord of Misrule," she said loudly enough for those sitting nearby to hear, and then she offered a manly bow.

"Arise, Ealdorman Aisley," Rheged cried, "and join your fellow thegns on the bench."

Behind her, applause rang out. Unwilling to turn to acknowledge the crowd, Aisley made her way around the head table to reach the spot Rheged had created for her. Brecc rose and offered her his hand. She took it, clinging to the anchor it represented as she slid onto the seat. Moments later, he was seated beside her, his fingers still wrapped around hers beneath the table.

Rheged tilted his head toward them and spoke quietly. "You may both thank me at a later date."

"Or I may mortally wound you for putting Aisley through that," Brecc replied through gritted teeth.

"A perfect opportunity for you to sit together for the remainder of the evening, with no one in any position to question it," Rheged said, his eyes sparkling with good humor. "It was too good to ignore." He glanced at Brecc and grinned. "And fully worth the risk of a blade at my neck tonight." He turned to face the room again. "And now, my friends, it is long past time for some music. Ealdorman Gimm, I have heard it said that you have a remarkable voice. I would have you sing us a song."

The portly gentleman seated next to Wulfhere rose on unsteady feet. "A song, you say, sire?"

"Aye." Rheged waved his arm expansively. "Entertain us."

Aisley felt the guests' attention shift from her to Ealdorman Gimm and allowed herself a small portion of relief.

"I pray you will find it in your heart to forgive him." Brecc spoke softly, his eyes facing those in the room.

Following his lead, Aisley kept her gaze forward and her voice low. "I will if you will."

"Ah, you desire a united front." His tone was thoughtful. "I am beginning to think that tactic might be our best course with more than one person." He gave her hand a gentle squeeze before releasing it to reach for his goblet. "It appears that Ealdorman Gimm's singing is an insufficient draw to capture your mother's attention."

Aisley forced herself to look to the table she'd left. Diera was watching the portly thegn, wincing at every untuneful note he bellowed. Her mother, however, was eyeing Brecc with a decidedly calculating expression. "What is she thinking?"

"I cannot tell, but I am most anxious that it not cause you difficulties."

The reason he had released her hand became clear. Whether or not her mother could see the placement of their hands beneath the table, Brecc wished to offer her no possible fuel for speculation. It was a wise decision, and Aisley could not fault it. Indeed, she should be grateful for his precaution. In her current discomforting position, however, it felt horribly as if she had been set adrift in a sea of overly interested onlookers.

She took an unsteady breath, and Brecc shifted slightly on the bench. Moments later, she felt his leg press against hers. Fresh awareness of his physical proximity—as comforting as it was disquieting—flooded through her in a warm rush.

"A united front, remember." His voice was gentle, reassuring. "By morning, most people in this room will scarcely recall your name, and your family members know full well that you were forced to play along with the annual Twelfth Night madness."

"True." He was right. After all, she was not the only one to have been targeted by the Lord of Misrule. "I am grateful that I was not asked to parade the room as a chicken or sing a ballad off-key."

"It is hard to believe you would have rendered a worse version of 'Caedmon's Hymn' than is being offered now."

Ealdorman Gimm hit a particularly unpleasing note, and at her other side, Rheged squirmed.

"Mayhap it is time for Ealdorman Gimm to rest his voice," Rheged muttered.

He went to rise, but before he was fully on his feet, the main doors to the great hall flew open. A young man wearing a dark cloak burst into the room accompanied by a blast of cold air. The fire surged, and the guests gasped.

"Vikings!" the young man cried. "They have entered the town and are breaching the estate walls even now!"

CHAPTER 14

BRECC PULLED AISLEY FROM THE table before the initial screams subsided. This was his nightmare. He had relived it too many times already.

"Run, Aisley! I beg of you. Whilst you yet can. Once they enter the great hall, you will be trapped." The Vikings were brutal opponents on the battlefield; he did not want to contemplate what they would do to the women in their midst.

"But what of you?" She was already moving toward the end of the table.

"I must stay with the king." Never before had the choice been so difficult. "Go to the stables. Find a mount. Any mount. And ride as far from here as you can."

The main doors slammed against the wall, and with a terrifying roar, a dozen Vikings raced into the great hall. The women's screams redoubled. Tables and benches thudded to the floor as the guests scrambled to escape.

Wielding axes and spears, the warriors made directly for the head table. A quick glance told Brecc that Aisley was gone, but the king and queen remained obvious targets.

"Rheged!" Brecc yelled, sidestepping Ormod to reach the king. "Protect the queen!"

His friend seized the queen's arm and drew her back as the Viking in the center of the pack raised his arm. "Death to the king of Wessex!" he shouted in heavily accented Saxon, and then he let his spear fly.

Lowering his head, Brecc barreled into the king, knocking him sideways as the weapon shot across the head table and hit its target with a thud. Ormod cried out, the wooden circlet he'd been wearing on his head dropping to the floor as he staggered backward, clutching the shaft of the spear that had pierced his chest.

"Ormod!" The king pushed back against Brecc.

"Forgive me, sire," Brecc said, fighting to keep the king from going to his adviser even as he was assailed with horror over the blood now staining Ormod's tunic. "There is nothing you can do for Ormod, but there is a great deal you can do—*must yet do*—for your people."

More spears flew. A few of the thegns were already engaged in combat. Armed with nothing more than the daggers they had used for their meal, the Saxons had little chance against the heavily armed Vikings, but they were doing what was needed. They were offering the king a chance to escape.

"Find me a sword!" King Alfred bellowed.

"There are none to be had here." Brecc had his dagger in one hand, and with the other, he continued to hold the king back. "You must flee, Sire. An opportunity for you to escape this ambush is what your thegns are fighting for. Your time to avenge Ormod's death will come only if you survive long enough to see it done."

Those of the feast's attendees who had somehow avoided the Vikings' attention were now pressing toward the main doors. In their eagerness to escape, they likely had not considered how many more warriors were awaiting them elsewhere in the estate. Based on their past behavior, Brecc thought it likely that there were men ransacking every building. He could only pray that Aisley would be gone from the stables before the Vikings turned their attention to it.

The head table toppled over, the platters, trenchers, and goblets landing on the floor with a crash. Food littered the ground. With a cry of agony, another thegn fell less than four paces away.

Brecc pivoted, his dagger ready. Rangvald. Guthrum's chieftain had reappeared in all too many of Brecc's nightmares of the Battle of Wilton. The large Viking raised a double-headed ax above his head, and with a terrifying howl, he swung. Brecc leaped to the right. The king anticipated the move, circling Brecc and letting his dagger fly. The blade entered the warrior's upper arm, and with a roar of rage, the monster of a man lunged for his ax. Unable to reach it before the Viking, Brecc thrust his leg wide, catching the handle and sending it skidding over the floor. Rangvald scrambled after it.

"Brecc!" Rheged's voice reached him over the melee.

He swung around. His friend was leading the queen behind a curtain that covered a door. Most likely one that led to the barn on the other side of the great hall. How Rheged had discovered the hidden exit in the midst of this chaos was beyond him. But he had, and he had guided Brecc to it.

"This way, Sire!" Brecc yelled.

A spear flew overhead, landing on the floor not more than three paces from where Rheged had been standing moments before. Brecc reached it first, yanking the tip out of the wooden floor and hurling it toward an oncoming warrior.

The king glanced at the devastation behind him. Bodies littered the room, and the roars of anger, moans of pain, and sobs of despair melded into a cacophony of suffering. "Dear heaven! What has my neglect of your warning done?"

"This is the Viking chief's doing, not yours." Another warrior was heading their way, ax in hand. Brecc grabbed the two large platters at his feet and sent them spinning toward him. "You must go after the queen," Brecc urged. "It is the only way to foil Guthrum's plan."

Brecc's words appeared to have their effect. A mask of resolution fell over the king's grief-filled face, and he slipped behind the curtain.

Brecc hesitated one moment more. Another thegn had taken on the approaching Viking. If Brecc stayed to fight, he might lessen the number of warriors by two or three, but that was nothing when compared to how many were undoubtedly involved in this attack. If he went with the king, he could feasibly facilitate the monarch's escape before Guthrum realized that the man they had so brutally murdered was not in actuality the king of Wessex.

He backed toward the curtain, his eyes drawn to Ormod's bloodied, lifeless body. The agony of loss burned in his chest. This defeat might be the most crushing yet, but it could not be the end of Saxon rule in Wessex. "You were the very best of men, Ormod," he said. "You will not be forgotten." And then he pulled back the curtain and followed after the king.

Aisley grabbed her sister's arm and pulled her up against the wall of the kitchen, praying her mother would follow. Pounding footsteps approached in the darkness. She pressed herself against the cold stone as a glint of moonlight reflected off the blades in the hands of the approaching Vikings. Brecc had been right. The heathens who had entered the great hall were merely the vanguard. The entire royal estate was now swarming with the enemy.

She'd reached her mother and sister within moments of leaving the head table. Shaking them from their shock had been her first priority. Urging them to leave immediately had been her second. They'd been sitting close enough to the main doors that they'd been able to slip out before most of the guests had gathered their wits. But reaching safety was another matter entirely.

"We must go to the stables," Aisley whispered, repeating Brecc's admonition. "Attaining mounts is our only hope for escape."

"Dressed like this, we shall freeze to death before we reach safety." Her mother's anxious voice reached her from the shadows.

"The stable has blankets." How many or how distasteful they were, Aisley did not know, but with their cloaks still in the great hall, any covering they could acquire would be a godsend.

Shouts and screams coming from the great hall punctuated the frigid air. Shadowy figures flitted past, most of them running in unbridled panic. Those, she attempted to ignore. It was the silhouettes moving with heavy, purposeful strides that filled her with fear. And every moment that passed seemed to produce more of them. A clash of metal sounded from somewhere nearby. A string of unintelligible words was followed by pounding feet and a cry of agony. More shouts and more running. Beside her, Diera tensed, digging her fingers into Aisley's arm. The fight in the great hall was expanding to include those outside.

Aisley could see the outline of the stable roof against the star-studded sky, but to reach it, they would be required to cross a wide-open space. "We must cross the square quickly," she whispered.

"The Vikings will see us." Diera's words ended in a sob.

"If we remain here, we shall doubtless be found," Aisley said. "I would rather take a chance at escaping."

"What of Wulfhere?" their mother asked. "He will not know what has become of us."

Aisley was quite sure that Wulfhere's focus would be on securing his own safety. "I have no doubt he will leave for Wiltshire at the first opportunity. We shall meet him there."

"But if he is injured, he will need our assistance."

Aisley fought back her irritation. Ealdorman Ormod was dead. There were indubitably more dead and injured littering the floor of the great hall. Was Wulfhere truly her mother's only concern? She swallowed the lump in her throat. Brecc had begged her to leave. It was what he had wanted. But if she thought on what was occurring in the building behind her, on what might already have happened to him . . . She pushed the thought away. He was protecting the king. God willing, he, too, would be protected.

"As you told me yourself, Mother, the king surely has healers he can call on."

"Yes, but—"

"Hush!" Aisley stopped her mother's argument midsentence. "Someone is coming." They waited, barely daring to breathe as the thud of more heavy footsteps came closer. A man's voice called out something in Norse, and the direction of the footsteps changed. Aisley waited only until the thuds faded behind them, then she moved away from the wall. "Now," she whispered. "We go now!"

They crossed the open area at a run. The icy air cut through Aisley's clothing, numbing her skin.

Diera faltered. "I cannot. It is too far in this cold."

"You can and you must." Aisley could now see the stable door. "We are almost there."

As they approached, the sizable door swung open, and a large silhouette slipped inside.

"Vikings!" Diera gasped, stumbling to a halt.

"No." Their mother tugged her forward. "He did not move like an invader."

It was true. Despite their good start, it seemed that they were not the first of the king's guests to reach the stables.

Aisley grabbed the door latch and pulled. "I pray the stablehands are ready for the number of people who will undoubtedly come."

A male voice, low and urgent, echoed through the stables. "Make haste, boy! I have no time to waste."

A stableboy entered the circle of candlelight, drawing a large horse behind him. "I'll 'ave 'im saddled right away, sire."

The man stepped out of the shadows. "This is taking too long," he said. "Give me the saddle. You take care of the bridle."

"Wulfhere!" Aisley's mother gasped.

Wulfhere swung around. "Mother! And you have Aisley and Diera with you." He placed his hand on his chest. "My relief knows no bounds. When I could not find you in the great hall, I did not know what had become of you."

"What are you doing here?" Aisley asked.

"Acquiring mounts so that we may escape this madness, of course." He took the saddle from the stableboy and began threading the straps through the buckle. "I am glad you were wise enough to come directly to the stable."

Aisley glanced at the horse before her, her indignation rising. "One mount, Wulfhere? If we had not come at this precise moment, were you planning on leaving without us?"

"That is quite enough, Aisley," their mother interrupted. "We should be immensely grateful that in all the commotion, we have found each other."

Aisley could barely speak. Was her mother truly so blind to Wulfhere's selfishness?

"Three more mounts, boy!" Wulfhere yelled. "And blankets."

The boy scurried off into the darkness, and Wulfhere went back to buckling the saddle. Diera was standing beside their mother, her arms wrapped around herself. Aisley could not tell if it was the cold or fear that brought about her sister's quiet whimpers, but whatever amount of those things Aisley may have experienced over the last little while had now been replaced by a burning fury.

"Tell me, Wulfhere," she said, "how is it that of all the king's thegns, you are the only one not battling the Vikings in the great hall?"

Wulfhere snorted. "If you believe I am the only nobleman to escape that madness, you are delusional."

"You kissed the goblet. You accepted the ring-giver's gift, and by so doing, you pledged your devotion. It is your duty to protect the king."

"Really, Aisley." Their mother's voice rang with disapproval. "Your understanding of such things is far too limited for you to judge Wulfhere's actions. He is fulfilling his duty to protect his mother and sisters. That is quite enough."

No, it was not. But at this moment, arguing was counterproductive. The boy hurried into the light, drawing three mares behind him. Aisley reached for the blanket on the closest horse and set it across Diera's shoulders. Her sister drew the malodorous covering closer—a sure sign that she had yet to recover from the chill outside.

"I thank you," Aisley told the boy.

He bobbed his head. "Of course, mistress."

The door flew open, and half a dozen people entered on the run.

"Mounts, lad!" The first man was out of breath. "As quickly as you can!"

"Aye, sire." The boy disappeared.

Keeping his back to the newcomers, Wulfhere helped himself to another of the saddles lining the wall. "Assist Mother and Diera onto the mares, Aisley," he said. "We are quitting this place directly."

CHAPTER 15

BRECC CRACKED OPEN THE BARN door and peered outside. The sounds of battle continued from the great hall, muffled by the thick wall that now separated them. The king stood at his side, waiting. Behind them, the cattle looked on in silence, their eyes shining eerily in the darkness.

"Are we clear?" King Alfred asked.

"It appears that way." They should move quickly. Time was against them, and Rheged and the queen had obviously made their escape already. Yet Brecc hesitated. If there was anything worse than leading the king into the unknown, it was doing so unarmed. Brecc turned to scour the barn. The sliver of moonlight entering through the crack in the door illuminated the nearest wall. Three buckets, a spade, and two pitchforks. Crossing the short distance between them in three long paces, he grabbed a pitchfork.

"I will take the other one," the king said.

Brecc passed the rudimentary tool to the king. "If we make our way to the stables, we should be able to acquire mounts."

King Alfred nodded grimly. "It will not take Guthrum long to realize the king of Wessex is no longer in the great hall. He will redirect his attack, and the stables will be his next target."

Brecc's thoughts immediately flew to Aisley. Had she done as he'd asked and gone directly to the stables? Had there been enough time for her to flee? And what of Rheged and the queen? He tightened his grip on the pitchfork. This was not the time for worry; this was the time to act.

Pulling the door open a little more, Brecc paused for two heartbeats, then stepped outside. "No one in sight," he whispered.

King Alfred grunted his approval. "Then, we go."

Keeping to the shadows, they hastened along the length of the building. Shouts and screams filled the air. Occasionally, running figures flitted in and out of view, their identities and destinations unknown. A clash of blades sounded from the direction of the great hall's main doors. Men's shouts followed. And then the clang of more blades making impact. There was no way of knowing who was involved or how long it would last, but any skirmish that drew the Vikings' attention away from locating the king was welcome.

"Now is our chance, Sire," Brecc whispered.

The king needed no further prompt. Leaving the safety of the wall, he started across the central square with Brecc matching him stride for stride. They were three-quarters of the way across when Brecc heard a familiar crackle. It was a sound he appreciated when sitting around a campfire; it was one he dreaded during a conflict.

"They've lit a fire."

"I smell the smoke." The king glanced over his shoulder at the great hall. "Where is it coming from?"

The words were no sooner out of his mouth than a gust of frigid air hit them, and then, like a newly released wild beast, flames roared across the stable roof, consuming the thatch and sending ash spiraling upward. The doors to the stable burst open, and the shriek of terrified horses cut through the groans of weakening timber.

Brecc dropped the pitchfork he was holding and broke into a sprint. A cluster of people stumbled out of the stables, a few of them leading horses. The animals were tugging wildly at their ropes. Moments later, more horses appeared, bolting for freedom across the courtyard and grassy area.

Weaving through the frantic cluster of men, women, and horses near the doors, Brecc entered the burning building. "Rinc!" he yelled. At least a dozen more mounts tore past him in a flurry of hooves. "Rinc!"

"Over 'ere, sire!"

The boy's voice came from his right. Lifting his arm so it covered his mouth and nose, Brecc ran down the narrow path between the stalls. Already, the smoke was making visibility all but impossible.

"I need two fast mounts, lad," he called. "Do you have any left?"

A thud at Brecc's right had him pivoting. The whites of Rinc's eyes shone through the gloom. The boy was tugging at a rope.

"This 'un, sire. I reckon 'e's the strongest charger in the stable, but 'e's got 'imself in a bind by tanglin' 'is lead rope through the wooden slats."

"Fetch me a knife."

"'E'll bolt, sire. The moment Forca senses freedom, 'e'll be gone."

"Let me worry about that," Brecc said. "A knife, lad. Quickly." With a cough, the boy disappeared, only to reappear moments later carrying a short-handled blade. "Good," Brecc said. "Now, listen closely." Rinc coughed again but appeared to be listening. "I need you to pass me the lead rope of the next horse you come upon. The moment I have the rope in hand, I'll cut Forca free and will lead them both out."

"Beggin' yer pardon, sire, but given 'ow upset they are, they're not goin' to take kindly to walkin' nicely."

"I realize that." It was going to take every ounce of strength Brecc possessed to hold on to two frantic horses. He could only hope that King Alfred would be in a position to help as soon as Brecc reached the doors and the horses smelled freedom.

"Hand me one of the ropes." The king's voice cut through the horses' shrill cries and the creaking roof.

Brecc straightened, relief coursing through him. The king had followed him inside. "You heard King Alfred, lad."

The boy's gasp produced another coughing attack, but he scuttled out of the stall.

"There's no time to saddle them, Sire," Brecc warned. With one hand firmly grasped around Forca's lead rope, he placed Rinc's blade against the portion trapped in the slats.

"I am aware." There was no hiding the stark reality of their situation. Above the shrieks and thuds, they could hear the voices of the other stable-hands working to free the last of the horses from the other end of the stables. "There is no more time for any of us. The servants must leave when we do." As if to underscore the king's words, the roof above them cracked, and a shower of sparks rained down on the straw-covered floor. Instantly, the straw ignited. "Fire in the stables!" King Alfred shouted. "Everybody out!"

"'Ere, Yer Majesty," Rinc wheezed, staggered up to the king and handing him the rope of a white horse.

"Outside, lad," the king urged, taking the rope. "Make no delay!" Flames were licking up the edge of a nearby stall. The horse on the other end of the rope reared, but the king held firm. "Brecc?"

One more slice and the rope in Brecc's hand gave way. The charger backed into the corner of his stall, his hooves pounding the hard floor wildly.

"I have him, Sire," Brecc said, wrapping his fingers more firmly around the rope. The stallion shook his head violently. Brecc felt it all the way to his arm socket. Gritting his teeth, he tugged at the rope. "Now is not the time to allow fear to overcome your courage, Forca."

Two more newly freed horses cantered out of the stable. The king followed, leading the skittish palfrey in his custody. With an anxious snort, Forca trembled.

Allowing his instinct to overrule logic, Brecc released his hold on the rope with one hand and set it on the stallion's shoulder. "Steady, boy," he said, willing the cough that threatened to erupt to subside. "We can escape this inferno together if you'll allow it." Forca shook his head again, but notwithstanding the rapidly encroaching fire, his quivering seemed to lessen a fraction. "We don't have time for a long discussion," Brecc continued, attempting to keep the urgency out of his voice. "But if you will behave nicely, we shall speak at length once we are gone from here."

Barely daring to hope, he lowered his hand from Forca's neck and set it below his other on the rope. Slowly, he backed out of the stall, steadily pulling the rope as he walked. Forca shifted uneasily, and then he took a few hesitant steps toward him. Another timber cracked. Forca reared, his nostrils flaring.

"Come, Forca," Brecc said, pulling the rope more sharply. "It is time."

Miraculously, the stallion responded. He stepped out of the stall and was soon trotting toward the open door with Brecc running beside him.

Brecc's lungs were burning, and the air outside was only marginally better than the air within the stables. Straining to see through the swirling smoke, he searched for the white palfrey the king had been leading. King Alfred had left the stables only moments before Brecc; he would not have gone far unless he'd been forced to. Setting his hand on the hilt of the dagger Rinc had given him, Brecc scoured the area. Had the Vikings set the stables alight and then left to do the same to the other buildings in the royal estate, or were they waiting nearby, watching for the king to appear?

"Brecc."

The low voice had come from his right. Guiding Forca in a slow circle, Brecc studied the area more carefully. Movement near a large tree caught his eye, and then he saw a patch of white appear from behind the trunk. Forca snorted. There was a responding nicker.

Unwilling to give away the king's location to anyone else who might be watching, Brecc slowly walked the stallion toward the tree. The white palfrey materialized from the shadows, and on her back sat King Alfred.

"Your Majesty." Keeping his voice low, Brecc inclined his head. "You are mounted."

"Aye. The tree helped. The mare is still unnerved by the fire, so the sooner we are gone from here, the more likely it is that I shall remain seated."

"I am twice amazed, Sire. Riding bareback is no mean feat and is most certainly not how you were taught."

"And yet, have we not all tried it at one time or another?" The king paused. "You have ridden without a saddle, I assume."

"I have." Brecc eyed the stallion uneasily. He'd made his previous bareback escapades early in his youth, and he would prefer a gentler mount for this attempt, but given their current situation, he was fortunate to have a horse at all. He led Forca to the tree and tied the remaining portion of the lead rope to the lowest branch. "Any sign of Viking warriors nearby?"

"None that I have seen," the king said. "I saw the lad who assisted us stagger out of the stables. I pray he will survive. I pray all these people will survive." His voice cracked. "Am I in the wrong to abandon them in the midst of this awful destruction?"

Desperately wishing that Ormod were here to advise the king, Brecc placed a foot on a large knot in the tree's trunk and pulled himself up. "If you do not flee, there is no hope left for your people. The loss they experience today will be but a small taste of what is to come if the Vikings are allowed to rule Wessex."

"I go so that I may return," the king said.

"Your people will cling to that truth, Sire."

King Alfred released a troubled sigh. "Then, we shall have to ensure that it occurs."

Brecc slid his leg over Forca's back. The charger startled, dancing away from the tree. Wrapping his fingers through the horse's mane, Brecc dropped into a riding position. Forca's muscles rippled beneath him. Should he wish to, the stallion could unseat him in an instant. Brecc could only pray that the horse would choose a different response.

"Steady, boy." Reaching for the lead rope, Brecc pulled it free. Forca skittered away. Brecc dug his knees into the horse's sides. "Steady."

The palfrey nickered, and Forca's ears twitched. King Alfred wheeled his horse around so that it faced the estate gates standing open against a burning orange sky.

Brecc lowered himself over Forca's neck. "Whenever you are ready, Sire."

"We ride for Wessex," he called, and then his horse was galloping toward the exit.

Clutching a portion of the lead rope with one hand and Forca's mane with the other, Brecc tapped his heels to the horse's side. Moments later, he was flying across the ground in King Alfred's wake.

Warning shouts filled the air. People scattered. A single spear sailed past, narrowly missing the white palfrey's rump, but both horses continued undeterred. Up ahead, two Vikings stepped into their path, racing to pull the gates closed before the horses and their riders reached them. Hunched over the stallion's neck, Brecc gave him his head, reaching the gates half a horse length ahead of the king and three horse lengths ahead of the Vikings. Their mounts thundered through the exit. With shouts of frustration, the Vikings let another two spears fly, but both weapons fell short.

Taking the path that followed the river, they continued around the first bend. The cries of consternation behind them faded. Brecc raised his chin a fraction and inhaled an icy breath. They had no secure destination and no knowledge of where Rheged and the queen had gone. Many of the thegns were likely killed, and Aisley's fate was unbearably unsure. But the king of Wessex was alive and free. Notwithstanding the losses in Chippenham or what lay ahead, that was what Brecc must focus on now.

CHAPTER 16

AISLEY DID NOT KNOW HOW long they had been traveling; she simply knew she could no longer feel her feet, her fingers, or her face. Wulfhere and her mother rode side by side several paces ahead of her and Diera. No one spoke. Every ounce of their energy was being exerted on staying upright in their saddles.

Hunched over against the cold wind, Diera tipped to her right and then caught herself. She moaned.

"Wulfhere," Aisley rasped. She cleared her throat and tried again, this time a little louder. "We must find somewhere to rest."

Wulfhere turned his head and scowled. "As I have told you twice before, there are no inns to be had anywhere near here. We have no choice but to continue."

"There are farmhouses." The squat buildings were difficult to make out in the darkness, but Aisley had noted at least three they had already passed, located not far from the road. She glanced at Diera again. Her sister had yet to lift her head, and Aisley's concern for her welfare was rising. "I do not think Diera can last much longer."

"Diera?" With a mumble of frustration, their mother wheeled her horse around and rode up next to Diera. "It would behoove you to show a little more fortitude, young lady. None of us is enjoying this experience."

Diera did not respond. Instead, she listed slightly to the left.

Their mother reached for her arm and shook it slightly. "Do you hear me, Diera?"

Aisley's chest tightened. "It must be the cold, Mother."

"How long has she been like this?" The irritation that had laced their mother's voice moments before was now alarm.

"I noticed her swaying in her saddle soon after we rode through the last village."

"That was at least six furlongs ago." She reached for Diera's hand on the reins. "Her fingers are like ice."

"She has a blanket just like the rest of us," Wulfhere said.

"For Diera, one blanket was obviously not enough," their mother said. "We must find somewhere where she can truly warm up."

Wulfhere gestured toward the open fields that surrounded them. "If you know of a nearby inn, I would welcome the suggestion."

"If we cannot find shelter, we can at least light a fire," Aisley said.

"Need I remind you that we were forced to make this excursion with nothing but the clothes we wore to the banquet on our backs." Wulfhere's tone was curt. "No coins, no food, and no flint."

"Then we must find a farmhouse forthwith," their mother said in a rare show of support for Aisley. "And until we reach one, Diera must have your blanket as well as her own."

With a disparaging mutter, Wulfhere drew the blanket off his shoulders and tossed it toward Diera. Aisley caught one corner before it fell between their mounts. Urging her horse closer, she passed it to their mother, and between the two of them, they settled it over Diera's head and shoulders.

"Not much longer, Diera," Aisley said. "We shall have you indoors soon."

"We must hasten, Wulfhere." Their mother had yet to leave Diera's side. "Your sister's condition is serious."

"As will mine be now that I have no covering," he grumbled. "You realize that even if we find a place, the inhabitants are likely sleeping off their Twelfth Night celebrations and will not even hear us at their door."

"They will answer," Aisley said. "They are sure to be farm laborers, and as soon as the sun rises, they must be up tending to the animals." She tightened her grip on the straps. "As hard as it may be for you to comprehend, they cannot afford to drink themselves into a stupor."

Wulfhere glared at her, but Aisley ignored him. Urging her horse into a trot, she started down the road. It did not matter if Wulfhere kept pace with her or stayed back with Diera and their mother. Diera's situation was dire, and Aisley would not stop until she'd found someone who would take them in.

The moon's position in the sky had shifted, but daylight—with its accompanying easement in temperature—was still hours away. Brecc flexed his stiff fingers still entangled in the charger's mane. Fleeing the royal estate on a horse without a saddle was exacting a heavy toll on his body. His back and thighs ached from holding his position during their race from danger. Even the more leisurely pace the king had set since they'd left Chippenham behind was more exacting than it would have been had he been seated on his saddle.

"What say you, Brecc?" The king kept his voice low even though they had not passed another person or dwelling in many furlongs. "Is that a settlement up ahead?"

Brecc peered into the darkness. Moonlight illuminated a short section of the road, outlining the hedgerows and trees on either side of them. Beyond that, a hazy gray filled the space where fields surely lay. "I have yet to see any buildings, Sire."

"The sound of the running river has increased," the king said. "We are riding closer to it now, and if memory serves, it cuts through several villages and small towns. I would wager we shall come upon one shortly." He paused. "We must acquire saddles and bridles there."

Brecc's aching muscles wholeheartedly concurred, but his head was less sure. "As eager as I am to be seated on a well-fitted saddle, I wonder how we might locate such things at this time of night and in an unfamiliar community."

"I have pondered the same," the king said. "An inn, I believe, is most likely to serve our purposes." He glanced at Brecc. "I assume you carry no purse."

"No, Sire."

King Alfred grunted. "A hard lesson for us both. We would do well to never attend a banquet without one attached to our belts again."

"Aye." Brecc had already spent far too long ruing the loss of his own mount, sword, purse, and cloak. The lack of each of those things had already proven to be critically detrimental. "It will be difficult to attain the supplies we need without coins."

"Difficult, yes. But not impossible." The king's voice became thoughtful. "I imagine there is a merchant or innkeeper about who would be eager to procure clothing as fine as ours in exchange for simpler apparel. Mayhap that same fellow would be willing to offer a couple of saddles, bridles, and supplies for a royal ring."

"Are you willing to offer those things to another?"

"I am," the king said. "Such an exchange will be doubly beneficial. It will not only aid us in gaining the items we need, but it will also allow us to continue our journey with a level of anonymity. The Vikings will be looking for a king and his escort. By the time the sun comes up, there should be no sign of either one. Our best hope for reaching our final destination is to appear like any other traveler on the roads."

"You have a place of refuge in mind, then?"

"I do."

The king offered nothing more, and Brecc questioned him no further. It was enough that they could claim a direction.

Barely resisting the urge to pinch her nose, Aisley took a breath through her mouth. The smell of damp wool and sheep droppings was so strong, it was hard to think of anything else. But she must. Discovering the shepherd's hut so soon after beginning her search for shelter had been a miracle, and although the flock of sheep filling the other side of the one-room structure were pungent companions, they also exuded warmth. A warmth they all—particularly Diera—desperately needed.

By a single candle's light, Wulfhere stepped over something on the ground and wrinkled his nose in distaste. "By all that is holy, Aisley, I do not think you could have chosen a situation any less inviting than this one."

Biting back her retort, Aisley turned away from him and tucked her own blanket over the two already wrapped around her sister's shivering body. On Diera's other side, their mother was rubbing Diera's hands between her own.

"Take this fer the young lady in distress, mistress." The old shepherd pulled a sheepskin off the pallet where he'd obviously been sleeping and offered it to Aisley. "There ain't nothin' warmer."

"You are very kind," she said, "but it seems wrong that after disturbing your sleep, we should now also take your bedding."

He clucked his tongue against his almost toothless gums. "'Tis nothin' mistress. It's not often that I 'ave company, so I 'ave little more than a refuge from the cold to offer ya, but such as it is, yer welcome to share."

"My mother, sister, and I are most grateful," Aisley said. "My brother may yet choose to remain outside with the horses, but I would not have you concern yourself if he makes that decision."

"Surely you will not do that, Wulfhere." Their mother turned her concerned expression from Diera to Wulfhere. "It is perishing cold outside."

Wulfhere scowled at Aisley before responding. "You have nothing to fear, Mother. As unfortunate as our current circumstances may be, I am fully aware that duty demands that I remain indoors with you."

Their mother offered a sigh of relief. "I will feel much better if you are here."

Aisley attempted to swallow her aversion. If her brother cared one jot about duty, he would not be with them at all. He would be at the royal estate, fighting beside the other thegns in defense of their king. Her thoughts returned to Brecc, and for the first time since fleeing Chippenham, she did not push them away. She pictured him as she'd last seen him, standing before her, his dark eyes claiming hers as he begged her to leave. A lump formed in her throat. She had fled, but what of him? Had he escaped the Viking attack, or was he lying wounded—or worse—on the floor of the great hall? She bit her lower lip, willing her tears to stay away. How long would she have to wait to learn Brecc's fate?

He had promised he would come to Trowbridge. God willing, if Diera was sufficiently recovered, they could be on their way again by morning and would be home by day's end. Once there, they would be obliged to wait for news. If the king had been captured or killed, word would reach them soon enough. They might not immediately learn the fate of all the thegns who had stayed to fight with the king, but until she knew differently, she would pray with all her heart that he was safe and well.

A single tear escaped. She swiped it away, grateful that the light was too poor for others to notice.

"Aisley?" Diera's voice was so weak, it was little more than a whisper.

"Diera, can you hear me?" Their mother paused her chafing of Diera's hands long enough to smooth her fingers over Diera's hair instead.

"Aisley?" Diera said again.

Wulfhere had stopped his pacing and stood watching.

Aisley reached for Diera's hand beneath the sheepskin cover. "I am here."

"I . . ." Her brow creased as though forming the words was difficult. "I am not so terribly cold as I was."

This time Aisley allowed the tears that had filled her eyes to fall. "That is good, Diera. That is very good."

Diera moved her head in a slight nod. "Yes," she murmured. "So much better."

Aisley squeezed her hand gently and then raised her eyes to meet the shepherd's. "We are indebted to you, shepherd. Your generosity has likely saved my sister's life."

The older man shifted his feet awkwardly. "The name's Borden, mistress. An' I'm right glad t' be of service." He hesitated. "I've a crock of milk in the corner. Won't take me long t' start a fire and get it heatin' up. Warm milk works wonders, it does, when my lambs get caught out in the cold. Mayhap, the young lady would benefit from some too."

Aisley looked to her mother, who nodded her approval. "I thank you, Borden," she said. "Some warm milk would be most appreciated."

👑

Brecc pounded on the door a second time. The noise filled the silence of the dark town square, yet it appeared that it was insufficient to rouse the innkeeper.

"I fear good fortune may have truly abandoned us, Sire," Brecc said.

"Crosdon," the king said. "That is the appellation you must use for me until we are safely away from here. There is to be no more use of my titles or proper name."

"Yes, Si—" Brecc caught himself. Barely. "Very well, Crosdon." Though he could see the wisdom behind it, the king's newest command was going to be especially difficult to obey.

"Knock again," the king said. "The man cannot ignore us much longer."

Brecc fisted his hand and pounded a third time. If the innkeeper would only rouse himself, this rural inn promised to be an ideal location for their needs. It appeared large enough that it would likely possess spare tack in the stables for their horses but was located in a town small enough that the Vikings hunting for the king of Wessex would ignore it.

From somewhere nearby, a dog barked. A second took up a similar baying.

"It appears that we have woken the animals in town, even if the residents are yet in their beds," Brecc said grimly.

"Someone will come to our aid." The king was adamant. "Again, Brecc."

Brecc raised his arm, but just as he lowered it to knock for a fourth time, a bolt thudded back, and the door flew open.

"Enough!" A burly man with a scraggly beard growled the words even as the blade in his hand glinted in the moonlight. "Who are ya that ya'd make such a din in the middle o' the night? D'ya have no common decency?"

Beside Brecc, King Alfred stiffened. Doubtless, he had never before been spoken to in such a manner.

"I beg your pardon," Brecc said, attempting to buy the king time to adjust to his new role. "I am the one guilty of knocking on your door at this unearthly hour. But I would have you take it as a tribute to your well-positioned and inviting establishment."

"A tribute?" The innkeeper's eyes narrowed. "'Ave ya been in yer cups, man?"

"I have not. And neither has my companion. We are the victims of a senseless attack that lost us our saddles and bridles, and we come seeking replacements."

The innkeeper picked up the candlestick he'd set on a table just inside the door and raised it so he could see the two bareback horses more clearly. "If what ya say is true, ya should 'ave been poundin' upon the doors o' the tanner an' blacksmith rather than an innkeeper."

"If time were our ally, we would most certainly stay at your fine establishment whilst waiting for the local tanner and blacksmith to provide us with the items we need." The king spoke for the first time. "As it is," he continued, seemingly unaware that his decision to take a pseudonym had done nothing to erase his royal bearing, "we must be on our way again before daylight."

The innkeeper shifted his candle again, this time to more clearly view the king. The gold thread on King Alfred's purple tunic caught the light, and the innkeeper shifted his gaze to Brecc's clothing. "Yer noblemen," he said. "Those 'oo usually travel with the king, I daresay."

"We are," Brecc responded.

The innkeeper's jaw twitched, and the look in his eyes changed from irritated to calculating. "D'ya 'ave coins enough fer the saddles yer wantin'?"

"We are willing to barter," the king said.

"With what?"

The king raised an eyebrow. "Unless I am mistaken, I believe you took a moment just now to admire our tunics. We are willing to offer you our finely spun woolen attire in exchange for plain linen clothing and two bridles."

"An' the saddles?"

King Alfred pulled a gold ring from his finger. The red gemstone at its center sparkled in the candlelight. "A gold-and-ruby ring for two saddles, two cloaks, and sufficient food to feed my companion and me for three days."

The innkeeper's eyes widened, but he set down the candle and folded his arms. "Nobles or not, I don' do business with strangers. 'Specially those 'oo don' give me their names."

"Ealdormen Crosdon and Edlin," Brecc said, assuming his father's name and giving the man King Alfred's new designation.

"Ealdorman Crosdon and Ealdorman Edlin," the innkeeper repeated. "An' where d'ya hail from?"

There was no point in dissembling. The fellow had already guessed that they were members of the royal entourage, and most locals would know the king and his followers had gathered in Chippenham to celebrate Twelfth Night. "We travel a great deal," Brecc said, "but most recently, we are come from Chippenham."

The skepticism in the innkeeper's eyes lessened. The truth had served them well. "I 'eard the king an' 'is party was there this week."

Brecc did not look at King Alfred. "You heard aright. And I believe the king will be most appreciative of any assistance you might offer his men."

The innkeeper stood a little taller. "'E'll 'ear of me 'elpin' ya out, then?"

"Most assuredly."

Stepping aside, he gestured them into the inn. "The name's Fitch, and ya'd best come in if I'm t' be findin' ya tunics."

"And the saddles and bridles?" the king asked.

The innkeeper grunted. "I'll 'ave me boy check the stables fer any spare tack we 'ave lyin' about." He shrugged. "It won' be what yer used to, mind, but I daresay it'll do the job."

With a nod, King Alfred entered the room. "We are much obliged, Fitch. The sooner we have the items we need, the better."

CHAPTER 17

TWILIGHT WAS PAINTING THE CLOUDS a dusky gray, and the daytime temperatures were dropping. Brecc urged his mount to the top of the peak and then reined it to a halt. Below him, the county of Somerset stretched out like a green blanket embroidered with blue rivers and decorated with patches of woodland. "It has been many years since I've climbed Burrow Mump," he said. "I had forgotten how unparalleled the prospect is from here."

"Aye." King Alfred guided his palfrey into a position to the right of Brecc's horse. "Ormod thought it would serve well as a lookout spot."

"A lookout spot?"

The king pointed to a piece of land below them. It rose above the marsh but was cut off by the River Tone on one side and a swamp and a flooded lake on the others. "That is Athelney," he said. "As you can see, it is surrounded by water. An island, if you will. It boasts two acres of woodland replete with stags, goats, and other wild beasts. There is fuel for fires and ample water, and it is accessible only by boat."

Brecc nodded slowly. "The best possible situation for an exiled king and a small group of devoted followers."

"That was Ormod's thought. Athelney is remote enough to slow a Viking horde's attack and yet close enough to settlements for Saxon warriors to get word out to those loyal to the crown."

Brecc looked at him then. "You and Ormod already considered this contingency."

"We did." The king sighed, and it was as if the weight of the deaths of Ormod and an as-yet-unknown number of other thegns suddenly pressed upon him. His shoulders drooped. "I prayed it would never come to this, but Ormod insisted that we have a plan in place. The queen knows to come here. She will tell Rheged."

Brecc was unprepared for the measure of relief he felt at that news. He and the king had been traveling alone for the best part of three days. Dressed in Fitch's ill-fitting but serviceable clothing and riding worn saddles, they had dropped the ealdormen titles they'd offered the innkeeper days ago and had successfully passed as commoners at the handful of stops they'd made along their way. To know that Rheged and other surviving thegns would join them when they learned of this place of refuge brought new hope.

"We have made good time," Brecc said. "I daresay we will be the first to reach Athelney."

"That is for the best." The king gazed down at the isolated island. "I would wish to know the lay of the land before making further plans."

Brecc glanced at the sky. The last rays of the sun were disappearing beyond the horizon. "It might be best to wait until daybreak to cross the river," he said.

"Agreed." King Alfred pointed to a small stone building at the base of Burrow Mump. Smoke was escaping through the thatched roof. "There appears to be some kind of dwelling between us and the water. We shall apply there for shelter for the night."

Brecc wheeled his horse around. Up until now, they had been fortunate to have clear skies and moonlit nights, but this evening's clouds would block any such illumination. If they wished to avoid riding the path downhill in darkness, they had no time to lose.

"I pray Rheged was able to find the queen suitable shelter along her path," the king said, his gaze lingering on the untamed marshland below.

"As do I," Brecc said, and it was true. There had been multiple times the last few days when he had entreated God to protect the king, the queen, Rheged, and his other comrades. But during those prayers, inevitably, his thoughts had lingered longest on Aisley, and he had quickly come to realize that not knowing her situation was the heaviest burden of all.

👑

Morning had broken, but the longhouse was quiet. Aisley raised herself onto her elbow and looked over at Diera. Her sister's deep breathing indicated that she was yet asleep. Wool blankets were pulled up to her chin, but there was just enough light for Aisley to see the faint pink in Diera's cheeks. Wulfhere's disgruntlement at being housed with a flock of smelly sheep notwithstanding, the shepherd's kind ministrations four days ago had worked miracles. Diera had recovered well enough to travel the next day and had shown no lingering effects from her harrowing experience since arriving back at Trowbridge.

Pulling herself into a sitting position beneath the covers of her pallet, Aisley gazed sightlessly at the shutters. Was Brecc out there somewhere, welcoming the new day with as heavy a heart and as many unanswered questions as she had? She would not wish it upon him, but the alternative was far worse, so she clung to hope as tightly as she'd clung to her mount's reins during their escape.

"Please, Father God," she whispered into the quiet room. "Let Brecc be safe. Let him be unharmed. And if it be Thy will, let me see him again."

She took a deep breath and dropped her head. How would she survive another day of awaiting news? Ever since their return to Trowbridge, her mother had hovered anxiously over Diera, scarcely allowing her to lift a finger even though Diera was more than capable of her usual needlework. Wulfhere had alternated between pacing the longhouse like a caged animal and standing statuesque while studying Aisley with unnatural intensity. Of the two, Aisley preferred the former. Her brother's narrow-eyed gaze sent shivers of alarm coursing through her, and not even exiting the room fully quelled her apprehension at his silent appraisal. He'd said nothing more to her about marriage, but it was not difficult to guess the direction of his thoughts. Ever since their altercation at Chippenham, Wulfhere had wished her gone.

A blackbird sang. It was close by. On the roof immediately above the shutter, most likely. Aisley tossed back her blanket, and as the chill of early morning touched her skin, she reached for her gown. She dressed soundlessly, and then she slipped out of the bedchamber, closing the door quietly behind her.

The cockerel greeted her arrival in the courtyard with a loud cry. The blackbird that had been singing moments before took off in a flurry of feathers, and a horse in the stables neighed. Aisley paused. Her burning desire to escape her thoughts had driven her to leave the longhouse with no fixed destination in mind. She was not dressed warmly enough for a walk. Cook was undoubtedly already about her early-morning tasks in the kitchen, and she would not wish for Aisley to interrupt her work. A second horse neighed, and with few other options available to her, Aisley started toward the stables. The stablehands would likely tolerate an unexpected visitor better than most.

Cracking the stable door open a fraction, Aisley slipped inside. The smell of horses, leather, and straw assailed her, instantly transporting her to another stable. Memories of her family's frantic escape from the royal estate flooded her mind. She shuddered, recalling the cries of fleeing Saxons mingled with the roars of the attacking Vikings. Rubbing her hands down her arms, she willed those memories to make room for others: standing in the stables with Brecc, a pungent horse blanket over his shoulders; the compassion in his voice and eyes as he spoke to her; the feel of his strong hand about hers. She released an unsteady breath. *Where are you, Brecc?*

"Someone 'as t' know."

Aisley gasped, turning to peer into the shadowy stable. A tuft of blond hair appeared over the top of a nearby stall. It was Garren, the youngest stableboy.

"Well, it's not like anyone's goin' to send word of 'is whereabouts to the likes of us." This voice came from the neighboring enclosure, along with the clang of a pail that echoed the pounding of Aisley's heart.

These stableboys were not talking to her but to each other.

"I know that. But the king runnin' off when the Vikin's attacked is all people 're talkin' about in town," Garren said. "It's likely the same all over Wessex."

Understanding dawned. The boys were discussing King Alfred.

"I daresay." Aisley recognized the voice now. It was Taber. He was older than Garren, but since he was half a head shorter, he remained invisible in the stall. "But if the king wants t' stay 'idden, 'e will. An' them Vikin's 'll 'ave a job findin' 'im."

"Unless someone 'appens t' see 'im and gives 'im away."

"Why would a Saxon do that?"

"I dunno." Garren's voice had become disconsolate. "The Vikin's 'ave gold. Most Saxons 'ave nothin'. People'll do all sorts of things t' put food on th' table."

"True enough," Taber said. "But not everyone's so bad off as us. Me older brother says things were better in all of Wiltshire when Ealdorman Kendryek wus alive."

Aisley's throat went dry. What had Wulfhere been doing—or not doing—to cause his people to suffer so greatly?

"It's 'ard to imagine it gettin' much worse, but I've 'eard terrible things 'bout the Vikin's."

"Aye." Taber was firm. "Don't wish them on us, whatever ya do. No food on th' table would be the least of our worries."

Garren was silent for a moment. "I 'ope King Alfred fights back soon."

"'E will."

"'Ow can you be so sure? They're sayin' 'e didn't even lift a sword afore 'e ran."

"First off," Taber said. "Don' be believin' everythin' you 'ear. Second off, Wessex is worth fightin' for."

Aisley's heavy heart lifted a fraction. If Taber's attitude was any indication of the mind-set of others, notwithstanding the Vikings' capture of the king's estate in Chippenham and their ever-increasing presence throughout Wessex, mayhap there was hope for the country and crown after all.

A latch lifted. One of the boys was exiting a stall. If he turned toward the stable doors, he would see her and would know that she'd been eavesdropping. Taking a tentative step backward, she reached for the door handle. Escape without detection would be impossible. While she'd been standing there, the sun had risen. The moment she opened the door, daylight would spill inside. Making a snap decision, she took hold of the door handle, pushed the door open a crack, and slipped outside. Without hesitation, she then pivoted, pulled the door open wider, and walked back inside.

"Good day," she called. "Is anyone about?"

A pail clanked to the floor, and a stall door opened. Aisley held her breath. Would the boys assume she was only now arriving?

"Good day, Mistress Aisley." It was Taber. "'Ow can I 'elp ya?"

With a blend of relief and appreciation for the loyal young man, Aisley smiled. "I awoke early and thought I might visit the horses. Is there one that needs a little extra attention?"

Taber smiled. "There's always plenty o' those, mistress. I reckon ya can take yer pick."

"Mayhap I should work my way down the stalls, then."

"Ya do that, mistress. These 'orses will be all the 'appier fer it."

Aisley approached the closest stall. The mount she'd ridden from Chippenham appeared at the gate. The mare sniffed the air, and then it lowered its nose to rub Aisley's arm.

"Good morning, young lady," Aisley said, running her hand down the mare's long neck. The horse nickered approvingly, and Aisley's shoulders relaxed. She had learned more than she'd anticipated by coming to the stable—some of it difficult to hear—but her decision to come had been a good one. If nothing more, she had new information to think on.

Brecc guided his mount along the narrow path that led to the swineherd's cottage. When he'd left this morning, the swineherd and his wife had been rising. Now the man was attending to a fence in the field adjacent to the lowly dwelling. His wife was also outside. It seemed she'd been washing clothing because she was lifting fabric from a tub at her feet and draping it over the bushes growing at the front of the cottage. It was surely a more hopeful than sensible endeavor, for even though the threat of rain had passed with the disappearance of the clouds, the likelihood of anything drying in today's cold temperatures was slim.

"Good day, Mistress Hocca," Brecc called.

The woman looked up from her work. "You're returned sooner than I thought," she said, setting her reddened hands upon her hips. "Did ya find Edris?"

"I did. He was at the small cottage beside the river, just as you said he would be."

She nodded. "And will 'e take ya both t' Athelney on 'is boat?"

"He will." Brecc neglected to add that persuading Edris to leave his nets long enough to row two men across the river had taken significant negotiation since neither he nor the king had coins to offer the fisherman. In the end, it had been the promise of a leg of venison from Brecc's first kill on the island that had swayed the fellow. It seemed that the fisherman was ready for a change from his usual fare of grayling or perch.

The woman grunted, reached for something in the tub at her feet, and then abruptly raised her head again. Sniffing the air, she tossed her husband's wet tunic back into the container, and with a cry of consternation, she ran toward the door of the cottage.

Brecc did not hesitate. In a trice, he was off the horse. Crossing the distance between them in half a dozen long paces, he'd almost reached her when she threw open the door.

"Ya good-fer-nothin' fellow!" she cried, racing inside and grabbing a small wooden utensil. "I allow ya t' sleep beneath me roof, and this is 'ow ya repay me?"

The smell of burning wafted through the door. With mounting alarm, Brecc entered. King Alfred was sitting on a small stool in the corner of the room, staring at the swineherd's wife with a stunned expression. The woman was furiously removing cakes of bread from the griddle above the fire and setting them onto a flat stone beside it. Each one was dark brown and ringed with black.

The king's gaze moved from Hocca to the burned cakes, and he rose to his feet. "Forgive me." He had never appeared so crestfallen. "I was so consumed in my thoughts, I did not notice—"

"'Ow could ya possibly not notice th' smell of burnin'?" Hocca cried. "It's so pungent, I smelt it from outside." She shook her head furiously. "One job. I gave ya one job. Not an 'ard one, mind. Simply watch th' cakes an' call me when they're ready." She tossed her hands in the air as though it would rid her of her uninvited guests. "Well, there'll be no bread for us this week. That was th' last o' me flour."

"I am truly sorry." It was a humble admission for the king of Wessex, but Brecc did not doubt his sincerity for a moment. "I shall ensure you are compensated for my inattentiveness."

"And just 'ow do ya propose to do that?" Hocca was still fuming.

"We cannot offer you bread." Brecc spoke from the doorway. "But I have promised Edris a leg of venison in exchange for transport to Athelney. I can offer you the same as payment for our lodging and the spoiled food."

She swung to face him. "You would do that?"

"I would."

She must have sensed his earnestness for she briefly bowed her head, her anger dissipating like the smoke from the burned cakes. "I thank you," she said, meeting his eyes again. "Venison would be most welcome."

"Consider it done," Brecc said.

"And in the meantime," the king added, "allow me to make up for my mistake by assisting you in some other way before we take our leave."

Without another word, Hocca handed the king a broom. "By the time ya've swept the room, the smell of burnin' should be gone."

King Alfred stared at the simple contrivance in his hand. It was quite possibly the first time the monarch had ever held one.

"I would start brushing the floor in the farthest corner and gradually work toward the door," Brecc suggested as casually as he dared.

"If 'e don't already know that, yer friend is in dire need o' far more than basic bakin' instructions," Hocca said, frowning at the charcoal remains of her bread.

"If the results of my pondering this morning are any indication, I fear that baking and sweeping are only a few of the many areas in which I must show improvement." The king carried the broom to the corner and swished it haphazardly over the dirt floor. "I thank you, Mistress Hocca, for your patience as I learn."

The swineherd's wife sniffed and then wrinkled her nose at the lingering smell in the cottage. "Ya can set the broom against th' wall when yer finished."

Brecc stepped away from the door to allow her passage outside. "Good day, Mistress Hocca," he said.

"Good day to ya both," she replied. "I pray it improves fer each of us."

CHAPTER 18

SOMETHING WAS DIFFERENT. AISLEY GLANCED around the marketplace. She'd visited this square in Trowbridge at least a dozen times in the seven weeks since she'd returned from Chippenham, but this morning, there was a new energy. A buzzing of whispered words. The heavy fear that had infiltrated the country after word spread that the king was gone and the Vikings were roaming the land unchecked seemed to have lightened.

"What could possibly be so exciting at the fishmonger's stall that Mistress Udela would leave her butter and eggs to join in the conversation?" Diera asked.

Aisley's gaze moved from the farmer's wife's empty seat behind her cart to the fishmonger's stall, where several of the locals had gathered. "I cannot say."

"Nor can I," Diera said. "But I should very much like to find out."

"Then, mayhap we should." Aisley tucked her arm beneath her sister's and drew her forward.

They approached from behind the small crowd, and before long, they were close enough to hear the fishmonger's voice.

"I tell ya, if me cousin weren't such a trusty fellow, I wouldn't believe a word o' it." He shrugged. "They're on an island 'ere in Wessex, the king an' 'is men are. That's what 'e 'eard."

Aisley's breath caught. Did they finally have news? She took a step closer, straining to hear more.

"Sounds 'bout right t' me." It was the tanner. "There's no reason fer King Alfred t' go abroad. 'Is 'ome and land are 'ere, aren't they?"

"You'd think 'e'd feel that way. But if 'e did, why did 'e run the moment them Vikings caught 'im unawares?" Mistress Udela chimed in.

The fishmonger frowned at her disapprovingly. "Not all stories are as sound as this one."

"Is that so?" Mistress Udela huffed. "And what makes you the most trustworthy person in town?"

"There's interest in any news o' the king," the blacksmith said, "but an eyewitness sayin' that 'e remains in Wessex an' is plannin' a return t' power, well, that's certainly worth sharin'."

"Aye," the fishmonger said. "Even if our own ealdorman won't want t' 'ear it."

Aisley squeezed Diera's arm, willing her not to make a sound. Diera's eyes had widened, but thankfully, her mouth remained closed.

"*Our* ealdorman." Mistress Udela's disdain was obvious. "Ealdorman Wulfhere's no more ours than is that proud hawk that sits atop the church roof lookin' down its beak at the other birds one minute and swoopin' in t' steal their food the next."

The fishmonger sighed. "'E's not the man 'is father was, that's fer certain."

"God rest Ealdorman Kendryek's soul," Mistress Udela said.

"Aye." The tanner looked grim. "And may God 'elp the king fight back against the heathens stealin' our land."

"'E'll need men," the blacksmith warned. "'E'll need the fyrd."

"An' so we wait fer further word," the fishmonger said. "If they 'ear in Hilperton afore we 'ear in Trowbridge, me cousin'll tell me."

"More waitin'," Mistress Udela grumbled. "Always more waitin'."

"We're used t' it," the fishmonger said, waving his hand over a large piece of fish lying on his stall. A swarm of flies took to the air. "It's the king 'oo'll be frettin' over all the time passin'. With no one t' stop 'em, there's no sayin' what them Vikin's'll do."

A tremor coursed through Aisley as the memory of the Vikings' maniacal howls when they'd burst into the great hall at the royal estate filled her mind. They'd been fully focused on killing the king, set on reaching the head table and targeting the man wearing the crown. She clutched her throat as the vision of Ealdorman Ormod crumpling to the ground floated before her eyes. She took an unsteady breath, desperately pushing the memory away. If the fishmonger's tale was true, it meant the king had escaped. And if he had escaped, it was possible that Brecc and others had escaped with him.

"I beg your pardon." Pulling her arm from Diera's, she moved forward. Diera gasped, and those gathered around the fishmonger's stall swung around, their expressions ranging from shock to alarm. "Did I overhear you say that the king may be fretting over the recent actions of the Vikings?" There was no point in them knowing she'd heard far more than the last few lines spoken among them.

The fishmonger cleared his throat, clearly uncomfortable. "Yes, Mistress Aisley."

"Is there news, then? Are King Alfred and his associates safe?"

"I cannot say fer certain, mistress. Word from Chippenham is that there were a great many 'oo died."

The merchant was evading her question. She needed no confirmation that the loss at the royal estate had been devastating. She had lived through it. What she desired was the names of the survivors.

"But the king? He is safe?"

His gaze darted across the street and then shifted to the tanner beside him. The tanner immediately looked away. The blacksmith had yet to raise his eyes from the horse's bit in his hand that suddenly seemed to require significant polishing, and sometime during the last few moments, Mistress Udela had slipped back to her cart. Aisley frowned. She had always maintained good relations with the townspeople and visiting merchants. Why was no one willing to tell her what they knew?

"Forgive me," she said, "but is something amiss?"

The fishmonger looked over her shoulder and swallowed. Aisley swung around in time to see Wulfhere approaching on horseback.

"Good day, sisters," he said. "I did not know you were in town this afternoon."

Wulfhere's statement did not come as a surprise; they rarely interacted. But he should know that given a choice, Aisley would be outdoors.

"We come as often as we can," she said. "There is always something new to see." For a small market, that was stretching the truth somewhat, but Aisley would prefer that Wulfhere think her interested in the fishmonger's wares than in any news he might bear from other towns. She pointed at the large fish that was once more gathering flies. "Do you see the enormous pike the fishmonger has today?"

Wulfhere gave the fishmonger's stall a calculating look before turning his attention to the merchant. "Did you catch the fish yourself?"

"I did, sire. Early this morning. On the River Biss."

Wulfhere grunted. "I hope you sell it for a good price and that your good fortune continues." He smirked. "Your increased income will be an asset when it comes time to pay taxes."

Aisley stared at him, a pit forming in her stomach as the fishmonger inclined his head politely. "As you say, sire."

Wulfhere brushed a speck of lint off his warm cloak. He had somehow procured a new one after their escape, even though Aisley and Diera were wearing ones they'd outgrown but had reclaimed from trunks upon their return. "I am glad we have spoken. It is always advantageous to be prepared for such things."

"Wulfhere! Surely you do not mean to penalize this gentleman for one day's good catch."

"Penalize? Not at all. I am simply enabling him to share his good fortune with others."

The pit in Aisley's stomach was rapidly developing into a severe case of nausea. This was her doing. Had she not pointed out the pike to Wulfhere, mayhap it would not have caught his notice. And the fishmonger would be no worse off for his encounter with the ealdorman. "Forgive me," she whispered.

The fishmonger offered her a resigned look. It suggested that he was unsurprised by Wulfhere's response to his catch. How long had Wulfhere been excessively taxing the people of Wiltshire? Was this the source of discontent the merchants had been alluding to? It would explain Wulfhere's ability to purchase extravagant clothing while those over whom he had stewardship struggled to eat. Memory of another conversation flooded her mind. When she'd entered the stable soon after their flight from Chippenham, the stableboys had been talking about a new level of impoverishment among the commoners. They'd also been discussing King Alfred's whereabouts.

A new determination settled upon Aisley. The moment Wulfhere was about his own business and Diera was happily situated near the fire inside the longhouse, Aisley would go to the stable. Over the last seven weeks, her need to escape her thoughts had taken her there more often than not, and she had developed a friendship with the stablehands. With Taber in particular. Her association with Wulfhere might prevent the locals in town from sharing information about King Alfred and his men, but she had a feeling that Taber might be persuaded to talk.

An hour later, she slipped through the stable doors. There was something wonderfully calming about the rustle of hooves, soft nickers, and the murmur of the boys' voices as they went about their work. Aisley closed her eyes and took a breath. It smelled of straw and horses, and it was blissfully free of her brother's discomforting presence. The muscles across her shoulders released a fraction, and she opened her eyes. She must find Taber.

"Taber." Keeping her voice low so as not to startle the horses, she walked down the aisle between the stalls. "Are you within the stables?"

"Over 'ere!" His head appeared around a gate, and he grinned. "Afternoon, Mistress Aisley."

"Good afternoon." Aisley joined him at the stall where the mare she'd ridden back from Chippenham was eating from the bucket Taber had just placed on the floor. "How is this young lady behaving?"

"Ah, she's a grand one." Taber patted the mare's rump. "I wish all the 'orses in 'ere were so well behaved."

"I wish I knew who she belongs to."

He looked at her. "D'ya think ya'll ever find out?"

"That likely depends upon how many of King Alfred's thegns survived the attack at Chippenham." She paused. "Have you heard anything?"

He took his time closing the gate. Aisley waited, feeling her heart pound harder with each passing moment.

"There was somethin' new goin' around yesterday." He faced her, his eyes sparkling. "I 'ope it's the truth. I really do."

"What was it?"

"They say the king's 'idin' away on an island, bidin' 'is time till 'is men 'ave all gathered together again afore goin' after them heathen Vikin's."

The fishmonger had spoken of an island. But where was it? A goodly portion of Wessex was coastal. There were any number of islands he could have chosen as his place of retreat.

"That is all you know? That the king is alive and has retreated to an island?"

"Yes, mistress."

"What of those who may have already joined him?" Her heart had yet to resume its normal rhythm. "Did you hear the names of any of his followers?"

He scrunched his forehead as though deep in thought. "Not that I can remember. 'Course, word of the king bein' alive and preparin' t' fight back is all anyone really wants t' 'ear."

"Of course." Aisley swallowed her disappointment. If Brecc had survived, he would be with the king. Of that, she had no doubt. "Will you inform me if you learn anything more?"

The creases on Taber's brow had yet to fully disappear, but he nodded obediently. "Aye, mistress."

Somehow, Aisley managed a smile. Fresh news would come. It had to if King Alfred wished for his support to grow. Until then, she could do nothing but feign patience and pray that the name she most wished to hear would be mentioned by the next messenger.

CHAPTER 19

BRECC STOOD AT THE WATER'S edge, watching and listening. The sun had set, and the marshland creatures were in full song. Bullfrogs croaked, their voices low against the lapwings' distinctive peewit calls. Overhead, a hawk cried, and the gentle plop of the wader birds' feet in the shallow water turned to a chorus of flapping wings as they took to the air in unison. Had it simply been the hawk's presence that had disturbed them? Setting his hand on the handle of his dagger, Brecc strained to see through the rapidly fading light.

The sound of murmured voices reached him first, and then he heard the distinctive sucking of a pole being drawn from the mud. He whistled. An echoing whistle floated back, and the fingers on his dagger relaxed. It was Rheged, and he had the king with him on one of the punts they'd acquired from Hocca's brother.

As the flat-bottomed boat appeared, Brecc knelt on the damp grass, waiting for the punt's squared end to reach him. The wood grazed the turf, and Brecc seized it.

"I have the punt, Sire."

The small craft swayed violently, and the king stepped onto the ground beside him. "I thank you, Brecc."

Rheged stepped off after him and then turned to help Brecc drag the punt out of the water. They pulled it under a nearby tree, and Rheged set the pole against the trunk.

"I trust your time at the church was uninterrupted," Brecc said.

"Not another soul in sight," Rheged said. It was a good thing, but Brecc received the distinct impression that keeping watch outside while the king communed with God inside the small church was not one of Rheged's most highly rated activities.

"It was a most fulfilling experience." King Alfred was already walking toward the woodland where the stone cottage that now served as the monarch's safe haven and the gathering spot for his most loyal men was located. "Come," he called. "You both must hear what I have to say."

Offering Rheged an inquiring look, Brecc started after the king.

Rheged quickly joined him. "Before you ask," he said, "I know nothing more than you do." He cocked his head to one side as though contemplating something deep. "Well, that is not entirely true. Having stood outside the Aller church for going on three hours, I can now unequivocally tell you that there are twenty-three paving stones leading up to the church's door, the current molehill count on the east side of the building is fifteen, and on the left side, it is twelve. Oh, and there is a very aggressive magpie who takes exception to anyone standing within its sphere of influence for that length of time."

Brecc chuckled. "You obviously used your time at Aller most productively."

"I hope you can say the same for your afternoon at Athelney."

"Enough wood cut to fuel our fire for a week, and three moorhens caught and prepared for supper."

Rheged grinned. "I approve. Although, before you think too highly of yourself and your accomplishments, I would remind you that with only three moorhens under your belt, I counted far higher than you did this day."

Chopping wood had helped release some of Brecc's frustration over the continued lack of information reaching Athelney—whether it be regarding the king's missing thegns, the Vikings' whereabouts, or Aisley's well-being. But Rheged's humor had already done far more. It had lifted his spirits. With a laugh, he placed his hand on Rheged's shoulder. "I am glad you are here, even if you are only truly good for punting and counting."

The fire was blazing inside the king's temporary abode. He and the queen were already seated on rustic stools. The eleven thegns who had arrived in ones and twos during the days and weeks following Rheged's arrival with the queen sat on the floor around the fire.

Rheged and the queen had taken a longer route to reach Athelney than the one the king and Brecc had chosen. Brecc had used the time to clear the vacant building of refuse and make some basic repairs to one shutter and a corner of the roof. While the king had hunted for game and sequestered himself in prayer, Brecc had cut firewood and gathered sufficient fir tree boughs to create makeshift pallets. When he'd delivered the promised venison to Edris the fisherman and Hocca the swineherd's wife, he'd also managed to acquire their first punt. At the time, he'd not known how many people would come or how often the king would wish to visit the church at Aller, but it was obvious that they could not be wholly dependent upon Edris for transportation to and from the island.

Thankfully, Rheged had used his circuitous route to pass along word of the king's place of refuge to as many of the king's surviving thegns as he could contact. Those who had relocated to Athelney were a small group, but they were devoted to the king and to Wessex. They were the warriors King Alfred most needed.

"Sit, gentlemen," the king demanded.

Brecc and Rheged took their places between the king's stool and Ealdorman Odda. Odda gave them both an acknowledging nod and passed them a basket of bread. Hocca had obviously made her weekly delivery.

"As you all know," the king began, "ever since my arrival at Athelney, I have repeatedly petitioned God to provide me with a way forward, a way to take Wessex back from a Godless leader, and to ease the suffering of my people." He cleared his throat. "Today, at the Aller church, I believe He finally made His will known to me."

Brecc lowered the piece of bread in his hand from his mouth, his attention fully on the king.

"Whilst I was in prayer, a passage of scripture shared with me by Saint Neot came forcibly to my mind," the king continued. "It is from the book of Hebrews and says: *For whom the Lord loveth he chasteneth, and scourgeth every son whom he receiveth.*" He gazed around the room. "Do you understand? It is not my place to despise the chastening I have received. Instead, I must rejoice in having been received by the Lord. I must learn from my mistakes and use this humbling experience for good."

Brecc pondered the king's insight. It was a rare thing to be led by a monarch so willing to learn and to teach. Indeed, had King Alfred not been born to the crown, Brecc thought it likely that he would have become a priest, for there was no denying the strength he drew from studying God's word or his burning desire to share that enlightenment with others.

Odda was the first to speak. "Have you ascertained the direction the Lord wishes you to take, Sire?"

"I have."

A new, higher level of anticipation hummed through the room. Out of the corner of his eye, Brecc noted Rheged's anxious glance, but he kept his gaze upon the king.

"First," the king said, "we shall go from here—alone and in pairs—to seek out those thegns who are loyal to the crown. Those who wish to join us at Athelney shall be welcomed. We shall also turn our attention to creating chaos within our enemy's ranks. As our numbers increase, so, too, will the number of sorties we embark upon. We shall seek out all Viking strongholds and encampments, learn what we can of their methods and plans, and then lay them waste.

"News of the successful raids made on our foes shall quickly spread. Our surprise attacks will feed the heathens' superstitious temperaments, fueling unease. Those who harbor Viking sympathies will also grow increasingly discomfited, whilst others will be inspired to do their part to resist the Viking trespassers. Their brave efforts will join ours." Conviction rang through his voice. "I wish to offer a poignant reminder to the people of Wessex that their king will soon return, whilst simultaneously issuing a firm message to Guthrum and those who follow him that I *have not* and *will not* abandon this nation."

The king's impassioned words had barely left his mouth before the room erupted with cheers. All the thegns were on their feet, clapping and shouting their approval. With a pleased smile, King Alfred raised his hand, and silence descended on the room once more.

"At least two thegns will remain at Athelney to protect the queen and welcome new arrivals. This assignment will be rotated." He paused. "Rheged and Odda, I would that you should be the first."

Brecc caught the flash of disappointment in Rheged's eyes, but it was quickly masked by his bow.

"As you wish, Sire," Rheged said.

"The honor is ours." Odda inclined his head.

"Not only is it an honor, but it carries with it the greatest responsibility of all," the king said. "I am entrusting you with the safety of the person dearest to my heart."

The queen blushed and lowered her head in an effort to hide it.

Rheged, however, stood a little taller. "The queen shall be protected, Sire, you have my word."

"And mine," Odda echoed.

"I thank you." The king looked at Brecc. "And you, Brecc, where would you have me send you?"

"To Trowbridge," Brecc responded without hesitation. "I have heard rumor that Ealdorman Wulfhere may not be the most reliable of men. With access to the entire fyrd of Wiltshire at stake, I believe it worth our while to discover his true leanings."

"A wise choice," Odda said. "I would be most interested to know why Wulfhere removed himself from the great hall in Chippenham before the fighting had truly commenced."

King Alfred frowned, this report on Wulfhere's actions during the Viking attack obviously new to him. "I would wish to know the same. I shall anxiously await your report."

♛

Aisley had been foolish to go into town alone. She knew that now. But an hour ago, when she'd been desperate to escape the four walls of the longhouse and Diera had refused to go out until the puddles formed by all the earlier rain had dried, it had seemed practicable. The maids had been helping prepare the evening meal and could not be spared. Even Taber had been unavailable. It would likely take him and the other stableboy working together to clean off the mud currently caked all over Wulfhere's horse. Where Wulfhere had gone to render his mount so dirty, Aisley could not tell, but she was as anxious as he must have been to leave the confines of the house.

And so, she had determined to make the short walk without a companion. It would give her the fresh air she craved and enable her to interact with other locals, albeit briefly. For years, she had wandered the fields and woodlands near the longhouse, gathering healing plants. There really should have been nothing to fear about this excursion, had not three Vikings chosen to enter the square just as she reached Mistress Udela's cart.

The older lady's gasp had been enough to cause Aisley to turn. Now, all around, people scattered, leaving an open path for the newcomers to follow into the center of the market. The tallest man led the others. His light-brown hair was plaited into two long ropes. His beard was thick and matted, and he wore a sheepskin across his shoulders. A long knife hung from his belt. The two who followed were lankier in build and appeared younger. They each carried axes and sacks, and where one had a scar running across his chin, the other had a nose that had surely been broken at least once. They were obviously men who had experienced violence and likely did not shy away from it.

Only this morning, Taber had told Aisley of the latest rumor regarding the invading horde. Word was that they'd had their fill of pillaging, looting, and raping in Chippenham and were now working their way farther into Wiltshire, setting up camps along the way. A recent traveler passing through Trowbridge had reported smelling the smoke of a campfire coming from an area beside the river not more than twenty furlongs from town. He'd not seen anyone, but many feared that such an encampment could belong only to Vikings. If the three men currently sauntering across the square were any indication, those people had been correct.

Like a breathy gust of wind, a ripple of fear spread across the uneasy spectators.

"'Eaven 'elp us." Mistress Udela's voice was more of a moan. "They 'ave come."

Aisley moved to stand beside her. The cart offered little protection, but it served as a barrier, at least. "It shall be well," she whispered, more to herself than to the farmer's wife. "A moment longer and they shall pass by."

"But they're comin' this way," Mistress Udela sobbed.

"Hush," Aisley warned. "Look upon your wares rather than upon them. You need not watch their progress. I shall tell you when they are gone."

With trembling fingers, the older woman reached for a pat of butter wrapped in cloth. She lifted it, only to set it down again in the same spot. "It's no good." Her voice wavered, though she had yet to look up. "It's like I'm a field mouse an' they're 'awks ready to pounce. I can sense 'em nearby, but there's no place fer me t' run."

Aisley pulled her overly small cloak around herself more tightly. This was likely not the time to tell Mistress Udela that the Vikings did indeed appear to be walking directly toward her cart. The fishmonger who ran the stall beside this one had disappeared. One of the shorter Vikings picked up a perch and lifted it to his nose. He said something, laughed, and then dropped it into the other man's sack. The second man grumbled a complaint, but he didn't remove the stolen fish. Instead, he followed after the taller one to Mistress Udela's cart.

"This!" The taller man pointed at the basket of eggs.

Mistress Udela was trembling so much Aisley feared the older lady's legs might give way beneath her.

"This!" the Viking repeated.

The farmer's wife opened her mouth, but only a squeak emerged.

Aisley reached for her hand beneath the cart and squeezed it. "How many would you like?" Aisley asked.

The Viking's attention moved from the eggs to Aisley. Slowly, his gaze trailed down her long hair to her ill-fitting cloak to her shoes. A shudder coursed through her, bringing with it an overwhelming urge to flee. Without dropping his assessing look, the leader of the trio gave the young man who'd taken the fish a curt order. The younger Viking reached for the entire basket of eggs and set it in the crook of his arm.

"Rangvald," the leader said, jabbing his broad chest with his thick thumb. Then he pointed to Aisley. "You?"

Mustering her courage, Aisley raised her chin and pointed to the basket of eggs. "You must pay for those."

Something that looked remarkably like shock flickered across the Viking's face, and then with a smug smile, he withdrew a coin purse from his belt. Swinging the purse over the cart with one hand, he pointed to her with the other. "You. Name."

"Give 'im yer name," Mistress Udela said. "Then mayhap 'e'll pay me fer all them eggs."

"He has no right to demand my name."

"'E 'as no right to steal me eggs neither," Mistress Udela retorted, her courage remarkably restored now that she was no longer the focus of the Viking's attention.

The Viking moved closer, leaning so far over the cart that Aisley could smell his putrid breath. She took a stumbling step back. Her heel hit the wall of the smithy behind her. Her breath caught, and she pressed her hands against the stones.

"Rangvald," he repeated, a wicked gleam in his eye. "You. Name."

This was a game to him. A horrible, terrifying game.

"Aisley!" Mistress Udela cried, snatching the purse from the tall man's hand. "'Er name's Aisley."

"Yer a greedy old woman, Udela!" Out of nowhere, the fishmonger appeared, and before Aisley could gather her wits, he was hurling fish from his cart at the Vikings. The three men roared their displeasure, and the one closest to the fishmonger lunged for his arm. But the fishmonger anticipated his move and tossed a fistful of minnows at his face. "Run fer it, Mistress Aisley," he yelled. "I can only 'old 'em off fer so long."

Aisley needed no second bidding. Before the Vikings knew what she was about, she rounded Mistress Udela's cart and bolted across the eerily empty square. Another shout was followed by the sound of pounding feet. At least one of the Vikings had taken up the chase, and she knew full well that if it came down to a race, her short legs would be no match for the Vikings' longer limbs. The maze of back alleys surrounding the square were known to disorient even the locals. Losing her pursuers there was her only hope.

Not daring to take the time to look over her shoulder, she veered left and entered an unfamiliar narrow lane. Stone buildings pressed in on her from both sides. Gasping for breath, she pressed on, desperately seeking another way out. The pounding footsteps had followed her, and they were closer. Up ahead, the lane bent to the right. If no other route manifested itself beyond the corner, her chance for escape was gone. She rounded the bend. The lane continued. Choking back a sob, she scoured the buildings. More running footsteps echoed off the stone walls, this time seemingly coming from the other direction.

A man burst into view ahead of her. She pivoted. On the left, there was an arched doorway, larger than the others on the lane. It might be wide enough to hide her but only if she reached it in time. She took off, but her toe caught a rock. She stumbled, and suddenly she was lifted off the ground.

"No!" she cried, flailing her legs wildly.

Instantly, a hand pressed against her mouth. "Make no sound, Aisley. The vermin are almost upon us."

Shock stole her breath, and before she knew what he was about, her rescuer had carried her across the few remaining paces to the arched entrance. He had barely set her on her feet when those chasing her turned the corner. Aisley shifted sideways, pressing herself into the narrow corner behind the stones that formed the archway. Then panic struck. There was space enough for her small frame but nothing more. She looked up, searching the shadowy area for her rescuer, but he was gone. She closed her eyes. It had been Brecc. No matter his peasant clothing, she was sure of it.

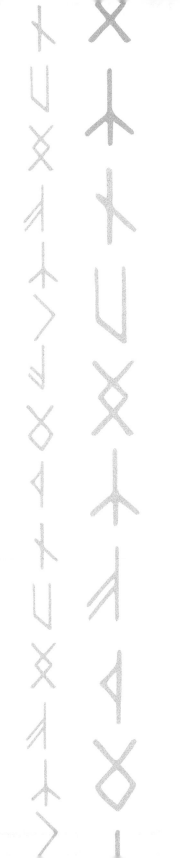

CHAPTER 20

WITH NO PLACE THAT WOULD conceal him from the Vikings, Brecc took the only other option available to him: to hide in plain sight. Seizing the broom leaning against the wall beside the arched entrance, he turned his back on the oncoming men and began to sweep the doorstep next to the one where Aisley was hidden. Aisley. He tightened his grip on the broom handle. He'd barely reached her in time, and even now, she was not fully out of danger. But Rangvald would have to contend with considerably more than a handful of cold, wet fish if he attempted to lay a finger on her this time.

The Vikings' voices, guttural and angry, drew closer. Brecc kept his head down. Rangvald operated within Guthrum's inner circle and had participated in the attack at the royal estate. Brecc did not know if the chieftain could identify him, but he'd rather not take the chance. He sensed someone behind him. Tamping down his instinctive response to draw his knife, he kept sweeping. The Viking spoke. Brecc did not need to understand the words to recognize the mocking tone. Moments later, a leg jutted out from behind him and hit the broom. Despite his overwhelming desire to use his tight grip on the handle to swing it across his tormentor's head, Brecc muttered a feigned exclamation and let the broom fall to the ground.

Laughter, cruel and callous, followed. And then an impatient shout sent the men running down the lane once more. Slowly, Brecc bent to retrieve the broom. He glanced over his shoulder. The lane was empty. Releasing a tense breath, he set the broom back against the wall, and after one more careful look around, he stepped into the archway.

Aisley's frightened eyes looked up at him from the dark corner. Aching to pull her into his arms, he reached for her hand. It was cold.

"Forgive me," he spoke softly. "I did not mean to treat you so roughly, but there was so little time, and I—"

"You came."

Those two simple words had never conveyed so much nor cut so deeply. It had been close to two months since he'd made her that promise. It had been too long.

"Would that I could have come sooner. I have been with the king, and only yesterday was given the opportunity to come to Trowbridge."

"How long will you be here?"

He did nothing to hide the regret in his voice. "Not long enough. I am on the king's errand to gather information. Only two hours ago, I stumbled upon a Viking encampment just outside town. I recognized Rangvald immediately, and when he and his underlings set off for town, I followed." Brecc's jaw tightened. "I should have stayed closer. He was already harrying you by the time I reached the square, and had it not been for the fishmonger's timely response, there's no accounting for what I might have done."

"The Vikings will seek revenge for what he did."

"Rangvald has far more interest in you than in the local fishmonger. I wager that if the fellow avoids the market for a week or two, the target of the Vikings' ire will move to another."

"I do not know how to thank him."

"I imagine your fleet-footed escape gave him a great deal of satisfaction. I was hard-pressed to reach the head of the lane before you entered it."

"But he lost all his fish."

"Aye." Brecc fought to keep his anger at Rangvald's blatant lasciviousness at bay. "But he undoubtedly knew that you were at risk of losing far more."

As soon as the words were spoken, he regretted them. Fear—raw and real—filled her eyes, and her gaze darted to the lane. "Are the Vikings truly gone? How did they not see you?"

He gestured to the unpretentious implement leaning against the nearby wall. "They saw only a simpleton wielding a broom outside his house and left even more irritated than when they arrived."

She released an unsteady breath. "You have not told me why it is that you are dressed as a peasant."

"The king has determined that, for now, it is best that he and his men be not readily identified."

"The king is well, then?"

He offered her the ghost of a smile. "He is."

"And the queen?"

"She, too, is safe and well."

Aisley smiled, and Brecc's heart warmed at the sight. "I am glad to hear it. The last few weeks must have been a terrible ordeal for her. May it not be long before she and the king can safely leave their island sanctuary."

He froze. "You know of the island?"

"The fishmonger heard word that the king had taken refuge on an island and shared the news with the townspeople. It was just enough to give us hope."

Brecc pondered her words. The king's impressions had been correct. If such token information—little more than an inkling that the king still lived and had not fled the country—offered vital hope to his people, how much greater would be the impact on Saxon morale when those same individuals heard news of gathering warriors and successful raids on Viking encampments?

"Were the rumors correct?" she asked.

"Close enough," he said.

There was a moment of silence, and when he did not continue, she offered an understanding nod. "I . . . I prayed that you were there with him. That you had survived the attack at Chippenham unharmed."

Her stunning, guileless eyes met his, and he felt his resistance falter. He drew her closer. "Not knowing what happened to you after you left the great hall that evening has been more torturous than I could ever have imagined." He shook his head. "And yet, notwithstanding how difficult it was then and how much I wish it were otherwise now, I must leave you straightway. It is imperative that the king learn about the Vikings' presence outside Trowbridge before Rangvald's men fully unleash themselves on the town."

"I know," she whispered, moisture shining in her eyes. "But at least I have seen you, have spoken with you, and know that you are well."

"And I, you," he said. "But if you are to remain safe, you must not leave your home alone again. Not with the Viking encampment so near and Rangvald so intent upon speaking with you."

She trembled, the memory of her recent escape still fresh.

Releasing her hand, he wrapped his arms around her. Without a word, her arms circled his waist, and she laid her head on his chest. He held her close, her long tresses flowing softly across his arm. "I must know that you are protected, Aisley."

"You have nothing to fear," she said, raising her eyes to his. "After today's encounter, I have no desire whatsoever to return to the market."

He searched her face, recognizing the earnestness there. Then his gaze shifted to her lips. As much as he desired it, he should not kiss her again. Chivalry demanded that of him. Until the king was restored to his throne, Brecc could offer her nothing more than friendship. He took a fortifying breath. Instantly, her unique scent of wildflowers mingled with herbs assailed his senses, bringing with it a fresh flood of memories: the compassion she'd manifest when she'd used her plants to create a remedy for Rheged, the joy on her face when she'd shown him the cowslip she'd picked. Gratitude for her goodness overwhelmed him, and before another thought—chivalrous, sensible, or otherwise—could form, he lowered his head and pressed a lingering kiss to her lips.

Slowly, reluctantly, he released her and took a small step back. He must go now, before it became even harder. "If you ever need me," he whispered, "send word to Athelney, and I will come."

"Athelney," she repeated, as though attempting to straighten her thoughts.

"Aye. It is a day's ride south of Trowbridge." He hesitated. "It's an island of sorts, although it is best that no one else knows that."

She nodded, and he knew she understood.

"Are you recovered enough that you can find your way home from here?" He caught the quiver of her lips that spoke of lingering fears and desperately wished he did not have to ask this of her. "It is best that you not be seen with me—for your sake more than mine—but be assured that I will be within earshot every step of the way."

She mustered a small smile. "Then I shall manage."

His heart swelled at her obvious bravery. "I shall wait only until you have reached the corner of the lane," he said, "and then I shall follow."

She squeezed past him to stand in the center of the arched entrance. After looking left and right and determining that the lane was empty, she turned back to him. "Godspeed, Brecc. My prayers go with you." And before he had a chance to respond, she was walking briskly away from the town square.

♔

Aisley tucked her trembling hands beneath her cloak and slowly approached the entrance to the alley. If she took this path, she could circumvent the marketplace and reach the road that led to her family's longhouse without returning to the center of town. The alley was her most direct route, but it was also long, narrow, and poorly lit.

She reached the turnoff and stopped. Up ahead, a woman stepped out of a house with a basket in hand. Aisley watched as she started down the lane toward the market. Aisley wanted to call her back, to tell her that it wasn't safe. But in all likelihood, it was. Brecc had told her the Vikings were gone. At least, for now.

Brecc. Her heart ached from the sweetness of his kiss and the agony of walking away from him. In his arms, the terror of Rangvald's chase had temporarily subsided, and she'd known true joy. That moment together, though painfully brief, had been real. And now, as she faced the shadowy alley and her fear came creeping back, she clung to the memory.

Turning to look over her shoulder, she scanned the lane. The arched entrance was no longer in view. Two children were chasing a dog the way she had come, and from somewhere nearby, a man whistled a tuneful song. A door closed, and a bird sitting on a rooftop took to the sky. Otherwise, the road was empty. There was no sign of Brecc. And yet, somehow, she knew he was there. Like the whisper of a summer breeze, she could feel his presence—comforting, steadying, and encouraging.

Summoning what little courage remained to her, she turned the corner and instantly felt the increased chill. The overhanging roofs on either side of the alley almost touched, blocking most of the sunlight and warmth of the day. Pulling her cloak around her, she picked up her pace. Refuse filled the center of the alley, its malodor trapped by the tightly packed buildings. Keeping to the left, Aisley lifted a corner of her cloak so as to breathe through the wool garment. It helped, but only moderately.

She pressed on. Up ahead, a door opened, and suddenly, a man appeared, standing directly in her path. He was tall and broad shouldered, but in the weak light, she could not make out his features. A small cry escaped her, and she stumbled to a halt.

"Brecc," she whispered, her eyes not leaving the shadowy form before her.

He was close. She knew he would not break his promise.

"Begin' yer pardon, mistress." The man lifted his hat in greeting. "Didn't mean t' startle ya. Didn't see ya there."

Aisley's pounding heart slowed a fraction. He was a local. Mayhap someone she would have recognized in better lighting. "Forgive me," she said. "I was in too great a hurry."

"Don' blame ya," he said. "Best t' spend as little time as possible in this stinkin' alley, I say." He tugged on his hat once more. "Good day t' ya."

"G-Good day."

He stepped around her and hastened away. Aisley set her cloak across her mouth and nose more firmly and continued on her path. After three more turns onto different, equally unpleasant alleys, a gradual increase of light and the distant sounds of voices and hooves announced an end to the labyrinth. Slowing her feet, Aisley approached the alley's exit cautiously. She lowered the cloak from over her face and studied her surroundings. Her circuitous path through town had led her to a spot farther along the main thoroughfare than she usually traveled, but it was reassuringly familiar. Grassy verges lined the rutted dirt road, and townspeople—some on foot and others on horseback—were traveling the lane, stopping to chat, and greeting each other as if it were any other ordinary day.

"All will be well." Aisley did not know if Brecc would hear her whispered words, but they brought her comfort. "The worst is behind me."

"Mistress Aisley!"

Startled by the shout, Aisley glanced around. Not more than ten paces away, a boy of her same height was guiding a brown horse by a long leather strap. He raised his arm to greet her.

"Taber!" Relief lent speed to her weary legs as she hastened to join him. "What are you doing here?"

"The master's 'orse threw a shoe when 'e was out earlier today," he said. "I've just come from the smithy."

"Then you are headed back to our stables."

"Yes, mistress." He looked at her, concern in his expression. "The smithy told me what 'appened today at th' market." He shifted his weight from one leg to the other. "If . . . if ya'd like to walk back with me rather than by yerself, I'd be 'onored."

Tears pricked her eyes at his thoughtfulness. "That would be most welcome."

He gave a pleased nod, and they started forward together. After walking a short distance, Taber broke the silence between them. "I'm right glad Nyle did what 'e did, mistress. An' so's all th' other people in town."

"Is Nyle the fishmonger's name?" she asked.

"Aye." He offered her a crooked smile. "Bein' treated like a bit of a champion, 'e is."

"He is a champion," Aisley said. "At least to me. But I wish his valor had not come at the expense of his source of income."

"Not t' worry, mistress. All them that was there cornered Mistress Udela and made 'er give 'alf of what was in that Vikin's purse to Nyle. They're sayin' it was more than Nyle would've made if 'e'd sold all 'is fish."

"I am glad to know something good came of the horrible experience," she said.

"Likely th' only good thing," Taber said. "Nyle told the smithy them Vikin's 're camped at the river on the east side of town." He gave a troubled sigh. "Seems t' me that whatever difficulties we thought we 'ad afore are about t' get a whole lot worse."

Aisley's thoughts instantly turned to Brecc. He'd given her few details of what he was currently about, but she had gleaned this much: King Alfred was going to fight this Viking scourge, and he had already initiated a plan to route the invaders from Wessex.

"The king has not forgotten us, Taber. Of that you may be sure. He will need us to show courage and loyalty, but if we do that, I believe he and his men will triumph."

"Seems like ya showed that kind o' courage t' everyone in town today, mistress."

"I was more scared than I'd like to admit."

"Don't matter," Taber said. "You stood up t' the heathen anyway."

She pondered that thought. "I suppose I did."

A wagon approached, and Taber led the horse onto the grassy verge to let the vehicle pass by. Stepping aside, Aisley turned to look over her shoulder. Two elderly women carrying baskets were not far behind them. They shuffled out of the way of the oncoming wagon. Following after them came a merchant pushing a cart laden with bolts of fabric. As Aisley watched, one of the cart wheels hit a rock, and the oversized barrow veered to the right. Grunting his annoyance, the merchant bent low to control his wayward contrivance, and by so doing, he revealed the man walking in his wake. For three long heartbeats, Brecc's eyes held hers, and then the wagon rolled by, and he was gone.

"I will have courage, Brecc," she promised in a whisper. "We shall be brave together."

CHAPTER 21

THE ENCAMPMENT WAS QUIET, AND the number of Vikings seated around the campfire had dwindled to two. The assigned watchmen. Having monitored the Vikings' movements around the clock for the last two days, Brecc knew what to expect. The two Vikings assigned to night duty would stay near the fire, playing bones and tossing an occasional log on the flames so the fire remained burning until morning. Approximately every hour, they would stand and do a brief circuit of their encampment before returning to their positions beside the fire. It was a token effort at defending their position, which played into the Saxon warriors' hands perfectly.

One week ago, this particular group of Vikings had ransacked the nearby village of Dinton before the local residents had even known the invaders were about. Brecc and his companions were ready to return the favor.

An owl hooted. Lufian and Bertwin were in position. Brecc turned to his right. The whites of Rheged's eyes glistened in the darkness.

"They've released the horses," Rheged whispered.

"Aye. As soon as the guards rise, we move."

They waited. A horse neighed. One of the Vikings looked over his shoulder to the area where the invaders' stolen mounts were tied for the night. Or, where they had been tied. If Lufian and Bertwin had done their jobs, most of the horses were now scattering throughout the nearby woodland. The Saxons needed only two of them to complete their work this night.

An owl hooted again. The men were on their way back.

"It's time," Brecc murmured, willing the guards to move.

As though the tallest had heard the prompt, he muttered something, gathered the bones, and slipped them into the purse at his belt. He rose to his feet. With a grunt, the shorter one joined him. Moments later, they started toward the outer edges of the camp.

Brecc waited only until their backs were turned. "Now!" he hissed. Keeping their heads low, he and Rheged raced across the open area to a large, dark shadow on the fringes of the firelight. "First the flour," he said. "Then the vegetables."

Rheged pulled back the blanket that covered the mound of supplies the Vikings had seized from the local people and reached for a sack of flour. "Bertwin better get those horses to us," he said, hoisting it over his shoulder. "We're not going to get far without them."

Brecc lifted one of the other sacks, his feet shifting as he adjusted the weight. Rheged was right. These sacks were even heavier than he'd anticipated. But this was Brecc's third time conducting a raid with Bertwin in as many weeks, and the fellow had yet to fail him. "He'll be there," Brecc said and took off for their appointed meeting spot.

He heard the swish of a horse's tail hitting a tree trunk before he saw the gleam of their eyes.

"Over here." Bertwin's whisper reached him as he drew closer.

"Start tying them on," Brecc urged, moving the sack on his shoulder to the horse's back. "We're going for more."

Not waiting for Rheged, Brecc raced back to the pile of provisions and reached for another sack. The Vikings had stripped the nearby mill of its flour. The miller had barely enough grain left to feed his own family, let alone those in the village who would need flour to survive.

Another bird call. This time, a nightingale. That meant Lufian had spotted the guards approaching from his position near the woodpile. Brecc's heart rate increased. The Vikings were making quick work of this circuit. He and Rheged needed to move faster.

"They're on their way back," he panted, lifting a sack of vegetables under his free arm while the other steadied the sack of flour on his shoulder.

"I heard." Rheged reached for two lumpy sacks and tucked one under each arm. "Time to go."

They ran for the woods. Bertwin already had the first flour sacks strapped to one horse. Brecc set the lumpy sack on top of them and lowered the other flour sack onto the second horse's back. "Get them secured as fast as you can, Bertwin," he said. "Rheged has two more."

"Devil take it!" Rheged dropped his load. "One of the horses Bertwin and Lufian released has wandered back into camp."

Brecc swiveled. Sure enough, a white horse was idly grazing within the light of the fire. If one of the guards spotted it, he would take it back to join the others. And discover that they were all gone. There was no telling what he would do at that point, but it most assuredly would not work in Brecc and his men's favor.

"Take these horses to the road, Bertwin," Brecc urged. "I'm going after the wanderer. Rheged, go with Bertwin. As soon as you reach the road, signal Lufian to start the blaze."

Brecc did not wait for a response from either man. Keeping to the shadows of the tree line, he worked his way around the edge of the camp until he was directly behind the horse. A quick glance across the campfire showed no sign of other movement. If the guards were returning, they were doing it more quietly than usual. Weaving between a handful of woolen tents, Brecc approached the wayward horse. It looked up and sniffed the air.

"Steady, boy," Brecc whispered.

The horse turned its head, and the straps that had been used to tie it to a tree rattled across the ground. It nickered nervously.

"Steady," Brecc repeated, stepping closer.

The horse danced away, and Brecc released a tense breath. Men's voices sounded. The horse snorted, and Brecc lunged for the straps. With a neigh, the animal reared back. Brecc pulled on the reins, drawing the creature out of the campfire's circle of light. But he wasn't fast enough.

"Oy!" It was one of the guards.

Footsteps pounded toward him. Brecc released the straps and swiveled. Both guards had him in their sights, and both were armed. Brecc eyed the glinting ax blades and darted into the shadows.

"I have the one on the right." Rheged's low voice came out of the darkness behind him. "You take the one on the left."

Not questioning his friend's directive, Brecc stepped left. The ax-wielding Viking raised his arm, and with a grunt of exertion, he tossed his weapon. Brecc dropped to the ground, the whoosh of air catching his cheek as the blade whistled past and landed with a thud in the trunk of the tree immediately behind him. Leaping to his feet, he pulled his dagger from his belt and charged at the Viking. His opponent crouched low and withdrew the knife strapped to his leg.

Vaguely aware of grunts and the clash of blades at his right, Brecc circled the Viking before him. Cruelty was etched in the man's face. His lips turned up in a sneer, and he pounced. Brecc anticipated the move and dodged left. The Viking lost his footing. Brecc lowered his shoulder and shoved it against his opponent's chest. With a cry of frustration, the Viking reeled and backed into the campfire. Sparks flew, and with a shriek, the Viking dove for the ground and rolled across his burning sleeve.

More shouts filled the air, and all around them, men began pouring out of tents. An owl hooted yet again. It was Bertwin's signal. Within moments, Lufian would have the Vikings' stack of fuel and several of their tents alight.

A man cried out in agony. Brecc whirled. Rheged was standing over his fallen foe, breathing heavily. But before either of them could do anything more, a sudden movement at Brecc's left had him spinning around once more. His assailant's blade slashed downward, slicing through Brecc's hose. He felt the sting and knew it had pierced his leg. Lunging forward on his uninjured leg, he thrust his blade into the Viking's side. With a scream, his enemy doubled over.

"Leaving now would be good," Rheged panted.

"Agreed." Gritting his teeth against the shooting pain in his leg, Brecc ran for the trees with Rheged right beside him.

"This way!" Rheged said, grabbing his sleeve and tugging him to the right. "I had Bertwin take our mounts with the pack horses. They'll be waiting for us at the road."

Brecc grunted. It was all he could do to keep moving. The smoke was thickening, impeding his vision and tightening his chest. "You lead," he gasped.

Tree limbs snagged his cloak, roots tripped him, and his leg pulsed with pain, but Rheged kept moving, and Brecc followed.

"Up ahead." Rheged slowed long enough to point to a gap in the trees. "I see movement."

Brecc stopped and leaned against a tree. "Make sure it is Bertwin and Lufian," he said. "I don't want any unpleasant surprises."

Rheged whistled and then continued forward. He disappeared into the darkness. Brecc waited, breathing through his pain.

Moments later, Rheged reappeared. "Come quickly. It is them, and the Vikings have started after us."

With a grimace, Brecc pushed away from the tree trunk. Rheged had stolen up on him unawares, and Brecc had not even thought to listen for the sounds of pursuit. He was in worse shape than he'd feared.

They broke through the trees and onto the road. Bertwin and Lufian were already mounted, and each held the reins of two other horses—Brecc's and Rheged's and the pack horses. Brecc eyed his charger grimly. Mounting would be a challenge.

Rheged glanced at him. "How bad is it?"

"Bad enough." Brecc did not bother asking how he knew. They understood each other too well for that. "But I'll manage."

The crack of branches and angry shouts were becoming louder. Their pursuers were dangerously close. Brecc placed the foot of his uninjured leg in the stirrup and prepared to swing himself up. They were two days' ride from Athelney, which meant he was in for a torturous journey. But it was a better option than walking or being captured by the Vikings.

Rheged hurried over to his mount and was in the saddle before Brecc had finished breathing through the agony of lifting his wounded leg over the horse's back.

"To the miller's straightway," Brecc called. "Once the delivery is made, we ride for Athelney."

👑

Aisley poured the last of the dried chickweed into the crock on the wooden table. With April less than a fortnight away, new plants would be making their appearance in the hedgerows again. She needed to gather more and hang them to dry before her current supply dwindled to nothing. She frowned. It wasn't only the chickweed crock running low. Almost all her containers of dried medicinal plants needed to be replenished.

It was the same at the end of every winter, but this time, restocking her supplies was proving to be more challenging. Over the last fortnight, the Vikings had gone from keeping to themselves at their encampment by the river to loitering in the town, stealing from the merchants, and threatening anyone who did not do exactly as they said. Aisley's fear that Rangvald would find her again had yet to fully abate. He knew her name, and anyone in town could tell him where she lived. Since her return with Taber over three weeks before, she'd not dared go any farther from the longhouse than the stables and the cold storage room off the kitchen.

She'd felt the loss of Brecc's presence the moment she and Taber had entered the courtyard that day. It had left a void that no amount of distractions had fully removed. She thought on him daily—wondering where he was and what he was doing—but her own world had become very narrow.

With a sigh, she sealed the crock and set it beside the others. A small pile of linen bags lay beside them. Her newly required time indoors had forced her to take up a needle more than ever before, and creating little sacks for transporting the dried plants had seemed a more productive use of her time than embroidering linens. Over the last few days, however, she had accumulated so many of them, it might be time to contrive a new project. Brushing the lingering flakes of chickweed off her fingers, she moved to the door. The sun was reaching its zenith; she had been away from the longhouse all morning.

Voices reached her from outside. Curious, she tilted her head to better hear. One speaker was most certainly Wulfhere. The other was a man, but his voice was more indistinct. Lifting the latch, she pulled open the door just wide enough to see across the courtyard. Wulfhere was facing her, speaking to a broad-shouldered man wearing a sheepskin. His brown hair hung long and limp down his back, but it did not need to be in plaits for Aisley to recognize him. Her fingers froze on the doorlatch. What was Rangvald doing here? And why had Wulfhere not sent him away?

Wulfhere laughed, and the Viking joined in. The sound sent a shudder down Aisley's spine. This was not the interaction expected of men from opposing forces. Pressing her shoulder against the wall, she leaned forward to peer around the doorjamb. Another Viking stood waiting near the stables, holding the straps of two horses. He shifted his feet as though he'd been standing there for some time. How long had Rangvald been here? Had he been invited into the longhouse? The questions swirled through her head in a never-ending eddy, leaving her feeling more and more nauseated.

At last, Wulfhere slapped Rangvald on the back, and the men grasped each other's hands in an unmistakable sign of solidarity. The language barrier between them, it seemed, had been successfully crossed. Rangvald left Wulfhere's side and walked briskly to his waiting horse. With a brief word to his companion, they both mounted.

"Two," Rangvald said, holding up two fingers. "Two days."

"Aye." Wulfhere acknowledged the directive with a nod. "Return then."

Return? Horror clawed at Aisley's throat. Not only had Wulfhere received the Viking warmly, but he had also invited him back. She leaned against the wall, attempting to calm her racing thoughts. She did not know what Wulfhere was about, but she meant to find out. And the best place to start was with their mother.

She waited until the sound of hooves had faded and then peeked outside again. The courtyard was empty. Slipping out of the cold storage room, she closed the door behind her and ran directly to the longhouse. In the great hall, two chairs were positioned beside the fire, and a couple of goblets sat on a nearby table. No one was in the room, but the evidence of recent occupancy was clear.

Crossing the great hall, Aisley made for her mother's chamber. The door was ajar, so she knocked once and then pushed it open. Her mother was sitting beside the fire, a new needlework project upon her lap. Across from her, Diera was sewing something that looked suspiciously like yet another gown.

"Good day, Mother," Aisley said.

"Aisley! Where have you been this entire morning?"

"I was in the cold storage room." Her response should not have been a surprise, especially now.

"Then you'd best come in and warm up," her mother said. "I cannot imagine what kept you there so long."

Her desire to avoid any type of needlework would not be a welcomed response, so Aisley opted to change the subject. "There was a Viking in the courtyard."

"So, I believe." Her mother picked up her needle and kept her eyes on her fabric.

Aisley stared at her. "He was talking to Wulfhere. Congenially. As if they were friends."

"Mayhap they have found common ground."

"Common ground?" Aisley fought to maintain her composure. "Have you so soon forgotten what the Vikings did at the royal estate? What they are now doing across Wessex?"

Her mother released an exasperated sigh. "We left the royal estate far too quickly to know exactly what occurred there. Hearsay is always exaggerated."

"Thegns died! Ealdorman Ormod was murdered before we left the great hall. There is nothing hearsay about that."

There was another rap on the door, and Wulfhere walked in. "Am I interrupting something?"

"No," Aisley said. "As a matter of fact, I am very glad you are come. Mayhap you would be willing to explain to me—since mother appears unable to do so—why you were speaking so amiably to a Viking chieftain in the courtyard and even went as far as to invite him back to our home."

"First." Wulfhere took on a steely expression. "I would remind you that this is not *our* home, but *my* home. I am the one who determines who is welcome and who is not."

Aisley clenched her hands. "You are consorting with the enemy."

"Incorrect. I am forging agreements and creating pacts that will protect the people of Wiltshire."

"Protect them from what?" Aisley could scarcely believe this conversation was happening. "The only threat to our people comes from the very invaders with whom you are choosing to associate. Have you seen what they have done in town? How they have robbed and plundered and raped? Do you even care? Even if you have no feelings for the people you are supposed to watch over, you are surely aware of their devastating losses in income. How do you propose to collect your precious taxes when the Vikings have left them with nothing?"

"Aisley! That is quite enough." At her mother's shocked scolding, Aisley turned to her.

"Forgive me, Mother, but I disagree. If Father were here, he would be doing everything in his power to assist those who have been crushed by the Norse marauders, and he would be fully supporting King Alfred in his quest to evict the Vikings from our land."

"Father was a fool," Wulfhere said. "He was killed because he gave blind obedience to an incompetent king."

Tears pricked Aisley's eyes. "Father knew he was dying, and yet he willingly went to serve his king because he wished his last acts to be those of courage, honor, and integrity."

Wulfhere snorted. "You are as big a fool as he was. The Vikings are too strong. Look at what they have accomplished in Mercia and Northumbria. What makes you think Wessex is any different? We shall be living by Danelaw in no time. Our only hope for safety and security is to ally ourselves to the winning side." His expression became smug. "And you, my dear sister, have secured that for each of us."

As far as Aisley was concerned, the self-satisfied gleam in her brother's eyes was far more terrifying than his earlier reddened face and flared nostrils. A frisson of fear shot through her, leaving her heart pounding. Her mother and sister were unnaturally quiet. Ignoring them, Aisley raised her chin a fraction. "I assume you intend to explain what you mean by that."

"I shall spare you the details," Wulfhere said, "but suffice it to say, Rangvald will return two days hence to add a ridiculously heavy purse to the pledge he has already made. I am to retain my position of power in Wiltshire in exchange for offering him my full support and for giving him my redheaded sister to wife."

Aisley grasped the back of the chair Diera was occupying and clung to it with all her might. This could not be happening. It had to be a nightmare. "You . . . you would sell your own sister to a plundering heathen? To a man who cares nothing for our God, our people, or our customs?" Her voice broke. "To one who does not even speak our language?"

"In truth, Rangvald has a remarkably good grasp of the Saxon tongue." Wulfhere acted as though he were discussing a toddler who had learned to talk earlier than most.

Two. Days. You. Name. The words echoed through her head in a mocking taunt. She turned to her mother, her grip on Diera's chair so tight that her knuckles hurt. "Mother," she cried. "Surely you will not allow this."

The fabric in her mother's hand trembled slightly, but she met Aisley's pleading look with disturbing calm. "Neither Wulfhere nor I are willing to place our trust in King Alfred again. If it had not been for Wulfhere, you, Diera, and I would have been homeless and penniless after your father died. He is doing this to secure our future."

Aisley stared at her in disbelief. "Do you truly care so little for my happiness?"

"You are strong, Aisley. Stronger than me or Diera. Marrying Rangvald may not have been your choice, but for the sake of your family, you will make the best of it."

The best of it? There was no best—nor anything remotely good—in any of this. She was being sold to feed Wulfhere's overarching desire for wealth and power. She looked to her sister. Diera's face was pale, her eyes brimming with tears. But she said nothing.

"Wulfhere cares nothing about anyone's future but his own," Aisley said. "Do you not see that?"

"Enough!" Wulfhere growled. "The time for discussion is over. The agreement has been made."

"Then unmake it!"

He curled his lip contemptuously. "You tout the virtues of integrity and would have me break my word to a Viking chieftain. I think not. My decision is made and will stand firm. You have two days to prepare for your departure. Be grateful for that. If it had been up to Rangvald, you would have left with him this very morning." And then he offered their mother a token nod of acknowledgment, turned on his heel, and marched out of the chamber.

Complete silence fell upon the room. Aisley stood alone. One part of her heart ached with hurt; the other part was utterly numb. Diera sniffled.

Their mother cleared her throat. "Let us talk on a different subject entirely," she said.

Both crushed and confounded by her mother's emotional detachment, Aisley looked away. "You and Diera may take upon yourselves that task if you wish, but it is currently beyond my supposedly *strong* capabilities." She walked to the door, keeping her head high even as tears threatened to fall. "Good day, Mother. Good day, Diera."

Closing the door behind her, Aisley took two short steps before her first sob escaped. A second followed. With her shoulders shaking uncontrollably, she pressed one hand to her mouth and ran from the building.

CHAPTER 22

THE SUN WAS LOWERING IN the sky. Aisley did not know exactly how long she'd been sitting on the ground beneath the old willow. Long enough to cry herself into exhaustion only to rise from the damp earth with her situation unchanged. The small grove of trees located near her home had long been her place of sanctuary. As a child, she'd escaped there whenever she'd received a parental scolding or needed time away from her brother's bullying or her sister's pestering. Life had always seemed better after an hour among the trees. This time was different.

She drew up her knees and wrapped her arms around them. Soon it would become too cold to remain outdoors. Before she returned to the longhouse, however, she needed a plan. Her brother's cruel edict might be in force, but she still had time to thwart it. Forcing herself to push past her personal anguish, she attempted to think things through logically. The chances of escape once she was in Rangvald's custody would be slim. He was surrounded by men willing to do his bidding—no matter how inhumane. She shuddered. She would not leave with the Viking chieftain; she could not marry him. That meant she must leave Trowbridge before Rangvald returned. But where to go? Her resources were few, those who knew her well enough to take her in, even fewer.

Slowly, deliberately, she reviewed all that Wulfhere had said. There was more to this arrangement than simply a brother ridding himself of a sister he disliked. It was bigger than his significant financial increase. The agreement Wulfhere had struck with Rangvald shifted Wiltshire's official allegiance at a time that King Alfred needed every able man fighting for the Saxon cause. Taber had kept her abreast of the news filtering through the towns. Alfred's men were making regular raids on Viking encampments and were ambushing the invaders as they traveled the roads of Wessex. Their successes had done much to boost morale among the common folk, and speculation was running high that the king would soon be calling for the fyrds to assemble.

The fyrds. Aisley gasped as the ramifications of what her brother had done to the balance of power in Wiltshire settled upon her. The ealdormen of each county were charged with gathering men to ride with them in answer to the king's call to arms. She'd seen her father fulfill this duty several times. The gathering of Wiltshire's fyrd had been the setting of their last farewell. But if the king sent word to Wulfhere now, not only would the desired fyrd not materialize, but her brother would also likely warn Rangvald that the Saxons were mobilizing. The consequences of such information reaching the enemy would be devastating to the king's forces.

She scrambled to her feet. The king had to be warned. And if, as Taber had suggested, royal messengers were expected to contact the ealdormen soon, she had no time to waste. She had already determined that leaving Trowbridge within the next twenty-four hours was a necessity. Now she knew where she must go. She would travel to Athelney, and God willing, she would arrive there in time to prevent the king from stumbling into a trap her brother's appalling perfidy had created.

But how? She paced in a tight circle, her thoughts whirling. These last three weeks, she had considered going into town to be unsafe. Taking a horse and riding all the way to Athelney unaccompanied was far more dangerous. There was no accounting for who she might meet along her way. And if she were to have the misfortune of encountering Vikings, her fate—and the fate of the Saxons' uprising—would likely be sealed.

She pivoted, frowning in frustration. If she were a gentleman, a full day's ride would be nothing, and the threat to her person would be minimal. Her thoughts stuttered. She was too small in stature to pass as a man, but could she pass as a youth? Surely, a young man riding alone would not be the target of many ne'er-do-wells. An image of Taber leading her brother's mount from town filled her mind, and a sliver of hope pierced her heavy heart. She and Taber were of a similar height and build. If she covered her head and was wearing his clothing, it was possible that travelers on the road would all but ignore her.

At last, she knew hope. Pausing at the edge of the grove of trees long enough to ensure that no one else was in sight, she flew across the meadow and down the lane. A few paces from the entrance to the courtyard, she stopped. She needed calm. If she encountered a family member, she must act subdued. Unwilling to enter into conversation, even. They would expect those things and would likely overlook what would normally be considered rude behavior. So much the better. Her priority was to give Wulfhere no cause to suspect that she was hatching a plan of escape.

She brushed off the dead grass from her gown and entered the courtyard. It was empty. Offering a silent prayer of thanks, she made directly for the stables. The door was ajar. She pulled it open and walked in. The light was dim. She blinked, giving her eyes time to adjust. The stables seemed unusually quiet. No whistling, soft voices, or even the rattle of pails or shovels.

"Taber," she called softly.

Taber appeared from one of the nearby stalls, a pitchfork in hand. He inclined his head. "Afternoon, Mistress Aisley."

"Where is everyone?" she asked, looking around.

"Garren 'as gone with Tilian t' fetch more feed," he said. "Can I 'elp ya with somethin'?"

Relief, swift and warm, filled her. She might not have long with Taber before someone interrupted them, but she would seize what time she had. "Do you own another tunic and hose?" she asked.

"Why, yes." He glanced down as if to reassure himself that the one he was wearing was not too terribly soiled. "One of each."

"What of shoes?"

Taber's expression became even more perplexed. "I've one other pair of shoes, but they're a mite small, an' I'd rather not wear 'em unless I 'ave to."

The smaller the shoes, the better. "May I purchase them?"

Taber blinked. "Ya wish t' buy me old clothes?"

"I know it's an odd request, and I would explain my need for them further, but it is best that you not know."

"In case someone comes askin' 'bout it," Taber guessed.

Aisley did not respond. Taber was a quick thinker. He would likely piece things together without her assistance, but she refused to willfully place him in a position where he would be forced to dissemble on her behalf.

He set the pitchfork against the stall gate. "I'll fetch 'em." Not waiting for a response, he hastened across the stable to the ladder that led to the attic, where the stablehands slept. Almost before Aisley knew what he was about, he had reached the top and disappeared. She heard the rustle of straw and a few soft thuds above her head. A horse nickered, and Aisley glanced at the stable doors. Still no sound from without, but she did not know how much longer her good fortune would last.

"Make haste, Taber," she whispered.

As if he'd heard her, his feet appeared on the top rung of the ladder, and moments later, he was on the ground.

"This is them," he said, offering Aisley a small bundle. He shifted uncomfortably. "There's a tear on one leg of the 'ose. I was goin' to ask the seamstress in town t' stitch it fer me, but I was waitin' t' see if I could save enough t' buy a bigger pair instead."

"I am most grateful." Aisley clutched the items to her chest. "Truly. I will come by just before dawn on the morrow." She hated to ask more of him, but she would likely need his assistance with a horse. "Will you be here?"

"If ya need me 'ere afore dawn, I'll be 'ere."

Swallowing the lump in her throat, she nodded. "You are the very best kind of friend, Taber."

His smile was crooked, but pleasure shone in his eyes. "I don' know 'bout that, but I thank you, regardless."

"When I come in the morning, I shall bring you some coins. I wish I had more to offer you, but I pray it will be sufficient for replacement clothing."

"Not t' worry, mistress. If needs be, I daresay Garren 'as somethin' I can use what 'e's outgrown." He looked over the stalls. "Which mount will ya be wantin' saddled first thing?"

"I believe the brown mare I rode from Chippenham would serve me well." Taking the first available mounts from the stables at the king's estate had not sat well with Aisley. Even now, months later, it felt wrong to claim them. But if she was going to take any horse from the stable, it seemed best to take one that Wulfhere was not overly attached to.

Taber nodded. "I'll 'ave 'er ready fer ya."

The stable door creaked. Voices accompanied the shaft of light that entered. Aisley wadded up Taber's bundle and stuffed it under her arm.

"We'll unload th' cart 'ere." It was Tilian giving Garren instructions.

Releasing the breath she'd been holding, Aisley moved toward the doors.

Tilian saw her for the first time and offered a startled bow. "Beggin' yer pardon, Mistress Aisley. I didn't know ya were 'ere."

"Do not let me interrupt you," she said, angling her way through the door so that the bundle remained out of his line of sight. "I am just leaving."

He gave her a vague nod. "Very good, mistress." It seemed that one benefit of having frequented the stables often was that her unexpected appearance was no real cause for inquiry.

A cart full of hay was parked outside the stables. Garren was approaching it, pitchfork in hand. With no one else in view, Aisley crossed the short distance to the cold storage room. Once inside, she pushed a stool up against the door. It would not prevent anyone from entering, but it would give her a little extra warning if she needed it. Ensuring that the shutters were firmly closed, she lit a candle and set it on the wooden counter before looking around. She needed somewhere to hide Taber's clothes.

There was a barrel near the door that appeared to be empty. She tipped it upside down, and a few dead apple leaves fell to the floor. Cook must have used the last of the fruit from this barrel for the baked apples she'd served last week. Setting Taber's clothes at the bottom of the barrel, she scoured the room. Cook would not have emptied a barrel this early in the year unless there were more apples stored elsewhere.

Large sealed crocks of pickled vegetables lined one wall. Pieces of dried, smoked pork hung from hooks on the ceiling above. Two more barrels sat in the corner. She crossed to them. One contained a mixture of carrots and onions. The other was full of apples. With a satisfied smile, she loaded her skirt with about a dozen, carried them over to the barrel containing Taber's clothes, and poured them on top. Another half dozen apples, and the fabric was completely covered. Moving over to the counter, she set out a row of the small linen bags she'd made only last week. If she was to be turned out of her own home, she was taking her medicinal plants with her.

She was filling her third bag when the door latch rose and the stool legs scraped across the floor. Her fingers froze around the string as she watched the stool slowly move forward and the door open. Her mother walked in, her glare instantly shifting from the stool to Aisley.

"Whatever are you doing in here? You have been gone from the house for an age. And why is the stool against the door?"

"I am bagging up some of the herbs," she said, choosing to ignore the second question while working to keep her voice even. "I have cried enough for one day and needed an activity to keep my thoughts on something other than my forced marriage to a pillaging Viking."

Her mother's indignation deflated a fraction, and her gaze shifted to Aisley's eyes. Aisley had no need of a looking glass to know they were red and puffy. They stung every time she blinked. She was fortunate that the light had been so poor in the stables that Taber and Tilian had not seemed to notice.

"Your future husband is a chieftain. You will want for nothing."

In truth, she would want for *everything*, but she was not willing to reenter this futile discussion. She raised the half-filled pouch in her hand. "When I leave, I should like to take some of my dried plants with me."

"Of course." Her mother glanced at the tidy row of crocks and released a troubled breath. "I would have you know that regardless of what you may currently believe, Aisley, you will be missed."

It was possible that her mother would wish Aisley there on the days she was forced to resume her own gathering and drying of plants. Or when Diera demanded that someone must accompany her into town. But those trifling reasons were hardly enough to make Aisley feel valued or loved. And she would rather not prolong this conversation only to learn for a certainty that her mother's genuine affection for her oldest daughter was unreservedly lacking. The time had come to protect herself from further emotional harm.

"I shall not be eating with you this evening," she said, unsure which was the most repellent: the thought of consuming food or the thought of being in the same room as Wulfhere. "When I am finished here, I shall retire for the night."

Her mother frowned. "I do not think that is wise. It would not do to leave here in a weakened state."

Regardless of the consequences, partaking of a meal with her family was an impossibility. "I shall have plenty of rest, at least."

"Hm." Her mother appeared unconvinced. "I shall check on you later this evening."

"Very well."

Returning her attention to the small bag in her hand, Aisley drew the string around the top and tied it tight.

Her mother watched while she set the filled pouch on the counter, and then she opened the door and stepped outside. "Good night, Aisley," she said.

Aisley waited until the door closed behind her. "Good night, Mother," she said sadly. It was likely the last time she would ever say it.

♕

Brecc leaned his head against the tree trunk and closed his eyes. The pain in his leg was worsening. Not surprising given how long they'd been riding, but it did not omen well for his night's rest. Exhausted or not, unless the discomfort subsided, he would be hard-pressed to sleep at all.

"Here!"

Brecc opened one eye.

Rheged stood over him, a piece of bread and a small chunk of cheese in his extended hand. "You must eat."

Wearily, Brecc accepted the food. "You have my thanks."

"The bread is stale." Rheged dropped to the ground beside him. "But it is better than nothing." He inclined his head to the left, where Bertwin and Lufian were already stretched out under a nearby pine tree. "Bertwin took care of watering the horses before bedding down for the night. If we get an early start on the morrow, we should reach Athelney by evening."

Brecc nodded, his gaze falling to his injured leg. Another day in the saddle would undoubtedly aggravate the wound further, but he had no choice. Remaining in the woods with no provisions would be even more detrimental.

"Have you looked at it?" Rheged asked, following his gaze.

"Not yet." Their narrow escape from the Viking encampment had precluded him from giving his injury any attention immediately after it occurred. And although they'd stopped at the mill long enough to drop off the reclaimed flour and vegetables, Brecc had chosen to remain in his saddle. It had been too dark to see the large reddish-brown stain that had manifested itself once the sun had risen, but the wetness of his hose had been clue enough. He'd lost a significant amount of blood, and the less he moved his leg, the better.

"It will not serve you well to ignore it," Rheged warned.

"True, but I would rather not risk reopening the wound by tugging at the fabric of my hose when I have nothing with which I can stem the blood or treat the incision."

Two deep lines appeared on Rheged's forehead. "I fear such supplies are limited at Athelney also."

"There will be more than there is in this woodland." Brecc lifted his leg and set it down again with a wince. "It is possible that Mistress Hocca will be willing to assist me."

"You will be hard-pressed to recompense her in the manner with which she has become accustomed. Unless you have a secret talent for sweeping a floor upon one leg, of course."

Brecc chuckled. The story of King Alfred's debacle with the burned cakes and lack of experience with a broom had been retold on Athelney more times than he could count. It was a credit to the monarch's humility that he had used the tale to illustrate the importance of making improvements. "I do not think Hocca has the patience for new sweeping techniques, and I do not think the king intended for us to focus our learning on housework."

"Fair enough," Rheged said. "But what do you think he does wish us to learn? What are all our raids and ambushes and spying ultimately for?"

Brecc rubbed his thigh absently, his thoughts on all the king and his men had undertaken during the last few weeks. "I think he wishes us to help unite Wessex."

"Has that not always been the case?"

"It has, but this time feels different. People of every walk of life are hearing how the king and his men are working together for the good of all Saxons. News of our successful attacks on the Vikings is lifting morale. The return of precious commodities to those who have so little reminds them that they have not been forgotten. The king's determination to oust the invaders offers hope. Our victories—no matter how small—prompt courage. King Alfred has seen the devastation a lack of preparation causes, and he will not make that mistake again. He wishes his people to be physically ready to fight, but even more than that, he wishes their hearts to be ready."

"That is why he has waited to call up the fyrds," Rheged guessed.

"Aye. They will join together from different parts of the country and with a variety of experience, but they must be one in conviction and purpose before we go against Guthrum again."

"How long do you think it will be before the king believes the people are ready?"

"That, I cannot say." Brecc eyed his leg grimly. "But I pray we are all prepared when the day comes."

CHAPTER 23

AISLEY DID NOT KNOW THE exact hour, but the deepest darkness of the night was beginning to fade when she arose from her pallet. With fumbling fingers, she donned her gown. She'd left her shoes beside her pallet for easy access. Sliding her hand beneath her pillow, she withdrew her small purse and dropped it into one of her shoes. The coins she'd taken to town the day Rangvald had hounded her were still there. It was what she would use to compensate Taber for the loss of his clothing.

She'd retired early the night before but had lain awake for a long time. Sleep was difficult to summon when one was overwhelmed with memories and sorrow. As promised, her mother had entered the chamber to check on her. Aisley had kept her eyes closed and her breathing steady. Her feigned slumber must have satisfied her mother, for she'd left the room soon afterward and had not returned. When Diera had come to bed, she'd gently touched Aisley's back, but Aisley had not responded, and with a small sigh, Diera had settled down on her own pallet. Aisley could only hope that she was now deeply asleep.

Aisley rolled up her blanket and tucked it under her arm, then carrying her shoes, she tiptoed across the room to retrieve her cloak from the chair beside the door.

"Aisley." Diera's whispered voice cut through the darkness. Clutching the edges of her cloak as if it were her courage, Aisley stood completely still. "Aisley," Diera repeated. There was a rustle, and the shadowy form on the nearby pallet shifted. "You have nothing to fear. I shall not ask where you are going. I only wish to offer you Godspeed." Her voice broke. "I am glad you are leaving. You deserve happiness, and I pray you find it."

Tears welled. Setting her blanket and shoes on the chair, Aisley crossed the short distance to her sister's pallet and knelt. She reached out her hand and found Diera's shoulder. Diera raised her hand and took Aisley's in hers. Aisley did not speak. She was not sure that she could.

Diera pressed their clasped hands to her damp cheek before releasing Aisley's hand. "Go," she urged. "Whilst you still can."

Aisley rose and walked back to the chair. Picking up the blanket and shoes, she ran her fingers across the door until she located the handle. She lifted it and carefully pulled the door open. All was quiet without.

She took a step into the narrow passage and then turned back to Diera. "I wish you happiness also," she whispered, and then she slipped through the door and closed it behind her.

Thankfully, she knew the house and its furnishings well enough to move through it with very little light. She reached the front door without encountering anything unexpected, but when she set her hand upon the handle of the bolt and pushed gently, nothing happened. She tried again, this time with more force. The sound of grating metal filled the great hall. Aisley did not wait to listen for the sound of movement from one of the bedchambers. If the noise had woken Wulfhere, her best course was to reach the stables as quickly as possible. Letting herself out, she closed the door tightly behind her and then raced barefoot across the courtyard.

Moonlight lit her path to the cold storage room. She hastened inside, scrabbling for the candle and flint she'd left on the counter. With the door closed, she lit the candle and pulled out the barrel where she'd hidden Taber's clothes. A new sense of urgency added speed to her actions. Stripping herself of her cloak and gown, she pulled on the hose and tunic. The hose was too long and the tunic worn, but they would suffice. Putting on Taber's shoes, she unhooked the satchel she usually used for gathering plants from its place on the back of the door. She wadded up her gown and placed it and her shoes at the bottom of the satchel. Her rolled-up blanket went next, followed by the small linen bags full of dried plants. She added three of the apples she'd taken from the barrel and her coin purse. There was no room for anything more. With trembling fingers, she pulled back her long hair, split it into three portions, and plaited it into a thick rope. Tossing it behind her shoulder, she donned her cloak once more. Then she slid the satchel strap across her shoulder, blew out the candle, and left the room.

She crossed to the stables at a run. On the other side of the courtyard, the longhouse loomed. A large, dark oblong on a gray backdrop, watching her every move. A chink of light showed beneath the stable doors. Aisley pulled on the latch and slipped inside. Taber was there, holding the straps of the saddled and bridled brown mare.

"Bless you, Taber," she said.

He offered her a lopsided grin. "It's right odd t' see you in them clothes, mistress, but it seems like they might work fer ya."

"They are exactly what I needed," she said, pulling two coins from her purse. "Take these. I hope it is sufficient to purchase another tunic, at least."

He shook his head. "The one I gave ya is full worn out. There's no need—"

"There is every need," Aisley said. "And I have no time to argue."

He glanced at the stable doors, the first hint of worry appearing on his face. "What more d'you require, mistress?"

"A boost into this saddle and your silence if anyone questions you about my disappearance," she said.

He cupped his hands beside the mare, and a moment later, Aisley was seated with the reins in her hand.

"As soon as yer gone, I'll be about me duties," he said. "If anyone comes 'round, they won't find anythin' unusual in that. An' I won't have anythin' unusual t' report." He stepped back and reached for the stable door. "Whenever yer ready, mistress."

Aisley raised her hood and tucked the satchel behind her. "Now."

He swung the door wide. The pale-pink rays of early morning were painting the horizon and chasing away the darkness. Across the courtyard, a flicker of candlelight shone behind the shutters to Wulfhere's chamber. Aisley's throat tightened.

"Farewell, Taber," she said. "I shall not forget your kindness and service." And then she touched her heels to the horse's side and left the stables at a gallop.

Entering the lane, she turned toward town. If Wulfhere had heard the clatter of hooves and guessed what she was about, he would come after her.

Searching the town might slow him, particularly if tradespeople were filling the roads and square by the time he arrived. She lowered herself in the saddle, allowing the mare its head while she yet could. A day's ride south was what Brecc had said. At some point, she would need to ask for directions, but for now, her focus was on putting as much distance between her and Wulfhere as she possibly could.

♛

The sun had been up for at least two hours when Aisley spotted a group of merchants on the road ahead. With the town of Trowbridge behind her, she thought it unlikely that any of the merchants knew her, but as she drew closer, she tugged her hood a little lower over her face.

"Good day t' ya, lad." The burly man driving the cart at the rear of the small convoy called out his greeting as Aisley's horse came abreast of his vehicle. "Where're ya bound?"

Aisley cleared her throat. "South," she said.

The merchant raised an eyebrow. "Lots o' places south o' 'ere."

Aisley was reluctant to give this stranger her actual destination, especially as she had yet to discover exactly where it was located, but she could not afford to arouse suspicion. "I've a mind t' go int' South Somerset," she said, affecting Taber's manner of speaking. "Not sure 'ow far yet."

"Ah, a fellow out to make 'is fortune, are ya?" He jerked his thumb toward the cloth-covered cargo behind him. "There's money t' be 'ad in wool and linen, if yer willin' t' travel."

"'Ow far d'ya go?" Aisley asked, genuinely interested.

"Used t' be that we went all over Wessex. Sometimes int' Mercia. But nowadays, with them fearsome Vikin's all over the place, we don' go as far." He shrugged. "Yer right brave t' be on th' roads by yerself. Either that or daft."

Or desperate. The word echoed through Aisley's head, but she did not voice it. Mayhap it would be in her best interest to travel a little distance with these merchants. She'd passed a few other travelers on her way. None but she had been unaccompanied. Her safety notwithstanding, that fact alone was enough to fuel her desire to ride with others. Anything she could do to avoid unwelcome attention was worth her while.

"I confess, travelin' alone makes fer a lonely day," she said.

"Stick with us fer a bit, if ya wish," the merchant said. "But pay no mind t' Orvyn up there." He gestured toward the driver of the cart in front of his. "'E'll do 'is best t' persuade ya t' take up sellin' vegetables, but all 'e's really after is someun to 'elp 'im unload all 'is swedes an' turnips."

"I'm glad o' the warnin'," Aisley said, grateful that her hood hid the instinctive uptick of her lips at the merchant's cautionary words. It was the first time she'd smiled in a long time, and it had the rather remarkable effect of making her load seem lighter. "Where are ya headed now?"

"Shepton Mallet," he said. "It's market day there on th' morrow. Ya can continue south from there if ya don' want t' stop."

Aisley did not know how far it was to Shepton Mallet, but she would willingly accept the companionship of these merchants if it took her in the right direction. "I thank you," she said. "I'd be glad o' the company."

He nodded. "Shouldn't take us more 'un a couple o' hours t' get there."

A couple of hours. It was a good amount of time to be less noticeable on the road. Her mount had already adjusted its pace to match that of the cart horse, and Aisley allowed herself to relax a fraction. Mayhap, moving at this slower speed, she could finally eat one of the apples she'd brought with her.

♛

They'd been traveling for several furlongs when the merchant's vehement mutter broke the silence that had descended over the company.

"Curse those heathen invaders!"

The rhythmic gait of Aisley's mount had lulled her into an alarmingly dozy state. Now, however, her heart was racing. "What is it?"

"Vikin's," he growled. "Comin' 'round the bend. Ya'd best be hopin' yer not carryin' anythin' they want."

Aisley pressed her hand against her satchel. Her coin purse had little enough in it, and she couldn't imagine the Vikings would want her dried plants. But the gown. She swallowed against her fear. If they found the gown, would they question her? Worse, would they force her to pull back her hood?

"I do not wish t' speak t' them," she said.

"None of us do. Believe me, every merchant I know's prayin' King Alfred'll put an end t' this soon. A nightmare, it is. A livin' nightmare. We never know if we're goin' t' reach market with anythin' left t' sell."

A shout rang out, and the merchant at the head of their short caravan reined his cart to a halt. Each of the other drivers followed suit. Aisley kept her head down, the pounding of her heart keeping time with the clopping of hooves as the Vikings circled the merchants' carts. Surely it could not be Rangvald and his men. If he was planning to return to the longhouse early on the morrow, he would not be this far from Trowbridge today.

A Viking spoke. He was close by. Moments later, the cloth covering the merchant's cart beside her was ripped back. Aisley did not turn to look, but if the exuberant shouts were any indication, the invaders were pleased with what they'd uncovered.

"That don't belong t' ya." Frustration filled the merchant's voice.

Another horse drew up beside Aisley's. She fought her panic.

"This!" A hand reached out and tugged on her satchel.

The strap cut into Aisley's neck, but she did not relinquish the bag. Without meeting the Viking's face, she slid her hand under the leather flap and pulled out an apple. She held it out. His exclamation was likely a curse. He knocked the fruit from Aisley's outstretched hand, and it rolled under the cart ahead of her.

The Viking at the cart called out something, and with a grunt of annoyance, the one beside Aisley guided his horse in that direction. She forced herself to take a breath. And then another. At the cart, thuds indicated merchandise was being moved. Aisley hazarded a glance at the merchant. He remained on his seat, his expression stony. Another shout, this one from one of the Vikings at the head of the caravan. The clatter of hooves mingled with guttural voices, and then they were moving away.

No one in the merchant caravan moved. Aisley's horse's ears twitched, and then as if desiring to rid itself of the Vikings' undesirable presence, it shook its head and snorted. With a curse, the merchant climbed down from his perch. Aisley dared raise her head. The Vikings were already out of sight, and her new friend was studying the contents of his cart with a grim expression.

"Thievin' barbarians," he said.

Fabric of every color lay in untidy heaps in the center of the cart. The merchant climbed up and began sifting through the material, folding each piece into a tight parcel with efficiency that spoke of years of experience. Aisley slid from her saddle and walked to the end of the cart. The cloth that had once covered the fabric was on the ground, so she picked it up.

"'Ow much did ya lose, Benwick?" The vegetable merchant had moved from assessing his cart to stand beside the fabric merchant's.

"Me best linen and three bolts of finely woven wool." He set down the newly folded bundles. "What about yer produce?"

"Two sacks gone."

The fabric merchant grimaced. "It's a good job they didn't decide t' take one o' our carts or they'd 'ave left with much more."

"Aye." Glaring down the road the way the Vikings had gone, the vegetable merchant rubbed his chin. "They must've needed t' be elsewhere in a 'urry. It's small consolation fer all we've lost, but it could've been worse."

So much worse. Aisley rolled her shoulders, attempting to work out the strain that had settled there. "I am truly sorry," she said, handing the merchant his cover.

"Not yer fault, lad." He took the proffered cloth and set it over the top of the other fabric. "But I think we'll all be glad t' get t' Shepton Mallet."

Aisley nodded. Now that she was out of the saddle, she had no desire to return to it. But she must. And since she had a far longer journey ahead than did these merchants, the sooner they set off again, the better.

♛

It was early afternoon when Aisley bid farewell to the merchants, and she found that she was remarkably reluctant to do so. In the short time that they'd traveled together, she'd come to think of them as friends, and their encounter with the Vikings had only enhanced that sense of camaraderie.

"If ya change yer mind," the fabric merchant said, "come back. We'll be 'ere till the end of th' week, an' Orvyn can alwus use 'elp haulin' 'is swedes an' turnips."

Orvyn, who was unloading his cart one heavy sack at a time, grunted his agreement, and although Aisley rode away alone, she left Shepton Mallet feeling less abandoned than she had when she'd been in her own bed at the longhouse.

On the outskirts of town, she came upon an elderly woman sweeping the steps of a small cottage. Aisley needed directions, and to ask them of a woman who had likely lived in the area for some time seemed sensible. "Beggin' yer pardon," she called. "Can ya tell me th' way to Athelney?"

The woman stopped her sweeping and looked at Aisley curiously. "Whatever would ya want t' go there for? There's nothin' but a parcel of land risin' up out of the swamp. Can't even get t' it without a boat."

An island of sorts. Brecc's words circled Aisley's head, and her pulse increased. That was it.

"It does sound a bit peculiar," she admitted. "But I was told it's worth a visit just fer th' fishin'." She was stretching the truth rather a lot, but Aisley had no doubt the men staying with the king had resorted to fishing simply to put food in their bellies.

The elderly woman frowned. "Seems t' me there's places closer that would do just as well. The River Sheppey is known fer its trout."

The seemingly simple task of asking for directions was not going nearly as well as Aisley had hoped. "I shall 'ave to give th' river a try."

"You do that." The woman leaned on her broom looking pleased. "An' then, if ya still want t' go down to the levels, you'll want t' go east t' Glastonbury an' then south till ya see Burrow Mump. Ya'll know yer close then."

Relief filled her. "I thank you."

"I 'ope ya catch a big un, but it might be worth yer while to pick up a rod or net first."

Aisley's face flooded with warmth, but thankfully, the accompanying color was hidden by her hood. "Wise counsel," she said.

With a chuckle, the woman waved her off, and by the time Aisley had turned her horse to the south, the elderly lady was engrossed in her sweeping again.

CHAPTER 24

TIME AND DISTANCE HAD LOST all meaning. Aisley felt as though she had been riding forever, but in reality, the sun was only now beginning its descent behind the peak the locals called Burrow Mump. It had been almost thirty-four hours since she'd last had a meal. Her stomach had long since given up on issuing painful and noisy complaints and had turned to causing her limbs to tremble with weakness instead. Indeed, she was unsure which would finally claim her first: hunger or exhaustion.

Over the noisy calls of the area's waterfowl, a man's whistle reached her. It was a familiar tune. One that marked him as Saxon. Desperate for help, she scoured the surrounding grassland. The terrain was too rugged to be considered good pasture for cattle, but stone walls portioned off sections of it, suggesting they were used as animal enclosures. She nudged her horse closer to the wall. The horse nickered nervously, and from the other side of the wall, a large sow raised her head and grunted irritably. Half a dozen piglets took up their mother's cause, squealing their displeasure.

"Oy!" From halfway across the paddock, a man shouted at the noisy swine. "'Nough of that, ya ridiculous creatures. That 'orse ain't done nothin' t' ya!" He moved toward Aisley, and she reined her horse to a stop. "Sorry fer all the fuss," he said. "Anythin' out o' the ordinary seems t' set them off."

"It's a quiet lane," Aisley said. "I don't suppose many pass by."

The man glanced to his left, where a wooded area appeared to rise out of the marshland. "These last few weeks, there's been more than ever afore. But not so many that its noticeable to most." He cracked a smile. "Just the pigs."

She wished she were in a position to exchange pleasantries with the man and to admire his piglets, but despair was beginning to set in. "I am lookin' fer Athelney," she said. "I wus told it wus nearby."

It was as though a shutter came down over his previously friendly face. "Why would ya be wantin' t' go there?"

It was almost exactly what the woman in Shepton Mallet had asked, but Aisley felt sure that this time, a vague response about fishing would not suffice. "I 'ave a message fer someone and wus told t' take it t' Athelney."

"The island's been uninhabited fer years."

"So I imagine. But as o' several weeks ago, some gentlemen took up residence there."

Indecision flickered in his eyes. "Ya say there's someone ya know over there?"

"Aye." She wanted to beg, to plead with him to help a lady in distress, but instinct told her to hold her tongue, to maintain her false identity just a little longer.

His gaze shifted from Aisley to the piece of land. He mumbled something and then turned back to face her. "Yer only chance of gettin' there is t' find Edris and persuade 'im t' take ya in 'is boat." He pointed at her mount. "The 'orse'll 'ave to swim behind. The water's not deep, mind, but it's too much fer the likes of us."

"And this Edris, does 'e live close by?"

"Take a left jus' past th' big oak an' ya'll see 'is cottage. Can't miss it."

Aisley wanted to weep with relief. "I'm most grateful."

The sow's loud grunt eclipsed the man's response, but Aisley was already urging her horse forward for what she prayed were the last few furlongs of her protracted journey. She turned left at the large oak tree, and just as the swineherd had said, a small cottage immediately came into view. And seated on a short stool outside the front door was a grizzled old man filleting a fish over a bucket of reddened water. He looked up as she approached.

"'Evenin'," he said.

"An' to you." Maintaining a colloquial accent was becoming more and more difficult as her tiredness increased. Taking her courage in both hands, she pressed on. "I'm in need o' someone t' take me t' th' island."

"Now?"

"Aye."

He shook his head. "It's too late. I'm fixin' me evenin' meal. If ya come back in th' mornin', I'll take ya then."

Aisley's trembling hands tightened around the reins. "I cannot wait that long."

"Hm." The fisherman went back to his filleting. "Seems t' me ya 'ave to."

"Ya do not understand." Tears pricked Aisley's eyes. She blinked them back. "My errand's no trivial matter."

The fisherman gazed at her with narrowed eyes. "Who are ya?"

"A friend." She swallowed. "A friend t' you, an' a friend t' the gentlemen at Athelney."

"Yer name?"

"It's best that ya not know it."

"Is that so?" Rising, he dropped the fish into the bucket and set his bloodied hands upon his hips. "Why?"

"Fer yer own safety as well as mine." Her voice shook. "I . . . I can pay ya fer yer service."

For two long breaths, he said nothing, then he reached for a rag and wiped his fingers dry. "I'm not afraid o' what might come," he said, "but if ya truly feel that yer life's in danger, then I daresay I can wait another hour t' make me dinner." He stepped off the small porch and started down a narrow path toward the water. "Be warned though. Them men who's on the island right now, they don't take kindly t' me takin' people over there. If they won't let you get out o' th' boat, I'll bring ya back 'ere, but nothin' more. Yer on yer own after that."

Aisley slid from the saddle and set her travel-weary limbs upon the ground. Clinging to the saddle for stability, she willed her legs to work as they should. She had come so far, and now she had only to follow this old fellow down to his boat, yet she was not sure she could manage it.

"I thought ya said this was urgent?" His voice was punctuated with a splash, and Aisley looked up to see him dragging a small boat off the grassy bank and into the reeds.

She took one shaky step forward. And then another. Holding fast to the horse's straps, Aisley continued moving until she reached the edge of the grass.

"Hand me them straps and get in," Edris said, reaching for the reins. "I'll give 'em back t' ya once yer inside the boat."

Aisley eyed the small craft. It was floating, but it was impossible to gauge the depth of the water beneath. Channeling every drop of energy she yet possessed, she leaped off the bank. Her feet hit the bottom of the boat with a thud, and the vessel rocked wildly from side to side. With a small cry, she grabbed the sides.

"Steady," Edris warned. "Take a seat." Aisley eased herself onto one of the planks that traversed the width of the hull. The boat swayed again. She clung to her seat as Edris climbed in. He handed her the reins. "Yer goin' t' 'ave t' coax th' 'orse into th' water," he said. "I'll row you an' me across, but I can't pull anythin' that big. She's goin' t' 'ave to do 'er own work."

Turning slightly so that she was almost facing her horse, Aisley tugged on the reins. "Come on, girl," she called. "It's time fer a swim."

Her horse bent its head and sniffed the water before backing up two steps.

"Ya'd best be quick about this," Edris said. "We're losing light."

Aisley did not need to consult the sky to know how low the sun had sunk. "Come on, girl." She clicked her tongue, and the horse pricked up its ears. Edris set his oars in the water and pulled. The boat moved away from the grassy bank. Aisley clung to the straps. Edris pulled another stroke, and the straps became taut. "Now, girl!" Aisley cried.

Tossing its head nervously, the horse took a tentative step toward the water. And then, with a splash that rocked the boat, it plunged in.

"That's it!" Edris said, rowing faster now. "'Old on to 'er, an' she'll manage jus' fine."

Edris was right. After the first few floundering steps, the movement of the horse's legs fell into a steady rhythm, and as the boat cut through the swampy water, the animal followed with remarkable calm. Reassured that her mount would make it across, Aisley set her sights on the raised piece of land directly ahead. The woodland was turning black with the coming of evening, but at the water's edge, a single light shone.

"Someone's spotted us," Edris muttered. "Ya'd best be thinkin' up somethin' convincin' to say, lad, or ya'll not be settin' one foot off this boat till we get back t' th' other side."

"Who goes there?" A man's voice carried across the water.

"Edris, with a visitor to Athelney," Edris shouted back before giving Aisley a resigned look. "A name would've been 'elpful."

"Forgive me," she said.

Releasing a troubled sigh, he steered the boat toward the man on shore. "Not sure this fellow's goin' t' be so accommodatin' as me."

Aisley peered through the dimming light, trying to make out the guard's features. Medium height, broad shouldered, gray hair and beard. Her heart sank. Not Brecc or Rheged. She did not know how many others were here—but if this guard had not been in the great hall when Rheged had called her to the front, the chances were good that he would not know her.

The boat touched the shore with a soft bump. Torchlight flooded the small vessel.

Edris winced and averted his eyes. "Fer goodness' sake, stand back with yer torch. Ya know who I am."

"Aye, but not your companion." The light fell over Aisley. "Your name and the reason you are come, if you please?"

Aisley tensed. She could not give the guard her true name. Not with Edris listening. If Wulfhere and Rangvald were both searching for her, no one outside those living on this isolated island must know she had come here. "Avi," she said. "Avi o' Trowbridge. And I bear a message o' vital importance t' those livin' at Athelney."

"What proof do you have?"

"Ealdorman Brecc'll vouch for me."

"Ealdorman Brecc is not here."

The unexpected blow left her thoughts reeling. Even though Brecc had told her he would be about the king's business until Wessex was reclaimed, she'd not considered her course of action should he not be at Athelney when she arrived. "Then send fer Ealdorman Rheged," she said desperately. "'E, too, knows me."

"Ealdorman Rheged is not here."

Despair was rapidly consuming hope. "Then allow me t' wait fer 'em," she begged. "Or take me t' th' gentleman in charge." She dared not use King Alfred's name or title. Edris may have guessed his identity, but she refused to be the one who confirmed his suspicions. "Ya may isolate me from all else on this island, but do not send me away afore I've spoken to one of 'em. Yer leader's plans—indeed, 'is very life—'ll be greatly impacted by th' news I bring."

In the water behind her, the horse splashed, still scrambling for footing.

The torch shifted so as to illuminate the thrashing animal, and the guard issued a grunt of frustration. "Toss me the reins," he said. "I shall assist your mount out of the water."

Aisley handed the straps to Edris, who threw them toward the shore. The guard caught them, and within a few moments, the horse had circled the boat and was scrambling up the bank. With an anxious nicker, it reached solid ground and shook the moisture from its coat.

"What about the lad?" Edris was readying his oars. "I must get back afore it's full dark."

"Let him out." There was no mistaking the guard's reluctance, but it did nothing to quell Aisley's relief. "I am taking you at your word, Avi, and if I find that you have deceived me, you shall suffer the consequences."

Aisley stood. "Ya shall not regret it, sire." She took a hasty step forward. The boat listed, and she stumbled.

"Careful, lad." Releasing an oar, Edris placed a calloused hand upon her arm. "I'll not move away till yer off."

On unsteady legs, Aisley clambered over the boat's hull. One foot sank into the boggy grass. She pulled at it. Her wet foot emerged, but Taber's shoe was missing.

"My shoe!" she cried, bending over to retrieve it even as her other foot sank lower in the mud.

"Give me your hand," the guard said.

The mud released the lost shoe with a squelch of protest. Aisley tossed it onto the shore and reached for the guard's outstretched hand. He grimaced as her slimy fingers connected with his, but he gripped her hand tightly and pulled. Her feet slipped, and she found herself up to her knees in water.

"Where's your strength, lad?" the guard grumbled. "You're not being required to climb a cliff."

Clawing her way onto the bank, Aisley pushed herself into a sitting position. It was the best she could manage. "Forgive me." She reached for her shoe with a shaky hand. "I 'ave eaten very little an' traveled a long way."

The older man's disdainful look would have been more hurtful had she not been too exhausted to care. For now, all that mattered was that she had arrived at Athelney. Once she'd had some sleep and—God willing—some food, she would decide what was to be done if Brecc and Rheged were not expected back in the near future.

The rhythmic splash of Edris's oars traveled across the water, and Aisley swung back to see the gray silhouette of the boat disappearing in the distance. "Edris has left, an' I did not pay 'im fer 'is service," she said, tugging her satchel onto her knee.

"Have no fear, you shall see him again." The guard crossed the short distance to where the horse was now grazing. "He makes his appearance here more often than he's welcome."

"I am most grateful t' 'im."

"So, I imagine." He gathered the horse's reins and started walking away. When Aisley did not follow, he turned. "Remaining there is not an option. Get up and stay beside me. There's to be no wandering off."

What little pride she yet retained prevented Aisley from telling the guard that in her current state, placing two footsteps in succession would be a huge accomplishment. Wandering off was all but impossible. She tugged on her sopping shoe, and then placing one hand on the boulder at her left, she pressed down and pulled herself upright. She swayed.

The guard shook his head in disbelief. "I believe you may be the feeblest arrival on the island yet."

Indignation flared, warming her chest and giving strength to her weakened limbs. A reproaching retort rose to her lips, but then she remembered her position. Or at least, the position this guard believed she held. Clamping her mouth closed, she redirected her pique. Following after him without a fall would be proof enough of her fortitude. Until she knew exactly who she could trust on this island, she would be Avi, not Aisley.

"Your mount can stay in the enclosure with the other horses," the guard said, leading her to an area of grass bounded by a wooden fence. Two horses raised their heads and watched curiously as the man lifted a rope on the gate and led her mount in. She watched silently as he took off her mare's saddle and bridle. "The tack can stay with you," he said, carrying it out of the enclosure with him.

"Very well." He had not offered her an alternative, but keeping the saddle and bridle nearby seemed wise.

"You can sleep here," he said, dropping the tack at the entrance of a small tent pitched beneath a large pine tree. He inclined his head toward her satchel. "Did you bring a blanket?"

"I did."

"Good."

For the first time, it appeared she had given the correct response. It was a small thing, but it gave her the courage to ask a few questions of her own. "Ya said that Ealdormen Brecc and Rheged are away. D'ya know when they're expected back?"

"No."

Aisley had hoped Brecc, and possibly even Rheged, would be willing to accompany her when she first approached King Alfred. The thought of facing the king alone filled her with dread. There could be no doubt his anger at what Wulfhere had done would be swift and fierce. And as a member of the traitor's family, she would be considered blameworthy. It was quite possible that she would be subjected to the full measure of the king's ire and punishment. Yet after so desperate a journey, she could not delay delivering her news out of fear. "What of th' king?" she asked.

The guard stared at her stony-faced. "Not here."

His response, although disheartening, was not wholly unexpected. Aisley had the distinct impression that even if the older man knew more, he would not share it with her.

"An' I'm t' stay right 'ere till they come?"

"Either that, or you may return across the marsh first thing on the morrow," he said grimly.

Surely he would not place her here if he knew she could be waiting for weeks. Having to monitor her for an extended length of time would be sufficient incentive to come up with an alternate plan.

Silently praying that she was right and that Brecc's or the king's return would not be long in coming, Aisley lowered her satchel from her shoulder. A gown, shoes, bags of healing plants, and a blanket. She was grateful for each one of those items, but she was in desperate need of something else. "I shall abide by yer rules," she said, "but I would ask one thing more afore ya leave me 'ere." He raised his eyebrows, but before he could respond or her wounded pride could interfere, she continued. "Some food. It don't need t' be much, but if ya have any yer willin' t' spare, I'd be most appreciative."

One look at the guard's face told her that whatever redeeming points she'd garnered by bringing a blanket had been lost.

"I shall see what I can find," he said.

"I thank you." Aisley wrapped her arms around her satchel and pressed it against her empty stomach. Until Brecc or Rheged returned or she was miraculously granted audience with the king, the guard's grudging assistance was the most she could hope for.

CHAPTER 25

THE FLICKERING LIGHT GUIDED THE punt toward the island. It had taken the men longer to reach Athelney than Brecc had hoped, but he was deeply grateful that their journey was finally nearing an end. A few hours later than he'd anticipated was far better than a full day or two.

Standing on the small platform at the back of the punt, Lufian gave the pole in his hands a sharp twist and then pulled. With a reluctant squelch, the mud beneath the water relinquished the long shaft. Lufian raised it clear of the water, waiting until their forward momentum slowed before dropping the pole into the water again. He pushed against the pole, and the boat glided on.

"You have become an expert punter, Lufian," Rheged said. "We are fortunate that Brecc did not insist on taking charge of the pole this evening. We may have all taken a dip before reaching the island."

It was a poor attempt at levity. Brecc's skill with the punt was not so lacking as all that. But given how tired the men were, Brecc could not fault Rheged for trying. And truth be told, he would rather listen to them tease him about his inexpert performance with the punt pole than to lie in the bottom of the boat dwelling on the seriousness of his leg injury.

"If we each arrive on the island with dry feet, I shall consider my captaining the punt a success," Lufian said.

"Do not blame yourself if I enter the cottage trailing water behind me," Brecc said. "I am not sure this leg of mine will sustain an elegant exit when we dock."

"He has been riding so long, he wishes to remain at one with his mount," Rheged said, turning to watch the four horses swimming after the punt.

At the front of the craft, Bertwin chuckled. It was no secret that they'd each been more than happy to dismount when they'd reached the marsh. Two full days in the saddle was too long for any man.

"Looks like it's Radolf who's come to meet us," he said.

"Once again, fortune has smiled upon us," Rheged said dryly.

The darkness hid the humor in Brecc's eyes. "I am glad you think so."

"But of course. Who amongst us would not wish to be welcomed home by an ill-tempered guard?"

"Who goes there?" Radolf's voice filled the short distance.

"Rheged, Brecc, Bertwin, and Lufian," Rheged called back.

The flaming torch moved in a slow arc. Keeping his eyes on the light, Lufian steered the punt left. An instant later, it thudded against the bank.

"Nicely done, Lufian," Brecc said.

Bracing himself against the pole, Lufian gave him an acknowledging nod. "I'll keep it as steady as I can whilst you alight."

"Truly, Lufian's concern for our feet is remarkable." With one foot on the end of the punt and the other on the shore, Rheged straddled the water below.

Placing his weight on his uninjured leg, Brecc pushed himself upright. The punt rocked, and he took a moment to steady himself. Behind him, Bertwin had taken charge of the ropes attached to the horses. The animals were splashing impatiently, but Brecc knew Bertwin was waiting on him. Pushing past the discomfort, Brecc limped to the front of the punt, and Rheged grasped his arm.

"One firm step is all it will take," Rheged said.

"One, I can do. Firm, I cannot promise."

"Then simply do one," Rheged said. "I shall be behind you."

With no desire to delay the challenge, Brecc leaped onto the bank. He landed on his strong leg. It held his weight, but his balance was off, and without thought, he lowered his wounded leg to make up the difference. Pain shot from his knee to his hip. His leg buckled, and he lunged for a nearby shrub. The branches dug into his fingers, but they held him. He took two deep breaths.

"You are on dry ground." Rheged appeared at his side and took his arm again, this time to pull him upright. "The rest will be easy."

The horses were scrambling up the bank around him, and water was spraying from their glistening bodies.

"Could you not have released the animals one at a time," Radolf grumbled. He was holding the torch aloft to protect it from the unanticipated shower.

"We are happy to see you again too, Radolf," Rheged said.

Before the older ealdorman could respond, Lufian and Bertwin appeared in the circle of torchlight.

"I have tied up the punt," Lufian said. "It's the second one."

Over the last few weeks, the king's men had acquired three punts. They endeavored to have at least one available on each shore.

"Has the king returned?" Brecc asked.

"Not yet," Radolf said. "Odda and his men arrived this morning. They brought the other punt in."

"Were they successful?"

"Two Viking parties ambushed, stolen coins and merchandise returned to their original owners, and Guthrum's campsite ransacked." Radolf offered a rare, craggy smile. "To hear Odda tell it, word of the raids is spreading rapidly throughout Wessex."

"As it should be," Rheged said.

Radolf eyed Brecc's leg. His bloodied hose and obvious limp were impossible to miss. "What of you?"

"We accomplished what we set out to do," Brecc said. Details could come later. For now, his priority was to finally attend to his wound.

As though he'd followed Brecc's train of thought, Rheged gathered the reins to his horse and Brecc's. "Lufian, Bertwin, and I will take care of the mounts," he said. "Go to the cottage and see to your leg."

Brecc took a few limping steps. "At the rate I am moving, you might reach it before me regardless."

"If I do, I shall make sure there is water ready."

Brecc grimaced. He'd likely have to soak his hose just to pull it away from his damaged skin. And if his current discomfort was any indication, he was not in for a pleasant sight when the wound was exposed.

Holding the flaming torch aloft, Radolf led the way across the grass toward the horse enclosure. The other men guided the horses after him. Brecc followed more slowly. He was passing by the enclosure when Rheged's raised voice caused him to stop.

"Radolf! What is my mare doing in here?"

The older man scratched his head. "Why, you just put her in yourself."

"Not that one." There was something in Rheged's tone that caused Brecc to deviate toward the horse enclosure. "This one!"

Rheged was standing inside the gate. The horses the men had just released had wandered farther into the paddock and were already grazing. Another horse had approached Rheged and was nudging his arm with her nose. Brecc grasped the closest fence post and leaned on it to watch. Rheged had only ever owned one horse that singled him out in such a way. And he'd not seen it since he and the queen had fled the royal estate in Chippenham.

"Is it truly Bracken?" Brecc asked.

"Of course it is." Rheged ran his hand down the mare's neck before swinging back to face Radolf. "But how?"

"He came with the young lad who arrived an hour or two before you."

"What young lad?" Brecc asked.

"Avi, he said his name was. Edris brought him over on his boat. The lad insisted that he had a message for Brecc that was of utmost importance."

"And you're only now telling me of this?"

Radolf glared at him. "It seemed like you had more pressing matters—like a wounded leg—to see to first."

"I appreciate your concern," Brecc said, "but in the future, I wish to be told such things immediately so that I might decide for myself which should take priority." He shifted the weight onto his uninjured limb. "Tell me more about the fellow. Did he indicate where he came from?"

"Trowbridge."

Trowbridge! Brecc pushed himself off the fence. "Where is he now?"

"Resting in the tent under the pine tree. After he got here, bedding down for the night was about all he was good for."

Brecc was already hobbling across the short distance that separated them from the tent. Behind him, Rheged shut the gate, and by the time Brecc reached the small shelter, his friend was at his side.

Brecc banged his hand on the side of the wool cloth. "Show yourself," he called.

There was a soft moan and then a rustle. The flaps to the tent twitched, and a young man crawled out, his head covered by the hood of his cloak and his body wrapped in a blanket.

"Forgive me." The voice was bleary. "I was asleep."

"Who are you, and how did you come to have my horse?" Rheged asked.

Stumbling to his feet, the lad turned to face him. "Rheged!" he gasped.

"Remember your place, boy," Radolf growled. "It's Ealdorman Rheged to you."

The stranger pulled back his hood, and by the light of Radolf's torch, Brecc caught the shimmer of copper-colored hair. His heart thudded in his chest. It could not be. But the newcomer was the same build as the woman who so often filled his dreams, and who else would know exactly where to find him?

"Aisley." Her name escaped his lips before he'd formulated another thought.

She swung around. "Brecc!" Tears filled her green eyes. "You are here."

He took an unsteady step toward her, and her gaze flew to his leg.

"You are hurt!"

"It is nothing."

"Do not believe him," Rheged said. "He was injured two days ago, and I pray that despite your curious garb, you brought your remedies with you."

"I do have them." Aisley disappeared into the small tent, and Brecc barely had time to scowl at Rheged before she reappeared carrying a leather satchel. "I have much to tell you, but it can wait until I have treated your wound."

Brecc shook his head and reached for her hand. "I do not wish to wait. You can tell me whilst you tend my leg."

"I do not understand." Radolf looked from one to the other. "Who is this person?"

"Radolf, may I introduce Aisley, daughter of Ealdorman Kendryek of Wiltshire," Rheged said.

Still holding Brecc's hand, she inclined her head toward Radolf. "Forgive my deception, sire. My errand is of so sensitive a nature, I could trust my true identity to no one but Brecc or Rheged."

"A young lady." Radolf almost choked on the words.

"A rather remarkable young lady," Brecc said, tightening his grip on her hand.

Radolf bowed. "I beg your pardon, mistress. I would not have treated you so harshly had I known."

"You treated her harshly?" Brecc tensed. "What in the name of all that is good did you do to her, Radolf?"

"I . . ." The older man appeared distinctly uncomfortable.

"He took his duties as guard seriously," Aisley said, coming to his rescue. "He also offered me a place to rest and brought me some pottage."

"Just so." Radolf and the light he bore inched away. "And I'd best go back to watching the water."

Aisley was obviously glossing over some significant and damaging details. A quick look at Rheged's frowning face told Brecc that his friend's opinion mirrored his own. But if Aisley was willing to overlook Radolf's inhospitable behavior, Brecc would let it go. For now.

"Very well." Brecc turned the other way. "We shall go to the cottage. My slow pace will likely give you time to tell us how you arrived here before we enter."

"And how you came to have my mare," Rheged added.

"Is she truly yours?" The warmth of her response was discernible. "In the madness of the Viking attack on the royal estate, she was given to me as a means of escape. I always wondered who her rightful owner was. She has been well cared for at Trowbridge, but I am sure she has missed you."

"I have missed her," Rheged said with feeling.

"Then I am especially glad you have been reunited."

"As am I," Brecc said, "but I should like to hear the story behind your arrival here. From the beginning, if you please."

"The beginning." All trace of pleasure disappeared. "Remarkably, that was not so very long ago. Two days, to be precise. But so much has happened since then . . ." Her voice faded to nothing.

This was going to be difficult for her. He felt it. "Take as much time as you need. If you would rather wait until we are situated indoors, we can do that."

"Aye," Rheged said. "And if you need a distraction in the cottage, Brecc's fine-looking leg will surely provide you with one."

Brecc was not sure who was most fortunate: Rheged because he was not close enough for Brecc to punch him or Brecc himself because the darkness covered his flaming face. "Ignore him, Aisley."

"Or mayhap it would be better to use him," she said. "Once mixed, some of my salves are excessively pungent in the worst possible ways. We could place him in charge of holding the bowl whilst we talk."

"I politely but firmly decline the assignment," Rheged said.

"Understandable, although most ungallant," Aisley said.

Brecc could not help but chuckle. Aisley's ease with his friend's ridiculous banter was refreshing. Whether or not he benefited from her gift of healing, this evening was improved simply because she was there.

CHAPTER 26

THE COTTAGE WAS LARGER THAN Aisley had anticipated. Built of stone, it was protected on three sides by woodland. A chink of light shone under the door, and when Rheged opened it, the murmur of male voices floated out to greet them. Almost a dozen men sat around a fire, and most of them looked up as they entered.

"Welcome back, Brecc," one of them called. "Lufian here was just telling us about your raid on the Viking encampment—and how you came a little too close to an enemy blade."

"It was a knife?" Aisley whispered.

He gave a tight nod but faced his comrades with a smile. "One chance is all I allowed him." Releasing Aisley's hand to set his gently on her back, he introduced her. "This is Aisley, daughter of Ealdorman Kendryek of Wiltshire."

"Ah, yes, the honorary thegn."

A few of the men laughed. For better or worse, it appeared that they remembered her brief time at the head table.

"Aye," Brecc said. "She has come to deliver a message to the king but has agreed to dress my wound whilst she awaits his return."

"So, we are to disregard any cries of agony coming from the corner."

Brecc lowered his hand and began limping toward the far end of the room. "I shall endeavor to keep them to a minimum," he said.

The laughter redoubled. The men were happy to be back, pleased to share their stories of success. Aisley wished she felt the same elation. She glanced at Brecc's bloodied leg. A deep knife wound that had been left unattended for two days was a serious matter.

"Rheged," she whispered. "Do you have access to honey, vinegar, or eggs?"

He gave her a wary look. "Do they take upon themselves a powerful odor when mixed?"

"No." She opened her satchel and began rummaging through the small bags. Now that she knew how Brecc had attained his injury, she did not feel like teasing. "But they may be beneficial to Brecc's cut." She withdrew a bag. "I shall also require some water, clean rags, and a small bowl."

He must have sensed her concern, for his expression sobered. "I shall see what I can find."

Brecc was lowering himself onto the floor in the corner when she reached him.

"Rheged has gone for water and rags," she said, setting her satchel down beside him.

"That will be helpful." Now that they were indoors and the firelight illuminated his face more clearly, she could see the pain in his eyes. He looked at his hose and grimaced. "This is not going to be pleasant."

"I fear not," she said, "but the sooner we tend to it, the better."

He pulled his knife from his belt and handed it to her. "Cut the hose away from around the injury, and then we shall see what we are up against."

Aisley knelt beside him. Taking off her cloak, she set one hand on his thigh and used the other to guide the tip of Brecc's knife into the fabric. Beneath her fingers, his muscle tensed. She swallowed. "Am I hurting you?"

"No."

He was bracing himself. That was all. She released a nervous breath. She had cared for countless wounds over the years, but never had her fingers felt so unsteady. "I shall try not to cause you undue distress."

His hand came down over hers. "I trust you, Aisley."

She looked at their overlapping fingers. Weeks before, his appearance in Trowbridge had strengthened her just when she'd needed it most. Now it was her turn to offer what little she could to him. "If it becomes too awful, tell me, and I shall stop."

He nodded and removed his hand. "Cut away."

Brecc's knife was sharp. It took only six cuts to peel away the sodden fabric from his leg and expose the wound beneath. About the length of

Aisley's forefinger, it was impossible to tell exactly how deep the cut went, but the flesh around the incision was red and swollen.

"It's angry with you for neglecting it so long," Aisley said.

"I daresay." Brecc's head was against the wall, and his arm was across his eyes. "Can you do anything to calm it down?"

"That is my hope."

Rheged arrived at her side, carrying an assortment of items. "One egg, honey, vinegar, three small bowls, a large bowl of water, and three rags," he said.

"Bless you." Aisley took them gratefully. "These are exactly what I need."

"Vinegar?" Brecc lowered his arm. "I do not like the sound of that."

"You said you trusted me," Aisley said, dunking the first rag into the water.

"That was before I heard the word *vinegar*."

"Then we shall start with water," she said.

"I understand your disquiet, my friend." Rheged took a seat on the floor beside him. "She was equally domineering while she was forcing me to drink her awful tonic in Chippenham."

Brecc raised his eyes to the roof. "If you aim to stay with us, I would ask that you remain silent. It is Aisley's turn to tell her tale."

"Agreed."

Aisley swabbed the dried blood around Brecc's wound and returned the cloth to the bowl. She rinsed the cloth and then resumed her washing. Brecc was right. The time had come to share her story.

"Very well." Gently, she wiped off more of the blood. "Two days ago, my brother informed me that he had come to an agreement with Rangvald. For an undisclosed sum, he had arranged to give me in marriage to the Viking chieftain."

Brecc bolted upright from his reclined position. The empty bowl closest to him fell to one side and rolled away with a clatter. "He did what?"

Red water ran off his muscular leg and onto the floor. Aisley hurried to mop it up.

"Great heavens." Rheged stared at her. "Why would he do such a thing?"

It was the question that had haunted Aisley for days and one for which she had yet to settle upon a comfortable answer. "I cannot say for certain. Wulfhere is driven by avarice and power. He and I rarely agree on things.

I think he saw this marriage as a way to rid himself of an undesirable sister whilst also lining his own coffers."

"He deserves a knife at his throat for the very idea." Brecc clenched his fists, his expression one part horror, the other part fury. "But to actually consider implementing it . . ." His jaw worked as he attempted to control his heightened emotions. "If he had somehow prevented you from leaving . . ."

"Had he known of my plan, it is certain that he would have."

"How did you escape?" Rheged asked.

"It would not have been possible without the aid of our stablehand," she said, and then as she resumed her washing of Brecc's wound, she proceeded to tell them about Rangvald's appearance at the longhouse, Wulfhere's unyielding announcement, her personal preparations that night, Taber's kindness, and her eventful ride from Trowbridge.

"I am grateful to all those who assisted you," Brecc said.

"As am I." Aisley set aside the bowl of water and doused a rag in vinegar. "In truth, the traveler Radolf met at the shore was physically and emotionally spent but overwhelmingly thankful to have reached her destination." Before Brecc noticed what she was about, she set the rag on his wound.

Instantly, his eyes widened, and he released a penetrating hiss. "By all the Saints!" He spoke through gritted teeth. "Tell me you do not need to do that again."

"Twice more," she said.

He groaned, and closing his eyes, he leaned his head against the wall again.

As Aisley cleaned the entire wound with vinegar, Brecc's muscles became iron, his face alabaster.

She set down the rag. "I am finished." He did not reply. Beads of sweat lined his forehead. Anxiously, she reached out to cup his cheek. With his eyes yet closed, he leaned his face into her hand.

"I believe I may be finished also," he mumbled.

She smiled. "The worst is over, I give you my word."

"For now, at least," Rheged added.

Brecc's eyes opened. "You are the very worst kind of friend."

"But at least you can count on me for honesty." He glanced at the other bowls. "Fair warning, she still has honey, an egg, and a pouch of a mystery ingredient in her armory."

"None of them will hurt so much as the vinegar," Aisley promised. "Honey and garlic are known to aid healing. My hope is that the egg white will help seal the skin. If I had attended to the cut soon after it occurred, I likely would have stitched the skin closed, but that is harder to do now." She poured some honey into a small bowl and stirred in a small portion of dried garlic. "After I have applied the egg whites, you must limit your movement," she warned. "I will wrap your leg, and then we must all pray that the swelling recedes."

"I thank you, Aisley," Brecc said. "Despite my moaning, I am most grateful."

At the look in his eyes, Aisley's heart warmed. "I am glad to be of assistance."

"Aye," Rheged said, all hint of amusement gone. "Along with enabling you to escape your malicious brother, I daresay God guided you here to help Brecc."

Aisley gasped. How could she have neglected to mention the most important reason for her journey to Athelney? "I would like to think that He did, but there is more. And it is perhaps the most terrible news of all."

"I defy anything to be as terrible as forcing your sister to wed a Viking," Brecc said stiffly.

"It is something that the king must hear first," she said. "Something that will deeply affect his ability to rid Wessex of the Vikings."

Brecc frowned. "The king is expected back within the next two days. I imagine the queen has already retired for the night. She and King Alfred use the small chamber adjacent to this larger room so that they might have some privacy."

"When he returns, do you think he will grant me an audience?" she asked.

"Undoubtedly. No matter what your brother has or has not done, your father was beloved by the king and all the thegns who knew him."

Aisley set down the bowl of honey and garlic and reached for the egg whites, the familiar ache that came with memories of her father filling her chest. "Would that he were still here."

Brecc gave her a knowing look. "Your dreadful news would not exist if he were, am I correct?"

"Yes."

He nodded grimly. "You shall speak to the king the very day he returns. I shall personally ensure that it happens."

"You have my thanks." She knelt next to him, waiting for the egg whites to dry so that she might wrap his leg. In an odd way, she wished that she had more still to do. It felt good to be close to him, and her assigned tent was cold and lonely.

"Shall I take these away?" Rheged asked, pointing to the bowls and rags.

"That would be most helpful." She smiled at him. "And, Rheged, despite your qualms, you are a worthy assistant."

He grinned. "It is far better than being the patient."

She waited until he'd gathered everything, and when he moved away, she began wrapping Brecc's leg with a long strip of linen Rheged had included among the rags. "Promise me that you will rest," she said.

"You have my word. My leg feels as though it is on fire. It's hard to imagine ever moving again."

Aisley tied the linen in a knot above his knee and attempted to push aside her lingering worries. It was a clean cut, but that did not guarantee that it would heal well. If it festered, Brecc's condition would worsen very quickly.

"Would you like me to make an infusion for the discomfort?" she asked.

"No. You have done more than enough already."

She studied the bandaged leg anxiously. "The pain should subside as the honey and garlic do their work. I shall come back and check on you first thing in the morning."

"Come back? Where are you going?"

"To the tent."

He looked at the blanket, cloak, and satchel lying in a small heap behind her. "Did you leave any items there?"

"Only the horse's saddle and bridle."

"Then you have no need to return. The tack will be safe enough overnight."

"But the men . . ."

He pointed to a small partition up against the opposite corner. "The queen's maid sleeps there. I have no doubt there is room for another pallet behind the partition. If you are willing to endure a chorus of snoring men, I would feel better about having you nearby."

Relief filled her. "In truth, the background noise in the cottage would be reassuring."

"Then, it is settled," he said. "As soon as your worthy assistant returns, we shall have him locate a pallet for you."

"Poor Rheged. If these obligatory errands continue, he will come to rue the day that I arrived."

Reaching for her hand, he drew her closer. "He might as well become used to it. If I am forced to contrive a chore for him every time I wish to spend a few moments alone with you, he is destined to be a very busy man." His thumb ran a gentle circle across the top of her hand, and Aisley's pulse responded. "I have yet to come to terms with what Wulfhere aimed to do to you. It is possible I never will. But I am more grateful than I can express that you escaped his machinations and traveled to Athelney in safety."

"I cannot deny the miracles that attended me during my flight," she said. "And if you had not come to Trowbridge and told me where I might find you . . . where I might find the king . . ." She looked away. The ramifications of what Wulfhere had done were almost too much to bear.

"Aisley." His voice was gentle. "Look at me." Slowly, she turned back to Brecc. His eyes that had been so full of pain earlier were now filled with concern. "Whatever it is, you need no longer carry it alone. If it would ease your burden, you can tell me and can count on my full discretion."

She knew he spoke the truth. They had promised each other as much. The king deserved to be told before all others, but it would be safer if she were not the only one aware of Wulfhere's treachery. She marshaled her courage. Saying the words aloud, admitting that a member of her family had committed such an act of betrayal, was horribly difficult. "It is Wulfhere," she began.

He nodded. "That much I had guessed."

Behind her, the low buzz of men's talk was interspersed with laughter. No one was close enough to overhear. Indeed, no one had shown much interest in her after she had begun attending to Brecc's wound.

She swallowed and forced herself to continue. "My brother has formed an alliance with Rangvald. If King Alfred calls up the fyrd of Wiltshire, he will receive no assistance. Wulfhere has pledged himself to the Vikings and their cause."

Brecc's stunned expression was quickly replaced with one of tightly controlled anger. "He pledged his devotion to the king at Chippenham under three months ago. He kissed the horn and accepted the ring-giver's gift."

"I know."

"Dear heaven, Aisley." Brecc released a tense breath. "The Wiltshire fyrd is vital to the Saxons' counteroffensive against the invaders. The king could rightfully take Wulfhere's life for this."

"I know that too." Shame over her brother's perfidy hung over her, but she kept her head up. She would not take upon herself Wulfhere's misdeeds. "He must answer for what he has done, but even more importantly, the people of Wessex must not lose the battle for their own land simply because of his self-seeking actions."

"You are right. And they shall not. Especially with the forewarning you have offered the king."

"But what can be done?"

He met her anxious eyes with a thoughtful look. "Would you say that the general sentiment in Wiltshire is in favor of the king?"

"Most assuredly. Taber kept me abreast of the news in town. There was always much excitement when word came of a raid the king's men carried out against the Vikings. The men have been anxiously awaiting their call to arms."

He nodded as though her account corroborated his own belief. "That insight alone will help offset the enormous blow your intelligence will be to the king." He hesitated, and when he spoke again, it was more cautiously. "Would you allow me to broach the subject of Wulfhere's allegiance with the king first? King Alfred is a God-fearing, mild-mannered ruler, but I fear that he will not take the news well. If you are willing, I would wish to spare you from witnessing his initial wrath at your brother's duplicity."

She stared at him, scarcely believing her ears. She had desperately hoped that she would not have to face the king alone, but to have Brecc be the one to initially deliver the devastating news was more than she had thought possible. "You would do that for me?"

"Most certainly. He will likely wish to speak with you himself afterward, but by then, he might have had time to consider the situation fully and have a more measured response to it."

Since arriving at Athelney, Aisley's trepidation over telling the king had been multiplying with every passing hour. "I do not know how to adequately thank you."

With a small smile, he lightly patted his injured thigh. "I believe you already have."

CHAPTER 27

BRECC STARED UP AT THE rafters, willing the dawn to come. The dark shadows above his head had deepened as the last remaining coals from the cottage fire had faded from glowing orange to dusty gray. He had watched it happen. Despite his desperate need for sleep, the precious commodity had eluded him most of the night.

At first, he had blamed it on his discomfort, but as the night had worn on, the searing pain he'd experienced when Aisley had tended his wound had subsided to a dull ache, and he'd been forced to admit the true cause of his insomnia. His head had yet to relinquish the intelligence Aisley had shared, and his heart had yet to recover from its reaction to almost losing her to a Viking chieftain.

He groaned and closed his eyes again. If his overwhelming desire to pummel Wulfhere into the ground for what he had done to Aisley was not sufficiently telling, the fact that he'd volunteered to be the bearer of disastrous news to the king in order to spare her any further distress was proof that her well-being had come to mean more to him than his own. He flexed his fingers, remembering the feel of her small hand in his. It belonged there. He knew that as surely as he knew that morning would eventually come. But just as this night seemed interminable, so, too, did his commitments to the king. He could only pray that she would be sufficiently patient to wait for him.

The door to the cottage creaked open, and Brecc turned his head to see a man's silhouette framed against the moonlight. He walked in, and another man silently rose from his pallet. It was the changing of the guard. They would not leave the shore unmanned for long, especially as the king was expected back anytime. After a brief whispered exchange with Radolf, the new guard left, but to Brecc's surprise, Radolf did not immediately lie down to rest. Instead, he slowly made his way across the room toward the spot where Brecc lay.

"Radolf?" Brecc could barely make out the man in the darkness.

He stopped. "Aye. I didn't mean to wake you."

"I've been awake for some time. Is something amiss?"

"No." He stepped forward and set down something long and hard beside Brecc's pallet. "I made something for you."

Curious, Brecc rolled to his side and moved his arm in a slow circle, groping for what Radolf had set on the floor. "What is it?"

"A crutch. I found the branch soon after you headed to the cottage with Kendryek's daughter." He cleared his throat uncomfortably. "I swear, I had no idea that's who she was when she arrived here in a peasant boy's attire."

"I am sure that is so." If Radolf was this uncomfortable about his treatment of Aisley, for the older gentleman's sake, it was probably better that Brecc remained in ignorance about what he had done. "I am grateful that you were willing to grant her the opportunity to speak with me."

"Aye." He cleared his throat again, obviously anxious to move on. "When I saw your limp, I thought you might could use some assistance. And seeing as there's not much to do when a man's on watch duty at night, I was glad to have something that kept my hands busy and my mind alert. The branch would be too long for me, but I think it might be about right for someone of your height."

Brecc's fingers had finally found the piece of wood, and by the feel of it, Radolf had cut off the bark and sanded it smooth. "I'm much obliged to you," Brecc said. "That was most thoughtful."

"Think nothing of it." Radolf took a few steps back. "Well, I'd best get some sleep and let you do the same."

"Good early morning to you, Radolf."

The older man grunted. "I believe we'd both be better off if we pretended the night was yet young."

Brecc smiled into the darkness. His thoughtful gift notwithstanding, Radolf was still Radolf.

Sometime later, Brecc awoke to the sound of men moving pallets and benches. He opened his eyes, blinking against the light now streaming in through the cottage shutters. Sleep had finally overtaken him, and a new day had ultimately come.

"Ah! You are awake at last." Rheged stood over him. "How is the leg?"

Brecc attempted to move it. "It hurts but not so badly as before."

"I am glad to hear it. And Aisley will be especially pleased. She's been waiting for you to rouse yourself so she can check the wound."

"Where is she?" Brecc pulled himself onto his elbows and glanced around the room. Over half the men were gone, and if the sound of chopping reverberating through the cottage was any indication, some of them were already hard at work replenishing the wood supply. Those yet within the building were setting the room to rights in preparation for a meal later in the day.

"She's talking with the queen."

Brecc shifted so he could better see the entrance to the small chamber. Two women stood by the door. The taller one wore an elegant dark-blue gown, and her dark hair was braided into a coronet. The petite one's gown was pale green in color and simpler in design. Her coppery hair flowed freely down her back, catching the light of the morning sun. As he watched, she smiled at something her companion said, and Brecc's chest tightened.

"She's wearing a gown." It was a banal statement, but the best he could manage.

"She is indeed, and I should warn you that far more of the other thegns took notice of her this morning than they did last night." At Brecc's immediate frown, Rheged laughed. "I see it is just as I thought. The fiercely independent and heroic warrior Ealdorman Brecc has fallen hard."

Brecc's frown deepened, and Rheged's laughter increased. It caught the attention of the two ladies, and moments later, Aisley bobbed a curtsy to the queen and crossed the room toward them. Brecc could only imagine how disheveled he appeared, but as he could do nothing whatsoever to put himself to rights in the amount of time it would take Aisley to reach him, he pushed himself into a sitting position and greeted her with a smile. "Good morning, Aisley."

She returned his smile, a hint of pink on her cheeks. "Good morning. How does your leg feel?"

"I have yet to rise, but currently, the pain is better."

Obviously pleased, she knelt beside him. "May I check the wound?"

"As long as there is no vinegar in the vicinity, you may."

She laughed lightly. "You are in luck. Your trusted friend Rheged carried it all away." Carefully, she began untying the linen strip, unwinding the fabric until the cut was exposed. She studied it, silently and carefully.

Brecc's anxiety mounted. "Well?"

She met his eyes and smiled. "The swelling and redness have both diminished, and there is no sign of pus. We have a long way to go, but I believe we are on the right path."

His shoulders sagged with relief. He'd not verbally acknowledged the depth of his own concern for his previously untreated cut, but he knew enough to realize the seriousness of his situation. Too many good men died from wounds that festered. This early report, however, gave him real hope.

"I am most grateful."

Her shy smile returned. "I shall rewrap it now, but if you are willing, we should treat it with honey and garlic again later today."

He was not sure whether she had purposely omitted mentioning vinegar to win him over or if he was truly to be spared the fire water. Either way, he knew his best chance of recovery lay in her ministrations. "Agreed," he said.

She had just bent down to wind the linen around his leg again when the door to the cottage flew open and Lufian entered. "The king has returned! He and the men with him are approaching the island."

Aisley turned to Brecc with alarm-filled eyes. "He is come." Her fingers fumbled, and she dropped the linen across his leg. Hastening to pick it up again, she resumed the winding, but her previous calm was gone. He wanted to take her in his arms and reassure her, but there were men everywhere. Even the queen and her maid had appeared from the small chamber.

"It will be well, Aisley," he said.

She nodded mutely and tied a knot on the bandage.

"Rheged," Brecc said. "Help me to my feet."

"Should you be—" Rheged broke off to give Aisley a questioning look, but before she could respond, Brecc continued.

"I will stand for the king. Look to the side of my pallet. Radolf made me a crutch. Once I have that, I shall manage without needing to put weight on my injured leg."

Rheged reached for the long piece of wood. "Radolf made this for you?" He appeared as stunned as Brecc had been when the older man had set it beside him. "It's quite remarkable."

Now that he could see the crutch properly, Brecc could more fully appreciate the workmanship that had gone into it. It must have taken Radolf all night to peel away the bark and smooth the wood so well. The long part of the branch was almost straight, and at one end, it forked into two stubby pieces.

"How marvelous," Aisley said.

Rheged handed her the crutch and moved to stand over Brecc. Bracing his feet, he grasped his hand. "Whenever you are ready."

Setting the foot of his strong leg down, Brecc nodded. "Now."

Rheged heaved, and Brecc pushed upward. He rose and wobbled, but he kept his wrapped leg off the floor.

"Here." Aisley handed him the crutch. He slid it under his arm. It felt awkward, but it did offer him a new way to maintain his balance.

"I thank you," he said. "Both of you." Being dependent on others for something as simple as standing required swallowing an unpleasantly large dose of humility. "And although I have no right to ask anything more, I do wish to make one further request."

Rheged raised a curious eyebrow. "And that is?"

"I wish you to take Aisley out of the cottage. Show her around the island, visit Bracken and the other horses, check on the punts. Do what you must to keep her from here until I have spoken with the king."

Rheged's brows furrowed. "But does she not have something important to tell the king also?"

"She does. And I shall ensure that she is given an opportunity to speak with him. But I must see him first. Alone."

Brecc glanced at Aisley. Had Rheged noticed how pale she had become or how tightly her hands were clasped?

"If you are willing, Rheged," she said. "I should enjoy that very much."

"Of course I am willing," he said, looking between the two of them as though attempting to decipher a secret code. "Fetch your cloak, and we shall go directly."

Aisley hurried across the room toward the partition, and Rheged swung on Brecc. "Would you like to tell me what this is about?"

"I would, but unfortunately, I cannot. Trust me. This is for the best. I will send for you and Aisley when it is safe for her to return."

"Safe?" Rheged's eyes widened. "What is this, Brecc?"

Brecc set his hand on his friend's shoulder. "You will know all soon enough, I give you my word. Until then, you must trust me."

"Hm." Rheged reached for his own cloak and set it around his shoulders as Aisley appeared from behind the partition wearing hers. "I accept no responsibility if Aisley chooses me over you after I have escorted her so gallantly around this patch of land lying in a swamp."

Despite knowing that a fearful tempest was about to be unleashed, Brecc's lips twitched. "Fair enough. I shall simply have to hope that ultimately, the best man triumphs."

Rheged started across the floor. "In that case, your cause is lost. Aisley already loves my horse."

Brecc watched them walk out of the cottage and took a moment to collect himself. Rheged was intelligent enough to guide Aisley away from the royal party, even if he did not know why it needed to be done. He was giving Brecc the time he needed. But how was Brecc to inform the king of Wulfhere's treachery without it leading to the entire family's being condemned? Kendryek was the key. He had to be. The king would not disregard traitors, but neither did he forget those who were ardently loyal.

Voices approached. Brecc watched the door. It opened, and the king walked in. Instantly, those in the room stopped what they were about and bowed.

"Welcome back, Sire." Using his crutch, Brecc hobbled toward him.

"Brecc." The king eyed him critically. "You look terrible."

He was correct, but that was not very comforting. "I have had better days."

"So, I imagine." King Alfred pointed to his leg. "What happened?"

"A Viking blade."

The king grimaced. "Has it been properly attended to?"

It was the opening Brecc had hoped for. "It has. Fortunately for me, Ealdorman Kendryek's daughter arrived at Athelney yesterday. She is a skilled healer, and she cared for the wound last evening."

"Did she come with her brother?"

"No, Sire. She was alone."

King Alfred appeared dumbfounded. "How is that even possible?"

"Through a series of miracles. And she was driven by a desperate need to relay vital information to you."

"Well, where is she?"

"She is outside, waiting to be granted an audience with you."

The king heaved a weary sigh. "I am excessively tired, Brecc. Indeed, my exhaustion has gone so far as to rob me of all curiosity. Sleep is to be my first order of business. I shall speak with her this evening."

"Under normal circumstances, I would agree wholeheartedly," Brecc said, knowing full well that by openly disagreeing with the monarch, he was treading on dangerous ground. "But I believe the news she brings is of such import, you will not wish to delay hearing it."

King Alfred offered him a warning look. "Does this report directly impact my life and the lives of those I love?"

Given that King Alfred genuinely cared about his people, Brecc was able to answer without hesitation. "It does. And if you wish to be the judge of whether Aisley's news can wait until after you rest, I can offer you an abbreviated version."

"By all that is holy," King Alfred grumbled. "You would think a king might have full control over his agenda."

"Forgive me, Sire."

"You are not walking away, I see."

"No, Sire."

"So you seek forgiveness but are not truly repentant for imposing your will upon mine."

Brecc inclined his head. "So it would seem. Although I do fully understand your need for rest and shall make my delivery as brief as possible."

King Alfred grunted and started toward the small chamber. The few people remaining in the cottage scattered.

"You have only until I reach my pallet," he said.

Taking up his crutch, Brecc hobbled alongside him. "Aisley is cut of the same cloth as her father, Kendryek. She is fully loyal to the crown—to the extent that she was willing to risk her own life to save the king's."

"Her father was a good man."

"He was. Unfortunately, the same cannot be said of his son, Wulfhere."

The king stopped so suddenly, Brecc all but ran into him. "What has Wulfhere done?"

Brecc steadied himself with the crutch. There was no point in dissembling. He had promised to be concise. "He has made an alliance with the

Viking chieftain, Rangvald. Not only will he refuse to call up the Wiltshire fyrd when you issue the order, but he will also inform Rangvald of your intentions."

For the length of three heartbeats, there was total silence. A muscle in King Alfred's jaw twitched. "How sure are you that Kendryek's daughter tells the truth?"

"Completely sure."

Color flooded the king's face. "He swore allegiance to me! He accepted the ring-giver's gift no more than three months ago." The king's voice rose. "Has he no honor? This is a complete betrayal."

Brecc waited, knowing the king desired no response from him. He simply needed to release his fury.

With a muttered curse, King Alfred paced eight steps, swiveled, and paced back. "Mark my words, Brecc." His complexion remained mottled, but already, he had his temper in check, and his icy calm was far more unnerving than a shouted tirade would have been. "That blackhearted thegn will pay dearly for his actions. He will rue the day that he broke his oath to the Saxon king, and it will serve as an example to any other thegn who considers aligning himself with the Vikings."

As far as Brecc was concerned, Wulfhere deserved whatever fate the king meted out. His anxiety was not centered on the outcome for the deceitful, grasping ealdorman. "What of his family, Sire?"

"Each person will learn a necessary lesson." Anger laced his words, and Brecc's tension increased.

"If I may be so bold, it would seem to me that Aisley deserves commendation for bringing us the news rather than censure for her role in this affair. Like her father before her, she risked everything for Wessex and the crown."

Thankfully, his comment appeared to offer the king pause for thought. "Does her brother know what she has done?"

"No, Sire. To the best of my knowledge, he is ignorant of her whereabouts. If he had known her destination, he surely would have stopped her."

"Hm. Methinks I should hear from the young lady herself before I make any determination. If she is truly her father's daughter, in every sense of the word, I shall know it forthwith." He waved his hand toward the door. "Fetch her. You have ensured that I shall be granted no sleep even if I were to lie down. I will speak with her now."

CHAPTER 28

AISLEY AND RHEGED HAD COMPLETED a full circuit of the small island and were now watching the horses in the small enclosure. Throughout their walk, Rheged had done his best to entertain her with humorous stories about the men's misadventures when initially setting up camp on the island, but Aisley was quite certain she had been a poor audience. Rather than giving Rheged her full attention, she'd had her ears constantly tuned for the echo of angry words coming from the cottage, and the longer Brecc's lack of appearance dragged on, the more concerned she became that his conversation with the king had gone badly.

"What did you name Bracken when you had her?" Rheged asked.

Aisley tore her gaze away from the cottage and attempted to focus on the mare nuzzling Rheged's hand. "I did not give her a name," she said. "It never felt quite right. She went by 'lady' or 'girl' when I spoke to her."

"A sound solution," he said.

At the click of a door latch opening, Aisley tensed, her eyes turning back to the cottage. Others had exited earlier, but this time, it was Brecc who appeared in the doorway. He tucked his crutch beneath his arm and began limping toward them. "Brecc is coming."

"So, I see." Rheged gave the horse's nose a final rub, and they started across the grass toward Brecc. "What news?"

"The king would like to speak with Aisley," Brecc said. His face was grave but offered no further clue as to how his interaction with the king had gone or what the king's current mind-set might be.

Rheged raised his eyebrows. "It appears that you have been summoned, so I shall hand you off to Brecc. He is better at dealing with orders of execution than I am." Aisley felt her face blanche, and the humor in Rheged's eyes evaporated. "That was meant as a joke."

"It was in poor taste," Brecc said tightly.

"Aisley, you must know that King Alfred is a good and noble ruler. None of us would be here if that were not the case," Rheged said.

"True," she said, summoning a halfhearted smile. "I shall try to be brave."

Rheged gave Brecc a puzzled look. "Something untoward is in the air, and I should like to know what it is."

"You shall," Brecc said. "As soon as the king deems the time right." He inclined his head. "I think it likely that you will learn the whole of it before day's end."

"Very well." He took a step back. "I shall not delay you further."

"I thank you, Rheged," Aisley said. "For your patience with me and this difficult situation."

"Oh, what you see is not patience," he said, a hint of his normal joviality returning. "Rather, it is exceptional acting skills."

She managed a smile. "Exceptional, indeed."

"You have my appreciation also," Brecc said, and then he took Aisley's hand in his. "Come. We must not keep the king waiting."

Aisley wrapped her fingers around Brecc's, drawing strength from his touch. It would be well. Surely Brecc would not escort her in if he knew the outcome was to be a death sentence upon all members of Ealdorman Wulfhere's family. She glanced at him. He must have caught the movement because he looked down and smiled gently.

"Fear not, lady warrior. Once the king has heard the details of your story, he will quickly recognize your brave and loyal heart."

"I do not feel brave."

"Then focus on your loyalty," he said. "Your bravery will shine through whether you intend it to or not."

They reached the door, and Brecc released her hand. She felt the loss instantly. "Will you come in with me?"

"If you wish it."

"I do. Very much."

He smiled again. "Then lead the way."

The cottage's main room was empty, save for one man. The king was standing beside the fire, gazing at the low-burning logs. When they walked in, he turned, and Aisley dropped into a curtsy.

"Aisley, daughter of Ealdorman Kendryek," the king said. "We meet again."

"Indeed, Sire." Was it wrong that she'd hoped he would not know her from her ridiculous appearance at the head table on Twelfth Night? "I only wish it were under better circumstances."

"As do I." He studied her. "Brecc has told me of your claim that your brother has betrayed me, but I wish to hear it from your mouth. And I would have you spare no details. The whole of it, if you please."

Aisley's hands were clasped so tightly her fingers were hurting. She loosened her grip. The king's tone was measured, his gaze guarded. He would undoubtedly assess her every movement and word, but she would rather that than her being the target of his ire. *Show loyalty.* She repeated Brecc's counsel in her mind. This was something she could do. This was who she was.

Choosing to begin from the moment she'd spotted Wulfhere and Rangvald conversing in the yard outside the family longhouse, Aisley rehearsed the entirety of her dismay at her brother's plans, her struggle to have him change his mind, and her realization that his actions had the potential of impacting the very future of Wessex, followed by her determination to notify the king and her subsequent escape and journey to Athelney.

Keeping her head held high, she finished her account and waited for the barrage of questions that would surely come. To her astonishment, however, the king spoke directly to Brecc.

"Your power of discernment has not failed you. Once again, you have been proven correct. In both appearance and heart, Aisley does, indeed, take after her father."

Unbidden, tears sprang to Aisley's eyes. She blinked them away, but not before the perceptive monarch noticed them.

"My comparing you to your father affects you," the king said.

"I can think of no greater compliment, Sire."

"Nor I." He clasped his hands behind his back, his expression pensive. "Your father was well loved by his people. Can the same be said of your brother?"

"No, Sire."

He raised his eyebrows. "That took no thought."

"My brother continues to raise taxes even though many struggle to survive. He has little interest in those living beneath his station and shows no concern for the welfare of those over whom he has stewardship."

"A damning report," the king said grimly. "Particularly as I have seen no sign of additional revenue from Wiltshire."

"If I may, Your Majesty?" Brecc asked.

"Please." The king signaled for him to continue. "I would welcome your input. I confess, it is at times like this that I sorely miss Ormod's level-headed advice."

"I do not believe I shall ever be so wise as Ormod," Brecc said, "but it strikes me that if the people of Wiltshire begrudge their ealdorman, it is likely that their political leanings do not emulate his. You are in need of Wiltshire's fyrd to beat the Vikings. If the people are willing to fight, it might be possible to call up the fyrd without Wulfhere's involvement or knowledge."

"Brecc is correct, Sire. The local people in Wiltshire are anxiously awaiting your call to arms," Aisley said.

"I am gratified to hear it, but the fyrds are the ealdormen's responsibility. I cannot see how we could rally enough men without using the established system."

"Aisley," Brecc said, "can you think of anyone in Trowbridge whose influence is great enough that information given to him regarding the gathering of King Alfred's fyrds would then reach those willing to join the fight? Someone whose loyalty to the crown is so sure that there is no threat of any hint of it reaching your brother."

Aisley pondered the question. She had witnessed many ceorls come and go at the longhouse, but she could not be sure of their faithfulness to the king. Her thoughts moved to Taber. His heart was true, but he had little to no influence beyond the stables. He received all his news from the fishmonger in town. She gasped. He had no title or position of power, but the fishmonger was the obvious choice.

"Nyle," she said. "He is the fishmonger in town. His cousin lives in a neighboring town, and between the two of them, they fuel all the news and excitement about the raids on the Vikings and the movements of the king's men. As he was willing to sacrifice his entire catch to spare me from the unwanted attention of Rangvald and his men, I believe it is safe to say he harbors no love for the invaders."

"I witnessed this event and concur with Aisley's opinion," Brecc said. "Nyle, although in many respects an unlikely choice, may well be the best man, for that very reason. Wulfhere would never suspect the peasants at the market of disseminating any information of worth."

"And you believe that if the men of Wiltshire were given a date and a location, they would come, armed and ready to fight without the leadership of their ealdorman?" the king asked.

Aisley looked to Brecc, and he gave a slow nod.

"I believe it is entirely possible," he said.

"As do I," Aisley agreed. "It has been under three months, but the people of Wiltshire have experienced enough of life under the cloud of Viking rule to know that it is far worse than anything they have experienced before. They will fight to restore you to the throne and to reclaim Wessex for the Saxons."

"Entrusting the gathering of Wiltshire's fyrd to a fishmonger is a grave risk," the king said. "But if we are to muster sufficient warriors to take on the Viking horde, I see no other avenue available to us." He turned on his heel and started toward the small chamber. "Rally the men, Brecc. I shall rest for an hour, and then we shall meet to make assignments. We have bided our time long enough; the moment has come to call out the fyrds and take care of our enemies—foreign and domestic."

The flash of astonishment in Brecc's eyes was nothing to the shock that rippled through Aisley.

She took a few hurried steps so as to catch the king as he reached the door to the chamber. "Begging your pardon, Sire, but what is now to become of me and my family?"

"Your family members are no longer your concern. They shall be dealt with appropriately." He paused long enough to acknowledge Aisley's stricken expression. "For the good of the kingdom, traitors must be dealt with. I do understand, however, that although they are not blameless, in this instance, your mother and sister carry less culpability than does your brother. You may be reassured that I shall take that into account."

Aisley could hope for nothing more. Tears threatened once again, but he had yet to answer the question that affected her most. "What of me, Sire?"

"Do you have a preference?"

"I should like to stay here," she said. "I know the island was intended to house only your male warriors, but I am willing to help around the cottage, and I am skilled in the art of healing, should a need arise."

She looked down. She was all but begging, and it did not come easily. But she was desperate. If the king denied her request, she did not know what would become of her.

"You assisted Brecc with his wound."

"I did."

"How does it feel, Brecc?"

Brecc was so close that she could feel his warmth on her back. "Much improved, Sire."

"I am glad to hear it, but if that is so, you should clean yourself up."

A rustle of fabric sounded, and the queen stepped out of the small chamber and into the doorway. "I know nothing of the urgent business you have been discussing in the main room, but when you move your dialogue here, I feel that I may join it. My conversation with Aisley this morning, although brief, cheered me no end. I had not realized how much I have missed associating with other women." She looked to her husband. "If she is willing, I should like her to stay."

The king offered his wife a polite bow and then turned back to Aisley. "It seems that the queen demands your presence here at Athelney."

On trembling legs, Aisley managed a faltering curtsy. "I thank you, Your Majesties."

"I shall look for you when the men gather for their next meeting, Aisley," the queen said. And with a pleased smile, she walked back into the small chamber.

"One hour, Brecc," the king admonished, and then he followed after her and closed the door.

Aisley pivoted and fell into Brecc's arms. Brecc stumbled backward, his crutch clattering to the floor as he struggled to maintain his balance.

"Oh no, forgive me. I did not think." Swiping at her tears, Aisley backed away and reached for the long piece of wood.

"Leave it." Brecc had steadied himself against the wall. "And do not ever apologize for needing me to hold you." He extended his arms to her. "Especially as it is almost certain that I share the same desire."

Muffling a sob with her hand, she entered his arms. He pulled her close and pressed a kiss to the top of her head.

"I can stay." She raised her head to meet his eyes, barely able to take in all that had transpired in so short a time. "The king believed me, and I can stay on Athelney."

Smiling, Brecc lifted one hand to gently wipe away the tears on her cheeks. "Bravery and loyalty. I never doubted he would recognize those things in you, but I confess, to have him grant you permission to remain on the island with his closest associates is almost more than I had dared hope for."

"I agree. But I prayed exceedingly hard. And in the end, his permission sounded a little more like a command."

Brecc's smile widened. "Just so. And I shall be forever grateful for it." And then, almost before Aisley knew what he was about, his lips were on hers, his kisses sending her fears and loneliness fleeing.

"Aisley?" he murmured sometime later.

"Hm?" She pulled back slightly to discover his emotion-filled dark eyes gazing at her as though she were the most precious thing he had ever seen.

"I must go to gather the men," he said, regret evident in his low voice. "But before I leave, I wish you to know that I have fallen in love with you." He ran his fingers through her hair, leaving a tingling trail behind them. "I do not know when I shall be free to offer you more than my heart, but with the king's decision to call up the fyrds, I pray it will be soon."

Joy threatened to overcome her. "Since you are the one whom I always dream of at night and ache to be beside each day, I have begun to believe that I am in love with you also."

A new warmth filled his eyes. He lowered his head for another brief kiss before whispering in her ear. "I like that notion very much, but I shall enjoy helping you discover its certainty."

👑

The thegns sat around the fire in the cottage, awaiting the arrival of their king. Tension hummed in the air. Over the last couple of months, they had gathered often in the evening to exchange stories and receive instructions, but rarely had a meeting been called at midday, and never had it come so unexpectedly.

From his position beside the king's empty chair, Brecc could see Aisley and the queen conversing quietly in the far corner of the room. The queen smiled at something Aisley said, and Brecc marveled at the confidence Aisley had gained since the Lord of Misrule had forced her to approach the head table at the Twelfth Night banquet. In truth, Brecc was changed too. He had most certainly developed sincere feelings for Aisley while they had been in Chippenham, but those sentiments paled in comparison to what he felt now.

The door to the small chamber opened, and the king emerged. Everyone in the room rose and watched as the monarch crossed the room to take his position within the circle. After he'd taken his seat, he indicated that they all do the same.

"You are my most trusted men," the king said, taking a moment to survey those around him. "I thank you for your loyalty and steadfastness, particularly during this trying time. Your efforts over the last weeks have been significant. The information you have gathered from watching the Vikings' movements has been invaluable. Your raids and ambushes have not only frustrated our enemy but have also lowered their morale whilst raising the Saxon people's determination to overcome their oppressors. Because of your actions, the Saxons know it can be done. And I believe the time has come to involve them."

An excited murmur passed through the circle, and King Alfred raised his hand for quiet. Instantly, the whispers stopped.

"First, allow me to share with you some of the things I have learned during our sojourn at Athelney. More important than matching the Vikings in physical might is the need for us to match them in cunning. The chieftains are as crafty as serpents, but we can gain an advantage by combining shrewdness with nobility. The pagan invaders cannot conquer a country led by true noblemen, for if our motives and actions are guided by Christian principles, we cannot fail.

"My people have spent far too long living under the threat of Viking pillaging, looting, and rape. They are ready for a return to Saxon rule. Support for our cause is steadily growing. The common folk are ready and willing to fight for freedom from their oppressors. Our job is to prove that Saxon leadership is also ready, that we are as good as our word, and that we have God on our side."

He paused, and Brecc braced himself for what was surely to come next. A quick glance at Aisley told him that she and the queen were still fully engaged in their own conversation. He prayed she would be spared from hearing this portion of the king's report.

"Unfortunately," the king continued, his tone steely, "not all thegns demonstrate the fidelity that should be integral to the title. These men must be routed out from amongst us. I have recently learned that Ealdorman Wulfhere has broken his oath of allegiance to the crown and has aligned himself with the Viking chieftain Rangvald."

Shouts of shocked indignation filled the room. Brecc felt Rheged's stunned gaze, but Brecc's eyes were on Aisley. The men's loud and negative reaction to the king's news had interrupted her conversation with the queen. Both women were now looking at them, and he could tell from Aisley's pained expression that she had guessed the cause of the thegns' anger. She lowered her head. The queen said something to her. She nodded, and they both quietly rose and slipped out of the cottage.

Brecc rolled his shoulders, attempting to release the tension there. He wanted to go to her, but for now, his place was here. With the king and his men. Grateful for the queen's thoughtful gesture, he endeavored to focus on the heated discussions going on around him. Wulfhere surely had no notion of the full consequences of his treacherous decision. Not only had he broken with his king, but he had also broken with his fellow thegns. Those who considered him an enemy had just multiplied more than twentyfold.

"Enough." Once again, the king raised his hand, and once again, silence fell. "Wulfhere's time of reckoning will come. He will suffer for what he has done, but if we are wise, we shall gain from it. His underhanded cooperation with Rangvald has served as a reminder that we must be on our guard for traitors in our midst. Especially now, as we move into our final phase to reclaim the kingdom."

The king had every man's attention. The fury that had filled the room only moments before had turned to excitement.

"The time has come to call up the fyrds." A cheer sounded, and the king smiled. Imperviousness to the men's enthusiasm was all but impossible "That seemingly simple act may not be quite so easy as you imagine. For generations, the responsibility of gathering the fyrds has fallen to the local ealdormen. Wulfhere's perfidy has illuminated the need to assess the faithfulness of each ealdorman before they receive the order. And in cases where trust is lost, the fyrds shall be gathered by another means. We shall be mobilizing an army beneath the Vikings' noses, but no word of it must reach them. It is imperative that Guthrum and his chieftains know nothing of our plans until we are fully ready to face them."

"How do you wish this done, Sire?" Odda voiced the question every man was undoubtedly asking himself.

"I wish you to go out in small groups throughout Wessex, much as you have already been doing. But rather than focusing your efforts on crippling the Vikings, I would have you assess the mind-set of the local leadership. If there is any question of loyalty, discover someone in each community who can be trusted to pass along the king's command. Do not ignore those of lower station in life. They are often those who are most true to the king. Visit the folkmoots. That is where local business is conducted and where messages may be passed." He leaned forward in his chair. "Once our secret network of communication is established, our preparation for battle will truly begin."

"When do we leave?" Bertwin asked.

"Two days hence," the king said. "That will give those who recently returned from raids time to recover and will enable us to acquire any necessary provisions." He drummed his fingers on the arm of his chair as though pondering something. "Those of you assigned to Wiltshire must needs be especially circumspect in your inquiries. Rheged, I wish you to take two men to Trowbridge. Locate Nyle, the fishmonger, at the market there. Word is he is trustworthy. If you can confirm that, swear him to secrecy and prepare him for what is to come."

Rheged bowed his head. "As you wish, Sire."

"Brecc, until your leg is sufficiently healed, I wish you to remain on Athelney with two others of your choosing. You shall guard the queen and those others who remain here as well as maintain our supplies and gather the reports as they come in." He turned to look at the group as a whole. "Gentlemen, if we each do our jobs correctly, six weeks hence, my call to arms shall reach every able-bodied man in Wessex, with the Vikings none the wiser."

"What of our raids on Viking encampments, Sire? Do you wish those to continue?" Lufian asked.

"The invaders would likely wonder what had become of us if we halted those completely," the king said. "And I daresay an occasional well-targeted raid would be a good diversion from your fact-finding missions." He rose to his feet, and the men followed. "Do what you must to increase Saxon confidence and to leave the Vikings in a quandary." He strode across the room and into the small chamber.

The door had barely closed behind him before the room erupted with unrestrained exclamations and weighty discussions. Brecc situated his crutch more comfortably beneath his arm. He'd been glad of its assistance in helping him rise when the king had come and gone, and now he was ready to have it assist in his escape.

He'd traveled only three steps when Rheged appeared before him, his expression grave.

"This was the other burden she carried." He shook his head. "I suppose I should not be surprised since the marriage arrangement Wulfhere made for Aisley was so cruel, but this . . . this absolving of all that a king's thegn stands for . . ." He stopped, seemingly realizing that Brecc had no desire to revisit the king's damning revelation about Aisley's brother. "I have not spoken to Aisley since she met with the king. Did he direct his anger . . . ?" He stumblingly changed his approach. "Is she well?"

"Well enough, I believe. The king's initial fury had diminished by the time he spoke with her."

Understanding filled Rheged's face. "Your private conversation beforehand."

"Aye. I am sorry I was unable to tell you more at the time."

"No matter. It was a judicious move, and I am glad I could help facilitate it."

Brecc set his hand on Rheged's shoulder. "You are a good friend, and I am almost sorry that I cannot accompany you to Trowbridge."

Rheged's eyebrow rose. "Almost sorry? I did not think you would take kindly to playing nursemaid to the queen."

"Aisley will also be here. The king all but ordered her to stay on Athelney."

"Is that so?" A hint of humor replaced the worry in Rheged's eyes. "Well then, I shall offer you no pity whatsoever."

With a chuckle, Brecc shifted his crutch and took another step toward the door. "Good day, Rheged. I shall leave you to your planning."

CHAPTER 29

AISLEY PEERED INTO THE DARK corner where the roof met the wall. There had to be a spiderweb there. She was sure she'd seen one the evening before, when her candle had illuminated the spot directly above her pallet far better than this morning's overcast daylight was doing. Hopping off the stool she was using, she dragged it a little closer to the wall and climbed up again. There. From this angle, the gossamer threads were clearly visible. Offering a silent prayer that the spiderweb's resident was gone for the morning, she reached up and swiped at it with her hand. The hairlike threads clung to her fingers. Pleased, she climbed off the stool and held her hand over the stout crock she'd placed on the floor.

As carefully as she could, she scraped the cobwebs into the crock and replaced the lid. Few people would believe that spiderwebs could save a life, but Aisley knew full well how effective they were with healing wounds. The more she could collect, the more she would have at her disposal when the king's men needed them. She carried the crock to the small shelf Brecc had built for her behind the partition. The pouches of dried herbs that she'd brought from Trowbridge lay in a tidy row beside a pot of honey and three strips of rolled-up linen. She frowned. It was not nearly enough for what was undoubtedly ahead. The next time one of the men went to market, she would request more honey, garlic, and linen.

Setting down the crock of spiderwebs, she picked up her cloak and set it around her shoulders. It had been over four weeks since she'd arrived at Athelney, and despite the frequent coming and going of the thegns, her life had fallen into a comfortable pattern. On most days, she divided her time between caring for any who had made their way back to the island with an injury, conversing with the queen, assisting with a few of the household chores, and spending time with Brecc.

She glanced at the position of the sun coming in through the shutters and smiled. It was coming on noon, and that meant Bertwin would be relieving Brecc from his guard duty at the shoreline. A quick look over her shoulder told her that the door to the small chamber remained closed. The queen's newest needlework project had been consuming a great deal of the lady's time. Aisley did not mind. She had much to keep her busy, and although she had come to admire the monarch's wife very much and enjoyed their time together, their discussions—no matter how interesting—could not compare with the joy she experienced when she was with Brecc.

Slipping out of the cottage, she closed the door behind her and hastened across the grass toward the portion of the shore where the thegns docked the punts. She passed the small grove of trees that blocked the view of the dock from the cottage and caught sight of two men—one dark and one fair—standing at the shoreline. Bertwin had reached Brecc before her.

She slowed her steps, giving the men time to pass along whatever information needed to be shared and allowing herself the luxury of admiring Brecc's tall, handsome figure. It had taken several days for his nasty cut to fully lose its angry appearance and at least a week more before it had not pained him at night, but he had set aside his crutch two weeks ago, and was now walking with only a slight limp. To her immense gratitude, his leg looked to be on the path to a full recovery.

As though he sensed her approach, Brecc turned his head and greeted her with a warm smile. "Good day, Aisley."

"Good day," she replied.

Bertwin gave her a friendly nod. They had spoken not long ago in the cottage.

"I was just telling Bertwin here that if you are willing, I should like to take you out on one of the punts."

Aisley blinked. She had not left the island since the day she'd set foot on it. "May I, really?"

"Most certainly."

With the thegns' loathing of Wulfhere permanently fixed, Aisley had lost her fear of being discovered by her brother. She knew that he would not survive an attempt to reach her. Her dread of re-encountering Rangvald, however, had been more difficult to shake. There was something about the shrewd Viking that unsettled her still.

"Will we see anyone else?"

"Unless one of the groups arrives back unexpectedly, it is highly unlikely."

It would be rather wonderful to see something more of this area than the same view of the island she had every day. And the opportunity for a boat ride with Brecc was too good to ignore.

"If no one else is in need of the punt, I should very much enjoy going with you."

Brecc smiled and offered her his hand. "Come. Allow me to assist you into the boat."

Descending the bank with her hand in Brecc's proved infinitely easier than climbing up it in an excessively weakened state had been, and in no time at all, she was seated on the wooden seat inside the long, narrow craft. Brecc took his position on the platform at the end of the boat, set the pole in the water, and pushed. Smoothly and silently, they glided away from the island.

Clouds hung low over Burrow Mump, but to the south, sunshine and a patch of blue brightened the sky. Brown bracken and broken reed heads lined the shore, but the vegetation's annual transformation from the muted colors of winter to the verdant green of spring was well on its way.

"Look, Brecc," Aisley cried, pointing to a spot beneath a leafy birch tree. "Crocuses."

"Do you need to gather some?" His arms were poised on the pole, ready to adjust their direction if necessary.

"Not this time, but I am glad to know where to find them."

"What would you use crocus for?" he asked, pushing the punt forward again.

"It can be used for stomach ailments and smarting of the eyes."

He laughed.

"Why would you laugh at such a thing?" she asked.

"I am not laughing at the crocus's healing properties," he said. "I am simply in awe of your knowledge. I daresay I could ask you about any plant we pass and you would have an answer for me."

She felt her cheeks redden. "Not *every* plant. And I wish I knew a great deal more about other things." She pointed to an enormous gray bird with a black head and long, thin legs wading through the water ahead of them. "I do not know what that is called. Do you?"

"That is a common crane."

"There, you see? Common to you and many others, I wager. But I was ignorant of its name until this very moment."

He smiled. "I am glad we can learn from each other. If I see any of the only half dozen other birds I can recognize, I shall let you know."

It was Aisley's turn to laugh. She knew full well that Brecc's knowledge of birds was greater than that. The men used bird calls to message each other on a regular basis.

"Where exactly are you taking me?" she asked.

"There." He pointed to a small wooden structure sitting atop a gentle rise on the other side of the water.

Aisley studied it curiously. "What is it?"

"A church." Brecc guided the punt to the bank not far from a trail that appeared to meander up the rise toward the building.

"Truly?" There were no dwellings anywhere in sight. Indeed, as far as Aisley could tell, there were no people anywhere near this place beyond herself and Brecc.

"Aye." Favoring his uninjured leg, he jumped onto the land and tied the rope attached to the punt's end to a nearby sapling. "It has been all but abandoned by the local people, which has served the king's purposes very well."

Aisley gasped. "This is where the king comes to offer his prayers?"

"It is. I have brought him here more times than I can count. He feels a special connection to this humble place, and I believe he has been gifted heavenly direction during his many hours of worship." He reached for her hand and guided her out of the boat. "Would you like to see it for yourself?"

"Very much."

They walked the sheep trail hand in hand, and it was not long before they reached the isolated church. Brecc pushed open the door. It creaked. Aisley stepped inside and paused, waiting for her eyes to adjust to the muted light before moving any farther. Eight tidy rows of pews filled the modest structure, four on each side of a narrow aisle. At the front of the building, a simple wooden cross hung above a wooden lectern and a stone christening font.

Taking her hand again, Brecc led Aisley to the nearest pew, and they slipped onto the bench. For some time, neither of them spoke. A sense of peace—such as Aisley rarely felt in the midst of everyday life—filled her.

"Would you like to offer a prayer before we leave?" Brecc whispered.

She nodded, and they both slid to their knees between the pews. Aisley closed her eyes. Her mother had taught her a few prayers, but in this church, she felt that she must speak her own. "Father God," she whispered. "I am thankful." It was as far as she could go. A wave of gratitude swept over her, bringing with it the sting of tears. She had been granted her life, her freedom, a place on Athelney, and Brecc. What more could she possibly ask of God?

"Amen."

Upon hearing Brecc's softly spoken word, Aisley opened her eyes. His head was bowed still, and as she watched, he spoke again.

"Father God, I, too, wish to express my gratitude for all things. And as King Alfred leads the Saxon people into battle, I would ask that Thou wouldst bless the noble and good men fighting for their homes, families, and livelihoods."

"Amen," she whispered.

He looked up and met her tear-filled eyes. "It will be well, Aisley. I truly believe it."

She nodded, and together they rose to their feet and slowly made their way out of the church. Standing on the flagstone step outside, Aisley watched Brecc lower the latch on the church door. Then he moved closer. Wrapping his arms around her, he lowered his head and kissed her tenderly.

"I love the goodness of your heart," he said.

"As I love the nobility of yours," she responded. "I am thankful that you brought me here. I now understand more fully why King Alfred visits this sacred place so often."

"Aye," Brecc said, reaching for her hand once more. "It is reassuring to know that our king feels it necessary to commune with God, and methinks it likely that he feels what we experienced today on a far more regular basis."

"King Alfred wishes God to go with him when he leads you to battle against Guthrum."

"I do not believe there is a thegn on the island who does not desire that," Brecc said, leading her back toward the punt. "But I would like to think that God pays special attention when a monarch humbly petitions Him for such a blessing."

Aisley tightened her grip on Brecc's hand. Sometime soon, he would be tossed into the midst of that mighty battle. And no matter how valiant the warriors or how noble the cause, there would be some who did not survive. Despite the peace she had so recently experienced, her fears for Brecc's safety resurfaced.

"Would that no one had to go to battle at all," she said.

They had reached the boat. Without a word, Brecc pulled her into his arms and held her close. With her head on his chest, she watched a common crane take to the air. It sailed above them, its strong wings flapping against the slight breeze.

"I need you with me to teach me more about birds," she said brokenly.

"And I need you with me for more reasons than I could possibly name." He ran his hand down her hair, soothing her troubled heart with his touch. "It will be well, Aisley."

It was an echo of what he had said in the church, but she'd needed to hear it again.

"I shall try to be brave."

"Of that I have no doubt." He pressed a kiss to her forehead. "We shall be brave together."

She looked up at him. "My father used to say exactly that."

He smiled. "So you told me."

"And you remembered?"

"Aye," he said, releasing his hold upon her so that he might guide her onto the punt. "And I always will."

Brecc leaned over the table and studied the scrap of parchment. The appearance of the roughly drawn map of Wessex he'd fashioned six weeks ago had changed significantly. No longer was there clear space with dots marking the location of towns of significant population. Now the entire map was covered with crosses—almost the entire map. With no small measure of relief, he placed a cross over the last remaining blank space. Hingston Down. Radolf and his men had returned from Cornwall with just enough time to allow Brecc to make his report to the king within the monarch's prescribed deadline.

Rolling up the parchment, he carried it with him to the door of the small chamber and knocked.

"Enter!" The king's voice reached him through the door.

Brecc opened it and walked in. The king was alone in the room. The queen, her maid, and Aisley were taking a walk while the sun shone.

"Good day, Sire." Brecc bowed. "I have the final report from our men's scouting expeditions."

Setting aside the book of scripture he had been studying, King Alfred gestured Brecc toward the second chair in the room. "Sit. Tell me what you know."

Brecc sat down. "A communication network is in place throughout Wessex," he said. "To the best of our knowledge, the only ealdorman other than Wulfhere who is actively colluding with the Vikings is Gimm."

"Ealdorman Gimm of Dorset." Anger flashed in the king's eyes. "Another who sat at my table in Chippenham and accepted the ring-giver's gift."

"It appears that his integrity is as weak as his singing," Brecc said, recalling Gimm's awful rendition of Caedmon's Hymn at the Twelfth Night banquet. "He and Wulfhere are known to be close associates. It is likely that they chose this path together."

"And they shall suffer for it together." King Alfred rose. Brecc instantly did the same and waited as the king paced the narrow room three times. "Are we sure there are not others?"

"There are three more who have shown signs of weakened resolve, but as far as your men could ascertain, they have not entered into any official agreement with the enemy. In those instances, as you ordered, new contacts have been established in the community."

The king stopped his pacing and faced Brecc. "Then we are ready?"

Brecc's pulse quickened. "We are, Sire."

King Alfred glanced at his book of scripture. His jaw tightened, and he squared his shoulders. "Are all the men returned?"

"All but Odda and those who rode with him." Brecc had not been privy to Odda's assignment, which suggested it was of a clandestine nature.

King Alfred frowned. "No matter. If needs must, we have sufficient thegns to spread the message without them." He paused. "I would have you organize those already here into pairs. On the morrow, they are to travel to every established contact to deliver the royal command."

Brecc tensed. If he was to deliver this vital edict to the thegns, every word must needs be correct.

The king took one more turn around the small space and then spoke with a voice that rang with authority. "King Alfred of Wessex commands all fyrds to prepare for battle against the Viking invaders. The Saxon army is to gather at Egbert's Stone on the southern border of Wiltshire, east of Selwood Forest on Whitsunday."

Mentally, Brecc repeated the order, committing it to memory. Whitsunday. He took a moment to consider the date. It was three weeks hence. That would give the word time to spread and the men time to sharpen their blades, fashion spears, and travel to the appointed spot. But Brecc guessed that the king had chosen this particular date for another reason entirely. On Whitsunday, Christians commemorated the descent of the Holy Spirit onto Christ's disciples. For all who believed, it was a day of empowerment.

"That is all."

The king's curt reminder pulled Brecc from his thoughts. He bowed. "It shall be done, Sire. I will speak to the men directly."

Crossing to the door, he pulled it open. On the other side of the larger room, the outer door also opened, and Odda walked in. He took a quick look around the vacant space before marching purposefully toward the small chamber.

"It appears that Odda has returned and is anxious to speak with you," Brecc said.

"Have him enter." The king had yet to resume his seat. "And you'd best stay to hear what he has to report."

Stepping aside so that his associate could enter the chamber, Brecc noted the weariness on Odda's face and the mud on his hose and the lower portion of his cloak. He had been riding hard and long.

"Good day, Sire." Odda entered and bowed.

"Odda." The king acknowledged him with a slight inclination of his head. "I am glad to see you returned safely. A report of your doings, if you please."

"As you commanded, we traveled to Trowbridge in search of Wulfhere."

Brecc flinched. He had made no secret of his attachment to Aisley, but he'd presumed he would be told when the king chose to make Wulfhere accountable for his actions.

"And you found him."

"We did, Sire. With a Viking blade in his back."

This time, Brecc did nothing to conceal his shock. "A Viking blade?"

"Aye. According to the stablehand at the house, the ealdorman was found on the side of the road not more than three hours before we arrived, his horse and purse both gone."

"Did anyone know of a reason the Vikings would have turned on their erstwhile ally?" the king asked.

"The stablehand—Taber was his name—said the Viking went to the house to speak with Wulfhere repeatedly over the last few weeks, and each time he left, he did so in a fouler mood than before."

King Alfred gave Brecc a silent, knowing look. No one else on the island knew the full reason for Aisley's desperate flight from home, so Brecc remained silent, too, willing to follow the king's lead.

"They obviously had a falling-out," the king said. "The cause is immaterial. Rangvald did us a great service. Not only did he rid our land of an unscrupulous traitor, but he also left behind a powerful message for all those who might contemplate following in Wulfhere's footsteps. Let us pray that others quickly learn that a Viking chieftain's oath—no matter which of their pagan gods they choose to entreat—is worthless."

It was a lesson King Alfred himself had been forced to learn when the horde had attacked Chippenham.

"What of Wulfhere's mother and sister?" Brecc asked.

"They were yet at the house," Odda said. "We told them there was no longer a place for them in Wessex, but if they wished to live elsewhere, we would convey them to the nearest ship." He glanced at his muddy clothing. "We are just come from Portsea, where both women boarded a craft bound for Normandy."

A portion of the tension in Brecc's chest released. Aisley had been deeply hurt by her mother and sister, but she would not wish them killed. That the king had orchestrated this compromise—a dire punishment without the loss of life—was a credit to him.

"You have done well, Odda," the king said. "I thank you for your efforts on behalf of the crown."

Odda bowed. "Glad to be of service, Sire. And now, if you would excuse me, I shall attempt to rid myself of half of Hampshire's mud."

He left the room, and the king turned his attention to Brecc once more.

"And so, punishment has been administered—and the Vikings took charge of the worst of it." He sighed. "After you have given the men my charge, I would have you be the one to tell Aisley of her family members' fate."

"As you wish, Sire."

"It is, indeed," the king said, his expression softening slightly. "And I rather think it is also as Aisley would wish."

CHAPTER 30

AISLEY TIED A PIECE OF string to the end of her long plait and tossed it over her shoulder. She did not know the exact hour, but Whitsunday had just dawned, and on the other side of the partition, low voices and rustled movement told her the thegns were preparing for departure. Opening her satchel, she checked the contents one more time. Bandages, honey, pouches of her most effective herbs, a couple of small wooden bowls, a knife, needle and thread, the crock of spiderwebs, and her blanket. She was as prepared as she could be. Placing her cloak over her shoulders, she slid the satchel strap over her head, and with a last look around her small sleeping area, she slipped into the cottage's main room.

Almost all the thegns were gone. The last few were dragging their pallets into the corner of the room. There was no sign of Brecc. It had been too difficult to say farewell last night, so they'd not done so. Brecc had suggested that she come to the dock to see them off instead. She'd agreed. Not because she planned to see them off but because she planned to go with them.

Hastening out of the cottage, she followed the men heading toward the punts. It would take more than one crossing for each of the three crafts to transport everyone across the marsh. The horses would need to be guided across also. Not to mention the additional space needed to carry the weapons. For the last two days, the island had been filled with the sound of sharpening blades, and every man carried at least three spears with him.

"Push off, Radolf!" That was Bertwin, and it sounded like the transportation of men, horses, and weapons had begun.

Aisley reached the bank in time to see the punt carrying half a dozen thegns and drawing almost as many mounts behind it float away. The second punt was already loaded with men. Lufian was drawing four horses down the bank on long lead ropes. One of the horses slipped and pulled back anxiously. Another thegn reached for half the ropes and handed them off to Odda, who was seated at the rear of the punt.

"That's it!" Bertwin called. Immediately, the boat moved away, and with a splash, the horses entered the water behind it.

Aisley scoured the shoreline. There was no sign of the king. She guessed he'd been in the first punt. It was probably for the best. She intended to do all in her power to persuade Brecc to let her join the company, but if the king had denied her permission, she would have been forced to comply.

She followed the bank past a small grove of trees. A dozen uneasy horses stood awaiting the return of the first punt. Offering the thegn holding their ropes a brief greeting, Aisley kept walking, still searching for Brecc. And then she spotted him. He and Rheged were standing side by side, watching the punts float around the bend. Her steps slowed, and as the first rays of morning light touched the water, she took a moment to marvel at how deeply she had come to care for these men and their cause.

As though he sensed her presence, Brecc turned. His smile was instant, but then his gaze dropped to her clothing, and a worried frown appeared across his brow. She crossed the short distance between them and put her arms around him. He responded instantly, drawing her closer.

"I am happy to see you," he said, "but why are you wearing those clothes?"

"Because for the next little while, I am reverting to the role of Avi, a peasant boy."

His frown intensified. "Why?"

"Because I am coming with you."

He released her and took a step back. "Absolutely not."

She had rehearsed her argument multiple times during the night. It had been significantly easier to do without having to look into Brecc's horror-filled eyes. "You do not understand—"

"No," Brecc interrupted her. "*You* do not understand. I would not wish any woman to witness the atrocities of a battlefield. Ever. But of all kinds of combat, a war waged against the Vikings is the worst. Their cruelty and ferocity knows no end. The sights and sounds of such an encounter can haunt those who experience it for a lifetime."

"I am grateful for your desire to protect me," she said. "And you are correct, I have no place on the battlefield. But that was never my intention. I simply wish to travel with the company so that I may be close enough to care for the wounded." She pressed her hand to her satchel. "I have been collecting supplies. I could remain at the closest village or in a nearby woodland. All it would take would be a few strong men willing to carry the injured to me." She clasped her hands. "Please, Brecc. I wish to have King Alfred restored to his throne as badly as every thegn on this island. And I know it can be done only through a great battle, but I weep at the thought of how many will be left widowed and fatherless when it is all behind us. If I can help but one man return to his home who would not have done so otherwise, it is worth my joining you."

"She does have a point," Rheged said.

Aisley started. She had all but forgotten Rheged's presence, but now she looked to him for support. "It could be done, could it not?"

He glanced at Brecc's stony face, and his assurance dimmed. "It is possible. In a loosely possible way."

"Of course it could!" Aisley cried. In desperation, she took Brecc's hand and gripped it tightly. "I could not live with myself if you or Rheged or . . . or the king himself were to die from a wound that I could have treated."

"In truth," Rheged said. "I'd rather not have that happen also."

"Would you refrain from opening your mouth again," Brecc growled.

"I could. And I will. As soon as you are willing to look past your overarching fear for Aisley's safety and recognize the immense gift she is offering to every Saxon willing to fight for the king."

Brecc offered him an incredulous look, but Rheged responded with a stubborn glare, and he did not look away until Brecc released a heartfelt groan and pulled Aisley back into his arms. "You must give me your word that you will stay away from the battlefield. Nothing—not even word that I am injured—is to take you there."

"Brecc, I cannot—"

He placed his finger over her lips. "Not even that, Aisley. As much as you cannot countenance the unnecessary death of wounded men on your conscience, I cannot countenance your sweet goodness forever tainted by witnessing man's inhumanity to man on mine."

Swallowing the lump in her throat, she nodded. "I give you my word. But this may be the hardest thing I have ever done—or not done."

He offered her a grim smile. "Accepting the terrifying risk of taking you with us may also be mine."

She raised her hand to touch his cheek, running her finger gently across the scar that spoke of a previous hard-fought battle. There was no question, he knew of what he spoke. "Forgive me for adding to your burdens."

He turned his head slightly to kiss the palm of her hand. "You will never be a burden. Rheged is correct; you are a gift."

"Did you hear that?" Rheged's face shone with mock astonishment. "He admitted that I am correct." Brecc raised his eyes heavenward, but Rheged was undeterred. "I must take full advantage of this moment—for I know a fleeting moment is all he will offer me. So, whilst I am on this lofty pedestal, I should like to advise you both that although those in our company will know Aisley, those we shall meet along the way will not. That means there is to be none of that kissing when she is your young page, Avi."

Brecc muttered something under his breath that sounded suspiciously like, *I should dunk his head in the swamp*, and Aisley bit back a smile. At some point during their long ride to Egbert's Stone, she would thank Rheged for his assistance this morning, but for now, she would simply follow him to the returning boats.

CHAPTER 31

KING ALFRED AND HIS THEGNS sat around the campfire. All around them, the hillside was dotted with other fires, each surrounded by men who had come to join the Saxon army. Every one of the counties was represented, most by many hundreds of men. Brecc felt a surge of gratitude for their loyalty.

The journey from Athelney had been long, but the closer they'd come to Egbert's Stone, the busier the roads had become. Men of every walk of life had answered the monarch's call, and when they'd recognized him, they'd cheered as though they'd come to attend a carnival rather than fight to the death. But there was no question that they knew it now. As darkness had descended and the campfires had been lit, a somber camaraderie had fallen upon the gathering of almost five thousand. Voices carried on the light breeze. They were unusually subdued.

At this campfire, King Alfred was listening to reports from the thegns who had wandered the hillside, discovering the origin of each fyrd, assessing the weaponry they'd brought with them, determining the caliber of the local leadership.

"Nyle, the fishmonger, is here," Rheged said. He was seated to the right of Brecc, with Aisley in between them. "The fyrd from Wiltshire is large and strong."

Under the cover of darkness, Brecc reached for Aisley's hand. It was cold, but the moment he touched it, her fingers curled around his. She had to be exhausted, but she'd not offered a single complaint since she'd stepped onto the punt early this morning. She'd ridden beside him the entire journey, keeping her hood up and her head lowered whenever they'd encountered others on the road. Her hood had remained up since they'd arrived at camp. There were too many men wandering the area, and as Rheged had just reported, many of them were from Wiltshire.

Brecc squeezed her hand gently, knowing how pleased she would be by Rheged's report.

"How many of them are seasoned warriors?" the king asked.

"Not so many as we would like, to be sure," Rheged replied, "but what they lack in experience, they make up for in passion. The young men of Wiltshire are here to win back their king's crown."

The king's smile was fleeting. "We shall need that kind of determination if we are to win. I shall make a point to visit the men of the Wiltshire fyrd before we go to battle." He turned to Bertwin. "What of the Dorset fyrd?"

Bertwin began to reply, and Brecc felt Aisley shift a little nearer.

"Do we know where the battle will take place yet?" she whispered.

"Not to my knowledge." Brecc kept his voice low so as not to interrupt the conversation going on on the other side of the campfire. "By now, our element of surprise is over. It is impossible for this number of men to gather from every corner of Wessex without drawing the attention of Guthrum's spies. On the morrow, we will likely hear that the Vikings are on the move. The king plans to continue north toward Guthrum's stronghold in Chippenham, but if Guthrum comes to meet him, the battle could occur anywhere along our route."

She shivered, and Brecc caught himself just before he raised his arm to draw her closer. For the duration, she was his page. And now that so many others had joined them, for her safety's sake, he'd best remember it.

"After all this time, the battle for Wessex's future is truly upon us," she said.

"Aye." He listened. Beyond the crackle of fires and murmur of low voices, the night was still. "As hard as it is to picture when all is so calm, if the Vikings have mobilized, the confrontation is merely a day away."

"I am glad I am here with you for these last few peaceful hours."

He tightened his grip on her hand again. She did not belong here. Nor was she safe. And yet, he could not deny that he felt the same.

The king's scouts galloped toward them. At the head of the company, King Alfred raised his arm. Those on horseback at the front stopped, and the steady forward progression of thousands of marching warriors came to an unexpected halt. Aisley glanced at Brecc. He was watching the scouts with fierce intensity. One of them was gesturing to the ruined fortress sitting atop the hill ahead. The king responded by signaling for Brecc, Rheged, and Odda to join him.

"Wait here," Brecc said, touching his heels to his mount. "This should not take long."

Aisley waited. Those around her waited. And the tension mounted. The king, his men, and the scouts spoke together for a short time, and then the scouts wheeled their horses around and started back the way they had come. Brecc resumed his place beside her, and the king raised his arm again. They were on the move once more.

"What was it?" Aisley asked.

"Guthrum," Brecc answered. "When he heard the king was marching at the head of an army, he rallied his men and set off from Chippenham. They've made their base at Bratton Camp."

"Is that the name of the ancient fortress on the hill?"

"Aye." Brecc studied the distant structure. "It's a strategic position. You see how it sits on the northern edge of a long, flat ridgeline. On three sides, the slopes are too steep for us to mount an attack. That leaves us with only the southern side. Guthrum can consolidate his men in one area, knowing that we can breach their defenses only from that direction."

Aisley's stomach twisted. "What is to be done?"

"We meet them there," Brecc said. "Guthrum's scouts will have told him of our approach, so he is likely already setting up his shield wall."

Panic clawed at Aisley's throat. How could Brecc be so calm? The Vikings were here. They were waiting to attack. "I . . . I do not understand. If they are already in position, how do we—"

"The men will know what to do. Each warrior, regardless of his prior battle experience, has been told what is expected of him." He looked at her, a flicker of unease in his eyes. "As have you."

Aisley had not encountered Vikings since some of them stopped the merchants she was traveling with on route to Athelney. That interaction had been distressing, but the thought of witnessing thousands of bloodthirsty warriors filled her with abject terror. She had no desire to be anywhere near them. "Where would you have me wait?"

He pointed to a wooded area on the west side of the hill. "The king wishes us to leave our mounts there. We will approach the camp in formation from the south side."

At which point, the Vikings in all their ferocity would pour down upon them. On the reins, Aisley's fingers trembled. She could not think on it. It was too awful.

Under two furlongs later, they reached the woodland. The trees stretched out as far as the eye could see. Patches of grass showed between some of the branches, and the ground was littered with twigs, pine needles, and new growth. Overhead, birds sang, blissfully unaware of what was soon to come. At a signal from the king, the thegns dismounted.

"Secure your horses," he called. "As soon as the fyrds are assembled, we lead them into battle."

Brecc led his mount between two large ash trees. Without a word, Aisley followed, her horse in tow. All around them, others were making for the small grassy patches inside the woodland. A boulder lay ahead, partially covered by the long, tangled branches of a bramble bush beside it. Brecc veered right and entered the clearing surrounded by trees beyond. He tied his horse's straps around a low-lying tree limb and then reached for Aisley's horse's reins.

"If you remain in this vicinity, the boulder will lead me back to you. It will also serve as a marker for the wounded seeking your aid." He gathered the spears he'd strapped to his horse.

"Very well." Silently praying for whatever measure of courage she lacked, Aisley slid her satchel off her shoulder and set it beside the boulder. She dreaded staying behind in the woodland alone, but she knew it was what she must do if she truly wished to assist King Alfred and his men. "I shall be ready when the injured come." She swallowed. "And I shall remain here until you return."

He turned then and met her eyes. The air between them stilled, and the background noise of men and horses and weaponry faded to nothingness. Slowly, Brecc set his spears against a tree trunk. Then in four long steps, he crossed the distance that separated them and pulled her into his arms. "I will come for you." Emotion shone in his dark eyes. "I give you my word."

She leaned into him, her eyes not leaving his. "I love you," she said.

His groan was so soft she barely heard it before he was kissing her—desperately, fervently, deeply—unleashing a maelstrom of shared hopes, fears, and love that sent her mind spinning. She clung to him, drawing from him a strength she had not known she needed, and giving whatever comfort she could offer in return.

A horn sounded, and he drew back. "I must go."

With trembling limbs, Aisley stepped out of his arms. "My prayers go with you."

He reached for his spears. "As mine are with you." And then he was gone, racing between the trees toward the waiting men.

The Vikings' chilling call to battle grew louder as the Saxon shield wall advanced up the hill. Like an ominous heartbeat, hundreds of spears beat out a steady rhythm against the Vikings' wooden shields. Their screaming taunts and jeers rent the air, urging the men of Wessex to return to their hovels, to walk away from their incompetent king, and to drop their weapons rather than be slaughtered.

With their shoulders pressed together so tightly that they moved as one, the Saxons pressed on. Flexing his fingers, Brecc reset his grip on the handle of his shield and kept his eyes on the line of Viking warriors ahead. Sunlight glistened off their helmets and shield bosses. And behind them were more rows of warriors waiting to take their place. It was a formidable sight. But no more so than the enormous wave of Saxons now advancing upon them.

"Hold the wall, men!" The king's voice rose above the Norse chants. "The invaders have yet to discover our greatest strength. They cannot defeat us if we remain united."

They were within forty paces of each other now, and Brecc could hear the clank of the Norsemen's chain mail over the thud of marching feet.

"The time is right, Sire." Rheged's muttered words were likely not meant to be overheard, but Brecc acknowledged them with the tightening of his jaw.

An instant later, the king's voice rang out again. "Fire."

From three rows back, men launched their spears over the heads of their comrades. The Vikings released a similar volley. In a trice, the sky was darkened. Hundreds of spears blocked the sun. Brecc glanced upward. It was impossible to make out the trajectory of any one spear, but even if it were flying directly toward him, there was nothing he could do to protect himself. He was pinned so tightly between Rheged and Odda that there was no room to sidestep. And not even his shield could protect him from a barb coming at him from that height.

Suddenly, the Viking spears were incoming. A scream from Brecc's right confirmed a hit. With a thud, a spear entered the ground two paces before him, but they kept advancing. More screams. The clang of metal and the judder of movement in the line. Brecc kept his eyes forward, praying that the holes in the shield wall were being filled by those standing immediately behind them.

Another spear entered his peripheral vision. It was close. Too close. Brecc braced himself. The impact reverberated through his arms, but he felt no pain. Odda let out a frustrated cry. Brecc glanced to his right. A spear had pierced the man's shield. A six-foot-long shaft was projecting from the front, rendering the shield completely unwieldy and compromising the wall. There was nothing Odda could do. Releasing his hold on the shield, it fell to the ground, and he stepped back. Instantly, the man marching behind him moved forward, locked arms with Brecc, and set his shield over the hole Odda's damaged one had created.

Shifting his shoulder into position against his new companion's, Brecc hazarded a glance at the man's profile. He did not know him. Odda would take a spot in one of the lower ranks and would be an asset with his ax. For his part, Brecc could only hope that Odda's replacement in the shield wall was equally dependable.

The Viking shield wall was perilously close now. Someone released a blood-curdling shout, and while yelling pagan invocations to Odin, the Norsemen surged forward.

"For Wessex and our God," King Alfred shouted. "For our homes and families. Hold the line!"

And then with a horrific cracking of wood, the shield walls met. Linked as one, the Saxons pushed. Behind them, men holding longer spears drove them through the tiny gaps between the front line, aiming for arms, legs, necks, and shoulders. Viking ax blades flashed, slashing at heads. Cries of agony filled the air. The shield wall quaked but held. Quaked again.

Braced against his shield, Brecc continued to push. Immediately before him, a Viking warrior snarled with frustration, raising his ax even as he attempted to hold fast to his own shield. Brecc shifted his head a fraction to the right, praying the man behind him was alert to the danger. He was. A Saxon spear entered the newly formed gap with sufficient momentum to pierce the Viking's arm. He howled with rage, dropping the ax as he struggled to pull out the barbed head. He fell to his knees. Instantly, an ax sailed into the air over Brecc's shoulder, aimed at the Viking who was to take the fallen man's place. The ensuing scream manifested that it had hit its mark.

The Saxon line inched forward again. All around them, fallen men and their blood littered the ground.

"Stay true, men of Wessex!" The king's rallying call came again.

With a grunt of pain, Rheged jerked left.

"Rheged?" Brecc cried.

"My arm." He staggered, struggling to hold his ground. "For the good of the shield wall, I must retreat."

The next moment, the pressure of Rheged's shoulder against Brecc's eased. And then he was gone, and a fresh warrior took his place.

👑

The birdsong had ceased hours ago. The only noises in the woodland now were the rustle of the breeze through the trees, the nervous nickers and agitated shuffling of the horses, and the sounds of war.

At first, the distant clanging of weapons and screams of agony had reduced Aisley to tears. No attempt at covering her ears had helped. Eventually, she'd had no tears left to spill, and she'd been left feeling empty and horribly alone. Too anxious to sleep and too nauseated to eat, she'd wandered the woodland, talking to the horses.

Many of them she recognized from her time at Athelney. With each of those, she'd spent a little extra time, rubbing their noses and talking to them of their peaceful enclosure on the island. It had not been long, however, before she had run out of horses to visit. She glanced at the sky.

The afternoon was wearing on. How much longer would this harrowing battle—this agonizing day—go on?

She passed a young oak tree and spotted Rheged's horse.

"Well now, my friend," she said, running her hand down Bracken's neck. "I am happy to see you." The mare nuzzled Aisley's arm even as more cries of anguish reached them from the hillside. Aisley lay her cheek on the horse's neck and closed her raw eyes. "I was a fool for coming, Bracken. I sincerely thought that I was strong enough for this, that I could truly help. But instead, I find myself scarcely able to think above the sounds of suffering all around me."

Bracken nudged her arm again. Aisley raised her head and managed a weak smile. "I am to wait. Is that what you are telling me?" She sighed. "Other than prayer, I believe that is the only option left to me." She ran her hand down the mare's long neck once more. "I should return to the boulder and my bandages. There is little enough that I can do to prepare my heart for what may come, but I can at least have my supplies ready."

CHAPTER 32

BRECC HAD LONG LOST COUNT of the number of men who had fallen along the Saxon shield wall. He only knew that miraculously, their wall had remained firm and that the Vikings' endurance was waning.

The battle had become a test of resolution, and the men of Wessex had more to fight for than the invaders. This was their homeland.

"We have them, men!" King Alfred must have also sensed the change of mood along the enemy's line. "They cannot withstand us!"

With renewed determination, the Saxons pushed harder. A few cracks in the Viking line appeared.

"Now!" the king roared, and with a mighty surge, the Saxons broke through the faltering barrier.

The Vikings scattered, some falling to the ground, others running for cover as the enormous wave of Saxon warriors that had held their positions behind the shield wall burst forth. Wielding axes and swords, each man's fury over what the Vikings had stolen from them was unleashed. The clash of metal stung Brecc's ears; the shouts and screams were chilling.

Drawing his sword, Brecc assessed the immediate vicinity for signs of pending danger. Not far away, a small cluster of men were engaged in a battle of their own. The Saxons outnumbered the Vikings and appeared to have the upper hand. There was a flash of movement behind Brecc. He pivoted, raising his weapon just as the Viking thrust his sword at Brecc's chest. Propelling his arm upward, Brecc deflected the strike. He stepped back, circling slowly, his eyes not leaving his attacker. The Viking slashed. Brecc parried, catching his enemy's blade with his own. Caught off guard, the Viking loosened his grip. It was the opening Brecc needed. Before his opponent could recover, Brecc lunged forward. His blade pierced the Viking's chest.

"They're fleein'!" A young Saxon warrior raced up the hill toward him. "You see, sire! We routed 'em!"

Brecc turned. It did, indeed, seem that the Vikings who had not fallen had determined their cause was lost. Some were running, others were limping, but each one was leaving the hillside. The Saxons stood among the carnage, their expressions ranging from stunned to sickened to victorious. A cheer sounded. It was echoed by another, and Brecc's stomach sank. As much as he loathed what must be done, he knew there was no other way if they were to prevent history from repeating itself. He scanned the hillside, searching for the king as yet another cheer issued forth.

"Enough!" The king's roar was unmistakable. He stepped out from behind a couple of thegns at the crest of the ridge. "This is no time to celebrate. Our brothers lie dead and dying, and we have not finished the work we set out to do." He pointed to the ancient fortress. "After them! None must escape if we wish to prevent a second, even more deadly attack."

Brecc clutched his sword, a toxic mixture of relief and repulsion churning his stomach. It seemed that the king's memory of the Battle at Wilton was as painfully clear as his own. Brecc did not know how many friends he had lost this day. It had been hours since he'd seen Odda or Rheged. But there could be no doubt that if the Vikings were not stopped now, he would likely lose more, and the Saxons would also lose their victory.

All around, men were responding to the king's order. Most were hastening after the fleeing Vikings on foot. But the king and the thegns who were with him headed to the woodland. Brecc had no need to consider his options. Averting his eyes from the slaughter that surrounded him, he bolted down the hill toward the trees, his mount, and Aisley.

♛

"'Tis sufficient, Aisley," Lufian said. "I thank you, but there are others needing you more."

Aisley cinched the knot on the bandage she'd tied around the thegn's leg and glanced around the small clearing. Lufian was right. She was not sure how word of her presence in the woodland was spreading, but the number of injured who had managed to reach her was steadily growing.

Rheged had been the first to arrive. The cut on his arm had been so deep, she'd been forced to sew it closed to stop the bleeding. There had been no time to wait for a pain remedy to take effect; he'd lost too much blood already. That was likely the reason he'd lost consciousness after the first stitch. He'd awoken not long ago, still pale of face and weak of movement, but she was grateful to see him alert once more.

She moved to the young man seated on the ground beside Lufian. His hair was caked with blood.

"'Ow bad is it, mistress?"

Gently, she dabbed his head with a damp rag, searching for the wound. "The cut is not large, but heads tend to bleed rather a lot." She gave him a reassuring smile. "A few cobwebs and a bandage will help put a stop to that."

His relief was instant. "I'm most grateful."

She had barely finished wrapping his head when the crack of breaking twigs beneath lumbering footsteps announced the arrival of someone else. She looked up.

"Odda!" She scrambled to her feet. The thegn staggered farther into the clearing, a young man in his arms. "Are you hurt?"

"Not me." He lowered the warrior in his arms to the ground. "The Vikings are fleeing, and the king has ordered us to go after them. I came for my horse and stumbled upon this lad at the edge of the battlefield. I believe he is someone you know."

Aisley dropped to her knees beside the young man, and her heart dropped. "Taber!"

The stablehand's eyes fluttered open. "Mistress Aisley." His smile was weak but genuine. "We did it, mistress. We beat back th' Vikin's."

But at what cost? Taber's tunic was red with blood, and his fingers trembled as he felt for the gaping hole in his side.

"'Twas a spear that got me," he said.

"Did you pull it out yourself?" Aisley could hardly countenance the thought, but his deep, ragged wound spoke of extreme damage and pain.

"Aye." He closed his eyes. "I wasn't goin' t' die with a Vikin' spear in me."

Fighting back tears, Aisley looked up at Odda.

He grimaced. "Forgive me. I did not realize how bad . . ." He ran a bloodied hand through his hair. "I thought mayhap . . ."

"You were right to bring him," Aisley said. She could not think of all those dying alone on the battlefield. "I will take care of him."

With one more regretful glance at Taber, Odda moved away. He cut through the clearing, heading toward the spot where he'd left his mount.

"Wait!" At Aisley's call, he turned back. "Have you seen Brecc?"

He shook his head, his expression grim. "Not since this morning." And then he was gone, moving through the trees at a run.

He may be too wounded to reach the woodland. He may be dead already. The haunting thoughts circled her head. Her heart ached, but she refused to give up hope. He had promised he would come. Swiping at her traitorous tears, she gathered her discarded cloak, wadded it into a makeshift pillow, and carefully slid it beneath Taber's head.

She sensed movement at her right one heartbeat before a thick arm came around her, pulling her to her feet and knocking the wind out of her lungs as her back was pressed up against a mail byrnie. Gasping for air, she clawed at the arm that pinned her.

"Well now." The accented voice sent tremors of horror crawling down her skin even as a blade pricked at her throat. "I come to trees for horse and find a wife."

One of the injured men cursed, and a bird called.

"No!" She could manage nothing more than a raspy whisper, but it was enough to break the chilling silence that had descended on the grove.

"I say yes." Rangvald yanked her backward and spun her around so they were facing the cluster of helpless, wounded men. "And these fools. You see. They say yes."

Aisley's desperate gaze fell on the thegns. Rheged's uninjured arm lay across his torso as if he'd been reaching for his knife when Rangvald seized her. He did not look at Aisley. His eyes were on the chieftain, a look of frustration and animosity burning in their depths. Lufian's hand was on the handle of his knife, but he appeared frozen, his jaw tight and his face pale. Their unspoken message was clear. They could do nothing while a knife was at her throat.

Brecc pressed himself against the trunk of the oak tree and forced himself to think past the terror of seeing Aisley in Rangvald's clutches. Praise the heavens for Rheged's warning whistle. After three months of depending on those bird calls to stay alive during raids and ambushes, Brecc's response to the sound had been both instinctive and instant. He had stopped in his tracks when he'd been a mere handful of paces from entering the grove, and he'd deviated from his initial approach so that he might view the clearing before he entered it.

Tearing his gaze off Rangvald and Aisley, he counted the injured. There were eight men seated with their backs to trees or the boulder, including Rheged and Lufian. Eleven lay on the ground, at least half of them with closed eyes. Not one of them was capable of rapid movement. He would need to take on Rangvald alone. But he couldn't do it while the brute held Aisley. He needed a distraction.

With his attention on Rheged, he imitated a blackbird's call. The widening of Rheged's eyes was so subtle it would have been unnoticeable had Brecc not been watching for it. Rheged glanced at Lufian. His acknowledging nod was equally slight. The men knew he was there.

"Drop your blade, Rangvald," Rheged said. "She is unarmed."

The Viking chieftain laughed. It was a cruel, mirthless sound. "Fools." He pushed her forward.

"No!" she cried, planting her feet even as his knife hovered dangerously close to her neck. "I would rather die than go with you!"

Brecc tensed. Now. He needed something now.

Lufian struggled to his feet and extended the knife in his hand. "Let her go, and we shall each drop our weapons. You can walk out of here, take a horse, and join Guthrum."

"Your weapons." Rangvald spat. "They are nothing. You are weak. And fools." Contempt dripped from his voice. "I go with a horse *and* the woman."

He pushed Aisley forward again. She stumbled, and Brecc could wait no longer. He stepped out from behind the tree, knife in hand. "You should have taken Lufian's offer, Rangvald."

The Viking pivoted, slamming Aisley up against his body as he moved. She gasped, but Brecc dared not look at her. His eyes were on Rangvald and the blade in his hand.

"So!" Rangvald sneered. "There is one. One Saxon not bleeding." His eyes narrowed, and the fingers around his knife shifted a fraction. "Yet."

"Let her go, Rangvald." Brecc circled past the two men lying at his feet. He needed to get closer. "It's your only chance for escape."

Rangvald mirrored his move, dragging Aisley backward as he edged toward the treeline. Brecc stepped over a large rock, his foot landing on a twig. It snapped. There was an echoing crack in the trees somewhere to his left. He froze. Someone was approaching. But was it friend or foe?

"You hear it, Saxon?" Rangvald taunted. "Another comes. I think a Viking."

Whoever it was had stopped. No sound or movement came from the woods or the wounded. The air was still. It was as though the very trees surrounding them were listening.

Rangvald darted a glance at the entrance to the grove, and Brecc took another step toward him. How many of the chieftain's men had followed him into the woods in search of a mount? Was he truly expecting an ally, or was there another Saxon warrior nearby?

"You are trapped, Rangvald," Brecc said.

"Lies." He flicked his wrist. His blade flashed, slicing through the top of Aisley's tunic. "I go with my prize. You not stop me."

"I will not go with you!" Aisley writhed, attempting to break free.

Rangvald shifted his weight to pin her more tightly against him. And in that moment, the young man lying at his feet rose up on one elbow, and with his other arm, he plunged his dagger into the Viking's calf.

Rangvald roared with rage. Releasing his hold on Aisley, he pulled his ax from his belt and hurled it at the prone man a heartbeat before Brecc's knife entered the Viking's chest. For one long moment, Rangvald turned his shocked, soulless eyes on Brecc, and then his knees buckled, and he fell to the ground. Aisley screamed. Another twig snapped, and Brecc spun around. A deer darted out from between the trees. At the sight of the men, the creature bolted back into the woods. Rheged and Lufian were now both on their feet, weapons in hand. Leaving Rangvald to them, Brecc sprinted across the remaining distance to Aisley and scooped her into his arms.

"Brecc." Her voice broke, and she pressed her face into his chest and sobbed. Deep, wrenching sobs that tore at his heart.

"It's over, Aisley."

"You are here, and you are whole." Her tears were flowing freely. "I am so grateful." Her shoulders shook. "Taber . . . he . . . he gave everything for me."

Brecc looked to Rheged. He had pulled Aisley's cloak out from underneath the head of the young man who had attacked Rangvald and was spreading the fabric over him. Taber. Memory of Aisley's account of her flight from Wiltshire returned. The stablehand whose clothes she'd worn, who had saddled a horse for her in the early hours of the morning to facilitate her escape.

"Is that who it was?"

"He fought for the king." Another sob escaped her. "And he fought for me."

Brecc smoothed the strands of hair that had come loose from her plait away from her face. "He chose the noblest of causes, and we shall see that he is given a burial fit for a hero."

She looked up at him then, her eyes red and swollen. "You would do that for him?"

"Without question. He saved you—not once but twice. I am forever in his debt."

She wiped the moisture from her face. "He would like that." Still wrapped in Brecc's arms, she looked over at Taber's shrouded body and then seemed to recall their situation. "Forgive me." She pulled back. "Odda was here. I know you must join the king."

"I shall go when my work here is finished."

"Your work here?"

He looked around the grove. "These men have offered their lives for the king. When they are ready, I shall help them onto the carts that carried the weapons. Edington is no more than eight furlongs from here. King Alfred would wish them taken to the royal estate located there to recuperate."

"Your assistance with loading the carts would be welcome." Rheged joined them. "But once they are ready, Lufian and I are well enough to drive." He set one hand on Brecc's shoulder. "After all that has transpired today, I am glad to see you, my friend. Although, if you had given any thought to the welfare of my heart, you would have timed your arrival a fraction earlier."

"Believe me when I say yours was not the only heart to suffer." Brecc ran an unsteady hand across his face. Only now that the danger had been averted was the reality of Aisley's perilous situation truly sinking in. If he had survived the battle only to lose her to Rangvald . . . He cut off the thought. Rangvald was gone. He would never threaten Aisley again.

Placing his hand on the small of her back, he guided her away from Rangvald's body. "Come," he said. "Show me and Rheged what we must do to help these men."

"In case you have forgotten, I *am* one of these men," Rheged said.

"Indeed. But you are standing on two feet and supposedly capable of driving a cart. If I am going to entrust the safety of the woman I love to you, you'd best show that you can at least lift a pouch of healing herbs or a roll of bandages."

CHAPTER 33

THE SIEGE OF GUTHRUM'S FORTRESS at Chippenham was in its fourteenth day. Brecc sat before the campfire eating pottage, thinking of Aisley and their departure from Bratton Camp. He had ridden with the two wagons and the wounded men until they'd reached the royal estate in Edington. Leaving her there in the care of Rheged and Lufian, both wounded themselves, had been difficult, but knowing that any Vikings who had survived the battle had relocated to Chippenham had helped. He sighed and scraped the last of his food from his bowl. Surely this waiting could not go on much longer.

He rose to rinse his bowl in a barrel of water, grateful that the townspeople had responded to King Alfred and his men's return by supplying them with sufficient food to keep them fed and in good spirits for a long sojourn. Brecc doubted the same could be said for the Vikings. They had returned to Chippenham vastly depleted in numbers and with many wounded. Their winter stores would be running low at this time of year, and with the Saxons blocking all means of entering or exiting the fortress, their chances for survival were slim.

King Alfred exited the closest tent and looked around. "Our numbers are few this morning."

Brecc bowed. "I believe it is an illusion, Sire. Our numbers are great, but most men are not so slow to eat as I and have relieved the night guards of their duties. Those who watched during the night are already abed."

"Just so." He looked toward the fortress. "Still no word."

"No, Sire."

The king frowned. "Guthrum is a proud man, but he has lost too much to recover this time. He knows it. It is merely a matter of time before he is willing to admit it."

"I pray for all our sakes that he chooses to end the siege soon."

"As do I." The king studied Brecc a little too carefully. "Is there another reason—other than wishing to sleep in a more comfortable bed and don a fresh tunic—that you are particularly anxious to have this portion of the conflict behind us?"

"There is, Sire." Brecc had been reluctant to broach the subject when the monarch's thoughts were understandably consumed with weightier matters, but the king had offered him a direct invitation to share what was on his mind. "When the siege is over, I wish to take Aisley to wife."

"I see. And how does the young lady feel about that?"

"I believe she will be more enthusiastic about the notion than she was about Rangvald's proposal," he said.

King Alfred laughed. "I should certainly hope so. There are few men more despicable than he. You have my blessing. Both of you. Not that you need it, mind you, but a king can offer it regardless."

The clatter of horses' hooves moving at a rapid clip interrupted any further conversation. King Alfred and Brecc turned to see Odda accompanied by half a dozen guards gallop into the campsite.

"I have news, Sire." Odda was out of breath. He leaped from his horse and strode toward them. Pausing only long enough to bow, he continued. "Guthrum wishes to abandon the fortress in Chippenham. He is offering any number of hostages in exchange for safe passage for him and his men out of Wessex."

"He is surrendering without requesting Saxon hostages for safe passage?" Brecc asked. It had never been done before.

"I believe he is driven by desperation," Odda replied. "His men are starving. They have no fuel for fires, and many are still nursing wounds."

If Guthrum was desperate, King Alfred could exact almost any price—even to the loss of Guthrum's and his chieftains' lives—in exchange for the lives of his men. So costly a reprisal for losing at battle was not unheard of. Indeed, during Viking conquests, it was common. But King Alfred's Christian convictions had set him on a higher, nobler path, and he had yet to exhibit the vindictiveness necessary for such a penalty.

Brecc and Odda waited, watching the king as he studied the distant fortress pensively.

"I shall accept Guthrum's surrender," King Alfred said. "He and his men are to leave Wessex and are to take an oath that they shall never return." He paused. "I do have one further stipulation, however: Guthrum's oath may not be made in the name of one of the Vikings' pagan gods. Such an agreement is worthless. That has been proven time and time again."

"Do you have a suggestion for how you might obtain a more binding contract with the Viking, Sire?" Odda asked.

"I do." King Alfred straightened his shoulders. "Guthrum must swear to honor our treaty before the one true God. Not as a pagan but as a baptized Christian. If Guthrum agrees that three weeks hence, he and his chieftains will willingly be christened and that Guthrum himself will accept me as his godfather, then—and only then—shall he and his men leave unharmed."

Odda appeared as dumbfounded as Brecc felt. He cleared his throat, but presumably could find no words.

"That is it, Odda," King Alfred said. "There can be no other way. Give Guthrum my message. If he is willing to accept my conditions, the siege ends today. If not, we shall remain here until he and his men are dead."

Odda bowed. "I shall return forthwith, Sire." Returning to his horse, he mounted swiftly, and with the guards riding behind him, he took off down the road as quickly as he had come. The king and Brecc watched him go until he disappeared beyond the trees.

"What think you of those terms, Brecc?"

"They are bold, Sire."

"And foolish?"

"Unprecedented, most certainly. But I would find fault with anyone who claimed them foolish until they have been proven so."

"Having given the matter a great deal of thought," the king said, "I believe Wessex shall never know lasting peace until Guthrum and his chieftains accept that there is a higher power to whom they must answer for their actions. It may be that they are never willing to truly believe in the God we know, but unless we give them the opportunity to discover Him, we shall never know."

"It is a generous offer," Brecc said. "And an astute observation."

"Wisdom is a painfully hard-earned attribute for a young king," he admitted. "Ormod knew as much, but he stood by me regardless."

"I believe we have all missed his steadying presence, Sire."

"Just so. It is rare to find a thegn whose sound judgment is offered without overbearance or a desire for personal advancement. But it is a quality that you and Ormod share. And for that reason, I wish you to take on his former role—that of my special adviser."

Brecc stared at him. "I am honored, Sire, but you and I are of a similar age. I cannot offer you the wisdom that comes with experience or years of hindsight."

"That may be true, but I trust your judgment, Brecc, and decades of experience is worthless if it comes from an unreliable source."

There was no refuting the truthfulness of that statement. "If all you require of me is my thoughtful consideration of issues that face the kingdom and crown, followed by my honest opinion, then I humbly acc—"

"Wait!" King Alfred raised his hand. "There is more." The warmth in his eyes belied his stern expression. "Friendship. That is not a condition every monarch would set, but in this case, I must insist upon it."

Brecc's thoughts could have turned to the experiences he and the king had shared since their perilous flight from Chippenham on Twelfth Night, but instead, they flew back to his childhood, and the many hours he and the young prince Alfred had spent in play together. "In that case," he said, "I believe I am well qualified for the assignment. That requirement was met many years ago."

This time, King Alfred allowed himself a genuine smile. "I am glad to hear it. In truth, there are times when a king needs an adviser to help guide him, and there are other times when he simply needs a friend to sit with him whilst he awaits the response to a message of significant import."

With an understanding look, Brecc gestured toward the two wooden chairs positioned at the opening of the king's tent. "At the pace Odda set when he left, this time, at least, I do not suppose we shall have to wait very long."

👑

Aisley sat beside the queen on the front pew of the Aller church, awaiting the arrival of the men. Sunlight filtered in through the narrow windows, painting the wooden seats a golden brown and warming the flagstone floor.

Before them was the christening font filled with water. Behind them, the priest stood beside the door to the church, a basket of salt in his hand.

The latch clicked, and the door creaked open. The queen and Aisley rose, and the king, followed by Brecc and Odda, entered the building. The priest inclined his head and stood aside so that the men might make their way up the short aisle. Brecc's eyes met hers, the warmth in their dark depths bringing a shy smile to her face. He took his place beside the king on the row across from Aisley's, and then Guthrum entered the church.

The fearsome Viking chieftain was dressed in white. He stopped opposite the priest, and as a candidate for baptism, he opened his mouth for a portion of salt. The priest placed it under his tongue, and then Guthrum walked to the front of the church. Thirty of his closest associates—also dressed in white—followed. Each took their portion of salt before filing into the pews.

The king's most loyal thegns came next. Upon entering the church, they positioned themselves shoulder to shoulder along the walls. Guthrum's men watched them sullenly. Aisley studied the Vikings' faces. Their skin was weathered, and most had drawn their long beards into a single plait similar to the two hanging from their heads. Their blue eyes were alert, and their expressions ranged from puzzled to curious to defeated.

Many of the thegns appeared wary, and even though they were in a church, the knives at their waists were ever present. Rheged and Lufian stood closest to her. Their wounds had healed well, and that knowledge was a balm to her heart whenever she thought of the many men Wessex had lost in battle at Bratton Camp. Of the nineteen men she had treated, she had lost only four. Taber's death haunted her still, but Brecc had fulfilled his promise and had seen to it that the young man was buried in the church-yard at Edington with all the religious rites offered to a man of means.

She returned her gaze to Brecc, unable to contain the flutter of excitement she experienced whenever she set eyes upon him. Ever since his return from the siege at Chippenham, he and the king had worked tirelessly to bring about this event. But he had ensured that any time available to him between royal assignments had been hers. He'd sought her out every day. Sometimes they'd taken a walk or ride together. Other times, they'd sat side by side in the gardens at the royal estate and talked. Occasionally, when time had been truly limited, he'd brought her a flower and had kissed her soundly before hastening back to the king's chambers.

Her cheeks warmed at the memories of those favorite moments, and as she watched him standing beside the king, she offered a silent prayer of gratitude for the series of miracles that had brought her to this point.

"Please be seated." The priest's voice filled the small church, and with a rustle of fabric, all but the thegns lining the walls lowered themselves onto the pews. "Would Guthrum of Denmark and his sponsor please come forward."

Guthrum and King Alfred rose. Keeping his face forward, Guthrum followed the king to stand beside the priest at the font.

"Do you, Guthrum, renounce your previous pagan beliefs and embrace your newfound faith in Jesus Christ?" the priest asked.

"Aye." The Viking had yet to look away from the priest, so when the older man gestured toward the font, he obediently moved closer.

After a few quiet words were spoken between them, the priest anointed Guthrum's head and then plunged it into the font. King Alfred stepped up, and grasping Guthrum by the shoulders, he lifted him up from the water and embraced him.

Aisley was unprepared for the rush of emotion that accompanied King Alfred's unexpected act of fellowship, and it seemed that many of the thegns felt similarly. Their countenances reflected their wonder at what they were witnessing. And although others in the room appeared more skeptical, the atmosphere in the church had changed from one of suspicion to one of acceptance.

"Be it known to all assembled here and those far from this church," King Alfred said, standing beside Guthrum, "that from this day forth, my godson shall be known by the Christian name Aethelstan."

"Aethelstan," Guthrum repeated, and then with a dazed nod to the priest, he and King Alfred resumed their seats, and the first of his men walked to the front to repeat the ceremony.

One by one, the Vikings were baptized. The priest waited until the last one returned to his pew and then invited all to kneel. Everyone, including the thegns lining the wall, lowered themselves to their knees, and the priest offered a prayer over the congregation. When the last amens had been spoken, the king approached the aisle where the queen and Aisley sat and extended his arm to his wife. Smiling, she took it, and as they began their walk to the back of the church, the Vikings filtered into the aisle behind them, exiting the rustic building with a reverence rarely found outside a church of much greater size and splendor.

Aisley turned to watch the exodus, waiting until the last of the thegns had followed after the Vikings before moving.

"I wondered if you would ever choose to leave."

With a start, Aisley swung around. Brecc was standing at the end of the pew, an understanding smile on his face.

"Forgive me." She moved toward him. "I did not mean to keep you waiting. I thought you had gone ahead with the king."

He reached for her hand. "I told him I would likely be a little late in joining him."

"We can hasten." She wove her fingers between his, expecting him to draw her into the aisle. But he did not move. "Brecc?"

"I know you have an attachment to this old church," he said.

"I do, but we need not stay any longer."

He tightened his grip on her hand but still did not move. "This morning, it struck me that since we would be here together and the priest would be available, along with those on whom we could call to witness a private ceremony . . ."

Aisley's heart was suddenly beating so loudly she could barely hear what Brecc was saying.

The door at the rear of the church opened, and Rheged appeared. "Lufian, Odda, and I are still waiting. Is there to be a wedding or not?"

Brecc released a weary sigh. "Why do I even associate with him?"

Aisley laughed softly. "One moment, Rheged," she said, and then she took Brecc's other hand in hers. "Please continue."

Turning his back on the three thegns who were now standing at the rear of the room, he looked at her with such tenderness that tears pricked Aisley's eyes.

"I believe you know how deeply I love you and how desperately I wish to marry you. I have spoken to the priest who officiated at the baptisms, and if it pleases you, he is willing to also perform our wedding ceremony this day." He smiled uncertainly. "The king has decreed that the grand banquet he has planned at Wedmore to celebrate the Vikings' baptisms may also serve to celebrate our union."

"Brecc," she said, barely able to contain her happiness. "I can think of nothing that would bring me greater joy than to wed to you at the Aller church this day."

His smile was immediate. He released her hands to cup her face, and before she could so much as catch her breath, he was kissing her—filling her heart with his ardent love and sweet promises for their future.

"Well, men," Rheged said. "I have yet to hear from Brecc himself, but I think it is safe to summon the priest. All signs are that the wedding will take place."

The door creaked open again, and Brecc drew back just far enough to set his forehead against hers.

"When the wedding is over, would you like me to lead him to the shore so that you may dunk his head in the swamp?" Aisley whispered.

He laughed softly. "Other than the realization that I could marry you this day, that is the best notion I have heard for a very long time."

And then, because the thegns had gone in search of the priest and Brecc and Aisley were finally alone, he kissed her again.

EPILOGUE

Winchester, Wessex
Five Months Later

Brecc knocked on the door of the king's chamber.

"Enter!"

He walked in, and King Alfred looked up from the table where he had been poring over a map.

Brecc bowed. "Good day, Sire."

"I pray that it will be," King Alfred said, his tone grim. "What news do you have for me?"

"One of our scouts just returned from the north. Aethelstan and his men remain encamped at Cirencester, dangerously close to our northern border. The new band of Vikings camped just west of London sailed up the Thames two days ago. They have since joined Aethelstan's men."

The king thumped the table with his fist. "By all the Saints, Brecc, I am not so foolish as to think that all of Aethelstan's men were persuaded to abide by a higher law after their baptism, but I had hoped that with our newfound familial connection, Aethelstan would stay true to his word."

"I agree, Sire." Brecc was not sure that the Viking chieftain would consider the godfather and godson relationship as binding as did King Alfred, but Aethelstan had most certainly been treated generously by the king since the day he had taken upon himself Christianity.

"Well, agree or not, we cannot stand back and allow him to break his oath and attack Wessex again." He pointed to the map. "Show me exactly where their camp is located."

Moving closer, Brecc ran his finger along the line delineating the border between Wessex and Mercia. "Here, Sire."

"And our men?"

"We have a large band of warriors guarding the border. They have served well as a deterrent to those contemplating brief incursions into Wessex, but they will be insufficient if we are attacked by the merged might of both Viking armies. The nearest fyrd is in Wiltshire." He raised a questioning eyebrow. "Would you have me place the men there on alert?"

"Aye," the king said. "And we'd best prepare ourselves for departure. In good weather, it is two days' ride from here to Cirencester, and at this time of year, the weather may delay us further."

Brecc nodded. King Alfred was correct. On all counts. But that would not make informing Aisley that he would be leaving and likely entering a heated conflict any easier. "I shall see to it forthwith, Sire." He left the room and made directly for the great hall. Four thegns sat at one of the tables.

"Greetings, Brecc," Lufian said.

"Good day," Brecc responded.

"He does not look as though it is a good day," Rheged said.

Brecc frowned. "One of the king's scouts has delivered concerning news. Aethelstan appears to have joined forces with the group of Vikings who were previously encamped near London. The king needs messages sent to the Wiltshire fyrd and the men guarding the northern border."

Instantly, all four men were on their feet. "We can be gone within the half hour," Rheged said.

With renewed appreciation for his companions, Brecc gave each of them the king's message and specific assignments. They separated, and Brecc headed outside. If he had to take a guess on where to find his wife at this time of day, he would choose the garden.

He spotted Aisley straightway. Wearing a pale-blue gown beneath her new cloak, she was standing beside a tree, gazing up between the branches, a look of pure delight upon her face. His heart contracted at the sight. Dear heavens, how he loved her. And how torturous it would be to leave her.

He moved closer. She must have heard his footsteps, for she looked around, and upon catching sight of him, her face lit up with a warm smile.

"Good morning," he said. "I heard tell there was something fascinating in that tree, and so I determined to discover what it was for myself."

She laughed, and taking his hand, she dragged him closer to the trunk. "Look," she said, pointing upward. "A yellow wagtail has made a nest up there."

He looked at her curiously. "I thought you knew nothing of birds."

"Almost nothing. We had a family of yellow wagtails that made their home in our eaves every autumn. Their distinctive color and tendency to nest late in the year make them easy to remember."

His gaze followed the direction of her finger, and sure enough, a small round nest was just visible in the fork of one of the upper branches.

"I am impressed that you saw it at all," he said.

"I likely would not have had I not been trying to determine why the branches' shadows appear so odd." She did not wait for him to question her, but instead, she pointed to the flagstone path. "Do you see?"

Brecc studied the flagstones. The shadows were moving. Shimmering, even. It was as though they had become snakes and were writhing their way across the ground.

Just as Aisley had done, he looked up to the branches. They were completely still. In fact, now that he paused to take note, everything was still. The birds in the nest were silent. There was no birdsong in the nearby trees. No cow lowing from the nearby fields, no dog barking in the courtyard.

"Something is not right," he said.

"It feels like we are within Aller church," she said, looking around. "Do you sense it? That same aura of wonder? Of participating in something greater than us?"

"Aye."

"Brecc." He heard the uncertainty in her voice. "It is noonday. I am sure of it. But it is becoming dark."

All around them, the darkness was deepening. He looked up. One brilliant burst of light and a thin circle of white was all that remained of the sun, and suddenly that, too, was gone, and the sky was filled with stars.

"What is happening?"

At Aisley's hushed exclamation, he stepped behind her and wrapped his arms around her waist. From the courtyard, cries of fear mingled with exclamations of awe. Brecc tightened his hold on Aisley, his gaze fixed on the sky. He did not know what this was, but it was assuredly some form of heavenly sign.

They stood together, distant voices connecting them to the real world even as they participated in something that seemed to be of another. The darkness stayed for only a short time, and then the sky turned a new shade of dark blue, and a brilliant ray of light appeared.

"The sun is returning," he said.

Aisley leaned her head against his chest, and silently, they watched the world reawaken. Slowly, the shadows disappeared, and the colors brightened. Above their heads, a yellow wagtail sang, and a chorus of baby birds cheeped. As quickly as it had come, the astonishing feeling of wonderment fled.

Reluctantly, Brecc loosened his hold on Aisley and took her hand once more. "Come," he said. "There will be others wanting to speak of this."

Rheged met them in the courtyard. "Did you see? Of course you did." He ran his fingers through his hair. "The sun was gone! It was full dark at noonday. But what could it mean?"

"I cannot say," Brecc said. "I've never seen the like."

"Look around you." Aisley directed their attention to the many people who had joined them in the courtyard. They were gathering in small clusters. Some appeared fearful. Others were conversing rapidly, their excitement and amazement palpable. "We witnessed something miraculous, and for that reason, the answer to your question will likely be different for each person who experienced it."

Rheged watched a maid wipe tears from her cheeks. "We may never know what it means."

"Aye." Brecc's mind raced as he contemplated what impact the disappearing of the sun might have upon the mind-set of the Vikings. "And as Aethelstan and his chieftains are wont to be overly superstitious and are currently poised to make a dangerous decision, I would give a great deal to know what they will make of it."

"Aethelstan could see the heavenly sign as a portent for good or ill," Rheged said.

"Just so." Brecc gazed up at the remarkably normal afternoon sky and tightened his jaw. "And I daresay we shall all know which he chooses within a matter of days."

It was, in fact, five days later. Five excruciatingly tense days in which the king alternated between praying, pacing, and watching for the appearance of a messenger. Brecc was preparing to leave the king's chambers with a map of the Wessex border in hand and half a dozen battle scenarios floating through his head when the clatter of hooves in the yard announced the arrival of men on horseback. King Alfred moved to the window.

"Lufian and Odda," he said. "And they have one of our scouts with them."

Brecc's pulse quickened. Lufian and Odda were the thegns who'd been assigned to speak with the warriors at the northern border. They would have news.

"Would you have them come directly to your chambers?" Brecc asked.

"No." The king was already at the door. "I have completed sufficient pacing awaiting this one piece of intelligence. Come. It is time to discover my godson's true leanings."

Brecc followed the king through the great hall and out into the courtyard. Dusk was falling, and the air was chill. The men had dismounted and were passing off their mounts' reins to the stableboys.

"What news, men?" King Alfred said.

All three swung around and bowed.

"Good evening, Sire." Lufian appeared weary but not unduly worried.

Brecc's hope increased a fraction. He looked to Odda. The experienced thegn surely knew better than to extend polite greetings when the king's very presence in the yard spoke of his impatience.

"Aethelstan has been true to his oath," Odda said. "According to our contact at the Viking encampment, Aethelstan saw the darkening of the sun as a sign from the Christian God and has informed the newly arrived Viking chieftains that he refuses to attack Wessex."

Relief—pure and strengthening—lifted Brecc's heart and straightened King Alfred's shoulders.

"You are sure of this?" the king asked.

"Bowdyn here followed the departing fleet along the river for four furlongs." He gestured the young scout forward. "Tell His Majesty what you witnessed at the Viking encampment, lad."

"The newcomers weren't 'appy, Sire. Argued, they did. But Aethelstan wasn't 'avin' it. 'E pointed t' the sky over 'n' over, an' then 'e pointed t' their boats. Not long after, all them that 'ad just arrived got in their boats and rowed back th' way they come."

"And they showed no sign of setting up camp farther down the river?"

"No, Sire. They were movin' at a real clip. Wanted t' be gone, I'd say. It may be that Aethelstan made 'em wonder if Wessex wasn't such an easy place t' plunder after all."

"Praise the heavens," King Alfred muttered.

"Aye," Lufian said. "We offered our own prayers of thanks when we heard."

"As I must now do," King Alfred said. "I thank you all for bringing such good tidings."

He turned to return to the residence, and that was when Brecc noticed Aisley standing in the doorway.

Odda must have spotted her, too, for he chuckled. "Go to her. You have heard our news. In truth, we are more eager to change our apparel and rest than we are to engage in more conversation."

Brecc offered him a grateful smile. "You most certainly deserve that. Along with a good meal. I shall speak with you later this evening." And then, before Lufian could add anything, Brecc walked away.

Aisley saw him coming. Her smile was welcoming but anxious. "Well?" she asked.

"Aethelstan repelled the other Vikings," Brecc said, still marveling at the Viking chieftain's decision. "He will not go to battle with King Alfred."

She gasped. "Truly?" They had hardly dared dream of such an outcome.

He slid his arms around her waist. "If two loyal thegns and an eager scout are to be believed, then, aye, it is the truth."

Wrapping her arms around his neck, she smiled. "The trust the king exhibited in bringing Aethelstan and his men to the Christian faith rather than having them killed has taught his people more about how a monarch should reign than any number of fearsome retaliations would have done."

His smile matched hers. "I believe you are right, my love." This was likely not the time to tell Aisley of King Alfred's many plans to improve the lives of commoners throughout the land. That was a conversation—and another ray of hope—for another day. He kissed her gently. For now, it was enough that they had each other and that the people of Wessex would finally know peace.

AUTHOR'S NOTE

As a child growing up in the UK, the only thing I knew about King Alfred the Great was that his inattentiveness had caused some cakes to burn. Although I always thought it rather odd that a king had been placed in charge of watching cakes cook, I accepted the legend as one of the many anecdotal stories associated with ancient Britain. Many hours of research have helped change my childlike and somewhat simplistic view of the oft-told legend. I have developed a new respect for a monarch whose distraction was most likely due to his all-consuming concern for his people and who was humble enough to accept a scolding from a peasant woman.

Alfred was born in 849 and became the king of Wessex in 871, following the death of his older brother. He inherited a country rife with conflict. The Vikings had made significant gains in the neighboring countries of Mercia and Northumbria and were anxious to add Wessex to their conquests. The Norse chieftains were crafty, well-seasoned warriors who were known for their ruthlessness, and at only twenty-one years of age, the new king lacked the experience necessary to successfully defeat them.

The first few years of his reign were fraught with losses, and in desperation, Alfred offered the Vikings danegeld in exchange for peace. Royal coffers and churches were drained of their resources, but it was not long before the Viking incursions began again. Things came to a head when Guthrum and his men attacked Chippenham during the king's Twelfth Night celebrations. Guthrum's intent this time was not simply to rob the people of Wessex; it was to become its ruler. To that end, he had his sights set on killing the king.

King Alfred escaped the royal estate and went into hiding on the island of Athelney with his wife and most trusted thegns. The subsequent happenings in this book—from the weeks spent in prayer to the raids on Viking encampments, from circumventing disloyal thegns so that he might rally his people to the eventual gathering for the Battle of Edington—are all based on historical accounts. Remarkably, so, too, are the events that unfolded after the Saxons' victory.

Following the two-week siege at Chippenham, Guthrum begged for mercy. Alfred granted it on condition of him and his men becoming Christians. The Vikings were baptized at Aller church—the same church where Alfred had prayed so long and so hard during his exile—and Alfred took upon himself the role of Guthrum's (or Aethelstan, as he was called from then on) godfather. Deeply religious, Alfred took the role seriously, but he was wise enough to know that Aethelstan was unlikely to do the same, so he maintained a wary watch over the chieftain afterward.

Five months later, when another Viking army petitioned Aethelstan to join them in invading Wessex, the chieftain took the solar eclipse of October 29, 878, as a sign from God and refused. Interestingly, a few Viking coins have been unearthed in England from that time period, and they are marked with the name Aethelstan, which would suggest that the Viking chieftain went by his new name from that point on.

The fictional aspects of this novel center around the characters. Aisley, Diera, and their parents are fictional, and although King Alfred did surround himself with loyal thegns, Brecc, Rheged, and their associates are also fictional. Ealdorman Wulfhere of Wiltshire did exist, but I have fictionalized his character. The real Wulfhere—believing he was aligning himself with the winning side—did, indeed, make an alliance with the invaders. Already disliked by the people of Wiltshire, this act of treachery only made matters worse. He had broken his oath to the ring-giver, and everyone from the king to his fellow thegns to the common people despised him for it.

Alfred continued to rule Wessex until 899. During his lifetime, he is credited with championing literacy by having Latin books translated into Anglo-Saxon and setting up schools for children throughout Wessex, specifically to teach them how to read and write. He was an architect of towns and ships, a scholar, poet, and law-giver. By the end of his reign, he was a seasoned warrior, all the while remaining true to his Christian faith. Credited with saving the Anglo-Saxon nation and setting the groundwork for the creation of the United Kingdom, it is little wonder that of all the kings and queens of England, only Alfred has ever been named "the Great."

Enjoy this excerpt from

THE CALL OF
THE SEA

FROM BEST-SELLING AUTHOR
SIAN ANN BESSEY

CHAPTER 1

The Kingdom of Gwynedd, 1141

A SEAGULL'S CRY PIERCED THE air. Rhiannon raised her head to watch the large white bird glide in a wide arc over the sheltered bay and soar out to sea. What freedom such birds enjoyed. To ride the wind and the waves, to travel farther than the eye could see. Rhiannon could only dream of such unfettered liberty.

Stepping over the tide pool she'd been exploring, she turned toward the large house that overlooked the beach. Bryn Eithin's solid gray-stone walls and purple slate roof had protected her since her birth sixteen years previously. Its idyllic location, with the Irish Sea at its front and rolling pastures at its rear, was hard to equal. Indeed, compared to most young women in Gwynedd, she was fortunate. Her father owned land and retained servants. She was well cared for. Beyond the loss of her mother several years before, she lacked for nothing. Except, perhaps, the freedom of a seagull.

"Rhiannon!"

Her father, Iorwerth ap Gwion, appeared where the sand met the scrubby grass of the low dunes. He stood with his hands on his hips, his expression grim. Rhiannon spared the sky another glance, and her heart sank. The sun had lowered, and she had no need to consider the lengthening shadows to realize she was inexcusably late.

Lifting her skirts, she scrambled off the craggy rocks and ran across the beach toward him. "Forgive me, Father." She stopped to catch her breath. "I failed to keep track of the time."

"Clearly." He frowned. "I had hoped that today, of all days, you would not give me cause to seek you out, Rhiannon."

"I would have returned before the evening meal. Truly, I would have."

"The servants have their preparations well in hand, but you are still whiling away the afternoon beside the sea." His gaze traveled from her windswept hair to her sand-dusted gown and damp hem. He shook his head despairingly. "How am I to introduce you as a prospective bride to Owain Gwynedd's cousin when you resemble a foundling? And a wet one, at that?"

She offered him a contrite smile and slipped her arm through his. His frustration was born of concern for her. She knew this. Just as she knew that it would soon pass.

"Walk me back to the house to ensure that I cannot be distracted by the call of the sea again, and then place me in Heledd's expert care," she said. "Heledd will have me dressed and ready to greet your guests in no time."

"*Our* guests, Rhiannon." He was not yet ready to fully exonerate her. "Cadwgan ap Gronw does us a great honor by coming to dine with us."

"He comes because the king suggested it," Rhiannon said.

"And why should he not? Your mother was the sister of his wife, the queen. Your father is a member of the uchelwr."

"Your position as a member of the pedigreed aristocracy will undoubtedly influence who I eventually marry, but must that decision be made so soon?"

"Yes," her father said firmly. "Cadwgan may wait as long as he wishes for the wedding ceremony—you know that I have no desire to have you leave—but you have reached the age when a betrothal is both expedient and expected."

Rhiannon sighed. This was not the first time they'd had this conversation. No matter how much she hoped for her father's stance to alter, it did not. As his only daughter, it was her duty to marry well. Her father wanted what was best for her. He wished her to have every comfort and security. She should be glad. Mayhap, if she exerted a little more effort, she *would* be glad.

"This Cadwgan ap Gronw is handsome, is he not?" she said.

They started back toward the house together.

"I am not of a mind to consider such things, but I daresay he is pleasing enough. A little taller than I, with curly, dark hair."

"And young." That attribute alone was more than most young ladies in her situation could claim when meeting a potential spouse.

"Not more than eight and twenty. And yet, despite his youth, he owns a large parcel of land in Dyffryn Clwyd."

The district of Dyffryn Clwyd had been claimed by Gwynedd several years before, but with all the infighting that continued to plague the king, it was no secret that Owain Gwynedd was anxious for an ally within the uchelwr living in that area. As much as Rhiannon wished it were different, her role in this marriage was that of a prize or a bargaining chip.

"What will happen if Cadwgan decides against me?" she asked.

"He will not." Her father's expression softened. "Your lack of awareness of your natural beauty only enhances it, bach. Cadwgan cannot help but be captivated by you."

Her hair swirled wildly around her shoulders, and Rhiannon glanced at her wrinkled, salt-water-stained gown.

"Even if he were to come upon me now?" she asked.

Her father nodded. "Aye. As loath as I am to admit it, even now."

His words, which surely should have offered her greater confidence, in actuality, did the opposite. Rhiannon had oft been told that she had inherited her mother's silky tresses, dark-brown eyes, and flawless skin. Unfortunately, the same could not be said of her disposition. Whereas her mother had thrived as mistress of a sizable home and a hostess of large gatherings, Rhiannon preferred to wander the beach alone and quietly observe others from afar. If Cadwgan were to base his matrimonial decision upon appearances while paying no heed to her preference for solitude, he would undoubtedly be sorely disappointed in his choice of wife.

The feelings of apprehension that had sent Rhiannon to the sea in search of peace resurfaced. She wished to please her father. If she were fully honest with herself, she also wished to please Cadwgan. But only if she could also remain true to the person she was within. She took an unsteady breath. For now, she could only pray that when her upcoming meeting with Cadwgan was over, she could also claim some measure of pleasure for herself.

They had reached the front door. Her father paused. "A small portion of discomfort over meeting Cadwgan for the first time is understandable, Rhiannon, but I expect you to rise above it. A man of Cadwgan's rank deserves your respect." He glanced at her bare, sandy feet. "And that includes being dressed appropriately when you greet him."

"Yes, Father." Her stomach churned, but she somehow maintained a placid countenance. "I shall see to my wardrobe straightway. And I will have Heledd help me locate my shoes as soon as she finishes with my hair."

"Very well," he said. "I shall look for you in the great hall within the hour."

ᚼᚢᚷᚠ

The sleek longboat cut through the rolling waves. Dusk was turning to dark, and from his position in the bow of the agile craft, Leif breathed in the salty air and grinned. Returning home from a successful raid was an exhilarating experience, but unlike most of his companions, Leif's excitement came not from the value of their haul but from being out at sea.

Ahead of his craft, another longboat navigated the breakers. The Norsemen within were silhouetted against the sky even as the row of circular shields lining the craft's hull glinted in the last light of the setting sun. Although currently indistinguishable, Leif's brother sat in the bow of that boat. As the oldest son of Jarl Ottar of Dyflin, Bjorn was the designated leader of this raiding party. Leif did not envy him the position. At nineteen years of age, captaining the second boat was responsibility enough for him.

He pulled on his oar, feeling the water's resistance as his arms moved in unison with those of the other men. The steady, powerful rhythm powered them forward, increasing the distance between the Vikings and the monastery they'd pillaged. Later, if the wind was in their favor, they would raise the sail, but for now, the longboat hugged the coastline, fueled by oars in the hands of twenty Norsemen.

"It would have been nice if the monks had left us something to eat," the man sitting on the other end of Leif's bench grumbled softly.

"What ails you most, Knud?" Although Rune, the rower sitting behind Leif, kept his voice low, there was no mistaking his taunting tone. "Is it rowing all night on an empty stomach or the lack of gold beneath your seat?"

Knud's stroke did not waver, but his square jaw tightened. "You know full well that those goblets should have been mine."

Rune sniggered. "Not so. We each took a cupboard. You could have gathered more of the candles you found in yours had you wished to."

Knud growled his displeasure, but before he could speak further, a low bird whistle sounded from the other boat. A warning call. Other than the gentle splash of oars, all sound on the boat instantly ceased. Every man knew how readily voices carried on the water.

"A light. Over there, just above the bay," Rune whispered.

Leif spotted the flicker even as Rune spoke.

"Is it a traveler?" Knud kept his voice as low as Rune's.

"I think not," Leif said. "I see the outline of a building."

"Aye," Rune said. "Not tall enough to be a monastery or castle but no humble dwelling, to be sure."

Knud's teeth flashed in the gloaming. "What think you, Leif? Is it large enough to provide a meal for forty hungry Vikings?"

Leif glanced at the darkening water. If the decision were left to him, they would make use of the outgoing tide to put out to sea. Leaving the Kingdom of Gwynedd as stealthily as they had arrived was always his preference. Unfortunately, the choice was not his to make.

He kept his eyes on the other longboat, waiting for a signal. The birdcall came again, and with it came the unmistakable grind of oars lifting. Bjorn was turning his longboat toward the shore.

"Looks like you shall fill your belly after all, Knud," Rune said, satisfaction tingeing his low voice.

Smothering his frustration, Leif raised his oar. The men seated behind him raised theirs as well. Those on the other side of the boat lowered theirs and pulled. The dragonhead carved on the prow of Leif's boat swung right to follow the serpent tail carved on the rear of Bjorn's.

Leif gauged the direction of the wind. Already, it had shifted since they had begun their journey. Going ashore for another raid would delay their crossing of the Irish Sea significantly. They would need the wind behind their sails if they were to reach Ireland by morning. He frowned. With two monasteries and a church already looted along this stretch of coastline, news of the Vikings' uninvited presence on Gwynedd's soil would have reached the king by now. It was only a matter of time before Owain Gwynedd would send soldiers to oust them from his land.

"You may take the cupboards in the bedchambers, Rune," Knud said, his eyes on the outline of a substantial longhouse perched above the low cliff. "I am for the great hall. At this time of day, the evening meal should be ready for the taking."

Leif remained silent. His brother had opted to attempt one more raid. Whether Bjorn had oarsmen complaining of hunger, Leif could not tell. He only hoped that they would not pay too heavy a price for satisfying their appetites.

CHAPTER 2

"There now." Heledd stepped back to survey the plaited crown she'd pinned around Rhiannon's head and gave a satisfied smile. "That did not take long, did it?"

"No." Rhiannon spoke through stiff lips. "Not long." In an effort to prevent any cries from escaping, she had clamped her mouth closed some time ago. Giving Heledd a comb had been a risk, but with limited time to prepare for the banquet, it was one Rhiannon had been forced to take.

Somehow, she managed to resist the urge to touch her stinging scalp. Her tangles were gone, and her hair was dressed, so there was no point in looking for sympathy for her throbbing head.

"Well then," the older woman said, "you'd best join your father. I daresay he's waited long enough."

In the years that had passed since Rhiannon's mother's death, Heledd had become more of a companion to Rhiannon than a maid, and she was not beyond giving Rhiannon directions.

Rhiannon obediently rose from the stool where she'd been sitting. In this instance, Heledd was surely right. It would not do to disappoint her father again so soon after he'd been forced to come searching for her.

"Has there been any sighting of Cadwgan ap Gronw and his men?" she asked.

"Not that I've heard." Heledd chuckled. "Your father sent Eifion to watch for them. With how fleet of foot that lad is, he'll be back here long before the nobleman and his retinue ride into the yard."

Rhiannon nodded. Eifion was their stableboy. He was small and wiry, and at twelve years of age, he could outrun every one of her father's retainers—including men with far longer legs. Not only that, but he would take his responsibility as lookout very seriously and would return to report the moment he spotted the travelers.

Running her hands down her green gown, Rhiannon squared her narrow shoulders. The sky was clear this evening. If Eifion positioned himself on the bluff above the house, the moonlight would enable him to see a good stretch of the coast road. Since he had not yet returned, she surely had a few moments to compose herself.

"All will be well, bach," Heledd said. "Cadwgan ap Gronw will be mesmerized by you."

"Is that how it was for Dai?" she asked, referring to Heledd's husband who worked as her father's head groom. "Did you mesmerize him at first sight?"

"I hardly think my appearance would mesmerize anyone. I'm far too plain."

Rhiannon considered the older lady critically. Her skin was wrinkled, her fingers workworn, and her hips wide, but until now, Rhiannon had never noticed any of those things. "Whatever plainness you claim to possess is not seen by others," Rhiannon said.

"You have known me long enough to look beyond those things, bach. And I believe the same can be said for Dai."

"But what of his first glance?"

Heledd's brown eyes crinkled. "I believe he had eyes only for my fish pie. That was what won him over."

Rhiannon sighed. "I cannot make fish pie."

"A lady of your standing and beauty has no need to make fish pie."

"Perhaps not. But whether it is how well I make fish pie or something else entirely, I should like to have a gentleman come to know my likes and dislikes, my strengths and weaknesses, rather than to make assumptions based merely on what he sees."

Giving her an understanding look, Heledd crossed the room and picked up a small wooden box. She carried it back to Rhiannon. "There's no cause for you to feel any less than your mother, bach. If she were here, she would have stood beside you tonight, exceptionally proud of the young lady you have become." She opened the lid. "Here. Take something of hers with you and let it bring you an extra measure of courage."

Rhiannon gazed into the box. A silver brooch and a gold bracelet lay beside a ringed cross hanging from a silver chain. Reaching for the necklace, she fastened the clasp around her neck. The ornately carved silver cross rested against her chest. She pressed her hand against it and closed her eyes, picturing her mother standing in the great hall, wearing her burgundy gown and this necklace as she welcomed a party from Owain Gwynedd's court to her home. She swallowed the lump in her throat and opened her eyes. "I thank you, Heledd. I should have thought to wear Mam's necklace."

"It's a small thing, but mayhap it will make her feel nearer."

Rhiannon released an unsteady breath. "I must go to my father."

"Yes." Setting the jewelry box back on the table, Heledd gave her an encouraging smile. "It is time."

Leaving her bedchamber, Rhiannon walked the short distance to the great hall. Colorful tapestries hung on the walls, and fresh straw lay on the wooden floor. Three long tables had been positioned in a horseshoe-shaped configuration. Wooden trenchers and goblets lined each table along with flagons of mead, baskets of bread, and platters of fruit.

In the center of the room, meat sizzled on a spit above a blazing fire. The firelight was augmented by candles burning at the center of each table and in the windows.

Myfanwy, the young maid who helped in the kitchen, entered the room, another basket in her hands. The smell of baking bread followed her, coming from the oven across the yard. Bobbing a curtsy to Rhiannon, she began taking knives out of the basket and setting them on the table.

Rhiannon crossed the room to join her father, who stood near the head table, talking to Dai. The groom had likely come to update her father on the state of the two foals born to her father's prize mare in the early hours of the morning. If it weren't for the pending arrival of his guests, her father would have undoubtedly spent all evening in the stable.

"Good evening, Father. Dai." She summoned a smile.

Both men turned to face her. Dai inclined his head politely.

"Good evening, Miss Rhiannon."

Her father took a little longer to respond, his gaze softening as he met her eyes. "You look lovely, bach."

"Thanks largely to Heledd," Rhiannon admitted.

Dai chuckled. "She knows what she's about, does Heledd."

"She tells me that she makes a rather memorable fish pie," Rhiannon said.

Dai's grin widened. "That she does, miss. If Nest would ever let her into the kitchen, I daresay she'd make one for you and the master if you asked."

"Well now," Rhiannon's father said. "We shall have to remember that the next time Nest decides to take a few days to visit her sister."

"Indeed," Rhiannon said. "Mayhap we could even go as far as to persuade Nest that another such trip should be made very soon."

Dai looked so pleased that Rhiannon's natural smile emerged. "It must be some time since—"

The front door swung open so far that it crashed against the wall. The resounding thud was immediately followed by the clatter of running feet. Everyone swung around in time to see Eifion stumble to a halt in the center of the room. His hair was windblown and his expression stricken.

He took a deep, ragged breath, then cried, "Vikings! Two boatloads of 'em. They just landed on the beach."

Rhiannon's father stiffened. "Are you sure, lad?"

"Yes, Master Iorwerth. I saw the shields along the length of their longboats shinin' in the moonlight. There's no mistakin' their craft, an' there's no mistakin' they're carryin' a lot of men."

"How many?"

"Too many to count, Master."

"Rally the men, Dai," Rhiannon's father barked the order, and Dai took off at a run. Her father turned to her. "Find Heledd. The two of you must leave immediately. Hide in the trees on the hill behind the house until you see the infidels' boats put out to sea. God willing, they will find nothing here worth stealing and will leave as quickly as they have come."

"But, Father—" Horror clogged her throat. Even if Dai were to round up every man and boy who lived and worked at Bryn Eithin, he would muster only five. Five farm laborers against a horde of pillaging Vikings.

"Now, Rhiannon." His tone brooked no argument. He withdrew his dagger from the small scabbard at his waist and pointed to the back of the house. "Go!"

Rhiannon fled the room. She ran directly to her chamber and pushed open the door. Heledd was laying Rhiannon's seawater-stained gown across the back of a chair to dry.

"Heledd! We must leave."

The older woman looked at her in alarm. "Whatever is the matter?"

"Vikings." Rhiannon could barely say the word without fear capturing her voice. Gwynedd's children were raised on stories of the devastating destruction the marauding Norsemen reaped. Vikings had no reverence for churches, monasteries, or holy relics. Gwynedd's men were considered no obstacle to their looting; Gwynedd's women were too often their prize.

Gripping Heledd's hand in hers, Rhiannon pulled her out of the room. Which way? They could reach the hill by running the length of the longhouse and going through the stable attached to the other end of the building, but the fastest route was through the front door and directly across the yard. Once they were beyond the yard, they could remain in the shadows until they reached the trees.

"How close are they?" Heledd asked. Her ruddy complexion had paled, but her tone remained calm.

"Eifion saw them on the beach."

The older woman nodded, her expression grim. "Then we have no time to lose."

Heledd's words propelled Rhiannon to the front door. She pulled it open and stepped outside. An eerie silence hung over the yard. No seagulls cried. No voices called.

A shadow crossed the open space, melding into the darkness beside the stable doors. Seconds later, two more shadows flitted across the yard. Rhiannon tightened her grip on Heledd's hand. Were the moving figures friends or foes? Where was her father?

"Hurry, bach."

Heledd's whispered warning drew Rhiannon's attention back to the distant trees. That was their goal. And they must reach it while it was yet attainable.

Turning away from the stable, they hurried along the length of the longhouse, staying in the darkest shadows beneath the eaves. Across the yard, a crack of light appeared, widening as the door to the kitchen opened. A narrow silhouette appeared.

"Myfanwy," Rhiannon gasped. "She must have returned to the kitchen before Eifion arrived back. She knows nothing of the Vikings on the beach."

"What of Nest?" Heledd asked.

Rhiannon released her hand. "Remain here. I will send Myfanwy to you. As soon as she reaches you, go to the trees. I will fetch Nest, and we shall follow."

"No, Rhiannon. Let me—"

"I am faster on my feet than you," she interrupted. "I shall join you again in no time." And then, before Heledd could argue further, Rhiannon left the protection of the wall and darted across the yard.

"Myfanwy!"

At Rhiannon's urgent whisper, the young maid stumbled to a halt. The mead in the pitcher she was carrying sloshed loudly. "Miss Rhiannon?"

"Yes." Rhiannon was close enough now that she could see Myfanwy's face. "Quickly. Put down the pitcher."

"Here, miss? In the yard?"

Myfanwy could not have sounded more mystified had Rhiannon asked her to place the pitcher on the moon.

"Vikings have come."

Significantly more mead spilled to the ground.

"V-vikings, miss?"

"Yes. And we have no time to lose." Rhiannon worked to curb her impatience as Myfanwy set the jug on the ground. "Run to the far corner of the longhouse. You'll find Heledd there. Go with her to hide in the trees. I must fetch Nest."

Now that she was free of the pitcher, Myfanwy took off running toward the spot where Heledd waited. Rhiannon did not watch her go. She picked up her skirts and crossed the remaining distance to the kitchen at a sprint.

CHAPTER 3

LEIF COULD NOT RID HIMSELF of the discomforting feeling that all was not well. He reached the scrub grass and paused to look back at the two longboats lying side by side on the sand. They were far enough up the beach to prevent the tide from reclaiming them but close enough to the water's edge for a speedy departure. With half a dozen men standing guard, the craft would be well protected. Three more men had been sent up the nearby hill to act as lookouts. But neither of those precautions fully offset the risk of storming the unknown longhouse.

He shifted to his right so that he was within arm's reach of his brother. "Are you sure this is wise, Bjorn?" Leif kept his voice low. He had no qualms about expressing his concerns privately, but it would not do for the other men to hear him questioning his brother's leadership.

"The men are hungry," Bjorn said. "They will row better with their bellies full."

Leif refrained from pointing out that if the wind were in their sails, there would be plenty of time for the men to rest. Bjorn knew that as well as he did.

"Do you truly believe that a single longhouse will have sufficient food to satisfy forty hungry men?"

"We will take whatever they have," Bjorn said, his eyes trained on the flickering lights ahead.

Leif frowned into the darkness. There was no reasoning with Bjorn when he was like this. He'd set his sights on the Cymry's longhouse, and like a hawk circling a field mouse in the grass, he was preparing to pounce.

"We go in as one," Bjorn said, raising his voice just enough for the waiting men to hear. "All food is to be brought out to the boats." He raised his arm and eyed the shadowed men sternly. "Is that understood?"

"Are you listening, Knud?" Rune's whispered taunts had yet to abate. "I am to share whatever spoils you remove from the pantry, but anything I discover in the bedchambers shall be mine to keep."

Moonlight glinted off Bjorn's silver armband as he dropped his arm, and Knud's growled curse was lost beneath the Vikings' chilling war cry. In a ferocious wave, they rushed toward the longhouse. Crossing the stretch of grass that separated them from the main structure, the men entered the yard and fanned out.

As far as Leif was concerned, they were there for one reason: to find food. Clutching his dagger, he made directly for the small building adjacent to the larger structure. If the aroma of baking bread emanating from the half-open door was any indication, it was the kitchen.

He was within a stone's throw of the structure when the door opened wider and two figures exited. Indistinguishable in the darkness, the rustle of fabric told him they were women.

"Make haste, Nest."

The female voice confirmed his guess, and Leif adjusted his thinking from his native Norse to Gaelic. His frequent interaction with the Irish people living around the Viking settlement of Dyflin had given him a good grasp of their language. There was enough similarity between the Gaelic dialects to enable him to follow a rudimentary conversation in the language of the Cymry.

The women ran toward the far corner of the longhouse. A dog barked, the frantic warning sounding uncomfortably close. Turning to gauge the canine's proximity, Leif saw four men burst out of the stables. Starlight caught the blades in their hands. Instantly, his forward momentum stalled. These men had not been caught unawares; they were wielding weapons.

Several Vikings veered to meet them, their shouts preceding the thuds of impact and the clash of metal.

Leif scoured the yard in search of Bjorn. Most of the men had already entered the longhouse. The clatter and rumble of voices now coming from the small building at his rear suggested that others had beaten him to the kitchen.

Another crash sounded as the shutters on one of the longhouse's windows flew open. By the light of a single candle flickering on the windowsill, Leif saw a man leap out and land catlike on the ground, not more than an arm's length from the fleeing women.

One of the women screamed.

The man came to his feet, towering over them. "Well, well, what have we here?"

Leif's stomach curdled at the tone in Rune's voice. With the Cymry at the stables outnumbered and the men in the kitchen having no need of his assistance, he crossed the short distance between him and Rune at a run.

The candlelight illuminated the pale faces of two women. The older one, whose brown gown was partially covered by a white apron, was pressed against the wall. The other was facing Rune with clenched hands. Her elegant gown indicated her elevated status in the household, and her stance spoke of anger rather than fear.

"Give me that," she demanded, pointing at a small wooden box in Rune's hand.

Rune grinned and took another step toward the young woman. "I daresay you are fair enough to make me wish that I understood your tongue." He raised his free hand and reached for the necklace around the young woman's neck. She slapped his hand away, and he laughed, grabbing her arm and yanking her closer. "Ah, there is some fire in this one."

"You are despicable," she said, her voice shaking with emotion. "First you ransack my home, and then you wish to steal all that I have left of my mother."

Leif could not tell whether Rune grasped the meaning of her words, but Leif had heard enough. He stepped out of the shadows. The older woman whimpered, but the young one instantly swung her head around to face him.

Her dark eyes met his, and she wrapped her hand around the circled cross at her neck. "You shall not have it," she cried.

"Let her go, Rune," Leif said, reverting to his Norse tongue.

Rune's grip on the girl remained firm. "I am not finished with her yet."

The shouts and clanks associated with deadly combat continued on the other side of the yard.

Leif met the man's eyes with a chilling stare. "We came for food—not women or trinkets."

Rune gave a derogatory snort. "To ignore such things when they are here for the taking is foolishness."

"I disagree," Leif said through gritted teeth. "True foolishness is to disrespect the captain of one's boat."

Rune's narrowed eyes told of his simmering anger. The man was five years Leif's senior. His broad shoulders hinted at his formidable strength, but Leif was a hand's width taller than him and had the advantage of rank. He stood completely still, waiting.

With a grunt of disgust, Rune released the young woman and pushed her away. She stumbled, righted herself, and then lunged for the wooden box in Rune's other hand. The Viking anticipated her move, raising the box out of her reach and hitting her across the head with the back of his other hand. She cried out in pain and staggered backward.

"Miss Rhiannon!" The older woman's shriek cut through the night and was answered by a roar of fury.

Leif pivoted. One of the Cymry had broken free of the melee at the stable doors and was running toward them, his sword raised. The muscles in Leif's arms tensed. Gripping his knife more securely, he shifted to the right. Out of the corner of his eye, he saw Rune step behind the young woman and reach for the axe at his hip.

"Touch her again and I shall run you through!"

The Cymry's shout had barely left his lips before Rune let his axe fly. The deadly weapon sailed through the air, penetrating the older man's chest with a sickening thud. Their assailant staggered sideways before doubling over and dropping to the ground.

"Father!" The young woman's cry of anguish reached deep into Leif's heart. She bolted to the fallen man's side, dropping to her knees in the dirt. "No. No, Father."

Leif crossed the short distance between them. The young woman had taken hold of her father's hand and was frantically smoothing back the gray hair from his face. The older man moaned.

"Forgive me, bach." His voice was barely above a whisper. "I . . . I failed you."

"No, Father. You have never failed me. And you never shall." Tears were streaming down the young woman's face.

Rune approached. With a curled lip, he looked down at the injured man. "One day the Cymry will learn that they are no match for a Viking," he said. And then he reached down and pulled his axe from the man's chest.

His victim moaned and gave one last faltering breath before falling silent.

"Father!" the young woman sobbed.

Rune turned his back on them, and from the hillside, a piercing whistle sounded a warning.

"To the boats!" Bjorn's voice rang across the yard.

The sounds of combat were replaced with shouts of urgency. In ones and twos, the Vikings exited the buildings at a run. Some carried bulging sacks. Two hauled a roasted pig, and four more held flagons of mead or ale.

As the yard emptied, the older woman left the protection of the wall and dropped to the ground beside the young woman. She began to wail, and Leif backed away. The lookouts had issued their warning. He must go.

As though she had only now realized that he was still there, the young woman looked up. Cradling her father's head on her knee, her tear-filled eyes met his.

"May God have mercy on your souls for what you have done," she cried.

Her tortured words penetrated his chest like a knife, and Leif took another unsteady step away from her.

"Leif!" Bjorn shouted. "The lookouts report mounted riders."

The young woman likely did not know what had caused the Vikings' sudden departure. Her grief was undoubtedly too great to truly care who came, but she deserved some measure of hope.

"Help is coming," he said.

A flicker of shock entered her eyes. She had understood.

"What good will that do now?" She swiped her hand across her damp cheek. "It is everlastingly too late." She covered her mouth to muffle a sob. "Go! And may you never set foot on Gwynedd's soil again."

To read the rest of *The Call of the Sea*, buy it at
https://shdwmtn.com/TheCalloftheSea
or scan the QR code below to purchase it:

DISCUSSION QUESTIONS

FOR *A KINGDOM TO CLAIM*

1. Were you familiar with King Alfred's reign and the Viking invasions of the British Isles before reading this book? How has the story enriched your understanding of this time period?

2. What insights did you gain into the lives of the Viking and Saxon peoples? What intrigued you most about their similarities and differences?

3. What motivates Wulfhere's actions? Do you think he would have acted differently if his father had lived longer?

4. Discuss the significance of Aisley's healing abilities and how they impact her relationships with other characters.

5. How does the initial Viking threat set the stage for the rest of the novel's events?

6. What role does Aisley and Brecc's encounter in the marketplace play in advancing the plot, particularly with regard to their relationship?

7. What is the overarching theme of this book? Does it resonate with you?

8. Discuss the concept of love and duty portrayed in the story. In what ways can these themes be applied to modern relationships and responsibilities?

9. How does the author use language and imagery to evoke the historical setting and immerse readers in the time period?

10. Are there moments in the story that surprised you with plot twists or character developments you weren't expecting? Discuss these instances.

11. Do you feel a connection to any specific character? Why?

12. How does the author's portrayal of the Viking attacks and their aftermath impact your emotional engagement with the story?

13. Are there any scenes or descriptions that particularly stand out to you as memorable or impactful?

14. Discuss the moral dilemmas characters face in the story, especially concerning loyalty, betrayal, and the consequences of their choices.

15. If you had lived in this era, what would you have found the most challenging?

16. Analyze the romantic tension between Aisley and Brecc. How does their relationship develop, and are you satisfied with its resolution?

17. Explore the dynamics between Aisley, Wulfhere, and Diera. How do family loyalties influence their interactions throughout the story?

18. Consider the impact of Aisley's involvement in King Alfred's cause. How does it affect the characters' futures?

19. Which of the secondary characters is your favorite, and why?

20. Analyze the relationship between Aisley and her mother? What do you believe causes the rift between them?

21. How might the outcome of this story—and history—have been different if King Alfred had not been so committed to his Christian faith?

22. Does a historical novel have greater emotional impact if it is based on actual events? Why or why not?

23. How does this historical fiction compare to other novels you've read within the genre? What sets it apart?

24. How does the death of Aisley's father shape her character and decisions throughout the story?

25. What role does humor play in a historical novel? Is it implemented well in this story?

HISTORICAL FACTS

THE VIKINGS

- The Vikings were a seafaring people from regions of present-day Denmark, Norway, and Sweden, collectively known as Scandinavia.
- The Viking Age had a profound impact on European history, particularly between the late eighth and early eleventh centuries. Beyond raids and invasions, Vikings contributed to cultural exchanges and shaping the medieval world by engaging in trade, exploration, and settlement.
- Vikings conducted numerous raids on Anglo-Saxon England during the ninth century, including the Wessex region. Coastal areas and monasteries were particularly vulnerable targets. Monasteries, often centers of wealth and learning, were targeted for their riches. The plundering of these monasteries led to the decline of some religious centers and the relocation of religious artifacts.
- Viking longships were crucial to their success in raids and exploration. The Vikings' advanced shipbuilding techniques and navigational skills allowed them to traverse both open seas and shallow rivers, making surprise attacks more effective.
- Vikings were skilled warriors who employed tactics such as hit-and-run raids, siege warfare, and pillaging. Their prowess in battle and strategic mobility made them formidable adversaries.
- Vikings are credited with the discovery of Iceland, Greenland, and Vinland (likely part of North America). Their spirit of exploration and

adventure contributed to the broader European Age of Discovery in later centuries.

- Danelaw was a region in England where Viking influence was particularly strong. It encompassed parts of East Anglia, Northumbria, and the East Midlands. Viking settlers in these areas contributed to the development of a distinct Norse-influenced legal and social system.
- The Vikings practiced Norse mythology, and their belief system included gods such as Thor, Odin, and Freyja.
- Vikings used runes, a system of writing with characters carved into wood, stone, or metal.

THE SAXONS

- The Saxons were part of a larger group of Germanic tribes who inhabited the countries now known as Germany and Denmark. They began migrating across Europe in the fourth century and settled England during the fifth and sixth centuries.
- Other Germanic tribes, the Angles and Jutes, also migrated to England. Collectively, they are known as Anglo-Saxons, and they established several kingdoms in England, such as Wessex, Mercia, and Northumbria.
- The Saxon kingdoms played a crucial role in shaping the early medieval history of England.
- The Saxons had a tribal society with a warrior aristocracy. They are believed to have practiced paganism until their widespread conversion to Christianity in the seventh and eighth centuries.
- The Saxons faced many invasions by Viking raiders during the Viking Age, leading to changes in political dynamics and power structures in England.
- The Saxons were skilled in metalwork, jewelry, and manuscript illumination. Remarkable artifacts from this era were discovered among the Sutton Hoo burial treasures.

- The Anglo-Saxon rule came to an end with the Norman conquest of 1066, when William the Conqueror defeated King Harold II at the Battle of Hastings.
- Long after the Norman conquest, the Anglo-Saxon influence persisted in England, contributing to the English language, legal traditions, and societal structures.

ABOUT THE AUTHOR

Photo by Melea Nelson

SIAN ANN BESSEY WAS BORN in Cambridge, England, and grew up on the island of Anglesey off the coast of North Wales. She left her homeland to attend university in the U.S., where she earned a bachelor's degree in communications, with a minor in English.

She began her writing career as a student, publishing several articles in magazines while still in college. Since then, she has published historical romance and romantic suspense novels, along with a variety of children's books. She is a *USA Today* best-selling author, a RONE Award runner-up, a *Foreword Reviews* Book of the Year finalist, and a Whitney Award finalist.

Sian and her husband, Kent, are the parents of five children and the grandparents of four beautiful girls and two handsome boys. They currently live in southeast Idaho, and although Sian doesn't have the opportunity to speak Welsh very often anymore, *Llanfairpwllgwyngyllgogerychwyrndrobwllllantysiliogogogoch* still rolls off her tongue.

Traveling, reading, cooking, and being with her grandchildren are some of Sian's favorite activities. She also loves hearing from her readers. If you would like to contact her, she can be reached through her website at www.sianannbessey.com. You can also follow her Facebook page, Sian Ann Bessey, or join her Facebook group, Author Sian Ann Bessey's Corner. Find her on Instagram, @sian_bessey.